Star of the Sea

The Cresswell Chronicles

— KATHARINE TIERNAN —

Sacristy
Press

Sacristy Press
PO Box 612, Durham, DH1 9HT

www.sacristy.co.uk

First published in 2023 by Sacristy Press, Durham

Copyright © Katharine Tiernan 2023
The moral rights of the author have been asserted.

All rights reserved, no part of this publication may be reproduced or transmitted in any form or by any means, electronic, mechanical photocopying, documentary, film or in any other format without prior written permission of the publisher.

Every reasonable effort has been made to trace the copyright holders of material reproduced in this book, but if any have been inadvertently overlooked the publisher would be glad to hear from them.

Sacristy Limited, registered in England & Wales, number 7565667

British Library Cataloguing-in-Publication Data
A catalogue record for the book is available from the British Library

ISBN 978–1–78959–288–7

Ave, maris stella,
Dei mater alma,
atque semper virgo,
Felix cæli porta.

Anon., eighth century

The
CRESSWELL CHRONICLES

Being the True History of a Family of North East England, comprising many Affecting discourses, Surprizing scenes and Romantick episodes, with Jacobites, Privateers and other Adventurers, a Voyage to the North Pole, a Spendthrift Heir and his Orphaned Daughters, a Resourceful Gentlewoman and the original Ghostly tale of the White Lady of the Tower.

As told by the late Gentlewoman's descendant, Miss Katharine Cresswell, having Recourse to Original Documents, Wills and the like, with a very Lifelike Portraiture of the Characters.

CONTENTS

Part One... 1745–50... The Forty-Five ....Chapters 1–9
Part Two... 1756–63... The Privateer ....Chapters 10–19
Part Three . 1766–68... A Clandestine Marriage .....Chapters 20–7
Part Four .. 1773–4.... The North-West Passage.....Chapters 28–32
Part Five... 1781 ...... The Orphans...............Chapters 33–5
Part Six.... 1785–7.... The Shadow of the Tower ....Chapters 36–41
Part Seven . 1788–92... Time's Changes ....Chapters 42–9
Epilogue... 1807
Acknowledgements

CRESSWELLS of CRESSWELL HALL

William Cresswell Snr **m**. Dorothy Stafford

Robert — Henry — William Jnr. **m**. Grace Forster

Surviving children of William and Grace (6 boys died in infancy):

| Catherine **m**. Wm. Johnstone | Dorothy | Grace | Elizabeth **m**. John Addison | Lelia **m**. Robt Sanderson | Juliana | Bridget **m**. Harry Parker | Alice **m**. Rev. Smalridge | John **m**. Catherine Dyer |

Grace **m**. John Easterby

Kitty **m**. Lt Brown

Fanny **m**. Frank Easterby (*Cresswell from 1807*)

Addison John Cresswell

ADDISONS

Francis Addison **m**. Mary Watson

John **m**. Eliz. Cresswell — Jane **m**. Francis Easterby

George Addison **m**. Susannah Forster

EASTERBYS of SKINNINGROVE

Francis Easterby Snr

Francis Jnr **m**. Jane Addison

John **m**. Grace Johnstone — Frank **m**. Fanny Cresswell

Note: This is not a complete family tree. For simplicity, only those members of the families directly featured in the novel are shown.

PART ONE

1745–50

The Forty-Five

CHAPTER 1

Cresswell, Northumberland

1745

On his return from Morpeth, William was curt with Isaac when he inquired, "Had Dainty ridden well over the fences?"

"Well enough," he replied, annoyed that the man had to interest himself in his affairs. It was not his place; William did not mean to stand in the yard gossiping to servants. Although, as a rule, it was his custom to do so when he came home from a race meeting and he even sometimes laid a bet on Isaac's behalf. But the enquiry laid salt on the sore of his disappointment, since the jade had baulked and thrown her rider. Worse, the manner of it had raised a laugh all along the fences. Two or three of his acquaintance had seen fit to tap him on the shoulder and congratulate him on his mare's skills. It rankled with him still.

When he came into the house, he could hear Cook's voice raised in the kitchen.

"You have over-churned it. I can never set lumps like that on the table."

"It was sour to start with."

"It would have been sweet enough if you had made it when you were bid."

He did not care to know about the butter either and kept his feet light on the flags past the kitchen. Once he reached the parlour, he closed the door behind him as tightly as its rickety hinges would allow and went directly to his closet, to let its spirituous darkness console him. He reached for the port, uncorked the bottle and drank off a glass at a swallow. The fruity sweetness slid down his throat with a pleasant warmth. He refilled the glass, took his accustomed seat by the fire, though it was yet to be lit, and stared down at the ashes. The truth was, there was more to trouble him than a wayward mare.

After the morning races, he had made his way to the Sun for a couple of chops and some ale. The parlour was in a roar when he entered, maids running red-faced and breathless from table to table, men standing in their shirt sleeves swilling ale and boasting of their winnings. He pushed through the crowd towards the bar. The landlord, a jovial corpulent man, was standing there with arms crossed, exchanging banter with his guests. But as soon as he caught sight of William, he turned away and came towards him.

"Mr Cresswell! Good day to you! Your wife is a Forster, is she not?"

"What of it?" William responded irritably, impatient to order his chops.

"Does she keep faith with the Stuarts like the rest of the family? You'd best take this home to her."

The landlord pulled a copy of the *Courant* from his pocket and thrust it towards him. When William went to take the newspaper, the man suddenly leaned so close that his sodden breath made William wince.

"You had best make your own views known soon," hissed the man into his face. "The papers say that Errington and many others of the Catholic gentry have already gone to London to protest their loyalty to King George."

He stood back as if assessing William, drops of sweat running one after the other down his jowls.

"Just a friendly warning!" he leered.

Then he was gone, back to the bar and the racegoers impatient for his attention. William was suddenly confounded. He took a quick glance around. Had anyone witnessed the exchange? It seemed not. The clamour in the parlour was just as before. Clutching the newspaper he made his way to the back of the inn, to the shadowy seclusion of the snug. Though there was barely enough light for reading he could make out the headlines well enough. Then he was grateful for the darkness, grateful that no one was there to observe him when he dropped his head into his hands and cursed aloud, when he struck out with his fist against the wall.

Once he recovered himself, he slid the newspaper inside his jacket, straightened his hat and made for the door. He would not trouble to take any refreshment after all.

Now, back at home after riding eight miles on an empty stomach, he was ill-tempered and peevish. His head was throbbing. Should he ask Cook to put him up a slice or two of pie, he wondered. But the mere thought of it caused a cramping in his belly. The whole business had quite put him from his food. He pulled the newspaper from within his jacket. How could it be? After thirty years of peace. After all the north had suffered. It could not be true, he told himself, even as he forced himself to read.

When a high piping voice at the door calling out "Father" distracted him some ten minutes later, he was tempted at first to curse her away. It was always a girl's voice, of course. That gave him no clues. He had eight daughters and these days he sometimes struggled to remember the name of whichever one stood before him. He swivelled round in his chair to look. He concentrated. It was Elizabeth. His middle daughter, near enough; bonny as could be and not a trace of the pox on her rosy skin. There was a sturdiness about her that was reassuring. Although young William had been sturdy enough too, he reminded himself. Strong as a young sapling, but it had made no difference. He pushed the thought away and looked at Elizabeth, standing before him in her pinafore and looking at him with her direct blue gaze.

"Well, what is it, child?"

"Uncle Robert has come from Bog End and you are wanted in the Tower."

"Uncle Robert, eh?" That could mean no good. "Tell your grandfather I shall be there directly when I have finished my business."

When I have emptied my glass, he meant, which Elizabeth comprehended without further explanation. She turned away and he heard her footsteps going hopscotch over the flags and off towards the kitchen. William took another gulp of port to brace himself. The news had not taken long to spread. Here was Robert post-haste with who knew what madcap schemes in his head and his mother would be ready to embrace them all.

"Folly!" he said aloud, banging his glass down on the table. "Mad misguided folly!"

*   *   *

The Tower formed one end of the house, an ancient square-built relic from the days of the Border wars five centuries ago. Earlier Cresswells had knocked through the thick stone and built a manor house onto it, with proper windows and fireplaces, where the family could live in comfort without keeping half an ear open for the clatter of steel-shod hooves in the night.

But even before William's family grew to its present size, his father had insisted on living in the Tower. The brick and timber construction of the manor house seemed to his father insubstantial. The Tower was the family's ancestral home; the very stones of the walls were a part of him. Sometimes it seemed to William that the old man's face was an outcrop of the masonry, chiselled into a form once sharply defined but now crumbling, wearing away into a blunt approximation of its original features.

As he made his way along the passage and started to climb up the worn stairs to the hall room, he could hear his mother's voice, all eagerness. She didn't notice him at first, so ardent was her exchange with his brother. He stood for a moment on the threshold. Despite the summer sunshine outside, the room was dim, the slit windows allowing only a few shafts of light to enter and brighten the long-faded tapestries that covered the walls. The familiar smell of his father's tobacco filled the air.

His mother was standing in front of Robert, close to him, a hand on her stick to steady herself. His father interrupted them.

"Do you mean to stand there all morning? Sit down, for God's sake," he said, stiffly upright in his black oak chair.

As Robert turned to draw up the settle, he caught sight of his brother in the doorway.

"Good day, William. I hope Grace improves?"

"She is weak still after the twins. Doctor Collins attends on her and would have her kept confined a little longer."

"Indeed, indeed."

Robert turned away, unwilling to hear more of women's matters. William took a chair further back in the dimmest part of the room. His headache was worsening, he decided.

"You have heard the news?" asked his father. William nodded, but Robert was not to be baulked of his announcement. He clasped his hands together like a priest readying himself for a sermon. As a young man Robert had been eager to take holy orders, but since he was the eldest and the heir his father had refused permission.

"As you have heard, Prince Charles Edward, our true and rightful monarch, is returned to claim his throne from the house of Hanover. It is a cause of great rejoicing and it is the duty of all true men to support him."

"Have you turned pamphleteer for the Pretender?" asked his father. Robert ignored him and continued.

"These past months I have met very often with other loyal gentlemen of our county who are in correspondence with the French court. We have expected this news for some weeks now. His Highness has chosen to raise his standard in Scotland and Edinburgh has declared for him."

"Edinburgh, maybe," said William. "Not Newcastle, so the papers say. They have declared for King George. Berwick too."

Robert glared at him.

"Why, William," said his mother. "Hear your brother out."

Robert turned to him.

"Newcastle? What does Newcastle count for? A rabble of Dissenters and tradesmen who think of nothing but their profits. The Prince has faithful men enough without them."

"What sudden start is this, Robert?" said his father. "You ate dinner here not a month ago and I recall no mention then of the Stuarts. Who are these gentlemen you speak of?"

Robert looked at his mother. She dropped her gaze. They have been scheming together, thought William, but she has not dared to tell Father.

"I believe John Hunter is known to you, Father. And Thomas Collingwood, and others. Tomorrow, they lead a force from Alnwick to join the king in Scotland. I mean to ride with them."

"You will not."

There was a long stillness in the room. Robert resumed at last.

"I am at fault, Father, in not speaking to you earlier of my intentions. I thought it best to wait till the Cause was afoot. But the news has come upon you suddenly. I see that I must give you time to reflect."

"I could reflect for a year and my conclusion would be no different. I want no stain of Jacobite on our name. Have you forgotten Derwentwater? And Widdrington? The greatest families in the north brought to ruin."

"Their sacrifice was glorious."

"Glorious? Dear God! You are forty-six, if my memory serves me right. It is too late for dreams of glory."

What if his own son had lived, thought William. Young William. He would be eighteen by now. Or nineteen. Would he have burned for glory and the house of Stuart? Would he be arguing with him now as his father was with Robert? Some part of him wished he could ignite the flame of passion that burned in Robert, but he could not. He felt only gut-sinking fear that Robert's righteousness would see the estate forfeited. His wife and all his girls homeless. Himself penniless.

An inadmissible thought came into his mind, of his brother Henry the lawyer, Henry handing down judgements at the Inns of Court in faraway London. Of the entail. The inheritance. What might he arrange if Robert would not yield?

"What about Henry?" he interrupted suddenly. Robert stared at him.

"Henry must examine his own conscience. As must you, brother."

Would his father catch his meaning? The old man pulled himself awkwardly to his feet.

"I will hear no more of this. I have more important matters to attend to. Give me your arm, William."

William leaped up to help him, eager to escape. As he helped his father towards the back room he muttered again,

"Henry, Father. He might . . . make arrangements. Re-assign the entail."

But his father gave no sign of understanding him. He was slower than usual and his arm was shaking. It has worn him out, William thought, and indignation with Robert filled him.

* * *

After she had given her father the message, Elizabeth loitered by the kitchen door to beg for pastry, but Cook was red-faced with a joint of mutton singeing on the spit and shook her head at her. She went on down the passage, dragging her feet. She was supposed to be helping her younger sisters with their lessons, but she wouldn't be missed yet.

She was curious about the meeting in the Tower. Uncle Robert didn't visit often. He was the eldest, but he preferred to live in the house at Bog End. He had no wife and the noise of family life was, Father said, obnoxious to him. Why he had come, she wondered.

That morning, when Elizabeth had gone to see her grandmother, she had found her in high spirits, her eyes bright, and she had caught Elizabeth in her arms.

"How great a day is this!" she exclaimed and held Elizabeth tightly to her.

"Is it your birthday, Grandma?"

"Better than a birthday; God bless us all!"

"Let the child be," said Grandfather and Elizabeth saw he was cross. Then she had glimpsed Uncle Robert standing in the shadow by the settle. She turned and curtseyed to him politely. Not a smile in return, for all her curls and dimples.

Grandfather sent her for Father. She had lingered outside on the threshold to see if she could hear any more.

"Will Grace come?" Uncle Robert asked.

"She is still confined."

And that was all. She dawdled down the stairs. She knew Mother wouldn't go, so that was no news. Mother sometimes didn't get up at all since the twins. It would take time for her to get her strength back, Doctor Collins said, after so difficult a birth. She suffered with low spirits.

Sometimes she broke down into tears and weeping in front of everyone and called on God to be merciful to her. Catherine would send to Cook for a fortifying potion. She was grieving for the babies, Catherine explained, although it was weeks now since they died. They had hardly lived any time at all. The vicar had been called to the house straight after they were born to christen them. Ephraim and Forster. They were very small and ugly with red wrinkled faces. Forster died two days later, but Ephraim had lived for a few weeks before he too was wrapped up in a white shroud and buried with the others.

Her eldest brother William had a gravestone, because he was six when he died and he had a soul, but the other boys who died after him had only a marker because either they were dead when they were born, or when they were tiny babies, and they hadn't had time to become proper people. There were six boys altogether in the graveyard. William would have been the eldest of the whole family, but now it was Catherine.

"Why do all the boys die?" she had asked Betsy the nursemaid.

"God loves them so much He wants them for Himself," Betsy told her.

It was clear to Elizabeth that girls were better at living than boys. Or perhaps God didn't love them as much.

She and all her sisters had lived, though Dorothy, who came before her, had nearly died in the smallpox outbreak that had taken William. The illness had left her with pockmarks on her face and all over her body, round red dents and leathery ridges and she was almost blind. Her sister Grace had taken it too; not so badly, but her face had as many pockmarks as Dorothy's. When Elizabeth looked in Grandma's mirror, her own face looked back at her smooth and clear and she said a special thank you to God and asked Him to protect her. No one was safe from it, ever. Queen Mary herself had died of it, Mother told her, despite having all the doctors in the land to care for her. Elizabeth stroked her face, just to make sure.

A sudden inspiration struck her. She would go to the chapel. There was no one about, no one to see her run along the back passage and push open the black door with its great brass handle. And if they did, she could say she was praying for the twins.

The chapel was full of shadows and Sunday smells, incense and sweet-stale wine and musty cloth. It was the family's private chapel, built onto the end of the house. There were windows on either side high up in the walls, the panes too dull to let the sun in, but hatched with small lozenges of stained glass through which the light fell in pools of green and blue onto the stone floor below. You could have played hopscotch from one to another, but games were not allowed in the chapel. On the altar was a special house covered in patterned brocade in which the host was kept and above it, suspended with three silver chains from the ceiling, hung a red light with a candle inside. It burned night and day to show that God was in His house.

On Sundays the chapel filled up with the family and servants and sometimes the people from Home Farm. If the curate from Woodhorn couldn't be spared, they said Matins and Father read the lesson. Sometimes a priest came to say Mass for Grandma. But Elizabeth preferred to come here all on her own, to sit in the strange shadowy darkness to see if God would talk to her. Grandma had told her that if you sat quietly for a long time, you might hear God speaking to you. He hadn't so far, but she liked to sit there anyway. As well as God in His house on the altar there was a statue of the Virgin Mary; she wore blue robes embroidered with stars and was holding baby Jesus in her arms. Did any of her babies die, Elizabeth wondered. She said three Hail Marys to the Virgin, one each for her mother and for the two dead twins. What would it have been like to have brothers? The boys down in the fishermen's huts chased each other with stinking fish or fought with sticks and shouted bad words. She didn't want brothers like that. They would be like the boys in picture books with pink cheeks and proper breeches and shirts. Or like Jesus going to the Temple with his parents.

The door of the chapel opened. It is Catherine come to look for me, she thought, and she pressed herself into the shadows at the back. But it was Grandma, tapping up the aisle with her stick, not looking around but heading straight for the altar. She didn't notice Elizabeth. When she got to the altar, she took hold of the rail to help her kneel down on the stiff cushion in front of it. She took something from her pocket and set it on the altar. Then she took out her rosary and started to pray. On and on she prayed, the beads clicking steadily. It was boring. Elizabeth's legs were getting tired from standing so still. At last she gave a little cough. The clicking stopped.

"Who's there?"

"It's Elizabeth."

Grandma swivelled round a bit to look.

"Why, child, why are you not with your sisters?"

Elizabeth hung her head.

"Well, since you are here, you can come and pray beside me."

Elizabeth went and kneeled as close as she could. Grandma leaned forward and took the picture from the altar. It was an oval miniature with a gilt frame showing a man with a white face, pink cheeks, high black eyebrows and a curly white wig. Grandma kissed the picture and then handed it to Elizabeth. She knew who it was. Grandma kept the picture with her always and was always happy to show it.

"He has come home to his people," said Grandma. "I am saying special prayers for him."

She put the picture back on the altar and took up her beads again.

"He will soon be king," said Grandma. "Soon he will."

CHAPTER 2

Cresswell and Newbiggin, Northumberland

1746

William had spent the morning in his father's office checking the accounts. It would be a quick enough task, he had thought; he would not trouble the servants for a fire. But now, after hours at the desk, the October chill had seeped into his bones. He shut the books and went to the window to stare at the grey clouds rolling past. There was no doubt, he decided. The whole business with Robert had affected the old man's brain. It was as if a tight-coiled spring had abruptly given way so that the whole mechanism was gone slack. The household account was overspent by more than seven shillings. He, who had always been so diligent over every farthing! And he was making other mistakes.

"The rent payment from Longframlington is wanting, Father," he had said, when the old man wandered in, halfway through the morning.

"Longframlington? I have entered it, look, it is here."

"That was last month's. You have entered it twice—see, there is no receipt against this one."

There was a moment's silence as his father stared blankly at the ledger, then looked away, already distracted. It was pitiful to see. He would have to take over, William was starting to believe, and to make no delay about it, before his father's wits deserted him altogether. He, William, understood the estate and what it took to run it. He had never been a scholar like his brothers, but he understood practical matters. Robert would sooner spend all day closeted in a Newcastle coffee house with his Jacobite friends than seeing to the estate. Did he care nothing for his inheritance? For his father? Robert was happy to leave William to take care of it all, to act as his steward, and then he would come back from his adventures without a word of thanks.

At least there was Henry. His younger brother had left the north for good years ago. He would rather labour his way through a pile of writs and stand all day in a dusty courthouse than take a gun wildfowling. But Henry had made his fortune from those piles of writs. He had married the Proctor's daughter at the Inns of Court, so he had a father-in-law well placed to help Henry to lucrative cases. Henry might be a scholar, but he was shrewd too. A man of the world. It was Henry they had to depend on now. His letter lay before them on the desk.

> *My dear Father*
>
> *I am sorry that the Occasion of this letter should be so Grave a matter for our Family and I pray that you are bearing it with Fortitude. The late Enterprise upon which Robert is now entered is Ill-judged. I fear it is no more than a romantick Phantasy that will be soon Crushed and brought to nothing. My Counsel is to act without delay to demonstrate our Fealty to King George and more, to make Payment to support his loyal Army. There is nothing so Convincing to the Public Sentiment as Fifty guineas. I plan to attend on Mr Pelham to present a protestation of Loyalty to the Crown and I counsel that you do likewise wait upon the Mayor and Council of Newcastle and make Publick to all observers the ground on which our Family takes its Stand, letting it be known that Robert's act has incurred your high Displeasure.*
>
> *Believe me, Father, your most Affectionate Son*
> *Henry Creſswell*

How much would they have to give? William pondered. Fifty guineas? A hundred? It was pointless to discuss it with his father. The old man had read through the letter twice, then stared at William with a kind of helplessness.

"Henry bids me go to Newcastle."

"He takes no account of the journey. He forgets how poor the road is. I will go in your place, Father, if you will write a letter to the Mayor and Council for me to take."

He would ride to Newcastle, but not yet. No need to rush into throwing away a fortune till they knew how the land lay. After a morning shut up like a counting house clerk, he meant to spend the afternoon more enjoyably.

*   *   *

When he was called down to the yard the next morning to see a man from Newbiggin, William could have laughed aloud. Had he not said to himself last night, a smugglers' moon?

He had taken a stroll down to Snab Point to smoke a pipe or two and stare at the sea. It was a mild night, just a ruffle of surf over the Skears and a southerly breeze, the moon still pale but starting to cast a yellow light on the water as the daylight faded. A perfect night for it, he thought.

And now, here was young John Addison standing before him. He knew very well before John opened his mouth what the message would be, but he feigned surprise.

"What brings you up from Whitby, John? Is there no work to be had for a sailor?"

"We had fair winds from the Nore that brought us early into the Tyne and my uncle needed an extra hand."

"Indeed."

To unload his cargo from the Netherlands, he thought. Although the Addisons were written down in the parish registers of Warkworth and Newbiggin as Sailors, no one grew as rich as they on cargoes of barley and worsteds. They had built fine houses for themselves and lived like gentlemen. One of the Warkworth Addisons had married Grace's sister, so they were cousins of a sort. Young John's father had moved down to Yorkshire to work on some great estate, but his son had the sea in his blood. John Addison had been apprenticed to a ship owner in Whitby before his voice had broken.

William liked to see John Addison. He was scarcely a year older than his dead son William would have been now. Watching John grow from child to youth was a ghostly reminder of how his son might have been, how the first bristle of beard might have hidden the softness of his skin, how his voice might have broken into a man's bass, how quick he might have been springing up into the saddle.

"He sent to tell you that there is a cargo that may be of interest down at Newbiggin," said John Addison.

William nodded.

"Come into the kitchen and take some breakfast with us. Let them know in the stables and tell them to saddle up Conqueror. I must see to the accounts first and then I'll ride back with you."

* * *

In the kitchen they had found the children at breakfast, Catherine sitting like a queen in her mother's place at the end of the table. She was seventeen now, wanting to be a woman, impatient of her sisters and their cries and arguments and contemptuous of her mother's long sickness. To her left sat Dorothy and Grace, always together, and now Elizabeth had joined them. At nine years old she was too old for the babies' side of the table. On the other side of Catherine were the four little ones in their bibs and pinafores, Betsy the nursemaid beside them, spooning bread and milk into any mouth that was open, scolding and cajoling. Lelia, Juliana, Bridget and Alice. Juliana had not yet noticed her godfather's entrance and was waving her spoon in time to the song Lelia was singing.

Godfather John. William had done it on a whim. Five years ago, when Juliana was to be christened, he had decided on his cousin Cuthbert from Heddon to be godfather to her.

"He is not fit to be godfather to her," Grace had objected. "He is a drunkard and a spendthrift."

"I'm sorry we have no more saints left in the family to please you. We have used them all up."

"Why should it be always your family? Why not from mine?"

She knew very well that William considered the Forsters beneath him. They might be as old a family as his, but they were reivers and farmers. Not gentry. It had not stopped William marrying her, since he was a younger son in any case and might do as he pleased. But it didn't stop his haughtiness. Now he shrugged.

"Very well then. Choose who you like."

That took Grace by surprise and she hesitated.

"Come on—who is it to be?"

She was flustered now and a sudden half-malicious impulse took hold of William. It was a morning just such as this, when John had called to the house with a packhorse loaded with brandy and port for his cellar.

"Let it be young John Addison then. He's a fine lad and likely to make himself a fortune. Let him stand godfather to her."

"John Addison? He is only sixteen!" she protested. "And nephew to my sister, but not to me."

But she agreed in the end for want of any other. So John Addison stood in Woodhorn church and swore in Juliana's name to renounce the devil and all his works, the vain pomp and glory of the world, with all the covetous desires of the same, and the carnal desires of the flesh, so that she would neither follow nor be led by them.

"I renounce them all," said John, and the image of that moment had stuck in William's mind, of his infant daughter in her white robes in the arms of the priest, and the fresh-faced young man in a new jacket, scarcely more than a boy himself.

"Juliana!" William cried out now and the table suddenly fell silent. Juliana turned and stared at him with wide eyes. "Your Godfather John is come and you must mind your manners."

John Addison came into the kitchen behind him and at once Juliana clambered up onto the bench and held out her arms to him, wanton for an embrace. John caught her up, tossed her into the air and kissed her before setting her back on the bench. The other girls stared, pink with envy.

"Have you eaten up your breakfast?" he asked her.

"Yes, yes, yes!" she lied and he put his hand in his pocket for a sugar plum. Bridget and Lelia set up a clamour of "me, me", till he pulled out the whole packet and sent them rolling down the table. Cook turned from the stove to see what the commotion was. There was a wild flurry of grabbing and argument till every child had one and their mouths were stopped.

They had not had so merry a breakfast for many a month, thought William.

*   *   *

He and John Addison rode out along the coast road, past Home Farm. The women were bent over the near field pulling weeds from the turnips, but the other fields were still bare stubble. It was a windy autumn afternoon, with streamers of pale clouds opening to sudden spells of sunshine that lit up the sea.

"Where next, John, when you are finished here? Another collier from Newcastle?"

"Not yet. First I must go down to Yorkshire to see my sister wed."

"Do you know the man she will marry?"

"Francis and I were apprenticed together in Whitby when we were twelve years old. He is like a brother to me already and now he will be so in law. I could not wish for a better man for her."

"Do you think of marriage, John?"

"I? No, I cannot think of marriage yet. Francis has land and family behind him. The Easterbys have a manor at Skinningrove with the neatest little cove you ever saw for bringing in a cargo. His father owns ships that lie at Whitby. But we Addisons have nothing but our wits. I mean to own land before I take a wife. I will be a ship master in a year or two and trade in Whitby never stops growing."

John paused and glanced at William.

"I mean to be a gentleman, Mr Cresswell. I run errands for my uncle now, but I will have men run after me before I'm done."

William felt John looking at him. What was he to say? He was half amused, half disturbed. How could he say to the boy, you will never be a gentleman. It is not something to be bought and sold.

"I wish you well, John. For sure, trade will carry us all forward."

The road circled past the fishing village at Lynemouth. The fields and hedgerows gave way here to a stretch of moorland where nothing grew but tall clumps of reed. The desolation of the moor had a lowering effect on William's spirits. There was something in John's ambition that he feared. The world was full of John Addisons, hungry for wealth and hungry for land. What if Robert was taken prisoner and attaindered? The estate was still his father's, not Robert's, but if the Crown wanted revenge that would not stop them. Look at the Widdringtons. All their lands confiscated and sold to whoever would have them.

What would become of him? How would he, William, fare at making his fortune? He shook off the thought. He was a gentleman. No one could take that from him.

When they rounded the headland at Newbiggin, he saw George Addison's ketch at once, anchored offshore and riding the swell. At once his dark mood fell away and he was full of joyful expectation. For sure, it would be a fine cargo and he would fill the cellar for the winter. Was there any trouble that could not be cured with a glass of brandy?

When the liquor had been inspected and a deal struck down in Newbiggin, William turned his attention to another matter.

"My wife Grace, George. She has been confined since the summer and I need something to raise her spirits. What have you got?"

George brought out a bolt of silk that was blue as cornflowers and packets of Ghent lace. The price of it made William wince. But Grace hadn't been out in company for months and the girls suffered for it. If she had a new gown? Or some lace trimming? Might it tempt her?

In the end, he settled for the silk and some ribbons for the girls, though it emptied his purse.

By the time he set out for home, it was growing dark. He was befuddled with the liquor he had sampled in Addison's warehouse and had to let his horse find its own way. When he got to the stables, he handed it over to Isaac and headed for the house, one thought in his mind. Grace.

The shutters were already closed in her bedroom when he entered and the candles lit. A low bed of coals glowed in the grate. She sat on the side of the bed closest to it, dressed only in her nightgown and a wrapper. Her fair hair was combed out over her shoulders; there was not a hint of grey in it. In the soft light, she was still the girl who had infatuated him twenty years ago, for whose sake he had ridden to Low Buston in rain or shine, week after week, till she would have him. He would do it all again, he told himself. She was still a beauty to him.

"Why, William! Are you home at last?"

"I've ridden to Newbiggin and back at the command of your relatives."

"Ah."

"I have bought something for you."

She turned towards him. He pulled the silk out of his pack and held up a length of it for her to see. The blue was deeper in the firelight. Not as bright as he had thought it. But she gave a little gasp and clapped her hands together.

"Oh look at that. Let me feel it."

She held the silk between her fingers and put it to her cheek.

"How fine it is! Oh, William . . . how could you afford it?"

He felt his heart lift with joy to see her smiling up at him. He bent down and kissed her head.

"I don't care what it cost."

She put out her hand to him and he sat down on the bed beside her, letting his arm slide round her waist.

"George Addison must have given you more than one glass of brandy!"

She was laughing. She was teasing him. How much he wanted her! But the doctor had been firm in his directions.

"If you want your wife to live, Mr Cresswell, you must leave her be. I could not vouch for her if she had another confinement like these last two."

He had been faithful to the doctor's instructions for months. The man had even insinuated he might look elsewhere for comfort. But he would not. If Grace had to suffer, then he would too.

But surely, he might kiss her, he thought now. He kissed her hair first, then her neck, then found his way to her lips. She didn't resist him. As his tongue slid into her mouth, he felt her lean towards him in the old way, felt her mouth firm against his. All at once he was overcome with desire. He drew her close to him, her body so thin now, so fragile, so precious to him. He could not stop himself; he wanted her beyond reason, beyond all thought of consequences. He pulled off his jacket and, as he did, he felt her hand on his breeches. Surely it was what God intended. They would be man and wife again.

CHAPTER 3

Cresswell, Northumberland

Epiphany 1746

Grandmother told the story of the White Lady every year at Epiphany. Epiphany marked the coming of kings, so that was the right time to tell the story, Grandmother said, since the stranger in the story had been a prince. Elizabeth first heard it before she could speak and all she understood of it was the sound of her grandmother's voice, the milky smell of her sisters pressed close against her and the taste of the Epiphany cake.

"Long ago," Grandmother began, "when the Tower had not long been built and the land was still lawless, there was a great storm at sea that wrecked a ship on the rocks at the head of the bay. Only a few men were brought ashore alive. One of them had rings on his fingers and a gold chain round his neck like a nobleman so the fishermen took him to the Tower. The lord told his daughter to look after the stranger and she cared for him night and day till he grew strong. She taught him to speak English and he told her many tales of his country, of the north and of the royal palace where he lived, for he was a prince in his own realm. "I will take you there," he told her and she dreamed every night of crossing the seas to his snowy palace.

"When he was well enough to leave, the lord of the Tower demanded a payment of him.

"'We have kept you here and fed you; my own daughter has cared for you. All this must be paid for.'

"'Give me a ship and a crew to attend on me,' said the stranger, 'and I will return with enough gold to fill your coffers. I will bring you one chest of gold as payment for my life and another as payment for your daughter, for I want her to be my wife.'

"When the lord's daughter heard his words, her heart was filled with joy, for she had grown to love the stranger. She begged her father to accept his offer.

"'I will give you three months,' said her father. 'If you have returned with the gold you have promised in three months, you may have her. But I will not wait longer for there are more men than you who would have her.'

"The stranger agreed his condition and set sail back to his country. Every day the maiden stood at the top of the Tower, looking out to sea for her lover's sail, fearing for every storm that might stay him. At last, when the three months were nearly up, his ship sailed into the bay.

"She ran down the stairs, wild with joy. But her brothers stood in her way and would not let her go out to him. They pushed her inside and locked the door against her. Weeping bitterly at their unkindness she ran back to the top of the Tower to watch for him.

"He came ashore with his men, who were carrying the two chests of gold he had promised. How tall and handsome he was! How noble in his bearing and how finely dressed! When he reached the door of the Tower, he looked up and called out his greetings to the maiden. The next moment her brothers, armed with swords and daggers, pushed open the door and fell upon the stranger and his men, greedy for his gold. When she saw their treachery, the maiden cried out to them, 'Stop, stop in God's name!' but they paid her no heed. Desperate that her lover should not believe she had betrayed him, she leaped from the top of the Tower, crying his name. With his last breath he caught her in his arms. They died together, stained in his blood.

"Ever since then, whenever a storm is brewing, the White Lady walks the shore, calling out for her lost lover and searching the sea for him."

When Grandma finished, there was a hush in the room. The candlelight flickered suddenly across the walls in the draught like a ghostly presence. The incoming tide was just audible, a faint roar from outside the window.

"Have you seen her, Grandma?" asked Dorothy.

"I can't be sure, child. When the surf is blowing above the water, I have fancied I have seen her. You must have a true heart to see her, for she died for love."

Then Cook brought up the Epiphany cake made with currants and nutmeg. It had a special bean inside that was supposed to be baby Jesus and whoever found it in their slice got a prize. You weren't allowed to break up your slice to look for it, you had to eat it properly and wait to bite on the bean. Elizabeth ate her cake very fast, but there was no sudden hardness against her teeth. Then Bridget cried out, "It's me! It's me!" and Elizabeth felt a cold clutch of disappointment at her throat. Why did there have to be so many of them? Now Bridget would have the prize and everyone would make an extra fuss of her because she was pretty.

While the others crowded around to see what the prize would be, Elizabeth slipped away, through the door and onto the twisting staircase. She climbed up past the dark chambers on the next floor and out at the top of the Tower, onto the flat roof with its blanket stitch of battlements. There were showers of sparks flying up from the smoke hole, hot and red, alive in the darkness. And above, the stars were spread across the winter sky, so many that they gave off their own cold light. She stood staring out to sea, half-frozen, looking for the ghostly lady, willing her to appear. The east wind blew and the distant roar of the tide filled her ears; she was lost in wind and sky and stars, till her grandmother's voice called out from far away below, "What are you doing up there, Elizabeth? Come down!"

And she turned back to the stairs, still in a daze of stars, and forgot that you had to stay on the outer tread, next to the wall, as the stairs spiralled down to the parlour. Her feet slipped and stumbled over the narrowing tread, unable to find their footing, and she tripped forward till she was flying through space with arms and legs flailing, tumbling headlong down the circling space, her soft body finding only stone, her fall too fast to check, rushing down into darkness. Then suddenly there was a light, not the firelight of the parlour, but a light pale as the stars, and all at once she was safe, caught in firm hands that stayed her, held her till the helter-skelter in her head came to rest and she was set back on the stair, her feet steady again on the outer tread. I am alive, I am alive! she thought and turned back to look up the stair, to find who had rescued her. There was nothing but darkness and silence.

"Come here this minute!" called out her grandmother. "Those stairs are not safe at night."

She ran down into the parlour to find all her sisters staring at her. She wanted to cry out, "It was her! I have seen her!" But how could she say so, for though she was certain, certain it was her, she had only felt her, not seen her. Then Grandma slapped her arm and scolded her for being a naughty girl to go running up there on her own and she was in disgrace.

The next day Elizabeth went down to the beach to look for the White Lady, but there was nothing but the fisherwomen stretching out the nets and a few gulls flying low over the waves. Perhaps Grandmother was wrong, she thought. It wasn't the shore she haunted. It was the Tower. She wanted to ask Grandma about it, but how could she now?

A week later snow came, falling thick and silent round the Tower and on the roof. No one could go up there. Father and Isaac shovelled a path from the front door round to the stables and the dairy and Elizabeth and Lelia rolled the snow up into a fat man with coal buttons. Mother said he should have a hat and gave her an old cap from the rag box. Elizabeth was tugging it down onto the snowman's head when she saw the Lady. In the field at first, then moving with all speed towards the shore. She was so pale against the snow that Elizabeth could not be certain at first that she had seen her, that she was not a slip of light escaped from the cloud. But it was her. Elizabeth looked again and was sure of it. She was like a mist, moving and shifting. Then she stilled, turned, seemed to look back towards the Tower and at once Elizabeth wanted to be with her again, to feel her body gentle as a snowflake on the air, floating, falling to the downy earth. But she was gone. Even as she disappeared, Elizabeth felt the wind start to tug at the hood of her cloak. That night the wind roared round the house, rattling at the windows so hard that she couldn't sleep. Down on the shore the Lady waited for her lover and in her bed Elizabeth waited too, her heart loud between her ribs.

CHAPTER 4

Marsham Street, London

1746

After five days on the road, every bone in William's body ached. The wheels of the post-chaise found out every rut and puddle, jerking him from any fitful doze he might manage. At first he had sat outside with the coachman, watching the wearisome progression of fields and hamlets, towns and villages, rolling past. Durham and Darlington, Topcliffe and Wetherby, Boroughbridge and Bawtry . . . the litany of towns continued day after endless day, punctuated by plates of greasy mutton at crowded inns and straw mattresses covered with grubby linen. No wonder Henry never came north, he thought. Or that he, William, never took Grace to London. Then soaking rain drove him inside and, by the time they rolled out of their last stop at Hatfield, he hardly knew whether it was night or day and was reduced to staring at a lone persistent spider working his web in the creaking corners of the chaise. He had thought the solitary journey would be a respite from his troubles. Instead, he found himself endlessly rehearsing them.

After Robert had left in August last year, there had been silence, month after month. No word. No letter. His mother had grown pale with waiting.

"Do you not think he might come home at Christmas?" she had asked him, again and again.

How could he explain to her? Everyone knew by then that Robert Cresswell was a Jacobite. If he had shown his face in Morpeth, he would have been arrested within the hour. Or shot. Worse, if they, his family, had opened the door to him, all their protestations of loyalty, all their lavish donations, would have turned to dust in a moment. They would have all stood guilty of treason.

He had schooled himself into a kind of indifference. The supposed Rebellion was nothing more than a handful of skirmishes, he had told himself. There was no sign of popular support sweeping the country. No sign of the promised French invasion. As far as he could see, it was all going to peter out ignominiously. Robert might suffer disgrace, even exile, but he would not die for his folly.

When Christmas came, he had taken his wife Grace and daughter Catherine to the Morpeth Assemblies as though his family had not a care in the world. Grace wore the new silk dress that brought out the cornflower blue of her eyes. The bloom had returned to her cheeks and as they danced together his heart lifted in spite of their troubles. He had seen with relief that Catherine had no shortage of young men to wait on her. None of them thought it necessary to remark on her Jacobite connections.

Epiphany was scarcely past when it had started to snow, thick flakes that piled up around the house and covered every track and pathway in an even blanket of white. It went on for two days and nights and by the time it was done the roads were impassable. Even his mother could see it. A kind of snowed-in peace had descended on the household; time suspended in the blank whiteness of the snow.

Two days after the thaw, towards the end of January, a postboy had ridden into the yard with a letter. William had snatched it from him and taken it to the parlour to read before anyone else should see it, though it was addressed to his parents, not him.

> *My Dear Father and Mother*
>
> *I send you Affectionate greetings and Trust that God preserves you in Health.*
>
> *Indeed, no Man could mistake the Providence of the Almighty at this present time in prospering the Forces of his most Gracious Majesty King Charles. I do not know what News you may receive from such scurrilous Pamphlets and newspapers as the Illegal*

Government may approve and so I Rejoice in Informing you of the True Progress of His Majesty's Army, which I have Witnessed with my own Eyes.

After leaving Edinburgh and taking the castle at Carlisle the King's Army advanced as far as Derby, with loyal acclamations from the People. However, with Winter now upon us we are returned to Scotland to join with the Scottish regiments besieging the Castle at Stirling. We are Informed that Ten Thousand French troops will presently be embarked towards our shores, together with the Supplies and Artillery which are most urgently required to effect the Siege. With so great a Force none of us doubt that the coming Year will see Success for our Hopes.

The arduous nature of the Campaign has till now left me with but little Leisure to spend upon correspondence, or to find a postboy. However I am quartered presently at Falkirk with other Officers in preparation for the Siege and this gives me Occasion to write to you and to assure you of my continuing Affection.

I suffer somewhat with a recurrent Ague that Forces me at times to keep Abed but I strive to bear such Afflictions with Patience, since we have no knowledge of what God requires us to endure. As Winter draws on it is no easy matter to find Food for all our Forces and this has led many of the Highlanders to return to their homes. We are Fortunate as Officers that some Fare may usually be found to furnish a Sufficient dinner, though with no such Abundance as I know your Hall will see for the Christmas Feast.

I hold you in the strongest Filial Regard and believe me your Obedient son,

Robert Crefswell

It was, William had thought, like receiving a letter from a lunatic. How could his brother persist in deluding himself? He took a spiteful satisfaction in the news of his brother's Ague. In truth, he thought, he was more likely to die of a chill than as a hero in battle.

But his mother had been wild with relief and joy, all her belief in the Cause refreshed and her terror for her son allayed. She had spent hours in the chapel following Robert's bidding, praying for the Pretender.

Then silence again, through all the long winter and into spring. Till Culloden.

Even now, whenever he said the word William felt sick. The very sound of it was like a skull split open. He would not think of it, he told himself, and turned his attention back to the carriage and to the spider. But it had disappeared into some dark recess of the canopy and the web hung empty. Even the horses' hooves at the canter seem to echo it. Culloden. Culloden.

Of course, the newspapers had been full of it, full of triumph at the great casualties inflicted on the Jacobite army, of the cowardice of the Stuart prince abandoning his followers. He was on the run and the Rebellion was over.

Surely, if he lived, Robert would come home, slink back to Cresswell with his tail between his legs. If he lived. As weeks passed, it had become harder not to believe him dead. And then, to cap all his troubles, even as his mother moved into mourning clothes, it became obvious to everyone that Grace was with child again. He had felt like a criminal.

"Don't blame yourself, William," she had said when she told him. "I'm forty-two. Nurse told me I'd never give birth again. No one expected it." The guilt was too much for him to bear. Was he to lose his wife as well as his brother? He laid his head on her breast and wept like a child. She took his hand and put in on her belly.

"This one will be different," she said. "Feel it. It's strong, it's kicking already. And am I not healthy now?"

He looked at her, grown plumper, grown solid and material. It seemed impossible to imagine she could ever not be there. But in the night watches, fears haunted his rest till he got up and went out into the dawn, down to the beach to let the hiss and retreat of the waves bring some calm to his soul.

He had found the best physician in Newcastle to wait on her and had sworn not to stir from the house till he had seen the labour through to safety. But now, instead of being at her side he was on the coach to London.

* * *

He hardly noticed that the chaise had come to a halt. The driver pulled open the door and bellowed at him.

"Here we are, sir! Marsham Street!"

Stiff from days of sitting, he half-staggered from the chaise, to find himself before a tall, terraced house, three storeys high, built, as his brother was eager to inform him later, in the Palladian style. The windows were very large and regular, framed in white to contrast with the dark red of the brickwork, and the front door was flanked by an elegant classical surround. As William stared, Henry appeared in the doorway, dazzling in his flowing wig and brocade coat.

"You are arrived at last! Come in, my dear fellow. You must be shaken to pieces—let us find you a glass of brandy. We will have dinner directly."

William followed his brother into a hall whose blue walls were covered with gilt-framed pictures and from which a graceful staircase curved upwards to the first floor. He had an impulse to flee up the stairs, but Henry led him into the drawing room. William could not help himself. He stared at the printed wallpaper, at the upholstered furniture, at the marble fireplace with its pale cherubs flying above the flames in the hearth below.

"You have a fine home, brother."

"I am newlywed again, you know. Sarah is a woman of very discerning taste—she decrees what we are to have and I write the cheques."

What can it have cost, William thought. Can the law be so profitable? His astonishment was completed when Sarah entered the room. His brother had been a widow for some years. His first wife had been of a similar age to him, but Sarah was much younger, William saw at once. Not many years older than Catherine, but so elegant and refined! Her hair was dressed and powdered, her cheeks rouged, her lace-trimmed dress so full she was obliged to turn sideways to pass through the door, and a perfumed fragrance hung all about her. A lady's maid must have been required to turn her out. All at once he was conscious of his soiled breeches and the threadbare elbows of his coat. He straightened his wig and bowed.

"Mrs Cresswell, I am honoured to make your acquaintance. I fear that I am not fit to meet you in my travelling dirt."

She let her eyes take in his provincial clothing before she smiled.

"Why, I am happy to meet any brother of Henry's, whatever his state. Welcome to 22 Marsham Street. I fear it is not as spacious as Henry's estate at Windsor, but it is convenient for Doctors' Commons."

Henry put a glass of brandy in his hand. He drank it at a swallow.

An hour later, loosely clad in a change of clothes belonging to his brother, he sat at the mahogany dining table set with silver and an epergne of Venetian glass. A neatly dressed housemaid served dishes that seemed to have no end: a side of salmon, a vermicelli soup, a raised pigeon pie, lamb's sweetbreads, braised celery, French beans, a lobster ragout. There were tarts and cakes, blancmange and custard, there was claret and Chablis and a sweet wine for the cakes. After so many nights of boiled mutton William's stomach was hardly equal to the task.

"No, no—I cannot! Such a feast—so delicious—but not another morsel."

No wonder Henry's clothes were so large, William thought. His brother had become quite stately in his girth. Sarah refused all but a few of the dishes and passed the meal telling him of the new play she had attended at the Theatre Royal and of the amazingly fine picture gallery at Stafford House where she had lately been invited.

"What of your family, William?" she asked. "What entertainments do you have for them?"

"I am blessed with eight daughters," he told her, "so there is seldom shortage of entertainment in our family, what with stories and play-acting and the like. We are more rustic in our tastes, I should say. The girls like nothing better than a picnic on the shore to watch the ships come in."

"Oh! How delightful, to live by the sea! How amusing that must be! Henry, I declare we must make a visit one day."

"Indeed, my love, though as William will tell you, it is a tedious journey. Three hundred miles or more."

"Three hundred! Why, it must be practically in Scotland!"

At last, the meal was done and all the dishes removed. Sarah withdrew to the drawing room and Henry took out the port. The brothers settled into their chairs with a certain relief and fraternal familiarity.

"Well then. Sarah has some notion of what is afoot with Robert, but we don't speak of it. I don't talk to her of my work at law either. She is often in society and I prefer she is ignorant of it all so that people do not try to draw her out."

He took a gulp of port, rolled it round his mouth and swallowed.

"Robert is in the Gatehouse Prison with a score of his fellows. He got word to me and I sent for you at once."

"He is alive?"

"He is indeed. You'll be surprised to hear that our brother never made it to Culloden."

"He didn't? Did he fear to fight?"

"Who knows? But he was not alone. It seems that Lord Murray, the prince's general, convinced the prince that their best chance of defeating Cumberland was a surprise attack. It meant an overnight march and the terrain was more difficult than they expected. Robert was with a party of officers and men who became separated from the main body of the army. As far as I can tell they spent the night marching in circles. By the time they got there it was all over, since it took Cumberland less than an hour to wipe out Charles' army. Well, to cut the sorry tale short, Robert and the other officers were taken prisoner. They have been brought to London to stand trial."

"Dear God!" William took his head in his hands. He could think of only one outcome for such a trial. It was too horrible to contemplate.

"Don't worry. I have undertaken to defend him and his comrades when it comes to trial. Strange to say, there is sympathy for the Jacobites in London. There is a kind of romance about their cause. I believe I can save him the noose."

William looked at his brother. They were both drunk, but the matter was too grave to mistake. There was a certainty about Henry that convinced William. But it must convince a judge and jury too, he told himself.

Henry leaned forward, a different harshness in his voice.

"But I cannot save him from attaint. He has brought that stain upon himself. He will never own land again. He will never vote. He can never be a member of society." He paused.

"I will not let him drag down the family with him. I have drawn up documents to alter the entail on the estate. In a year or two, it will be as if Robert never existed. The inheritance will be yours. The family will go on."

It was overwhelming, William thought. How could he grasp what his brother's words implied? He felt an urgent need to be at home again. He struggled for something suitable to say.

"He is—I mean, I am—forever indebted to you, brother. How will this all be paid for?"

"I am sure Robert and his company will give me some token of their esteem if they are spared the gallows. But there is no need for gratitude. I have my own reputation to consider in all this."

He uncorked the decanter and refilled both their glasses.

"You can see that I am comfortably appointed here. I would loathe to live in the north. What a wilderness! All coal and barley. No, my dear fellow, you are welcome to it. All I require of you is reputation. I need it to be known that the Cresswells are a landed family with a seat in the north and a good pedigree."

He raised his glass. "To Cresswell! We might even come and visit when I have an heir of my own."

He leaned forward confidentially.

"As for Robert, I believe he will go to France if he can. Turn Papist and become a priest at the Stuarts' court in exile. He'll love it."

CHAPTER 5

Cresswell, Northumberland

July 1746

Elizabeth came in from the garden early in the afternoon, tired of games with the babies. The house seemed empty without her father. He had been gone for days already, but he would not be back for weeks, he had told them. London seemed like another country, faraway and impossible to imagine. Before he left, he had embraced each one of them in turn.

"Take care of your mother," he had told them.

She wandered past the kitchen where Cook was asleep in her chair, snoring. It was warm even in the house and flies circled in the hall. She listened. She could hear Dorothy and Grace in the parlour, Dorothy's slow voice stumbling along and every now and then Grace saying look Dorothy, like this, you must stitch it tighter. Everyone said their names together, GraceandDorothy, as if they were one person. Grace looked after Dorothy. She was younger than her, but it didn't matter because Dorothy was simple. It was because she was almost blind, Betsy said, and she, Elizabeth, should be kinder.

It would be kind to go and see them now. But she didn't want to sit stitching and listening to Dorothy's slow stories. She listened again.

Mother was supposed to be resting, but Elizabeth could hear her voice upstairs, calling out instructions to a servant. She ran upstairs and along the corridor to her mother's room. She was watching the new housemaid hanging drapes over the bedroom windows. The girl had been sent over from Low Buston, where Elizabeth's other grandmother lived, to help

Mother out. But the girl was clumsy and the drapes kept slipping. Mother's voice was irritated. Although the afternoon was warm, there was a fire burning in the grate. Then her mother noticed her.

"Why Lizzie, have you come to help us? We are trying to put up the drapes, though if I had my way I would sooner tear them down than put them up."

She pulled Elizabeth close to her and squeezed her tight.

"How I hate a summer confinement! How hot it is already!"

Elizabeth wanted to ask, why is there a fire then? But it was all part of the baby coming and they were not supposed to ask questions. Her mother took her hand.

"I cannot bear it a moment longer! You can manage on your own now, Susan."

She pulled Elizabeth out of the room and along the passage as fast as her condition would allow, so that Elizabeth had to hop from side to side to avoid the full skirts of her dress. At the top of the stairs her mother turned to her, face flushed, conspiratorial.

"I have such a longing for something fresh and green! Cook cannot see a green thing without boiling it half to death. The room's not ready yet. We'll walk over to the woods and pick watercress. Tell Catherine."

Elizabeth went running down the stairs ahead of her mother, crying out for Catherine as she went. She found her out in the cool darkness of the dairy draining whey from a cheese. Catherine wiped her hands on her apron and considered.

"Why not," she said. "Poor Mother will be abed for weeks." She squatted down beside Elizabeth. "It's too far for Dorothy. She and Grace will have to stay and Betsy is with the babies. Just you and me and Mother, Lizzie. Fetch your hat and I'll find baskets."

Outside it was all July loveliness. The sun was bright in the sky but not yet hot and a westerly breeze lifted lacy lines of whiteness from the waves in the bay. How blue the sea was! How lovely and fresh the air! All three of them were seized with a giddiness that sent Elizabeth and Catherine running towards the woods, with their mother lurching after them, ungainly with her great belly. The beech trees were fully out in leaf, tendrils of bracken were uncoiling from beneath the leaf litter and the bramble thickets were in flower. Soon they were at the Lyne, a clear stream with shallow pools where the watercress grew, thick and green. Catherine could reach out and pick it from the bank, but Elizabeth pulled off her shoes and socks and tucked up her pinafore so she could paddle. Their mother sat on the bank, shoes off, feet in the water. When Elizabeth gave a bunch to her, she bit into the green leaves directly.

"Oh! It's so good! So good I could eat it all!" declared their mother.

After a while she hauled herself heavily upright and wandered further down the stream while the two girls worked through the thickly matted plants, filling the baskets. For a long while Elizabeth was conscious of nothing but the water flowing past her ankles, the sunlight filtering through the trees onto the stream and a cuckoo calling in the woods. Then a scream cut through the stillness of the woods. She felt a tight squeeze of fear in her chest.

"What was it?"

"It's Mother!"

Catherine dropped her basket and ran. Elizabeth scrambled out of the water and tried to get socks back onto her wet feet. By the time she was ready to follow Catherine, she had heard two more screams.

When she found them, she saw her mother was lying on the ground, her face red. Catherine was kneeling beside her, trying to undo her stays. She looked up at Elizabeth, her face white with fear.

"She has tripped, Lizzie."

"Is she hurt?"

"Her ankle, I think. But that's not it."

Elizabeth stared, baffled.

"The baby, Lizzie. The baby is coming and I don't know what to do. Run back to the house as fast as you can and tell them. Tell Cook and Betsy; tell anyone; they'll have to come now, quick, quick as they can."

Elizabeth turned and ran.

* * *

After she had told them, she wasn't allowed to go back to the woods. She had to stay and look after the babies because Betsy was gone with Cook and Isaac and the stable boy. It seemed like hours before Catherine came back. Her dress was streaked with dirt and leaves, and all her usual haughtiness was gone.

"She's had the baby," Catherine said. "It's a boy. I saw it coming out. It was all covered in slime and blood and Cook had to wash it in the stream." Catherine put her head in her hands and burst into tears. "Everyone's going to blame me," she sobbed. "Mother will die, and they'll all blame me."

She was still weeping when the doctor arrived from Morpeth, looking very grave. He shook his head at her.

"It was very ill-judged, Miss Catherine. Very ill-judged. We must pray to God that no ill comes from it, but it could have grievous consequences."

When the door at last swung open, late in the afternoon, the men were carrying their mother between them. At first her eyes were closed, but she opened them just for a moment to see the girls, and she managed a little smile for them. She was alive, for sure. Betsy was behind them carrying a shawl-wrapped bundle. Immediately, the doctor took charge, giving instructions to take her up to her room without delay, and the baby too; this was a very unfortunate turn of events; he would carry out his procedures straight away; he must have hot water and cloths at once. As soon as Betsy came back down the stairs, the shouting started.

"Why did you let her go?" Betsy screamed. "Everyone knows women take such fancies in their head when their time is near. It could have killed her!"

On and on she went. Although no one scolded her, Elizabeth felt burdened with shared guilt. But when Betsy went off at last to see to the little ones, Cook took them both into the kitchen and gave them pieces of bread and jam. While they ate it, she leaned over the table to Catherine.

"Don't you worry. Nor Lizzie neither. Your mother was better off out there than shut up in her room with that doctor. He's angry because he's not going to get his guineas. You did nothing wrong."

Upstairs, they could hear the baby starting to bawl, loud angry screams.

"Nothing wrong with his lungs," observed Cook.

*   *   *

At first their mother wouldn't look at the baby, wouldn't hold him, for fear of the grief of losing him. But on the third day the wetnurse took him into her.

"He's feeding so well. He's a fine little fellow. Just you hold him there a minute."

Once she had taken hold of him, she couldn't give him back, couldn't let him go, and the wetnurse came and stayed in the house. Soon Elizabeth and her sisters were allowed to go and look at the baby, one at a time. Her mother was still confined; when Elizabeth went in, she found her wearing only a nightdress and a shawl in the hot, airless room.

"Lizzie!" she said. "Come in and see your little brother. He has just had his feed."

The baby was lying on the bed. He wasn't wrinkled and ugly like the twins. He had hair on his head; his face was pink and smooth, and his eyes were open. She leaned over and gave his toes a little wiggle. His lips moved.

"Oh!" she cried out. "He smiled at me, Mother!"

Her mother laughed.

"What a good boy he is!" she said.

"What's he going to be called?"

"Father must decide, of course. But I think he might be John. What do you think?"

"Why?"

"Do you remember, in the Bible? The Virgin Mary had a cousin called Elizabeth. John was the child of her old age. She had given up hope she would ever have a son when God sent John to her. It was a miracle."

She bent over and nuzzled the baby's head.

"Just like him."

CHAPTER 6

Doctors' Commons, London

July 1746

Afterwards, when he counted back the days, William found that his son had been born on the very day that he and Henry had gone to Doctors' Commons for the witnessing of the entail documents. Had he had some premonition, some sense that the course of his life was about to alter, to flow into streams he had never expected? He had not.

He recalled only the low spirits that had afflicted him throughout his stay in London. He slept poorly, disturbed by the constant movement of carts and carriages outside and the shouting of the draymen. He kept his chamber window tight shut against the din, but in the early hours grew restless in the airless room and flung it open. By morning the sill had already collected a fine layer of soot, and he banged it shut again. Newcastle coal dust, here in London. How could people live in this city, breathing in soot and the foul seepings from the ordure in the street? There was such a tightness in his chest he could scarcely breathe, though whether it was the noxious air or his anxiety for Grace he could hardly tell. He was assailed with guilt that he was not at her side and wished every day to be returning, but Henry was not to be hurried. He had suits that could not be put off, he would attend to their business very soon, meanwhile why did William not take the opportunity to take a stroll around the town?

His brother, William soon learned, rose early and took breakfast. His carriage would be waiting from eight to take him to Doctors' Commons and the coachman then returned to wait on Sarah. William seldom saw her in the morning. Around nine o'clock, a housemaid took up a tray of hot chocolate and fresh muffins, soon followed by the lady's maid. It would be another hour or two before Sarah emerged, the ceruse-white of her face brightened only by rouged cheekbones, hair padded, curled and dressed, stayed and buttoned into her costume for the day, ready to take tea with her acquaintance. As far as William could tell, she had no part in the running of the household beyond giving the cook her orders for dinner. It was all very elegant, all utterly distant from the familiar pell-mell of life in his hall. How he missed it! How slowly the days seemed to pass!

One morning he took a stroll down to the Thames to see if he could catch a tang of the North Sea on the breeze. The river at Westminster was like a great highway, with small craft of all kinds ferrying passengers to and fro, dodging gilded shallops rowed by liveried oarsmen and loaded barges that lay heavy in the water. Light sailing ships caught the current and the breeze together, darting past the lumbering barges and down the river like pale birds, under the half-finished arches of the new Westminster Bridge. How different it was from the Tyne! The dark waters of Newcastle's river were filled from side to side with keels bringing coal downriver to the waiting colliers moored on the quayside, their high masts lining the banks. No gilded shallops for the Tyne. Nor palaces either.

He thought of John Addison, master now of the *Darling*. Where would the *Darling* anchor when she came to London, he wondered.

He put his question to Henry that evening at dinner.

"Down at Deptford," Henry told him. "Deptford, Rotherhithe, Wapping—all the business of the port is down there. The arches of London Bridge are too narrow for a sea-going vessel, so they must moor in the Pool below it or further down. There are scores of docks and warehouses down there. It is a mercy to the city since trade is become so great. We are spared the vulgar presence of the sailors."

So John Addison and the *Darling* were shut out of polite London. He thought of John's words when they had ridden to Newbiggin together: "I mean to be a gentleman, Mr Cresswell." How could he ever be? London Bridge split the town in two; on one side, all the palaces and pomp of Westminster, the courts of law, the theatres and the pleasure gardens. On the other, the beating heart of trade, the toil and turmoil that paid for the Palladian houses and the painted ladies. John Addison would never belong to the Westminster world. He was a Deptford man.

A few days later, Henry was free at last to attend to their business. The brothers took the carriage from Westminster to St Paul's and it deposited them beside St Paul's Churchyard, in the shadow of the walls of the cathedral reaching above them in its lofty glory, gleaming in the morning sunshine. In spite of his preoccupation William would have stopped, would have stared upwards at the pillared grandeur of the dome, would even have chosen to step inside. But Henry spared it not a glance, gliding briskly forward along the alleyway with hands clasped before him, robes sweeping the pavement and wig so curled and primped he could hardly have looked up even had he wanted to. Soon they were crossing a quiet and shady courtyard surrounded by red-brick houses, crossed now and again by clerks clutching bundles of papers.

"In here," directed Henry, and the notice above the entrance confirmed "Prerogative Office".

It was a long room lined with shelves filled with large volumes. Below the shelves were desks where clerks sat, copying deeds. Down the centre of the room were several high desks crowded about with people poring over documents. Wills, Henry explained. Anyone could come to this office, take down a set of papers and try to decipher the deeds and trusts that might bestow a legacy to them. There was a hush in the room, a tense attention at odds with the dusty documents. William suddenly felt his own desire mirrored and amplified by the urgent searching going on around him, shamed as if his own soul had been laid bare in all its venal yearning. He felt a flush rising up his cheeks. But Henry, unmoved, directed a clerk to bring him the volume he required and then sailed onwards, deeper into the building, to his private rooms. In the panelled coolness of his lair he took the will out, smoothed down the parchment and started to read.

At first, William listened with fierce attention. But as the will wound through sentences with no clauses and no endings, the messuages burgages lands tenements hereditaments and all and singular other, through the premises abovementioned with their and every of their appurtenances and every part and parcel thereof, he was unable to derive any meaning at all from it. His eagerness changed to a baffled blankness and frustration. He jumped up suddenly, slapping his fist down on the table.

"For God's sake, Henry! Can we not discuss this in plain English?"

"Patience, patience! You'll understand well enough in a moment."

"Don't tell me what I can understand or not!"

And he felt, suddenly, hot with rage against his brother, so accomplished and assured, with his Palladian townhouse and his country mansion, his young wife, and his coach and four. Henry could afford to turn his nose up at Cresswell. The inheritance was nothing to him, beyond a distant demonstration of his gentility. William would show him! He would show him what it meant to be the inheritor of a line that could trace its descent to kings. Henry was no more than a jumped-up clerk who used the law to bamboozle his way to a fortune. William turned away to the window, aghast to find himself close to tears.

There was a long silence. William returned to the table. Henry started to read again. The morning droned away, witnesses arrived, signatures were affixed, his father's attached, and it was done. When his father died, the estate would be William's.

CHAPTER 7

Cresswell, Northumberland

January 1747

One might have thought, in William's opinion, that God's gift to the family of a son, of an heir to carry on the family line, would have been for his mother a demonstration of the Divine even-handedness. It was true, in a sense, that He had taken Robert from her. But in his place He had given her a longed-for grandson. Indeed, it was hardly accurate to say He had taken Robert, since Robert was still alive, albeit exiled, and occasional letters still arrived from him. But no. All the brightness had gone out of her. She shut herself away in the Tower, growing frail before his eyes.

"Am I not enough for her?" William complained to Grace. "Is the babe not enough for her? What's the matter with her?"

"It's not about you. Or Robert even."

"About what then?"

"Ask to see her miniature of Charles Edward. Ask what she has done with it."

William stared at her. Grace looked down at the baby. He had fallen into a doze and his head dropped to the side of her breast. She leaned over, wiped his mouth and laid him to sleep on her lap. She looked back at William.

"She threw it in the fire and burned it. Do you know what she said to me? 'It is the death of all my hopes.'"

"The death of all her hopes? How can she say that?"

But he could see that it was true. She had lost all interest in life. There were no more stories and sugar cakes for the children. No matter how tasty the dinner she would push her plate away untouched. However cold the day she would take the same worn dress to put on, till Grace took to visiting her every day to coax her to take a warm shawl around her shoulders. When, after Christmas, she took a fever, no one had any doubt of the outcome.

* * *

Elizabeth was allowed to go and see her, to say goodbye, although her mother did not say that. As she climbed the circling stair to her grandmother's chamber, she remembered the Epiphany cake and the White Lady; how she had run up the stairs to go out on the turret, and how she had been caught ... but all of a sudden she was there, at the chamber door, looking at her grandmother lying in her wooden bed with blankets piled up high and only her face showing. It was very pale, and her long grey hair lay over the pillow in greasy tangles. The only sound in the room was her breath coming and going in low rattling gasps. Elizabeth went and sat on the chair beside the bed.

"Hello, Grandma," she said.

There was no reply. Grandma didn't even open her eyes. She would wait, Elizabeth decided. In case Grandma woke up.

The fire in the hearth started to sink down to red embers. The monotonous low gasp of her grandmother's breath and the warmth of the room sent Elizabeth into a dream. She was on the beach, and her grandmother's breath became the sound of the ebb and flow of the tide, of the small waves rushing up the sand and sinking back. She was looking out to sea, looking out, as she always did, for a sudden whiteness in the air, a movement of the light that would say, I am here! She could never tell when it would be. The breath-water gasped in, sighed out, in and out, and then there it was, a pale light, not on the shore but here, in the Tower room, beside Grandma, so close it was almost touching her. Elizabeth saw the old woman's face ease and soften. Her lips parted slightly, as if she meant to smile. She lifted her head and gave a little cry, then fell back onto the pillow. For a few moments the light filled the room, so that Elizabeth wanted to reach out and touch it somehow, to hold the gentleness and softness, but it was gone before she could. Then the room was empty and suddenly silent. It was a few moments before she realized that Grandma had stopped breathing.

*   *   *

Grandmother's funeral service was held in the chapel. Her coffin was raised on a stand before the altar, draped with green and purple silk and decorated with tightly bound posies of snowdrops and ivy that the girls had made. They sat in front of William and Grace, under the eyes of their parents and in their Sunday dresses, their fair hair scraped back into neat plaits tied with black ribbons. Eight pairs of plaits: my girls, thought William. Baby John was at the back, in Betsy's arms so he could be taken out if he bawled.

Grandfather sat beside William, his head sunk down between his shoulders, his wintry body statue-still and only William there to support him. Robert was gone to France and the roads were too bad for Henry to travel. In his brothers' absence he felt the full weight of family duty bearing down upon his shoulders and feared in his heart that he was unequal to the task. He had always known that he possessed neither Robert's moral strength nor Henry's wits; he was the supernumerary younger brother, good for nothing but keeping the estate accounts for his father. Robert and Henry had cast a long shadow over his prospects. He had always been "only William", the extra, the unconsidered son. Now he was the heir. He must be the support of his father and the upholder of the family honour. He edged himself closer to Grace and looked again at the row of pigtails in front of him, trying to feel anchored by his offspring.

Behind the Cresswells were the tenants from the farms, crammed in with their families, so that the servants had to stand in a row along the back. William felt a guilty pang of relief that the size of the chapel allowed no room for their wider acquaintance. What would they think? Everything about the chapel bespoke his mother's Catholic sympathies. The purple altar cloth she had embroidered with gold thread, the wrought silver and gilt candlesticks with bright wax candles reflecting light off the silver mass vessels below, the walls decorated with golden-haloed icons of the saints. The priest was the Anglican curate from Woodhorn, but he indulged William's mother in her Roman ways and today had robed himself like a Monsignor in her honour. William had forbidden incense, but he might have saved himself the arguments. The chapel was a Papist sanctuary. No wonder people talked of the Cresswells as Jacobites and Papists. All this, he decided suddenly—the icons, the mass vessels, all of it—would have to go. Just as soon as it was his. Just as soon—Then he caught his thoughts and bowed his head in remorse. How could he have such thoughts, in the middle of his mother's funeral? When his father still sat beside him? He drove his attention back to the service.

"Yet, O Lord God most holy, deliver us not unto the bitter pains of eternal death. Thou knowest, Lord, the secrets of our hearts; shut not thy merciful ear to our prayer . . . "

The priest's words seemed to be directed at him alone, as if God had indeed found out the secrets of his heart and was saying, "I know your thoughts, miserable wretch. Beware or eternal death will take you."

Forgive me, Lord. Forgive me, he mumbled under his breath, and prayed earnestly for his mother's eternal rest. Surely God would take her, Papist or no. Jacobite or not. Was He not merciful?

"I heard a voice from heaven, saying unto me, write, henceforth blessed are the dead which die in the Lord; even so saith the Spirit; for they rest from their labours."

Yes, he thought. Even if she was misguided. Surely she is blessed. As the servants came forward to take up the coffin and bear it out to the waiting cart to carry it to Woodhorn for burial, he felt a sudden moment of purest love for her. He stepped forward and kissed the coffin as it passed.

CHAPTER 8

Cresswell, Northumberland

May 1749

The desire to be rid of the chapel that had awakened in him during his mother's funeral did not leave William in the slow months that followed. Rather, it had planted the seeds of an even greater desire—a vision, even—that had grown to fill his entire attention. He had begun to understand Robert's possession by the Jacobite cause, how it might be to be preoccupied with one idea to the exclusion of all else. It had filled his waking hours, and sometimes his dreams too. To his shame, it had possessed him even while his father was still alive. He would be helping his father in some ordinary task, drawing up the rent bill for one of the farms and he would think suddenly, how much might it be mortgaged for? And for the passage of several minutes, he would hear nothing of what his father was saying to him, completely abstracted in mental calculation. His father had never noticed, of course. He had lived on for two years after his wife's death, but his tired old mind was winding down, wearing out, slipping and sliding away. At the end he had even forgotten that William was his heir. "Where is Robert?" he kept asking, again and again, in the days before his death. More than ever, William felt himself a usurper.

But now that the old man was finally gone and the mourning was done, he could pursue his vision without remorse. He could speak about it openly, could spend days in Newcastle sitting in the oak-panelled rooms of the bank, discussing figures. He could consult with architects. But there was a new problem, a problem he had not anticipated. Once again, he found himself unexpectedly in sympathy with Robert. No matter how clear, how compelling the vision seemed to him, he could not communicate it to Grace.

For the sake of decorum, he had forced himself not to mention it before his father's death, and indeed for months afterwards, so it should not seem that he was making changes with unseemly haste. But at last, he felt the moment had come. One afternoon he asked her to sit with him in the parlour, where they would not be disturbed, and gave her a glass of madeira. He was excited and a little drunk. He had been rehearsing this speech for several days.

"My dearest Grace! I want to talk to you. About the family."

Grace sniffed her madeira and waited.

"As you know, it was never my expectation to become the head of the family. But now that I am, it is my duty to do everything I can for its future. Not for us alone but for John in the future. To clear our name."

Grace was looking at him a little strangely now, but he didn't care to stop.

"Many people still believe the Cresswells are Jacobites. Papists even. The only way to stamp out those ideas is to demolish the chapel. You know my mind on that. But not the chapel alone, I have decided. Cresswell Hall is hardly more than a farmhouse. It is worn out, outdated, not fit to be the residence of a gentleman and his family. I mean to demolish it altogether and build again."

He paused for effect, but Grace's face was blank. He tried again.

"A new Cresswell Hall—how do you like the sound of that?"

Saying it aloud at last filled him with emotion. He had dreamed of the new hall for so long it almost seemed real to him already. His time in London hadn't been wasted. He had spent long enough staring at Henry's house and all the other fine London houses. The new hall would have a classical frontage, large windows and a pillared portico over the front door. It would lead into a gracious reception hall, utterly removed from the old medieval hall now in use, constructed for every purpose of the household from dining to dancing. Instead, the new hall would frame a wide staircase sweeping upwards and open on either side to well-proportioned dining and withdrawing rooms, while all the noise and tumult of the kitchen would be banished to the rear. In his dreams he stood before the house, his son at his side and all his daughters about him.

"Demolish the hall?" said Grace. "Dear God, what has put this into your mind?"

His attention returned abruptly to his wife. He felt as if she had flung a basin of cold water at him. It is all new to her, he reminded himself. She has had no inkling of it, at all.

"I have thought this over very carefully for many months. It has not just entered my mind, as you seem to suppose."

"I knew you wanted to do away with the chapel. But that could be done well enough without doing damage to the house."

"You don't understand me yet. If we were to demolish the chapel alone, it would stand out very strangely. It would be clear to everyone why we were trying to do away with it. But if it were demolished as part of a greater design, to rebuild the hall entirely, why then there would be nothing to remark upon."

He saw her opening her mouth and rushed to forestall her.

"In any case, that's not the point. As I have said, I mean to build a house more suitable to the family's reputation in the county."

"I can't believe what I'm hearing. Have you stumbled suddenly upon a pot of gold?"

"You have little understanding of how such things are managed, Grace."

"I understand well enough that we have nine children to feed and clothe and that there are marriage portions to be found if we are ever to see the girls settled."

"That's it, that's it precisely! Are we to spend the rest of our lives scrimping and saving as my father did, as if we were halfway to pauperhood? He never raised his head above the halfpennies. If it were used aright this is a good estate. Don't you think I can judge what it is capable of?"

"But where is the money to come from? Do you mean to sell one of the farms?"

He looked at his wife, her cheeks pink, her eyes flashing. She is a spirited woman, he reminded himself. Of course she is. But why could she not, just for once, take the part of a loyal wife and accept his judgement?

"Have some more madeira," he said. She shook her head.

"I will myself."

He sat back in the chair, swilling his glass. The finances of the estate were a matter for him and, one day, for John, not for Grace. But if she didn't understand how he meant to do it, these arguments would go on and on. She wouldn't give up. He sighed.

"Very well. I will explain it to you, although I am under no obligation to do so."

He glared at her. She composed her face into a semblance of wifeliness.

"I have no intention of selling land. That would be counter to all our interests. The money will be raised through an instrument known as a mortgage. What that means, simply, is that our agents will assist me to a loan secured on the estate. Over a period of years it will be paid off at five per cent interest."

He looked up. She was listening, at least.

"How are the repayments to be found, you will ask. You have heard me talk of the improvements I intend to make upon the estate, improvements that will greatly increase our returns. Moreover, my father has not raised rents for a decade or more. The money is there, in the estate. It is there for the taking."

A sudden moment of biblical inspiration struck him.

"The talents, Grace. The story of the talents. There is no reward for the man who buries his talent in the earth. The good and faithful servant is the one who works and doubles the value of what he has been given."

She was frowning slightly, staring at him. He felt a warm moment of triumph. Grace was silenced. For now.

CHAPTER 9

The Red House, Woodhorn Demesne

1750

He owed his acquisition to George Addison, William couldn't deny that, although it might have come to his ears through other routes. He had chanced to meet him in Newcastle. Emerging from his lawyer's office one afternoon, William's head was so turbulent with figures and forecasts and percentages that he decided on a stroll down to the quayside to clear his thoughts. One question was gnawing at him. It wasn't the first time the man had asked, but as he had no clear answer, he had preferred not to think about it.

Where were they to live while the new hall was being built?

At first it had seemed obvious to him. They would live in the Tower. It would stay, of course, since it was the ancestral seat of the Cresswells and the evidence of the antiquity of their lineage; the new hall would be attached to it just as the old one was. So they could live in the Tower while the building work went on. But when he had given Grace that answer she had raised so many objections that he had been forced to concede it might be difficult. There were only two chambers; where were they all to sleep? It was cold and damp and uncomfortable. There was no kitchen. On and on she went. He would have thought she might be prepared to put up with some discomfort; it was only for a year or two. But it seemed she was not, and he had started to doubt himself. And today, here was his lawyer asking the same question and he had felt a fool for not having an answer on the tip of his tongue.

William stepped out into the bustle of the street and turned into a narrow lane leading down to the river. A fresh breeze sent scraps of newspaper and frayed rope ends skittering over the cobblestones. A spiralling cloud of coal dust came blowing up the hill, half-blinding him; a gust of wind took the hat off his head and one side of his wig with it. He caught hold of the wig just in time and straightened it back on his forehead before chasing the hat down the hill. It blew into the doorway of a warehouse, where he pounced on it and rammed it firmly back on his head. He stood for a moment, catching his breath, watching as another gust took a loaded coal barge and swung it halfway across the Tyne, so that the two keelmen balanced on the stern had to snatch up their poles and shove them hard down against the current. William marvelled at their upright balance, at their casual deftness bringing round the heavy keel. No doubt the Thames was a more noble river, but he felt a perverse loyalty to the Tyne and its people. He looked along the river at the lines of masts pulled close to the dockside, sails reefed up tightly but still pulling and flapping in the wind. No doubt they were only colliers waiting for lading but still, he would like to take a look at them.

He righted his hat and coat and wandered along the quayside, looking at the names painted brightly on the side. *Beeswing . . . John and Mary . . . Hopewell Fortune . . .*

"*Brotherly Love*," he said aloud. He was suddenly aware of a presence beside him.

"Have you spotted the *Success*, then?" a man asked him. He turned to find George Addison at his right shoulder.

"Why, George!"

"We brought her in last evening. I've been paying my dues." He gestured up to the Customs House behind them and winked. "Will you take a coffee?"

When they were settled with a pipe in a snug corner of the coffee house, George told him the news.

"The Red House is for sale. You know the one. Hardly a mile from Woodhorn church. Fine prospects over Newbiggin Bay."

Of course he knew it. He knew every house, every property in the district. The Red House had been built the same year he was born, 1702. A dower house for Lady Widdrington, along with three hundred acres of the best grazing land in the district. After the '15 rebellion it had been confiscated along with the rest of the Widdrington estate and sold off by the Crown.

"What of it?"

"A London company bought it, but they have defaulted on the contract. It is to be sold by decree of Chancery. They are eager to be rid of it, so it seems." George took a slow pull on his pipe and turned his head to blow the smoke away. "My nephew, John Addison—you remember John?"

William nodded.

"He is become a shipmaster now. He has shares in a couple of ships, and it'll not be long before he owns one for himself. If any man can make himself a fortune, it'll be John Addison. Well, John got wind of this, and he is all taken up with the notion of buying the Red House.

"'Are you mad?' I asked him. 'How could you pay off a debt like that? What would you do with it? Your home's down there, down in Whitby.'

"'No', he says, 'I like it better here.'" George shook his head. "Just a dream," he said. "A young man's folly."

William hardly heard what he was saying. An idea had suddenly registered in his mind. He kept his voice easy.

"Give me the details of the agent, George. I might hear of someone."

As soon as he decently could, William rose to leave. He felt that Providence, in the unexpected form of George Addison, had given him a solution. He could save John Addison from his folly and solve his own problem at a stroke. As soon as he was clear of the quayside, he set off directly to pay the agent a visit.

* * *

When she first heard her parents talking of the Red House, Elizabeth imagined it as a fiery house in purgatory, like the pictures in Grandmother's book of Bible stories, burning red with flames leaping from the windows.

A shudder went through her at the thought of it. Why did her father want them to live there? It seemed a mad and terrifying idea.

"Is it painted red?" she asked her mother.

"No, it's not painted. It's called the Red House because it is all built of bricks. The windows and the front door have stone surrounds, but all the walls are brick." Grace looked at her daughter's anxious face. She caught her up in a quick hug and kissed her.

"Don't worry, Lizzie. It's a nice house. You and Catherine and Lelia will have a room together, away from the little ones. Dorothy and Grace too."

Elizabeth wanted to say, I don't want a new room, I don't want a new house; our house is here, this is where we live. But she hung her head and said nothing. Grace gave her another squeeze.

"It's not for ever, in any case. Just a year or two. We'll soon be home again."

Her parents must have discussed it, for after dinner the next day her father announced, "Next Sunday, after we have been to church, we will go and look at the Red House. If the weather is pleasant. Your mother thinks you should all see where we will live while the new hall is built."

So a few days later they were got up early in their Sunday dresses and shawls and bonnets. Isaac first brought the gig up to the door for Father and then went back for the old carriage.

"Mother and I will go in the gig," her father decreed. "Catherine, you had better come with us and John; you can keep him quiet. The rest of you in the carriage. No arguments," he added, seeing rebellion in the faces before him.

They were all squashed into the carriage, Betsy as well since she would have to look after John when they got to church. Elizabeth had to have Alice sit on her lap and with every bump in the road Alice fell back against her. They had hardly started out before the gig came to a stop in front of them and Isaac pulled up again. They could all hear John roaring. Catherine jumped out of the gig and ran back into the house.

"It'll be his soldiers," observed Betsy. "He won't go anywhere without his soldiers."

"And so, we all have to wait for John's soldiers," said Bridget tartly. It was always like that. Whatever John wanted he must have; the rules were different for boys. At least it might mean they were late for church.

But Isaac drove the horses on at a good pace and they had to sit through the whole of Matins and the endless sermon and there was nothing to do but stare at the coloured glass in the windows. While the sermon droned on, Elizabeth planned how she would escape if she was taken to the Red House. She wouldn't walk back along the road; they would look for her there. She would wait till low tide and creep along the beach, all the way back to Cresswell. And she would go and hide in the Tower, hide in the back of the inglenook where they would never find her, and she would live on the stores in the cellars. She would live there forever and never come back to her family. She could never leave Cresswell, because that was where the spirit of the Lady was, and she belonged to her, just as she had belonged to Grandmother. It was her destiny.

Then at last the service was over and they were leaving the church, running out into the bright air and sunlight, back to the carriage, and despite her fears it was impossible not to feel excited as they rolled down the narrow road to the house, past the trees that sheltered it to the north and east. As they hung out of the windows of the carriage they saw it suddenly, a tall stately house in mellow brick, warm in the sunshine, with a formal garden laid out before it and the walls of a kitchen garden to one side. The carriage came to a stop, the door was wrestled open and Elizabeth jumped out with her sisters. They ran across the gravelled drive, up the short flight of steps to the front door.

"Look! The sea! You can see the sea!" cried Lelia, and indeed, although it was not as close to the bay as Cresswell Hall, the house stood on a rise overlooking Newbiggin Bay and you could see far out to sea, you could see the brown sails of the fishing boats rise and fall on the glittering blue of the water and a line of red-roofed houses along the village street.

They ran inside and found the house was empty, just flagstone floors and high walls painted pale green, so that the inside of the house seemed like the outside, its white ceilings rimmed with plaster flowers. All the doors stood open, and it smelled of emptiness, a brackish dusty smell that would linger afterwards in Elizabeth's memory. A curving staircase rose out of the hall and Bridget, Juliana and Alice chased each other up it, shrieking with excitement. When Elizabeth followed and looked up to see where they had gone, she found there was a glass dome above her, set into the roof, so that the staircase was full of daylight. It led up to a landing, to a corridor with one door after another opening into bedrooms with high windows and polished floors, all empty, all waiting for curtains and chairs and beds, and how would they ever all be filled? Elizabeth stopped by a window and saw that it was half-open, that the bottom frame of wood and glass somehow slid upwards over the top frame so that there was a wide opening she could have squeezed out of, and a warm breeze was blowing through it, smelling of seaweed. She was transported at the wonder of it. Would she sleep here, in a room like this, where the windows slid over each other and the breeze blew in from the sea?

She ran out to find her sisters, to see where they had gone, and they were all stumbling up the narrow back stairs to see where the servants would live, in this high house with top windows that squinted out over a balustrade. But the servants' rooms were low-ceilinged and stuffy, so they ran down again, down the back stairs and out the back in search of the kitchen. Dorothy and Grace were there already, and Betsy, and John was chasing Alice as she ran just ahead of him around the kitchen.

"Cook will be pleased with this," said Betsy. "All conveniently laid out and the cool room and the dairy just to the back there. They've got some strange contraption over the fire though, Lord knows how that's going to work."

"Dorothy and Grace! Lizzie! Lelia! Bridget . . . " Catherine was out in the hall, calling for them. "It's lunch!"

Outside there was a bench overlooking the garden, where her father was sitting with a pipe and a bottle of beer. Isaac was lugging a hamper over from the carriage, and her mother was behind him with a rug and stoppered pitchers of lemonade. They were here, at the Red House, there was veal pie and curd tarts, the waves curled with white spray in the distance, and it was so far from Elizabeth's imaginings of the hellish Red House that she was utterly confounded by it all. She stood holding a curd tart in front of her mouth for so long that Lelia cried out at last, "Well put it in, Lizzie!" So she bit into the buttery pastry and the soft curds and currants and her mouth was full of sweetness.

Her mother sat on the bench beside her father and drank one of his bottles of beer. He put his hand on hers. She looked up and smiled at him. He leaned over and kissed her.

* * *

The next day William sat on his father's chair in the Tower room that he still used as the estate office. His father's desk still stood in front of the narrow window, but a large table now filled the far side of the room, covered with plans and folders and account books. It was another sunny summer's day outside and even in the Tower the air was mild. It had all gone very well yesterday; he had felt buoyed by the children's excitement and by Grace's enthusiasm for the place. But today the elation had drained away.

Buying the Red House had solved one problem, William reflected, as he shuffled through the bills. But it had created another. For sure, he had bought it for half its value; he had already let out the grazing and when they had moved back to Cresswell Hall, he would get a good rent for the house. He had no doubts; it was a good investment that would see a handsome return.

But it had used up part of the credit he needed for the building work. He got up and wandered over to the table to look again over all the bills of cost. They would pay nothing for stone, that was something. There was a good seam of sandstone close by at Bog Hall, next to the shore and the road and less than a mile from the hall. But it would have to be properly dressed. They would need six masons on site through the first stage of building, Amos said, and they would expect eleven shillings a week. Eleven shillings! Even the quarrymen and labourers would need seven shillings and as many pence.

Amos was the master builder William had chosen for the job. He had a good reputation in the district. He had done work for the Corporation in Newcastle and the handsome finish of the Banqueting Hall he had completed at Trinity House was admired. But a good builder was one thing. An architect was another. He had been recommended to one Daniel Garratt and had already visited Mr Garratt's office. They had viewed drawings of the mansions in the Palladian style Mr Garratt had constructed. He could even turn his hand to the Gothick and after a visit to his latest construction at Gibside William had notions for a while of using the Tower to lend a more fantastical feature to the new hall. But Mr Garratt had persuaded him otherwise and William was content with the elegant frontage proposed in the first sketches. Mr Garratt would be in attendance during the build to supervise the construction and to keep account of orders and supplies as required. His fee for this service had shocked William, but since Mr Garratt had no shortage of distinguished clients, he assumed that there was no alternative but to pay it.

Once the purchase of the Red House was done, he had sent word to Amos, desiring him to meet for a further discussion on building costs. When the man arrived, more than a week later, William found him in the kitchen enjoying a slice of cold mutton and talking to Cook. He was such a broad man he took up half the bench, his brawny arms bursting out of his shirt sleeves as he hefted the food to his mouth. When he half-turned to greet William, his curly black beard was covered in crumbs.

"Good day!" he roared, brushing himself down with a blunt-fingered dust-ingrained hand. "Here I am, at your service!"

He got to his feet to demonstrate his willingness and came over to take William's hand. Although William was not a small man, he found himself looking up to find Amos's face.

"Come upstairs," he said shortly.

William took the man up to the Tower and stood him in front of the table.

"I must find economies, Amos. I understand that you must pay the skilled men at their price, but can we not find labourers to work for a shilling or two less?"

Amos shook his head.

"It'll only cause trouble, Mr Cresswell. At the first wind of better paid work elsewhere they'll be gone and you'll be left with a quarry full of stone and no one to lead it out. I need a team of men I can rely on or we'll still be here in five years' time."

"You are very tender-hearted towards your people."

"There are ways of saving money, Mr Cresswell, and ways of losing it."

"Well, what do you suggest? If we cannot find a way to trim the costs, I will have to give up on the whole design and then there will be no work for anyone."

"There is one good way I know to save money, but the gentry don't like to hear of it and so I say nothing. If they want to throw away their gold, why, I'm not going to stop them."

"Say it out, man. What are you talking about?"

"I've been a builder since I was a boy and I've been a master for more than ten years. I've built every sort of building from almshouses to assembly rooms, and more than a few houses in between. But when Lord So-and-So wants a new wing on his mansion, does he call on me? No. He calls on his architect and they sit together staring at drawings, and my Lord pays him hand over fist for his cleverness. And then my Lord gives us the plans and tells us to get on with it, and when the architect feels like a ride in his carriage he comes down and tells us, no no, that's not what I meant at all, take down that wall, and we must start all over again. They're clever men all right. They know how to make themselves a fortune on my Lord's reputation."

Amos paused to draw breath. His lined and weather-beaten face had turned red with indignation and William was almost ready to laugh at him. But something in his words touched a nerve. Garratt's bill was almost as high as all the labour costs put together.

"If you want to cut down your costs here's my advice to you, Mr Cresswell, if you want it." He paused for effect. "Do without the architect." He stared histrionically at William and repeated himself. "Do without the architect. What do they do? Draw up plans? Well, you've got some plans over there already and between the two of us we can work them up. There's nothing there so different from any house I've built before. You know what you want. I can get another man in to help with the surveying. Managing costs and supplies? Well, Mr Cresswell, you've already got all the bills of cost worked out; I've never seen a gentleman so well prepared as you. You don't need an architect to do that for you, if you're prepared to do the work yourself."

Suddenly William felt he was right. How different could it be to the usual tasks of running the estate? He was used to figures and managing men. Amos had had years of experience. He knew how to build a house. Between them, they could do it.

But it would not do to let Amos see that he was persuaded. It must be clear who was master here and who made the decisions. He kept his face still.

"Well, Amos, I have every confidence in your abilities and I will certainly consider your suggestion. Let us meet again next week, when I have had time to go through all the papers."

Amos nodded and a sudden doubt struck William. "There is something sly about the man," a voice within him warned. "You must be careful." William paused for a moment, then decided to ignore it. He clapped Amos on the back and bid him good day.

PART TWO

1756–63

The Privateer

EXTRACT FROM THE *LONDON GAZETTE*, 17 MAY 1756

At the Court at Kensington
PRESENT
The KING's moſt Excellent Majeſty in Council.

His Majeſty's Declaration of War againſt the French King. The unwarrantable Proceedings of the French in the West Indies, and North America, since the Concluſion of the Treaty of Aix-la-Chapelle, and the Uſurpations and Encroachments made by them upon our Territories and the Settlements of our Subjects in thoſe Parts, particularly in our Province of Nova Scotia, have become ſo notorious, and ſo frequent, that they cannot but be looked upon as a ſufficient Evidence of a formed Deſign and Reſolution in that Court, to purſue invariably ſuch Measures as Would most effectually promote their ambitious Views, without any Regard to the most solemn Treaties and Engagements . . .

. . . **We have therefore thought proper to declare War, and we do hereby declare War against the French King, who hath ſo unjuſtly begun it, relying on the Help of Almighty God in our just undertaking and being aſſured of the hearty Concurrence and Aſſiſtance of our Subjects in ſo Good a Cause . . .**

Given at our Court at Kensington, the 17th Day of May, 1756

CHAPTER 10

Whitby, Yorkshire

1756

On a fine afternoon in August 1756 John Addison, shipmaster, took his hat off the peg and walked out of his office, ignoring the calls for him to attend to the carpenter's expenses, to sign off the bill of quantity for the spirits and wine, to look over the dockyard tallies, to check the new names in the muster book, and all the other tasks that went along with the *Friends' Desire* making ready to sail.

"I will be gone till Wednesday," he told his clerk and the man looked up at him close to panic.

"Two days, sir? Might you not return tomorrow evening so that we might spend an hour or two on the most urgent matters?"

"There's nothing you can't manage. Don't expect me."

And he was gone, out to the mews at the back of his house where the stable boy had a horse saddled and waiting for him. He swung up into the saddle, rode up the hill and out of Whitby, north along the cliff road. Out of habit he noted the ships out in the bay as he rode along—that would be the *Mary*, he thought, reefing down her topgallants as she drew close to the harbour—and then he shook his head once or twice, turned away, clapped his heels into the side of the horse and cantered down into Sandsend. He could see his grandmother's house, tucked into the side of the valley, his grandma who would totter out on her stick with shrill reproaches for his long absence, but he would not stop for her today, nor would he stop at

Easington either since his father and he had nothing to say to each other, but he would ride hard for Skinningrove and join the Easterbys for dinner.

The horse was lathered with sweat by the time he turned off the coast road into the valley that led to Skinningrove. It was formed by one of the sudden deep fissures in the cliffs found along the Yorkshire coastline, with a beck running through it, a strip of green meadow alongside, and hills rising steeply to either side. The hillsides were thickly wooded and in full summer riding down the valley was like plunging into a green tunnel. He had always the same sensation, familiar since his boyhood, of the world being shut out behind him as he dropped down into its leafy seclusion. It was a place where nothing could reach him, where there was nothing but the splashing of the beck and greenness all about him, where the clamour in his head could begin to calm.

After half a mile or so came the first glimpse of the sea; a sandy bay lying low between two rocky headlands, and in front of it the Easterbys' manor house, so strange a building that it increased the feeling of the otherworldliness of the valley. It was a high three-storey house built of dark brick that appeared almost black, with the windows and front door outlined in staring white, with geometric forms set around the front entrance. It sat, not looking out to sea to enjoy the pleasant prospect over the bay, but instead facing up the valley, back turned to the sea as if to deny that its existence had anything to do with the trade that came and went in the bay. For the Easterbys had been able to profit from the secluded location of their bay, far away from prying eyes. The long ride down the valley was enough to discourage the excise men from Whitby. And if they did come, why, the Easterbys were generous hosts to such travellers as made it to their door, and they had a free hand with the brandy.

As he rode up to the house, John shouted out a halloo and minutes later the front door was flung open and his two nephews came running out, racing to be the first to reach his horse and lead him down into the stable.

"I have a new pony! He is in the stable, I will show him to you!" cried out John, his namesake and the eldest. Frank, just turned six years old, clutched at the bridle and held up his arms to be pulled up onto the saddle.

"Oh! Have a care," called out his sister Jane from the doorway. She was too big with child to run after him, John saw. Another babe on the way. It was all family life now at Skinningrove, and there was a part of him that loved the noise and uproar of it all.

*   *   *

"How the boys love to see you, John!" said Jane. "You must come more often. We have hardly seen you since the winter."

John Addison smiled at his sister. He was too replete with roast mutton and oysters to defend himself against her reproaches, and besides, there was a sweetness in Jane that took any sting from her words. Jane loved him, that was all, and what could a man desire more than that? She had been both sister and mother to him after their mother's death; there was an unbreakable bond between them. He leaned back in the chair and took a pull on his pipe. There was nowhere he would rather be than here, he told himself, in the old, panelled dining room, with the oak table set in the middle and the last of the evening light coming through the windows and setting the crystal alight. The children were still awake upstairs, still excited, their footsteps audible on the boards and the nursemaid's voice scolding them back to bed.

He had once been a child in this house too, had run up and down the staircase as if it were his own, had sat at the kitchen table with a slice of bread and dripping and gone running helter-skelter to the beach when a sail came into view. Old Mr Easterby had let John Addison's father run ships out of the bay, had found him useful as trade grew with the Netherlands, and since their two boys were of an age it was natural for them to play together. When they reached twelve, the boys went to Whitby to serve their apprenticeship with the same shipmaster. There was just two months between them and they were often mistaken for brothers.

Now, as they sat at the table together in the twilight, there was still a physical likeness between the two men. They had both been seamen since their earliest youth,and were broad-chested, strong-built men who could work a ship's sail through two watches without tiring. John Addison had a couple of inches on Francis Easterby, but Francis had such an abundance of curly brown hair that he looked as tall. John had kept his fair hair, tied straight back from his head, and both men had taken to clapping a wig on their heads when ashore. Years of facing into all the storm and sleet the North Sea could provide had left them both with weather-worn faces that seemed older than their thirty-one years. That, and the trimmed beards that covered the lower half of their cheeks, made it hard for the observer to distinguish any difference in their features. The differences between them were only obvious to an observer such as Jane, who had known both men since their boyhood. She knew her brother John had always been the ringleader in their adventures, always the first to clamber into a boat, to carry off a musket, to go exploring further up the coast till they got lost in the caves. She saw that it was still there, that restlessness, harnessed now he was an owner and must oversee every tedious matter in his business, but perceptible still in the quickness of his manner, in his boldness before the mast, in his sharpness at driving a bargain. You could never be entirely sure of John; sometimes she wondered if he would ever settle down, would ever take a wife and make his own family. Francis Easterby, her husband, was as able a man but not as driven. He was steady and settled, content with his life. He had not altered since he was an apprentice and had declared that he would marry her. His father made him wait till he was twenty-one, but he had never wavered. When she gave birth to her sons, there was no question how they would be named; John first, then Frank.

The meal done, Francis set down his glass and looked across the table at his friend.

"So, John. You have made your mind up."

"How have you heard that?"

"All the town is talking about it. I dare say others will follow, but you are the first, I believe."

"I was lucky enough to hear news of the Declaration of War before I sailed for London. I thought, I shall waste no time in paying a visit to the Admiralty. Believe me, they were happy to see me. The Frenchies have been at the game long enough."

"Did they give you the Letter?"

"I have brought it with me." He reached for his bag. "Take care how you handle it! I have paid dearly enough for it with my bond."

He unrolled the document across the table. Francis leaned over it and Jane got up to stand behind him.

HIGH COURT OF ADMIRALTY: PRIZE COURT
Register of Declaration of Letters of Marque: AGAINST FRANCE
Owner: John Addison. Ship: Friends' Desire.
Burden: 400 tons. Crew: 80.
ITEM:
Commander: John Addison.
Lieutenant: John Broderick.
Gunner: Andrew Harper.
Boatswain: Hezekiel Newmatch.
Carpenter: John Hutchinson.
Surgeon: John Addison.
Cook: Thomas Presswick.
Armament: 10 carriage guns.
Date: 1756 July 31

"You must have spoken with these men before you left Whitby. John Broderick—Hezekiel—they are good men."

"They were ready to join me. Believe me, since it has become known in town that I hold a Letter of Marque, there have been men at my door from dawn to dusk. I have my pick of crew. And more than enough who can handle a musket."

"But eighty? There'll scarce be space for half of them to sling a hammock."

"I need prize crews. If we are fetching back a couple of ships to London, they'll not sail themselves."

Francis shook his head and stared at the document again.

"What of the gunner? Are you sure of him?"

"He was pressed for a year or more on a ship of the line. I have four others like him and they can train up the others. I brought up the guns from London from a prize ship lately brought in, a couple of twelve-pounders and the rest nine."

"You will not fight, will you, John?" said Jane.

"We'll let the guns do the work and the boarding party. I'll just be looking out from the quarterdeck."

"'Tis a risky business, though," Francis pitched in. "Terribly risky. Not just the fighting. You've got your own ship now, and to gamble it on such a venture! The bond, the guns, the provisioning . . . your credit must be strained to the limit, and for what?"

"For what?" John Addison suddenly lost his easy manner and thumped his glass down on the table. "Am I to spend the rest of my days running coal down the North Sea or freezing half to death on the Baltic run? And now, when the navy must sail all the colliers down in convoy for fear of attack from the Frenchies, so that every ship must make the same slow way till there's hardly a guinea to be made on the run—am I to stand by and watch myself decline? A single prize will pay off my credit and after that there's fine profits to be made. I'm not a fool, Francis. I can tell a merchantman from a fourth rate. I'll pick my fights."

"There's other ways, John," said Francis, unshaken by his brother-in-law's vehemence. "The government mean to send troops to the Americas, so I hear, and they'll be looking for transports. It's a long run and could bring you good money."

"Indeed, and I've no objection to a visit to Virginia either. I'll be out in the Channel till Christmas, I'll refit in London and then we'll see about a transport run."

There was a silence in the room.

"I had expected to hear more rejoicing at my news," said John, "but enough of that. Tell me of your plans, Francis."

"None like yours."

"What of the Whaling Company?"

"This year's sailings are not returned from Greenland. We have no news of them. I am minded to send out a ship next spring if other trade is suffering from the war. The bounty is forty shillings a ton now."

The conversation moved on till it was grown dark outside and the maidservant brought candles in. John Addison felt the exhaustion of the day wash over him and asked for his room. He carried his candle up the stairs to the end chamber where he always slept, set it down on a chest, and before he turned in for sleep sat for a moment on the edge of the bed. Francis was right. It was a risky business. Some privateers made a fortune, but plenty more lost their ships and their lives. He might not sit here again, in the familiar shadow of his Skinningrove chamber, listening to the beck running past outside. But nothing wavered within him. He was set on his course. If the fates gave him fortune, he meant to have a manor house of his own to match his friend's. But when his thoughts ran on to the wife that might be its mistress, he stood up suddenly, went over to the chest and blew out the candle.

CHAPTER 11

English Channel

1756

It was half past four in the morning, the moon still white in the sky and the air chill. The *Friends' Desire* was sailing out on the spring tide, carried down the Esk between the dockyards and close-packed wooden houses. The town was still asleep, and there was hardly a sound as the ship glided down the river, staysails up, till she reached the harbour mouth and was slipping out between the heads into the open sea. John Addison felt the wooden body of the ship come alive with the first dip and heave into the swell. The sailors of the first watch stood close together on the deck, waiting, watching.

"Away aloft!" he called to the bo'sun. His whistle shrilled out, and the ship was suddenly alive with men racing up the shrouds and out onto the yards. A second shout, "Lay out!" and the sails were unfurled and ready.

"Let fall!" The whistles piping again, the topmen shouting to the sailors pulling on the ropes below, the sudden whiteness of the mainsails falling down and filling out in the breeze, followed by the foresails and the mizzen sail. As the canvas filled out, the ship took the motion and John felt her starting to surge forward on the waves, the bow-wave cutting cleanly through the spray and the bowsprit stretching the ship forward into the easterly dawn light. They would have topsails on as well, he decided, and make the most of the lee wind. He sang out another litany of orders till she was in full sail, wings spread to the utmost. His spirits lifted with her movement. After all the days and weeks of preparation and planning, all the waiting in harbour for the wind and tide, at last they were out and away. A spring tide and a fresh nor-westerly. It was a good omen.

John Addison had sailed out of Whitby scores of times; he knew the North Sea and the English Channel better than the land of his native Yorkshire. He had been a sailor for twenty years. But today was different. He was used to a ship encumbered with thirty chaldrons of Newcastle coal lying heavy in the water, nothing more than a few squalls to worry about and a crew less than half this size. Now there were eighty men and more depending on him. He stood at the centre of the ship; he must not falter or show weakness, so that his people would follow him without question. There were no naval ranks and rules here, no floggings and chains, no admiral to lead the fleet and make decisions; there was only the hazard of the sea to focus minds and the promise of prize money that might put an end to poverty. That was the goad that drove every man on, that made them willing to spend weeks and months crammed close to the next man's hammock, to eat salt herring and biscuit full of weevils, to hang off the rigging in the blast of a northerly gale. They were young men, most of them scarcely into their twenties and many younger, reckless and thirsty enough to risk their lives. As the *Friends' Desire* sailed out of sight of land into the undistracted emptiness of the ocean, wild ambition possessed them all. It sang in the veins of their commander too.

John glanced up at the sky. The day was fine enough, but lines of cloud were straggling across the sun. The breeze was freshening. He might have to reef the topgallants later, but for now, she was running as sweetly as he could wish. *Friends' Desire* was a Whitby cat, a sloop little different from a score of other colliers, but something trimmer in the hull made her sit more lightly in the water, made her more responsive than others of her class. He had watched over her construction, had made sure that good oak was used in every strake and plank and no fir substituted, though he was happy enough to have straight Baltic pine for the masts and bowsprit. Since the yard where she was built was Quaker-owned, they had called her *Friends' Desire*; John Addison had no objection. She was his desire. Everything about her pleased him.

Satisfied with the sail, he turned off the quarterdeck and went aft to the helm to confer with his lieutenant, John Broderick.

"How's she running, Mr Broderick? Can you bring her up closer?"

"She's tight enough into the wind, I'd say."

"Bring her in a point or two."

The wheel came round, setting the ship closer into the wind. She heeled over in a sudden flash of spray over the rail. John Addison laughed.

"You're right. She's tight enough. Let her go."

He watched the deep water running past the bow, dark green and translucent.

"We'll hold this course for the present. I'll ask Mr Newmatch to have all hands up when the watch changes. I'll speak to the people then."

*   *   *

At eight bells the cry "All hands aloft!" went round the ship and the men crowded up from below decks, dropped down from the shrouds, came from every corner of the ship to cram onto the foredeck. John stood up before the mainmast with John Broderick and beside him, Mr Newmatch the bo'sun and gunner Andrew Harper. John Addison surveyed the men. They had just left port and they were still neat enough in their canvas trousers with pigtails tied back. It would all get rougher as they went along.

"Good day to you all. We have made a fair sailing this morning. Mr Broderick will speak to you about the order we mean to keep on board. Then I will make known the course we intend to make and what drills will be required of you. Mr Broderick."

John Broderick stepped forward. Now, while the men were fresh and might take heed, he would go through the ship's rules. What deductions would be made for drunkenness or insolence, what punishments for failing to turn up for duty, for slackness or negligence, what penalties for thieving or immoral acts. It was a code familiar to every sailor, a repeated ritual of shipboard life. John Broderick was a smart fellow with all his wits about him, thought John. The men could see he would stand no nonsense.

When he was done, John Addison took over.

"We are setting a course now toward Canterbury and then we will beat south along the Channel. The Frenchies will be bringing home their sugar fleet from the Indies and we mean to have a taste of it."

There was a low cheer from the men.

"The sugar fleet comes into Le Havre and St Malo on the Channel side. We will stand close to the ports for a fortnight or two. If we find no merchants there, we must go into the Bay of Biscay for La Rochelle and Bordeaux. But we'd like to meet them conveniently, eh lads?"

Another low roar from the men.

"They'll be West Indiamen and bigger ships than us, but they'll be heavy freighted and they've made a long crossing. If we can't outsail them, we'll all go home paupers. So it'll be no use taking your time up the shrouds on this ship. We must move fast, at twice the speed that they can make. We will be exercising every day. You will be beating to quarters on every watch and there will be sail set to speed every day. Mr Harper will be running out the guns with all the men detailed to them and the boarding party will have weapons practice. It will only take a couple of laggards on board to set us back in a chase. Every man must be ready. Do we mean to take a prize?"

A cheer.

"Do we mean to strike a blow against the Frenchies?"

Louder cheer.

"You are stout men all, and we will see good fortune!"

*   *   *

The ship was never still, never silent. Whatever hour of the day or night it was always alive, water slapping against the sides, wind soughing in the rigging, orders shouted to the masthead, a drunken brawl in the orlop deck, sheep bleating in the hold and always the creak and groan of the slakes against the movement of the sea. Long ago, since he had become a master, John Addison had given up slinging a hammock below decks. He enjoyed the comfort of a wooden cot in his cabin, but it was no less noisy than the rest of the ship. He slept undisturbed through the night and yet, somehow, through it all, in the early dawn he heard a cry that sent him bolt awake. Was it "Sail-ho"?

A knock at the cabin door, and one of the mates confirmed it. He pulled on his breeches and shoes, tucked in his shirt and was fully awake and on the quarterdeck in minutes, grasping his telescope. He looked up to the crow's nest and the man on watch pointed.

"Port and forrard!"

He scanned the horizon. With the telescope he could just make out the hazy contour of the French coast, a charcoal line in the pale dawn light. And then, close into the coast, yes! The distant gleam of sails. He lowered the telescope for a moment, turned to the mate.

"Yes. Sail. Fetch Mr Broderick."

He raised the telescope again. It was faint and distant in the half light, but there was no doubting it. Two masts, or was it three? Two; a coastal trader most likely, a brig or small sloop. Heading south, maybe for Le Havre or St Malo, and in no hurry. That would soon change.

"Good morning, Mr Broderick." He passed over the telescope. "On the port bow, south-easterly. A two-master, square-rigged I believe."

Broderick positioned the telescope, took his time, nodded.

"It's early yet, but it seems calm. Wind?"

"Sou-westerly."

"We'll go after her. Tell Newmatch to have the men put on all sail. We'll be up with her in a few hours. Run up the French ensign, so she doesn't take fright."

Broderick started shouting orders. John Addison sent a boy running for Andrew Harper. Soon men were running up the shrouds, the bo'sun's whistle started and the ship was suddenly alive. John watched for a few minutes. It was all helter-skelter, he thought; men were getting in each other's way in their haste to get up the ratlines, the sails were coming down in any order, it was all ragged and rushed. They would have to improve on this. Then Harper was beside him.

"We'll bring the guns up, the twelve-pounders as well though we most likely won't use them. It'll give the men practice. She's on her own, a merchant brig by the look of her, unarmed I should say. We'll fire a warning shot to start with."

Then he was away to the helmsman to chart the course.

"Take her as close into the wind as you can. We'll come up behind her to starboard so that she's against the lee shore."

He felt a pang of hunger for his forgotten breakfast. He sent for a coffee and went back to the quarterdeck.

Three hours later they were so close he could see the men hauling the ropes. The French colours had not deceived the *Etoile*; her crew were running for harbour with every scrap of sail they could muster, but she was loaded and lying low in the water. The *Friends' Desire* would be within firing distance within the hour. He trained the telescope again, scanning her sides. No sign of guns. An ordinary merchant brig doing a coastal run, no convoy, no armament. What was she worth? A few thousand guineas, maybe, and then the cargo. Not a great prize, but then she had fallen so sweetly into their path. And it would be first blood for the crew.

The helmsman had the *Friends' Desire* held so close to the wind that she was heeling hard to port and spray was flying over the deck. John called to Broderick, "Tell him to ease down now so we can get the guns rolled into place. We'll fire a warning shot over her bows as soon as Harper is ready."

They were coming close up behind her now and, with a sudden flash and roar from the gun deck, four cannonballs leaped across the space between the ships and splashed down into the water.

"Bring her up alongside! Boarding party ready!"

And then the two ships were suddenly close with sails heaving and cracking as the *Friends' Desire* came to alongside the brig.

"In the name of the King of England, strike your colours and surrender!" John bellowed across to the master. The man might not understand English, but he would understand very well what his choices were. There were a few minutes' silence before the colours slid slowly down the mast. The grappling irons were thrown across and soon the *Etoile* was rocking helplessly beside them.

"Boarding party over and take prisoners. Strike sail."

* * *

The master was a stout man with short legs and brawny arms who looked at John as though he would have liked to settle it all with a bout of fisticuffs had he not had a length of rope holding his arms tight to his body. A couple of sailors stood beside him in the cabin while John Addison went through the ship's papers. He must have the log and the muster book, the deeds if he could find them, the lading notes and anything else he would need in the Prize Court of the Admiralty. A ship had to be condemned as enemy shipping before it could be claimed as a prize, and while everything about the *Etoile* bespoke her Frenchness, he would take no chances. He glanced over the lading list. She was taking provisions to Le Havre for the French navy. Had they not struck a blow for their country as well as taking a prize? She was carrying flour, he saw, cured pork, hard cheese, onions. And wine. Fifty casks of it. The prize crew would eat well on the way to London.

He took the master prisoner on the *Friends' Desire* and put a prize crew of thirty on her, with a man who spoke French and one of the mates in charge. He didn't want to lose Broderick yet. The *Etoile* had been easy prey, but he meant to take a sugar ship if he could and there might be a fiercer fight.

CHAPTER 12

Guernsey, Channel Islands

1756

The *Friends' Desire* lay to for a few days off Le Havre and saw but a few dolphins and French fishing boats. They would round the Cherbourg peninsula and try their luck near St Malo, John decided, but they were hardly round the head when the wind dropped, leaving them becalmed, sails sagging on the masts. A heavy line of cloud appeared on the horizon to the west; by early afternoon the sky was dark and heavy drops of rain were starting to splash down on the deck. Mr Newmatch found the commander staring up at the mainsail.

"Storm coming up, sir," he observed.

"We'll head for Guernsey. See if we can get into harbour till it blows out. We could take on fresh water while we're there." He paused. "Have you been into Guernsey, Mr Newmatch?"

"No, sir."

"Ask the men—see if we've anyone who knows the island."

John Addison went down to his cabin to find his chart and calculate their course. It would all depend how quickly the storm blew up and whether it held due west. He would rather ride it out at sea than risk running close to a lee shore.

The ship lurched suddenly, sending the chart sliding into his lap and the inkhorn with it. The lamp above his head rocked sideways. The wind was getting up. No time to lose.

*   *   *

They ran before the storm with reefed sails, the rain pouring down onto the deck till every part of the ship was soaking and slippery and every man's clothes were soaked through, and the wind so gusty that the ship would suddenly keel half over and every man must cling to whatever rope or rail he could lay hands on. Sudden cracks of lightning flickered between the top masts, followed hard after by low growls of thunder. Only the bells for the watch told him they were still in daylight hours; it might have been midnight for all the light they had. In the thick of it all, a man appeared at John's side on the quarterdeck and stood, dripping, waiting to speak, leaning hard against the side of the ship.

"What is it?"

"I know the Guernsey ports, sir. St Sampson, sir. That's the one to go for. St Sampson's. It's on the north-east side of the island. Wide enough entrance and low ground to either side."

"Good man." John Addison clapped him on the shoulder and a small spray of water leaped from the man's jacket. "We'll make for it. Anyone else?"

"Don't think so, sir. Unless the other watch."

"Come down to the helm."

They staggered down, thrown side to side by the lurching of the ship, to the wheel, the helmsman spreadeagled over in the effort to hold the ship on course.

"St Sampson's," roared John above the blast. "This man'll take you in."

Their course held true; there was still enough light left for the watch to shout out "Land ho!", and once they slipped down the windward side of the island, they were sheltered from the worst battering of the storm. One final effort with all hands reefing sail and they were into St Sampson unscathed. He would give the fellow at the helm a guinea for his pains, John resolved.

*   *   *

PART TWO: THE PRIVATEER 79

By next morning all that was left of the storm was a fresh wind driving torn scraps of cloud across a clear sky and a heavy swell running out to sea. The decks looked like a laundry yard with trousers and shirts and blankets hung out to dry; there was a holiday mood among men lounging on the fo'c'sle playing dice and combing out their hair. He would have a boat dropped down and go ashore while they took on fresh water, John decided.

It was a tiny port, no more than a quay stretching out from the shore and a few houses clustered up against the bay. But to the north there was a steep mound with a circular fort on the top, a handy lookout he had spotted from the ship. He would climb up there with his telescope.

When he reached the top, he steadied his back against the wall of the fort. There was a clear view right across the Channel. Maybe, on a very clear day, you might see right across to Weymouth. But for now, it gave him all the view he wanted of the sea. He let the telescope move slowly right to left, half resting, half vigilant. Suddenly his arm tightened. He took a sharp breath in and straightened his back against the wall. No. Surely not, after such a storm. Impossible.

But it was.

For fully ten minutes he stirred not a muscle, save for the movement of the telescope. Then he turned and suddenly was all movement, half running, half stumbling down the mound towards the waiting boat drawn up on the beach.

"Back to the ship. Make haste."

As soon as he was back on-board ship, he sent men running for Broderick, for Newmatch and the bo'sun's mates and for Harper to come to his cabin without delay. They came one after another, pulling on shirts and coats, puzzled at the sudden haste.

"I took a walk up the castle mound this morning. There are five ships under French colours making down the Channel, all square-rigged sloops. They are half a day's sail from us, I should say, and look to be holding a northerly course for Le Havre. They have all taken some damage from the storm, but one has lost her mizzenmast and the top of the mainmast. Her sails have suffered too. She is lagging behind the others."

He looked at them. Intent faces looked back at him, struggling to take in the news.

"We'll cut off the straggler and take her. Mr Broderick, take two men as signallers with you and a telescope to the top of the mound. Signal to us when the first four ships are past. We'll follow the fifth. We are close to the top of the island here. If this southerly holds, we'll be out to sea within an hour of your signal. Mr Newmatch, all hands aloft and beat to quarters. Mr Harper, bring up the guns and have powder ready."

The loungers on the fo'c'sle were suddenly galvanized into action. There was a flurry of shirts and trousers being pulled off the rails and a rush of bare feet across the deck, so that the ship pulled slightly against her anchor as the noon watch came to attention in front of Mr Broderick.

The *Friends' Desire* weighed anchor an hour later, but it was late afternoon by the time the signal came for her to clear the island and make out to sea. By then her prey, the *Acheron*, was lying ahead of her, just within sight. The evening sun hung low over the water, lighting up the wounded ship but keeping the *Friends' Desire* in shadow from the other ships ahead.

"Every man keep silence!" John had ordered. They would do nothing to draw attention to themselves as the sea miles fell away between them. There was not a sound but the wind in the rigging and the steady rushing of the bow wave, as if every man on board was holding his breath. Then, suddenly, the *Acheron* sighted them and there was a violent commotion of extra sail being run out, men hurrying up and down the rigging, the ship heeling over as they set their course closer to the wind, but they were outrun already, they had no hope of escape and *Friends' Desire* was on their heels. In less than an hour she was only lengths away.

"Bring her alongside!" The ship pointed into the wind and came around till they were directly parallel to the *Acheron*. Within firing distance.

"Fire the starboard guns!" A crash of cannonballs hurtled towards the *Acheron*, but the gunners had not yet found their range and they splashed down into the water.

"Reload! Fire low!"

A burst of answering fire came from the *Acheron*, two cannonballs skimming the rigging and one taking down the fore staysail, before the *Friends' Desire*'s second firing found its mark. A shudder of cracking timber broke along *Acheron*'s side and a bright orange explosion burst out of a porthole.

"Fire!" John Addison counted scarcely three minutes between the reloads. The gunners were doing better than he could have hoped. The third volley exploded across before *Acheron* managed her second return of fire. Hers was a ragged affair this time, but they landed a hit across the fo'c'sle that sent the *Friends' Desire* lurching over. From the shouting below deck John knew that it had overset one gun at least. The carpenter and his mate went pelting across deck.

"Bring her round!" he yelled to the bo'sun. There was a frenzy of orders and whistles and hauling of ropes till the flapping sheets were steady and she was broadside on again. Within minutes of the ship steadying, the rhythm of the volleys resumed. All guns were firing, he saw, elated; they had managed to get them all forward. He loved every man of his gun crew as brothers at that moment. Their aim held good, shearing off the bowsprit tackle and putting another hole through *Acheron*'s side.

"Fire!"

And they were off again, one volley after another in a regular rhythm of assault. It was clear *Acheron* was struggling now, returning fire from only three ports and aiming too high. There was no more damage done to the *Friends' Desire* than a couple of sails torn.

He put the telescope to his eye to check the horizon. Had her companions seen what was happening? Would they try to return to her defence? The sea was wide and empty to the furthest distance. If they had noticed, they must have decided to abandon her to her fate.

At that moment a particularly violent volley shook the instrument from his hand. He bent down to retrieve it. When he looked up, he saw with a sudden lurch of the heart that one of the cannonballs had finished the work from the first hit. A wide hole had opened out in her side and powder burst alight, sending flames billowing out.

"Hold fire!" he yelled. She must surely yield now, and he must get men aboard before the fire took hold of the gunpowder stores. The crew of the *Acheron* would be able to think of nothing else now if they wanted to save their lives.

There was a sudden silence, both ships rocking in the water, and the brilliance of the flames reflected in the dark evening waters. The master of the *Acheron* hailed them, the incomprehensible French voice floating across the water. John Addison could guess well enough what he was saying.

"Strike your colours!" he bellowed back. "In the name of King George, surrender your ship!"

At last the colours slid down the mast.

"Lower away boats!" he shouted. "Boarding party!"

He would keep the *Friends' Desire* clear till the fire was out and leave Broderick in charge. He stepped down into one of the rocking jolly boats, clapping the men on the back as he went aft. Then the oarsmen were pulling across, the men were up the side of the *Acheron* and away, on orders to go directly for bailing buckets and water to get the fire doused. On deck, John found there was hardly a French crewman to be seen, only a group of officers huddled over by the helm. He sent his men below to start baling and took a quick look aloft. She had suffered badly in the storm; there were cracked and broken yardarms hanging like broken pinions, several sails were torn and ropes were hanging loose. Had she lost men as well, he wondered.

The master came over with a couple of his officers. As they drew close John Addison felt sudden pity for the man. He looked utterly exhausted. He had sailed through the storm only to lose everything: his ship, his cargo, his freedom. It steeled John's resolve. Never, he thought. We will never let ourselves be taken.

"We'll go to your cabin," he said to the man, gesturing below.

CHAPTER 13

High Court of Admiralty, London

1756

"I am asking for two ships to be condemned as enemy shipping," said John Addison, having been admitted through the marble entrance hall of the Admiralty Court, along dusty passages to the recording office.

"The first is the *Etoile*, a two-masted brig, burden 240 tons, registered Dieppe, estimated at £5,000, cargo provisions and liquor. Second, the *Acheron*, a square-rigged sloop, burden 500 tons, registered Le Havre, estimated at £8,000, cargo sugar. Prisoners returned to London."

The young man in front of him wrote it all down in his ledger in a careful flowing hand, dipping his pen in and out of the inkhorn. He was scarcely twenty, John thought, a fresh-faced pink-cheeked youth in a wig and a brocade waistcoat over his linen shirt. No doubt his father was a navy man who had found a place in the Admiralty offices for his son.

"The papers, Mr Addison?" said the young man. "We'll need to check those over to make sure all's in order."

John Addison untied his bag and laid out all the documents on the table, the *Etoile* to the left, the *Acheron* to the right.

"Why, you have made a capital job of it, sir. I dare vouch that the Prize Court will not hesitate above five minutes in agreeing the case. They will see to it before the end of next week."

He smiled at John with such enthusiasm and good humour that John couldn't help but smile back. He might see this young man again, he thought. It would do no harm to further his acquaintance.

"You've been very helpful," he said. "Do you care to take a coffee?"

The young man glanced round the office. Two clerks were working in a corner, heads down. Otherwise the room was quiet.

"Thank you, Mr Addison. There is a pleasant enough place close to the Cathedral."

As they walked into the high airy rooms, fragrant with tobacco smoke and the smell of coffee, John saw how unlike it was to the coffee houses in Deptford. The houses there were filled with merchants like himself, men he often knew by name, who he had made deals with and who breathed the same air of the docks as he did. Going into this coffee house at St Paul's he felt as if he had stumbled somehow into the Inns of Court or a university, where men in full wigs and starched cravats were arguing in loud voices about Mr Pitt's conduct of the war and the latest despatches from the palace of St James or reading aloud to one another from *The Gentleman's Magazine*. Some were in robes, fresh from the law courts, holding forth to their neighbours as if they were still standing at the bar. These were the men who decided his fate, John thought, with a sudden spasm of resentment; the men who decided from their comfortable offices whether John Addison and his crew might have their prize. Master and commander though he was, he felt suddenly humiliated.

When they were seated, his companion leaned over.

"My name is Harry. Harry Parker, Mr Addison, I am very pleased to make your acquaintance."

Why should he feel grateful for this youth's attention? But he was.

"I am so much in admiration of sailors like yourself, Mr Addison. I might have gone to sea myself—my younger brother is a midshipman already—but my father was set on making me an Admiralty man."

"Your father is in the navy?"

"He is an admiral—Admiral Sir Hyde Parker. Perhaps you've heard of him? When war was declared, he was sent to India to defend our possessions against the French."

The man's father, an Admiral! A lord or a baronet! John kept his face still.

"Do you have no desire to follow him?"

"I hardly know. My father wanted a scholar in the family. He sent me off to Eton at an age when I might have been aboard a ship and now I scarcely understand one word of his naval jargon. I would make a poor sailor."

"Are you his eldest son?"

"I am. But enough of me, Mr Addison. I wish you will tell me of your sea adventures, of how you were able to capture a ship like the *Acheron*. I fancy it would have taken great courage and daring."

The young man looked at him with such eagerness and interest that John found himself making a tale of it, of the sighting from the castle mound, the lying in wait in St Sampson, the chase, the skill of his crew, and all the while Harry Parker seemed to hang on his words. He let his voice grow louder, let these lawyers and judges hear what action was, what seamen did for their country and their fortune.

A man got up from a table behind them, bewigged and waistcoated.

"Now then, young Parker, I can see you like to hear tales of our brave sailors. But you have duties elsewhere, I believe."

"Oh, yes indeed, sir. I was quite forgetting myself."

He jumped up, shook John's hand and picked up his hat.

"It was so pleasant to make your acquaintance, Mr Addison. I hope we will meet again."

And he was gone, leaving John Addison to settle the bill. He hardly knew whether to be annoyed or amused.

* * *

As John Addison walked through the narrow streets towards the river, Harry Parker and the coffee house faded from his mind and his thoughts returned to his prizes. As both owner and commander of the *Friends' Desire* half the prize money was his. Six and a half thousand pounds, and he had not yet had a price for the sugar cargo. On a coal run he would count himself satisfied with a profit of six or seven hundred. Broderick and the other officers would get eighth shares and the rest would be divided between the men. When *Friends' Desire* had made harbour, he had paid them all an advance on their prize money; he did not expect to see them sober for a week or more. But he knew there was not one of them but would sail with him again if they could keep clear of the pressmen.

He had other business to see to in London; indeed, his head was moiling with schemes for his prize money and his next voyage. The war had changed everything. Suddenly there were possibilities he had never dreamed of. He was undecided as to *Friends' Desire*'s next voyage. For sure, there was money to be made in the dockyards; the Navy Board was ready to charter any ship it could find to carry troops and provisions. He might do a Home run, carrying ordnance and provisioning from London to the Out Ports, then beating home along the French shore on the lookout for a prize. But for the winter he had a mind to stay close to the Channel Isles. He would get to know Guernsey better, all her inlets and bays where a ship might stay hidden till it was convenient to attack. There would be no sugar fleets sailing home in December, but even a coastal brig like the *Etoile* was worth taking. And had not those casks of wine given them some merry nights besides?

But before all this he had another appointment to attend to. He took a river boat across to Deptford and walked for a mile or more till he came to a street set back from the river, a street of undistinguished two-storey brick-built terrace houses where children played in the street. He had called at 16 Mill Street the previous evening, but a maidservant had come to the door and told him that Mrs Dillon could not take visitors now. He gave the girl his name; would she find out when Mrs Dillon could see him? She scuttled back into the house. He could hear laughter inside, and a man's voice. The girl returned. Mrs Dillon would be pleased to see him tomorrow afternoon.

The wait had set him on fire with impatience. He could hardly restrain himself from running down the road, banging on the door and bursting inside. But he stood on the doorstep toying with the guineas in his pocket and rang the bell.

As the girl opened the door, he could see Amy behind her, tripping down the stairs as she pulled at her dress. He brushed past the maidservant.

"Why, Mr Addison! How impatient you are! I have scarcely finished dressing!"

And indeed, her dress was half unfastened still, so that her breasts showed white and round above the bodice, and there was still a curling paper in her long red hair. Her face was flushed pink. He stepped into the hall.

"Do not trouble to finish on my account."

He took hold of her waist and pulled her close, feeling the stuff of her gown against him and her soft breasts and wiry hair. He smelled her sugary breath and when he kissed her, her tongue tasted of chocolate.

"Will you not dine, Mr Addison?" she said, trying to push him away.

"Later. I will have you first. I cannot wait one minute longer."

He leaned down, gathered up her legs and gown and carried her back up the stairs.

CHAPTER 14

Lloyds Coffee House, London

1758

"Have you had your fill of piracy yet?" said Robert Spicer. "There are other ways to grow rich, you know."

John Addison looked down at the scored wood of the table, at the hot steam rising from his coffee. He took a long breath, savouring the smell of it. How he missed it during the long freezing weeks on the *Friends' Desire*! But it would take more than a cup of coffee to lure him away from the sea. He grinned at Robert.

"Are you envious of my prizes? Wish that you could take a French brig broadside on and fetch her home?"

"You won't escape harm for ever. If you get your legs shot off, there'll be no pension from a grateful nation. And even if you do keep your limbs, where will you be when the war is over? Back where you started."

There was a clatter of men getting up to leave, shouting for their bill and making their farewells. Robert shifted back against the wooden screen that sheltered their table and waited. John sucked a piece of sugar against his teeth and drank the bitter coffee through it. When Robert started speaking again, his voice dropped conspiratorially.

"You'll never have another chance like this to set up a business. Pitt wants four thousand troops taken to Halifax and the Navy Board is paying good money for transports. Then they'll need supplies. Horses. Ordinance. Mr Pitt means to win this war and he'll not stop until he has."

John Addison looked at his friend. Robert Spicer had never been a seaman; his face was smooth and close-shaven, his hands white. He was a merchant to his fingertips. He loved ships only for the profit they brought him. John had dealt with him over more loads of coal than he could remember, and he trusted the man. But he had come to talk with him about a cargo of spirits from a prize ship. Not about his future.

"Listen to this." Robert jabbed at the newspaper in front of him and read out:

> "*This day 30th Nov 1758. According to the instructions received from His Majesty's Government the Admiralty has ordered the Navy Board to charter 10,000 tons of transports to carry troops to the Americas.*

"See what I mean? That's thirty ships they're looking for, at the least. And this:

> "*Notice is hereby given of the Board's intention to treat for ships on Monday next 4th Dec instant at Lloyds.*"

"How much will they pay?"

"The Foreign rate? Anything between 12s and 15s a soldier, monthly. One man to every two tons."

John shook his head.

"I've no taste for a voyage to Virginia. A bad passage over winter and you lose half the crew with scurvy."

"You don't understand me. I don't mean for you to sail the ships. I mean for you to send them. Buy them. Or charter them."

John Addison felt the coffee singing in his brain. Every nerve in his body sprang wide awake.

"I know you love to stand before the mainmast. But how much can you make with one ship?"

"Speak on. I'm listening."

"You went to sea with what—eighty men? You'll never do that again. The Press are all over the docks taking men for the navy. You know that. If you can't take prize crews, you'll not take more than one prize a voyage.

You need to carry cargo too, and the Navy Board will give you steady money. It'll pay you for every month the ship's away, and it'll pay for the ship if the enemy take it or damage it."

Robert Spicer paused.

"I'll lay you a bargain, John. There's a ship up for auction in Deptford docks, *England's Hero*. Come in with me on her. We'll get Letters of Marque for her so she can take a prize if she falls across one, but she'll be hired out as a transport. I'll put the tender in to the Navy Board. You find her a master and a crew. Her burden is reckoned at three hundred tons, and they allow five men and a boy for every hundred tons.'

John Addison stared at him. Of course merchants invested in ships. A good shipment and they took half the profit. But was it what he, John, wanted—to send out a ship with a hired master on it, without his hands ever touching a rope?

"Come on, man. Use your talents. Everyone knows you can talk the birds down from the trees. Come in with me first and see how it's done. We'll see where we go from there. Look, all those Whitby masters—they could be making money with the Navy Board, but they don't know how to do it. They need someone to tender for them. Make all the arrangements. You know the masters and the ships. I know the Navy Board. We can work together."

Become a ship broker. That's what he meant. Buy and sell ships. Charter ships. Spend your days in offices in front of papers, dealing with endless tedious business. He shook his head and stood up, meaning to bid Robert Spicer good day.

Then, in a sudden, unexpected moment, standing there in the middle of Lloyds Coffee House, the merchant's words resolved into perfect clarity within his mind. Within a few instants a revolution came about in him. Of course. Robert Spicer was right. He would do it. By the end of the war, he would be a ship-owner. He would have the means to be wealthy. Was that not what he wanted?

He sat down again.

"I'll come down to Deptford with you."

CHAPTER 15

Cresswell, Northumberland

1760

William could not have said, now that the Hall was finished at last and they had moved back the last of the trunks and hampers and chests and dressers, that his dearest wishes had been fulfilled in all particulars. Perhaps it was a misfortune that the Red House had so pleasant a situation and was so convenient in every way. Instead of looking to their return to Cresswell with eager impatience, the family had rather delayed their departure with every stratagem imaginable.

And what a labour the new Hall had proved! He could never have conceived what an endless throng of matters there were that required his supervision, how many supplies were constantly called upon and found to be wanting, how many tasks were discovered to be ill-done and required repeating. There was scarcely a straight line to be had in the house. And if the workmen encountered too much objection, the next day he would discover they had wrapped up their tools and departed, since there was no shortage of employment for them elsewhere.

The greatest failure had come when Amos had somehow contrived to put in the first-floor landing without noticing that the back staircase had yet to be constructed and incorporated into it. The memory of it still woke him sweating in his bed. Half the work had to be taken down and the whole business recommenced.

There were some faults too with the chimneys that they were still unable to rectify and for which Amos had no explanation. Depending on the direction of the wind, different hearths smoked ferociously and when it rained heavily water would come cascading, black and sooty, into the room and ruin the carpets. It was exasperating. Indeed, the whole business had cost him more grey hairs than he could count, and he had wished a thousand times he had signed an agreement with Mr Garratt.

But from the outside at least the house looked well enough. The dressed stone had a pleasant mellow tone that gave the house a welcoming appearance, and after months of struggle the windows were perfectly symmetrical to either side of an unpretentious but elegant front door. He had received many compliments; "A fine new house, Mr Cresswell," was the usual comment. Its flaws were obvious only to the more discerning and there was no need to point them out to others. And he thanked God that the work had been close to completion before war was declared. Prices were rising everywhere, men were hard to find, and taxation was becoming ruinous. He would have been hard pressed to raise the capital now, with the government borrowing at such iniquitous high rates.

And he had, after all, achieved the essential purpose of the enterprise. There was no more talk of the Cresswells' Jacobite leanings. The Papist chapel had gone, the Cresswells attended the parish church as loyal members of the Church of England, and the family had re-invented itself, with a son and heir looking forward to the future. There would be no taint on John's name.

* * *

Although there was a parlour in the house which he had intended to use as his office, during the building work he had got into the habit of using his father's office room in the old Tower. It was convenient when he needed to be on hand during the construction work. He could even stay there if things were particularly intense. When at last they were able to move back, more than six years after the old house was torn down, he had continued to use the Tower room. In spite of all he had done to bring the family into the present age, he found a secret preference in himself for the old. For the familiar. Besides, it gave him some respite from the hubbub of the household.

Nor was he alone these days. Most mornings Elizabeth would come up to the Tower room and enquire, "Any business for me, Father?" and he would say, "There are a couple of bills here for you to look over. And that pile from yesterday to be entered into the ledger."

She would sit down at the desk, settle her skirts around her and pick up a pen. He would never have expected one of his daughters to undertake such tasks. But while the hall was being built, all the costing and ordering and bills to be paid for the house drove him distracted. It took up all his time, and the estate was neglected.

"Let Lizzie help you," Grace had said. "You'll be surprised. She's the quickest of all at them at her lessons. She can reckon a row of figures faster than I can. Since Catherine got married, I have had her do the household books. Who knows, she might have a great household one day. It's good practice."

It was the kind of task he would expect of a son, but of course John was still too young. If William were honest, he would admit also that the boy lacked application. For his lessons, at least, but he had learned well enough how to make a whole household, family and servants alike, depend upon his every whim. Any upset, any discomfort, and there was always a sister at the ready to comfort and coax him, or Cook to find a cake, or Betsy to divert him with a toy.

"John is getting spoiled. He should be checked," he complained to Grace, but she would see no fault in him. He was too precious to her. The boy would go to the Grammar School in Morpeth at Michaelmas, he comforted himself. There would be other boys to knock the corners off him and schoolmasters to din the lessons into him.

Dinning had never been necessary with Elizabeth. She seemed content to work away, hour after hour, producing a wonderfully neat and orderly ledger. Grace was right; she had a natural aptitude for figures. She could grasp a debit sheet in minutes, was quick to see when they needed to extend their credit for a week or two, understood when to put pressure on a tenant slow to return their rent. It was doubly surprising to him because he had always thought of Lizzie as a dreamer. As a child she had been full of fancies, always hiding away somewhere or running after her grandmother for tales and legends. Now she was grown into a woman she would often spend her evenings curled up with a candle at her side and some lady's magazine before her, filling her head with nonsense. Her grey eyes seemed to be looking far away, searching for something just out of sight. But he had learned that she could, nevertheless, bring them to bear on a ledger.

He had come to like her quiet presence in the Tower. It made the conversation he must have with her later this morning, concerning a certain Reverend Sanderson, doubly unwelcome to him.

* * *

William had noticed nothing, of course. After they had moved back to the Hall, the family continued to attend divine service at Woodhorn church. So he had taken little notice of the arrival of a new vicar in Morpeth, a young man named Robert Sanderson. However, the fellow had taken to calling at the Hall, though it was hardly in his parish. Grace and the girls made tea for him in the new drawing room and listened to his plans for the church. There was something about the young man that reminded William of his brother Robert. Like all schooled men, he seemed to have an insufferable belief in the rightness of his own understanding. When the Reverend Sanderson managed to engage him in conversation, the man had started on his theme at once.

"Why not bring the young ladies to a concert or an assembly one Saturday, Mr Cresswell?" he began. "We see them so seldom in town. You could put up at The Sun overnight and join us for Sunday worship at St Mary's."

"I fear I have another appointment in town most Saturdays," he responded. "I am very fond of the racecourse, and I am seldom ready for divine service the next day."

The young vicar went red, whether with anger or embarrassment, and Bridget started to giggle. Grace gave her a little slap. Afterwards Grace remonstrated with him.

"You should be more encouraging, William."

"Why should I listen to his sermons, when we have our own parish to think of?"

"It's not your presence he cares for, William. He wants to impress Lizzie with his learning."

"Lizzie?"

"He likes her. He brought over a copy of some sermons for her, though I don't suppose she's read it."

"What would Lizzie want with a prosing parson?"

"The man is on his best behaviour, William. He might be better company when he's had a glass of wine. The Sandersons are a well-respected family and Morpeth is a good living."

There was a lot of sighing and shrugging, but once a month Elizabeth, Lelia and Bridget went to Morpeth in the carriage with their parents and enjoyed an afternoon and evening at the Assembly Rooms.

Now the man wanted to ask for Lizzie's hand. Damn the fellow! Why should such a dull bore carry off his daughter? At least Catherine had found herself a gentleman. More than found, he had to admit; had set her cap at William Johnston Esquire of Woodhorn Grange till Mr Johnston found it more convenient to make her his wife. Now Mr Johnston's household was run far more efficiently than it ever was before, he had a baby daughter, and he might bid farewell to a quiet life forever, if William were any judge of the matter.

But Lizzie! He had not thought Lizzie so eager to make a match. He would have to tell her of the man's offer, but he would not force it on her, he decided. It should be her choice entirely.

* * *

Elizabeth bent down to light her candle from the one already burning there, then pushed it down onto the spike. She looked up at the dark face of the Virgin, who stood to one side of the chancel, half hidden by a pillar. She was carved of oak, so old that it had grown almost black. Only the upper part of her face was still distinct, with a wide brow and open eyes. Below her worn nose the wood was smooth and expressionless. The infant in her arms was hard to make out, only his head and an arm showing.

"She is the Stella Maris," the Woodhorn vicar had told her. "Star of the Sea. An incarnation of the Blessed Mary, after whom the church was named by the monks who built it long ago. The land was given to the Community of St Cuthbert by a king, and since the Saint was believed to have a particular affinity with the Blessed Virgin, they named their church for her. Perhaps our statue was carved all those centuries ago."

The vicar was a kind old man who never minded her coming and sitting in the church during the time they lived at the Red House, just as she had used to sit in the chapel with her grandmother. The Virgin and the candles and the illicit rosary whose beads she liked to tell reminded her of Grandma. Sometimes, when the weather was bad, she was joined by women from the village come to light candles and hold vigil for their men out at sea. Once a year the vicar held a special service to intercede with the Blessed Virgin to protect their ships.

Sometimes, when Elizabeth kneeled before her, light would flicker over the darkness of the statue as if sunlight were resting on it, or there might be a movement in the air and a smell of salt, like a ghostly breath of surf washing through the church. The beads of the rosary ran like a trance through her fingers, on and on, while the Virgin stood watch above her.

But when the Reverend Sanderson had accompanied them to church one Sunday, he had singled out the statue for his particular displeasure.

"They should get rid of it. Superstitious papist nonsense. I'm surprised Vicar Hardy allows it."

She had felt another door slide shut over her heart. Why did he have such definite opinions on everything? He liked to talk about doctrines and theology and all the other things he had learned about at Oxford. His sermons were so long that her father threatened to bring a pack of cards to service with him. She thought him very clever, so she was flattered that he had chosen to pay his respects to her, but when he asked for her opinion on a matter, she found she did not care very greatly to give it. One day, to provoke him, she asked, did he know that her Uncle Robert had become a Catholic priest? He turned white, but he rallied.

"It is of course deeply to be regretted. But since your family has made plain their adherence to the Church, there is no need for us to discuss him further."

To her surprise, he was a good dancer. When he partnered her at the Morpeth Assembly, she found herself carried away by his springing steps and lively moves. When he danced, he seemed handsome to her, with his strong shoulders and well-cut waistcoat, his lips open wide and his eyes upon her. She could almost forget his sermons. Could almost fancy that she loved him. But then, he would hand her back to her seat and almost before he had caught his breath would be talking again, reminding her of Mr Priestley's essay that he had loaned to her and of his views on it. Could he never be silent?

And now he had asked Father for her hand. Although he had been paying her attention, still she was surprised. He seemed to have so little real interest in her. It was hard to imagine that he loved her. Perhaps he did not look for that in a wife. Sometimes she felt his choice was simply a matter of form, that she was of good family, and one should start with the eldest available, since her older sisters Grace and Dorothy were pock-marked and not expected to be wed.

She thought of her own mother and father, of the arguments and disagreements that went on between them, but where each took account of the other. Where, in the end, each loved the other.

She turned back to the statue.

"Holy Mary, Star of the Sea," she prayed. "Shed light on my heart."

CHAPTER 16

Appleton-le-Street, Yorkshire

1760

John Addison found Appleton-le-Street to be a long straggle of cottages, stone-built houses with red-tiled roofs at one end and low thatched hovels at the other. Children played along the empty street in front of the houses and a couple of geese waddled towards the pond. There was an inn, but he was not minded to make his presence known there. Nor did he inspect the old church with its Saxon tower. But when he had ridden out of the village along the dusty lane that led to the neighbouring hamlet of Easthorpe, he reined in his horse and dismounted, staring about him. He needed to look, to take it in. To take possession.

The horse dropped his head and started grazing on the mossy turf at the side of the lane. It grew into an untidy hedgerow full of honeysuckle and half-ripe blackberries and beyond it was pasture, where cows grazed on yellow buttercups and grass. It was upland country, and from where he stood the land fell away from him in an endless vista of meadow, woodland and long cultivation strips of wheat and barley. In the furthest distance was a long low line of hills marking an end to the valley. Above was a wide sky filled with pale grey ruffles of summer cumulus cloud. If he had been aboard ship, he would have reefed down the topsails. But he was here, some thirty miles inland; a landsman now, standing in his new possession. It seemed like the Garden of Eden. The trees were in full summer leaf, moving and rustling in the wind; there were even a few oaks that had escaped the shipwright's axe. A small flock of finches rose suddenly into the air from the hedgerow. A buzzard hung in the air above the wood that lined the pasture. He felt like God Himself looking upon his Creation; he found that it was good. He glanced back at the road; there was no one around. He dropped to his knees and took hold of the grass, the little stones, the very soil itself in his hands. He rubbed them against his face. It was his. His land.

The previous day he had sat in York with the lawyer's clerk, going through the deeds clause by laborious clause. He had learned patience with the ways of lawyers. He accepted that their work was necessary. To him at that moment, the tedious, obfuscating language was strangely intoxicating. Every phrase, every paragraph added to his rights and privileges. The township of Appleton-le-Street with Easthorpe contained 1,559 acres of land, it affirmed, and its owner John Addison Esquire was the latest possessor of the ancient title of Lord of the Manor, with all its long-accumulated rights and perquisites, endlessly enumerated. Within the township, the deed further related, was the hamlet of Easthorpe and the residence known as Easthorpe Hall. It was the hall he was now riding to inspect.

The lane brought him up to the gates of the hall after a couple of miles. The solidity of the dressed stone pillars lent dignity to the entrance, he saw, although there was no enclosing wall around the house. He could see it plainly enough from the road. It was built of York stone, with three storeys and a grand front door with pillars to either side and a portico above. It was, he reckoned, a little larger than Skinningrove, and in every way more elegant in appearance. No doubt masons from York had been employed to build it. Everything about it bespoke balance and symmetry.

He would not venture to go inside, since it was let out to a gentleman and his family and he had no wish to intrude upon them. They might stay there for a year or two, or even more, till he was ready to become a country gentleman. He stared across at the house, at the gardens and fruit trees that surrounded it. It was every man's dream to own such a property. Yet he felt no spring of yearning within himself to walk at once through its doors. In truth he had only the vaguest imaginings of how it might be to live there, day after day. Perhaps a woman was what it needed. A wife and children to fill it up with noise and laughter. Certainly, that was what he planned to tell Jane, who longed for him to settle to a home, to a family. As soon as he had settled the purchase, he meant to ride north to surprise her and Francis. He had hardly seen them since the war began and he was eager to see their astonishment at his news.

The Hall was only fifteen miles from York with all its genteel attractions and scarcely four miles from Castle Howard, the Earl of Carlisle's great palace. He could not expect to be on visiting terms with Lord Carlisle, for sure, but the proximity of the palace lent distinction to the neighbourhood. He felt himself warmed in the reflected glow of so much gentility.

* * *

He had sent word on ahead of his visit, and he rode down the valley towards Skinningrove with a light heart. The boys would be halfway to young men by now, he thought, and was eager to see them run out of the door at his arrival.

But it was their father, his brother-in-law Francis Easterby, who came to the door. Alone. A servant took his horse to the stable.

"John," said Francis and embraced him without more words. When John Addison stood away, he saw his friend's face was grey.

"Come to the parlour first," he said. "I have news I must tell you before you see the boys."

They went inside. The house was strangely silent. Where was his sister Jane? Where were the children? Francis Easterby poured him a glass of brandy and took one for himself.

"You come to us at a sad time, John. I can hardly tell you of it." He took a gulp of brandy and rubbed his head.

"It is your sister. Jane." He looked down at his knees. "She was with child. Nothing was right with it and she came to term early. The babe lived at first, but Jane took an infection that turned to fever. The doctor could do nothing to bring it down." He drank again. "I do not blame him, John. The man tried everything."

"What are you telling me?"

Francis Easterby stared back at him.

"Is she dead?"

Francis nodded.

"Dear God!"

John hurled his brandy glass into the fireplace, sending a shower of glass glittering into the air.

"No!" he shouted. "No, no, no!"

He pushed back his chair and sat spreadeagled for a moment against the first anguish of the news, then pulled himself to his feet. He lurched over to the fireplace and knocked his forehead against the stone as sobs broke out of him. At last he turned his head back towards Francis.

"When? When was it?"

"Two months ago now. She spoke of you, John. She knew you would grieve for her. She asked that you care for her boys."

He returned to the table and slumped into his chair, tears still coursing down his face, fumbling for a handkerchief. He knew he must master himself for the moment. He must see the two boys. The other children, too, but John and Frank first.

When he was steady enough Francis called them in. Even in the first stupefaction of grief John saw how changed they were; that his nephew and namesake, John, was a youth now, more than a boy, and his younger brother Frank was half-grown too. There were none of the high spirits and excitement that usually met his arrival. They stood stony-faced before him.

"Uncle John," said John and came to him. John Addison caught hold of him and held him close, little Frank in his other arm. None of them spoke. He felt the warmth of their small bodies against his. When they stepped away, he searched their faces for traces of their mother, and yes, she was there, he saw her in them. He schooled himself to speak.

"God give us the strength to bear this. I never heard news that grieved me more."

Only their eyes fixed on his prevented him from falling back to the table in a further storm of sobbing. Francis went over to his cupboard and set more glasses on the table.

"Come," he said. "Sit, all of you." He poured a glass for each of them, even little Frank.

"We will take hands together and swear an oath and drink a toast upon it. First—join hands—now: we will be faithful to her memory. Her memory!" and they drank, Frank screwing his face against the strong alcohol.

"We will make her proud of us!" They drank again.

"We will never forget her."

Then they sat, together, John and Francis, John and Frank, the small hands in the large, around the table, and in their grief a bond was sealed between them.

* * *

When John Addison returned to Whitby he found the deeds of the Manor of Appleton-le-Street waiting for him at his office, the York lawyers having completed their business. He looked at them without interest. He should go through them, he knew, and check that all was in order, and he would do that. It was an investment and he needed to be sure of it. But it no longer held any attraction for him. The summer morning, the ride through his fields and meadows, the fine mansion at Easthorpe Hall, seemed like a memory from a distant time. From another life. It had been for her, he realized. For his sister. He had dreamed of showing Jane his fine estate, the manor house where he might for her sake settle down one day and raise a family. He wanted her to see how he had surpassed even the Easterbys. That was all over now. He cared for none of it.

He did not regret the purchase. Land was a good investment; he would get an income from it that would be steadier than trade. But it was no more to him than that.

He found himself restless back in Whitby. It was too raw, too close. Everyone in the town knew of Jane's death and wanted to offer their condolences. It kept the pain fresh, day after day, and for the first time in his life he felt alone. He would return to London, he decided. He meant to keep his promise to Francis and the boys, and already plans were forming in his head for how he might help them forward. But that was for the future. Now he wanted to throw himself into work—to be with men who knew nothing of death and loss—to sit in a tavern and drink till he could feel nothing. He was for London.

CHAPTER 17

London and Cresswell

1762–3

Two years later there was a new King, a third Hanoverian George, on the throne, Pitt's power was over and England was eager for peace. But there were still troops in foreign lands and ships on the high seas, and the Admiralty Court still had business to conduct.

On a dark dank November day in London, the streets filthy and the air heavy with smoke, John Addison and Harry Parker concluded their business with the claims put forward on behalf of *England's Hero*—at which Harry sucked in his cheeks and gave a little whistle—and took a stroll along the gloomy streets. Over the years, they had settled on a coffee house in Fleet Street that was more to John Addison's taste than the Inns. They were hardly settled at their table before Harry leaned towards his friend with some urgency.

"I have news for you too, John," he said. "Perhaps it will not surprise you as much as me." He looked around with unusual furtiveness and kept his voice low. "It is about my father and his recent posting."

He took a gulp of coffee.

"You know that since France made alliance with Spain they have profited very greatly from gold from the Americas. My father was sent out in command of several vessels to stop the treasure ships reaching the Spanish ports."

John Addison nodded.

"So for some months now he has been in the East Indies. He had another vessel with him when they came upon a treasure ship in the Pacific, sailing from Acapulco to Manila. Although it was heavily armed my father and his companion vessel engaged it. There was a long battle, but that is a story for another time. Suffice to say they took the ship, and whole. It has been declared my father's prize."

John felt a quick shiver of envy. A Spanish treasure ship! Their wealth was legendary. But then, only a ship of the line, an Admiral's flagship, could have engaged it.

Harry's voice dropped. His face seemed tense rather than elated.

"It is a huge prize, John. It was loaded with gold and silver plate. It is worth at least £600,000."

"Good God!"

"It will make him a wealthy man. Make us a wealthy family. I cannot grasp it yet. Although Father is an Admiral, we have never had wealth. My father only came into the baronetcy because his cousin died. There was never a house or an estate or any of that. My father will not want that. He is only happy in front of a mast."

"He may learn to like it."

"So there it is. What do you think, John?"

"I think your father a bold and worthy sailor deserving of his prize. May you all enjoy his good fortune."

"Nothing will change, you know. I will still be an inky clerk behind a heap of papers."

John Addison laughed.

"For now. But everything will change. Just give it time."

"He was lucky. There'll be an end to prizes soon. The talk in the Admiralty is all of peace treaties. By February or March, the war will be over. I am to be sent up to the Admiralty Court in Newcastle in the spring to deal with all the claims and cases waiting to be settled. Will you be up north then? Newcastle is not so far from Whitby, is it?"

"Not so far. And I might have a transport coming into Newcastle around then."

"Come and bear me company, John. I know not a soul up there and I am a miserable fellow left on my own."

"With all my heart," said John Addison, and they shook hands on it.

As he rose to leave an idea struck John.

"When you have seen your fill of the town, I will take you to meet my god-daughter's family. I have neglected them since the war began. They have an ancient tower house that will give you a taste of the Border feuds."

"I should like that very well."

* * *

A few months later the two men were riding out from Newcastle, along the coast road, past Newbiggin and into Cresswell.

Everything was different, John Addison saw, as they approached the house. The dark stone Tower was still there, but the old hall had gone, and the chapel. In their place was a frontage of freshly dressed stone, a front door topped with a portico and windows marching regularly away from it to either side. Of course, he had known this, known that Mr Cresswell was building himself a new hall, but it had not entered his imagination that it might be here and finished already.

When a maid opened the front door to them, they found themselves in a well-lit hall with a curving staircase leading upstairs, and then there were voices; first it was Alice, the youngest, skipping through the door with her mother, and then three girls coming down the staircase—and he was distracted for a moment by his shipmaster's eye, did he imagine it or were the banisters off true?—and then he forgot the banisters in his astonishment at the three daughters. It must be Juliana, and Bridget, and Elizabeth, but he had no notion which was which, although one was his god-daughter and he must show her proper remembrance. She was a child when he last saw her. They all were.

"Juliana!" he exclaimed to all three in general, and the middle one responded, "Godfather John!" and he moved forward to take her hands. He had brought a gift for her, but he would keep it till the introductions were done. Then he turned to his friend.

"Harry, let me introduce you. Mrs Cresswell, my honourable friend Harry Parker."

"At your service, madam," and he bowed over her hand so politely that the girls stared. And then it was their turn—Elizabeth, Juliana, Bridget and little Alice, one by one, and Harry smiled at each of them with such guileless pleasure that they were all in love with him at once.

Mrs Cresswell was equal to the occasion.

"Mr Parker, we are delighted to welcome you and Mr Addison. Is it your first visit to these parts?"

"It is, Mrs Cresswell, but I like it so well that I hope it will not be my last. I am engaged at the Admiralty Court in Newcastle for a month or two, and I mean to make a grand tour of the north while I am here."

"I'm sure Mr Addison will be a good guide for you." She turned to her daughters. "Juliana and Bridget, take the gentlemen to look over the garden while Elizabeth and I arrange some entertainment for you."

Bonnets were pulled down from their pegs and tied securely against the fresh wind blowing from the sea, and the little party tripped down towards the garden. John took his god-daughter's arm, leaving Harry to walk with Bridget.

"So, Juliana! You are all grown very much. When I left, you were in pinafores and now you are become young ladies."

"You have been away a long time, Mr Addison. We have scarcely seen you since I was a child."

"It is true, Juliana. I have been a poor godfather to you. But I mean to make amends today. See, I have a parcel for you." He pulled it out from within his coat and proffered it to her. She looked at him with bright eyes and a smile. For a moment he saw again the child holding up her arms for sugar plums.

"It is very kind of you, Mr Addison. Shall I open it now?"

"Let's sit on the bench for a moment so you can."

While she untied the ribbons, the work of a Bond Street draper's nimble fingers, he glanced back at his friend. Harry was talking with his usual enthusiasm and forgetting to check his long stride, so that Bridget was half-running to keep up with him, her face turned up towards him with eagerness to match his own. How pretty she has become, he thought. She still had the fair-haired curls of childhood without any need for the artifice of a hairdresser. She had grown into a shapely woman with a fine figure. He could see Harry was finding plenty to enjoy in her company.

Juliana had unwrapped the fine paper and drawn out the embroidered brocade enclosed within it. Her face was a picture of astonishment.

"Oh, Mr Addison, it is so beautiful! I had not expected . . . I don't know how to thank you! The embroidery is so fine!"

She held it against her cheek. He smiled at her.

"I hope it may set you off to perfection," he said. Her innocence pleased him.

When their tour of the garden was done, they returned to the house to sit in the new drawing room and take madeira and cake with the ladies. There was a good Turkey carpet on the floor, but John Addison noted the uneven line of the skirting board against the floorboards. He would have had the carpenter do the job again. And the curtains couldn't conceal the small blisters of damp where the windows didn't fit properly. Did Harry notice any of this? Of course not. He was delighted with the family and they with him.

"Are there only four of you at home now?" asked John Addison. "I tempted Harry here with tales of eight sisters."

"Dorothy and Grace do not come into company very much. If we get to know Mr Parker a little better, they'll join us. Catherine married some years ago and has a daughter of her own over at Woodhorn Grange. And Lelia has just married the Reverend Sanderson, the vicar of Morpeth."

"It rained all night before the wedding," said Alice, "and the chimney flooded into the hall."

"Yes, it did," said her mother, "and very inconvenient it was!" She smiled at the two young men. She was flushed with madeira and enjoying the male company.

"We have a brother now as well," said Elizabeth, and as if he had been waiting for his cue the door opened and John Cresswell was there, his face sullen.

"Where have you all been?" he shouted at them.

His mother rose and went over to him and cuddled him against her, grown youth though he was.

"This is my son. He shares a name with you! He is John Cresswell. You must forgive his bad manners."

"The fault is ours for stealing away your sisters, Master John. I am a sort of cousin of yours; my name is John Addison, and I am godfather to your sister Juliana. This is Mr Harry Parker, a good friend of mine from the Admiralty."

The boy forgot his sulks and stared at the two newcomers. Harry Parker doffed his hat to him.

"Good day, Master John. I am very happy to make your acquaintance."

"Perhaps you can give me some advice," said John Addison. "I bought myself a new knife in Newcastle, but I cannot get the way of the clasp on it. Here, see what you think."

He pulled out the knife, and soon the boy was beside him, trying the blade against his thumb and talking as easily as if John were a familiar acquaintance. Though Grace feared he might cut himself, she held her peace.

When the time came for the men to leave, Harry Parker took Mrs Cresswell's hand very earnestly.

"Indeed, Mrs Cresswell, I cannot express how much I have enjoyed our visit! I am to be in Newcastle for a few more weeks. Would you and your daughters do me the honour of attending an Assembly in my company — and with Mr Addison too if his business will allow?"

"I will speak with my husband, Mr Parker, but I believe we will be delighted to accept."

It was arranged that the three eldest girls should go to Newcastle in the company of their parents the following Saturday, and that lodgings should be taken for the night, or maybe two, since William might take the opportunity to escort the young people to a race meeting if it were fine weather and make a holiday of it.

The Newcastle Assembly Room was larger and more elegant than Morpeth could boast, the walls coloured light blue and ornamented with paintings and carvings. At one end was a recess fitted with mirrors which reflected the bright candles in the chandelier; to Elizabeth, the whole room seemed to be glittering and shining. She believed she looked well enough in her watered green silk and ribbons, though it was clear it was Bridget's golden curls that had won Harry's attention. He was unfailingly well mannered in partnering all three of the sisters when they wished to dance, but by the end of the evening there was no mistaking that it was Bridget's company he most desired. When supper was served in the tea-room, he was at her side and by the end of the meal had given up the pretence of talking to anyone but her.

It was left to John Addison to look after Juliana and Elizabeth. He might have abandoned them for the card tables as their father had, but he did not, and Elizabeth was grateful for his attention. The recollection of Lelia's wedding, only a few weeks before, still rankled with her. She could not get the image of the ceremony out of her mind. Robert Sanderson had looked so handsome in his flowing wig and velvet coat as he waited at the altar in Woodhorn church. Lelia tripped up the aisle to join him, complacent as a cat supping cream. Had she, Elizabeth, been wrong to refuse Robert, she had asked herself a hundred times. She would have had a fine vicarage to call her home and a respected husband. Now it was all Lelia's and Robert hardly spared her a glance. She was twenty-seven years old, and her younger sister was wed before her.

So she was pleased to have John Addison at her side, though she hardly knew how to address him. He had changed so much. She remembered him from years ago, the young sailor who used to call with liquor for their father and bring them all sweets. The merry youth had been everyone's favourite then. It was hard to fit that memory with the man before her now. He seemed quite old. His face was worn weather-brown so that the grey wig looked incongruous against his complexion; Elizabeth had a momentary fancy of him standing before the mast in a pigtail with the surf-crested waves tossing around him. There was a stiffness in his movement; a slight limp in his left leg. Perhaps he had been injured in some storm. Or fighting against the French.

"Are you still a sailor, Mr Addison?" she asked him. "Did you fight in the war?"

He smiled at her, and for a moment in his smile she saw a flash of that younger laughing self.

"You've seen me limp," he said. She blushed. "I took a flying piece of shot half through my thigh when we were broadside on to a French brig."

She couldn't resist glancing down at his leg, wondering what the wound might look like beneath his breeches.

"I was Master and Commander on the ship, but since there wasn't a surgeon to be had in Whitby, I set myself down on our Letters as Surgeon too. So I was forced to be my own doctor."

"Did you . . . what . . . ?"

"Yes. I knew the shot must come out. So when we had won our prize, I took to my cabin with a bottle of brandy and a sharp knife, put a napkin between my teeth and did the job. But a true surgeon would have done it better, and I have left myself lame."

"Oh! I can hardly bear to think of it!" She clasped her hands tight and stared at him.

"There's no help for it, on a ship. You must make do as best you can. But enough of all that. My fighting days are over, and I am a shore man now."

Beside the slim young men on the dance floor, with their coats pinched in tight to their waists and their close-fitting breeches, he seemed broader, stronger, almost ungainly. Although he was not especially tall, his wide chest made him seem bigger than his friend Harry. When he led her out to dance a cotillion, she could see he was not a practised dancer. He often made mistakes, and Elizabeth lost her shyness; felt even that she was helping him, her hand on his, guiding him through the moves. When it was over, he lifted her hand to his mouth and held it close for a moment before he kissed it. She felt a little shock run through her body.

"How well you dance."

She looked up and found his eyes looking at her very directly.

"Mr Addison," she said, then hesitated.

"Yes?"

"Might I . . . that is . . . I have never been on board a ship. A proper ship, I mean, not a coble."

"Do you want to? Would you like me to take you down to the dock? You might find it rough."

"Yes. I don't care about that. I would like to. Very much."

CHAPTER 18

Newcastle-upon-Tyne

1763

Their mother enjoyed the services of a lady's maid at the lodging rooms, but although the sisters had a breakfast of tea and muffins brought to their room, they did their own dressing.

"Not so tight," said Elizabeth as Bridget tugged on her stays. "I need to walk this morning."

"Why?"

"I'm going to see Mr Addison's ship. Do you know, he has called it after himself! The *Addison*."

Bridget released her hold on the laces.

"Go down to the harbour?" she said. "It is not at all respectable, Lizzie. There will be all sorts of rough types down there."

"Tie them, Bridget. Be quick. They will be calling for me, and I won't be ready."

Bridget finished tying off the laces. Elizabeth climbed into her blue petticoat.

"Who is 'they'?"

"Mr Addison and Mr Parker. Harry has to go to his office, but he will accompany us first. You can come with us if you like."

Elizabeth stuffed her fichu down her stays and pulled on her gown, glancing back at her sister as she pinned it in place.

"I shouldn't like it at all," Bridget replied.

"Nor me," said Juliana, "although you didn't ask me. We are going with Mother to visit the shops."

Then her cloak was on, her bonnet tied, and she was ready. It was just her! She wouldn't have to listen to all her sisters' protests and silly questions. She, Elizabeth, was going down to the harbour with Mr Addison, she was going to see his ship, and more. She would feel it move on the water beneath her and imagine how it might be to sail far away.

*   *   *

The carriage bumped down the cobbled street that led to the river and came to a halt close to the bridge. Harry Parker jumped down first and handed Elizabeth out of the carriage, then John Addison was beside her. Before she had time to stare at the bridge, with its shops and tenements packed close together above the narrow arches, they were walking briskly down the harbourside. The weather was overcast with an occasional spit of drizzle. Elizabeth turned her cheek away from the breeze towards the river. There were ships moored all along the harbour, their tall masts and crossbeams like winter branches against the sky, sails reefed up neatly. Men stripped to the waist were working on the decks, hauling at tangles of ropes, shifting barrels and sacks to the hold, banging and hammering at beams and planking, and all the while shouting orders, laughing, cursing, so that the air was full of the noise and din. Her shoes would get dirty, she realized. The roadway was grimy with coal dust and mud and mounds of dark rotting stuff that might be seaweed or something worse. The stench of it all brought her close to retching but her companions seemed not to notice it. She hurried along beside them.

"Here we are," said John Addison.

He shouted an order to the men on the ship for a gangplank and, while they waited, Elizabeth stared at the ship. It had a long bowsprit stretching out beyond the ship and beneath it the carved figure of a woman, her hair and dress blown back behind her, her breasts naked and one arm reaching out before her to the horizon. The sailors' Stella Maris, she thought.

Then she was on board, on the deck, with the great timber mainmast stretching away above her, and oak boards beneath her feet. Wooden decks, wooden steps, wooden sides. She felt the slight motion of the river beneath them, the gentle rock and heave of the ship. It was at once unsettling and elating.

"Welcome to the *Addison*. She's a good ship though she's had a few troubles. On her first voyage she sailed as a transport across the Atlantic. To Halifax." He looked at Elizabeth.

"Did you hear of the battle of Quebec?"

She wasn't sure. She looked to Harry for help.

"In Canada," he said obligingly. "Four years ago, was it, John?"

"Yes. 1759. A famous year for victories. Well, the *Addison* was there. She took one hundred and fifty soldiers ashore for the assault."

He turned to Harry. "She took some damage too, but not from the enemy."

"How so?" asked Harry.

"On the way back down, the *Pembroke* lost her bearings and rammed her broadside on. Her captain was a Whitby man, James Cook. He has a great reputation now for his charts and navigation, but his clever eye failed him then. The *Addison* had to be laid up for repairs and I had the devil's own job finding men to prove Cook was in the wrong of it."

While the two men talked, Elizabeth stared around her, up at the masts and crossbeams and the unintelligible netting of the ropes. A man in canvas trousers and a loose shirt came up to speak to John. She could hardly understand him for his thick dialect. Something about the windlass and John nodded, gave instructions, listened again. He was different here, she saw. He was at home. He was master.

"How do you like to be aboard ship, Miss Cresswell?" said Harry to her while they waited for John.

"I like it very well—though I am not sure how it would be out on the open sea."

"Nor I. I deal with ships every day, and my father is an Admiral, but I am dreadfully ignorant of the seafaring life."

"You must start early if you mean to go to sea," John Addison said, turning back to them. "While you are still young enough to learn it all. So that it is second nature to you. Boys must start at ten or eleven."

Elizabeth thought of her brother, John Cresswell. He would never manage at sea! He would be crying out for his sisters before the ship left harbour.

"Let me show you below decks."

Down in the dim light and low ceilings below decks she saw row upon row of wooden cots, each with a blanket on it.

"They're for the soldiers. *Addison* has been fetching the Fusiliers home from Germany after their victory at Wilhelmsthal. The King's soldiers can't sling a hammock like a sailor; they must have a bed to sleep on."

How ignorant she was, Elizabeth felt. All these battles in faraway places that she had hardly heard of and wars that she knew nothing of. The *Addison* had sailed halfway across the world; she had never been further than Newcastle.

John Addison turned to Harry.

"Once Mr Parker here has looked over all our paperwork and discharged her from service, we'll have all those cots out in no time."

Elizabeth tried to imagine John Addison going to sea.

"Do you sleep in a hammock, Mr Addison?"

He laughed.

"You have me there. No, the master has a cabin and a bed. The other officers too. Look up here."

They went aft to the semicircle of cabin doors at the stern end of the ship. He opened the door into the master's cabin. Elizabeth saw a low room, lined and floored and ceilinged with planks. There was a narrow dining table and six chairs, a desk covered with charts and papers and in the corner a box bed. At the back was a pair of windows opening out onto the sea. This was his kingdom, she thought. When he opened his eyes every morning, he would look out at the waves rushing away from the stern of the ship. Or did. He told her he had come ashore.

"Do you miss your life aboard?"

"I have another life now. But I like to stay close to the sea."

"If it were not for shipmasters and merchants like Mr Addison, we should never have won the war," said Harry earnestly. "All the transports and shipping they have provided us! You cannot imagine what a business it has been. Horses, soldiers, provisions, guns all needing to be got halfway across the world, to the Americas, Europe, the Indies and the like. The navy gets all the glory, but believe me, Miss Cresswell, it is only half the story."

"We've kept you busy, Harry, for sure. I have sent to the cook for some chocolate for us. Let me see what is become of it."

They sat in the cabin and drank chocolate, listening to John's stories of the sea. She saw how he sat, always upright, away from the back of the chair, as if he might at any moment need to spring up. The small cabin was filled with his energy. She felt as if she were coming under his spell—and that he knew it too—but that he held back from her. His will, she saw, was very strong. Was she equal to it? A confusion came about in her of wanting him and resisting him, all together. And all the while she felt him watch her.

"What are you planning for her next voyage?" asked Harry.

"Now the war is over she can do what she was built for. She's a whaler, you know. But it is too late now for the Greenland season; they must be away before the end of April. So she'll ship coal down to London for the sake of a cargo, and we'll see what comes up."

Bells rang somewhere in the ship.

"Noon," said Harry. "I had best away. I don't need the carriage, John, I'll walk up to the offices. I hope to see you later, Miss Cresswell, and Bridget too, perhaps?"

She smiled her acceptance and thought, he is disappointed that Bridget did not come. She felt no pique; their preference for each other was so evident that envy was immaterial.

"We'll come with you. I will bring you back to the carriage, Miss Cresswell. I must not keep you too long from your family."

She would have liked to stay there all day, she felt, feeling the slight rocking of the ship beneath her. But it would not do to be tête-à-tête with Mr Addison in his cabin. Once up on deck she paused, looking about her.

"I love to see all the ships about us! I wish I was bound for the open sea!"

He laughed.

"I'm sure you would make a fine sailor."

She smiled at him, her face flushed with the sea air.

"I fear I will be always watching from the shore. Did you ever hear the tale of our ghost at Cresswell? She walks the seashore looking for the ship that will bring her lover to her. When I was a child, I used to walk for hours watching out for it, imagining myself in her company. It is our own Gothic tale to match Mr Walpole's."

He looked puzzled.

"We have lately had *The Castle of Otranto* from the lending library. It is full of ghosts and haunted towers and murdered maidens. It has kept us all awake at night. But perhaps you are not a reader."

"No," he said. "I never found time for it. But you'll find sailors have many tales to tell of ghostly visitations at sea. I have seen one or two strange sights myself. But never a ghost at Cresswell. I will keep my eyes open."

Once back on dry land he took her arm, steering her through all the hubbub of the harbourside, past the men gathered outside the alehouses taking their midday ale, and she felt herself pleasantly secure beside him. Then they were back at the carriage, he handed her in, doffed his hat to her and was gone.

CHAPTER 19

Cresswell, Northumberland

1763

On a pleasant early summer's morning a few weeks after the Assembly, William sat in the cool stone chill of the Tower office. Elizabeth was working through a pile of papers, and her brother John Cresswell sat fidgeting beside her. At last, the boy threw his pen down on the table and burst out, "Why do I have to do this? You've got Lizzie to help you."

He stared at his father defiantly, cheeks pouted. He looked like a child, though the boyish pink-and-white cheeks were sprouting a pale bristle now. William felt intense irritation and controlled an impulse to slap his son. Would he ever have spoken thus to his father?

"You do it so that you understand the running of the estate. When I am gone, this will be your task, not Lizzie's."

"A clerk could do it."

He stood up and stood over his son, trying to keep his voice even.

"Don't bandy words with me. Do what you're told."

His father's closeness was enough to intimidate John Cresswell, and he bent his head back over the ledger. There was a long silence in the room. William returned to his seat. When his father was absorbed again John glanced up at Elizabeth.

"What do I put here?" he mouthed at her. She leaned over and pointed the figure to him. Slowly they worked through his task, Elizabeth prompting, John giving long sighs and slumping over the bench. At last, it was done. Without a word to either of them he swung his legs over the bench and strode out of the room. William turned and looked at Elizabeth, shaking his head.

"I despair of him."

He got up and walked over to the corner cupboard and took out the port.

"God knows how he will ever keep the place going. You've made too good a job of it, Lizzie. He thinks he doesn't need to bother."

"He's young, Father."

"He is." William took a pinch of snuff. "I have not mentioned this to your mother yet, but the Master at the Grammar School has made a suggestion to me."

Elizabeth waited.

"He thinks your brother would not be suited to university. He suggests a year or two at the Inns of Court in London. It seems that many young men finish their education there and get a taste of London life."

"It would be a long way from home."

"It would do him good. Get away from all you girls. And Uncle Henry can keep an eye on him."

"And Bridget, perhaps."

"Indeed! Bridget! I had not thought of that."

They both leaned back in their chairs for a moment, suddenly distracted from thoughts of John Cresswell. Bridget was at the centre of the family's attention. The past weeks had seen a constant flow of visits to the Hall and to Newcastle. Ordinary life seemed to have been suspended altogether. Bridget was in a state of constant rapture, and when Harry Parker had asked William for his daughter's hand the whole family felt the same euphoria.

"She will be Lady Parker!" said Grace, again and again, trying to accustom herself to the grandeur suddenly bestowed upon them.

"What an honour it is for the family," said William. "But Bridget will have to be patient. Harry must return to London and the Admiral must get home from the sea and his prize money claimed. Then there must be a visit to London and a dowry decided upon. It might be a year or more before they are wed."

Another thought struck him.

"We have John Addison to thank for it, for introducing Harry to the family." He paused, looking at his daughter.

"Has John Addison spoken to you?"

"No."

"I shouldn't be surprised if he does. He has made sure that I know every detail of his business and his property. All his ships and cargoes, his houses in London and Whitby, his estate in Yorkshire. Remarkable."

"Should you object that he is not a gentleman?"

"If money can make a gentleman, he is fast on his way to becoming one."

Elizabeth bent her head low over the ledger.

"I like him, Lizzie. He's got his wits about him. Even if the rest of the family are no more than ordinary sailors."

Ordinary sailors, she thought. Would that be her company if John Addison were to speak for her? Then she thought of Harry. Harry would be a baronet one day. He was happy enough to call John Addison his friend.

* * *

But John Addison did not speak for her. When the two men came to make their farewells, Bridget and Harry spent an hour together alone in the parlour, but John sat with the family and talked with all of them. Elizabeth felt a singing wire of tension in her head so that she could hardly look at him. Was he going to leave without a word to her? She felt somehow deceived in him. Had she been mistaken in her feelings? Had not her father seen it too? And she was humiliated because he, and maybe her mother and her sisters too, would know, know that he had seemed to like her but had turned away. By the time they were saying their farewells, the tension had turned to anger. When it came to her turn, she stood very straight before him and looked directly at him.

"Goodbye, Mr Addison." His eyes looked back into hers with equal directness and the two of them stood arrested for a moment. For a moment, she saw a flash of his usual easy openness, but it was at once restrained and held back, like a flame suddenly doused.

"Goodbye, Miss Cresswell." He hesitated. "My ships are not so often at Newcastle, but at Whitby. Or London. Perhaps . . . ". And then his voice trailed off in so uncharacteristic a way that she almost laughed.

"Goodbye," he finished. He let go her hand, turned and was gone.

*　*　*

If he had been riding alone, John Addison might have pulled the reins around within half an hour of leaving the house and cantered back up the road. But Harry's presence restrained him.

Why had he stayed silent, he demanded of himself as they rode along together. Why so indecisive? Here was Harry beside him, who three months earlier had known nothing of the north, nothing of Cresswell Hall and its daughters, and was now engaged to be married! He seemed to have not the slightest reserve in committing his heart and his future estate into the hands of Miss Bridget Cresswell.

Harry's ardour had cast a romantic cloud over the whole visit. There was a giddiness in the air that infected all of them, that had made him inclined of a sudden to chance his heart. There was no shortage of female company at Cresswell, and it was easy to be taken with the candid grey eyes and direct gaze of Bridget's elder sister, with her boldness and unexpected thoughts. He could not resist exerting himself to charm her till he felt confident she would have him, should he wish. In the same way, he found himself working upon her father. John Addison knew that in William's eyes he was little more than a common sailor. The Addisons might have some connection to his wife's family, but they were certainly not gentry. Not a suitable match for one of his daughters. It stung John's pride. He had set himself to remove William's objections—to impress him with his newfound wealth and influence and to remind him that he kept company with the likes of Harry Parker. By the time his stay in the north was coming to an end, he was confident any suit he might want to make would be favourably regarded.

But now, at the last minute, he had walked away with not a word spoken.

If only his sister Jane were alive! Jane, who loved him without calculation or reserve; Jane, whose counsel was always trustworthy. What would she say to him now? For sure, she would be eager for him to marry. Eager for him to have a family of his own, though he had always been a part of hers. But I am not in love, he wanted to tell her. I know there is passion enough between Elizabeth and myself to make me want her. But I am not besotted with her like Harry is with Bridget. Not deep in love like Francis Easterby was with you.

Love will come, she would say. Married love is a different thing to romance. If you will but open your heart to her, then love will come.

But if it doesn't? he insisted. If I find myself as stony-hearted a husband as our father?

She would have laughed at him, he knew, but the thought sent a chill through every part of him, despite the pleasant warmth of the day. He would think of it no more, he told himself. He set himself to ride onwards to Newcastle and attend only to Harry and his plans.

PART THREE

1766–8

A Clandestine Marriage

CHAPTER 20

Inns of Court, London

1766

Marsham Street, City of Westminster
February 1766
My dear William

Sarah and I Rejoice to see the Announcement in the London Gazette of Bridget's marriage to Sir Harry Parker, a most Suitable Union of great Advantage to the Family. We understand the Parkers are to Live at Newman Street in Marylebone and we anticipate with Pleaſure their Cloſer Acquaintance.

With regard to my nephew John Creſswell, I heartily Endorse your Suggestion in relation to the Inns of Court and will lend it Every Support. A year or two at the Inns will complete his Education both in Study and in Manners. It is Invaluable for young Gentlemen who have known only a Country acquaintance to gain Familiarity with London Society and it can only be Helpful to their Advancement. Should he prove to have an Aptitude for the Law we may then Conveniently Arrange for him to Continue at the Inns.

Since Sarah is so Occupied with the Children I will not venture to Offer Lodgings here at Marsham Street. However I am happy to Recommend to you Lodgings for him with one Reverend Dyer, a Perpetual Curate at Paddington Church and a most Amiable and Cultured Gentleman. His Family numbers a Dozen at least so John would Find himself in the Circumſtances of Domeſtic Intimacy to which he is Accuſtomed.

Your Affectionate Brother,
Henry Creſswell

CHAPTER 21

Cresswell, Northumberland

September 1766

All the trunks and boxes were strapped on, the baskets stowed, the last kisses given, the farewells made, and the carriage rolled away down the drive. They were gone at last.

Elizabeth stood with Grace, Dorothy, Juliana and Alice outside the front door. Suddenly it was all over, all the commotion of packing, all John's storms and tempers, all her mother's lists and instructions. It was all quiet. Elizabeth could hear a bird singing in the garden. None of them spoke. One by one they turned back into the house. Elizabeth went to the kitchen, but there was no sign of Cook. The remains of breakfast still lay on the table; she had scarcely eaten before the departure and now she was suddenly hungry. She picked up a roll and dipped it into a half-empty pot of chocolate. The chocolate was quite cold, but the sweetness of it was comforting. Still munching, she went upstairs to her mother's bedroom. It was all in disarray, the bed unmade, discarded petticoats and shawls strewn on the bed.

Her mother had never been to London. For the last month the dressmaker had hardly been out of the house. There must be gowns suitable for dining with Admiral Sir Hyde Parker and Lady Parker, with Henry and Sarah, for visiting the Inns of Court, for promenading in the London parks and gardens. You are sixty-two, Mother, Elizabeth wanted to say; no one will care how you dress. Perhaps her father thought the same, but he remonstrated to no avail. Between her mother and John, the house seemed to have been in uproar for weeks. Elizabeth supposed that she would come to miss her brother's presence, but for now it was only a relief to have him gone. She dawdled through her mother's room, folding and tidying.

At least all the uproar had distracted her from her thoughts. There was a dreariness in her spirits since Bridget's wedding. It had been a family affair in Woodhorn church with a boisterous wedding breakfast afterwards at the Hall. Elizabeth had found it hard to enter wholeheartedly into the rejoicings. Bridget had always been the beauty of the family with her curls and dimples; it was no surprise to see her wed, but now Elizabeth had watched two of her younger sisters stand at the altar before her. She was twenty-nine. Would soon be thirty and in all her life had received only one proposal of marriage. Was she to spend the rest of her life with Grace and Dorothy? Perhaps, she consoled herself, Bridget's marriage would help her prospects. Perhaps she too might go to London one day, might stay with Bridget and meet Harry's friends. Sometimes another thought slipped in. Was the lowness of her spirits due in some part to her disappointment in John Addison? No, no indeed. I did not care for him, she retorted to herself. He is no more than a common sailor; indeed, some of his family are disreputable.

She looked out of her mother's bedroom window. It was still early; the sky was cloudy, but occasional shafts of sunlight broke through and lit the sea with a shimmering light. She would go down to the shore, she decided.

It was low tide, and the fisherwomen were laying bait lines down by the rocks. The women stooped over the ropes with their buckets of squirming lugworms, slipping them one after another over the hooks, moving steadily up the beach. They wore woollen mittens with the ends cut off, but their hands must still be cold, she thought, though it was only September. When a line was completed, they secured the rope around an iron stave and drove it into the sand near the top of beach. Some days she might have gone and spoken with the women; bid them good day and asked how the boats were faring. But today a pale mist was blowing in off the sea and she wanted to walk alone, watching for her spirit self. Halfway along the shore she fancied she saw a form, a gleam of whiteness brighter than the mist—but in a moment it was gone. She looked upwards at the clouds to see if a storm might be coming in. Surely it is, she thought. There was an angry, dark grey look to the cloud stack building at the horizon and the wind had gone round. It is a childish fancy, she reproved herself, but still she wanted to imagine herself close to the spirit, to her more-than-sister, wanted to run with her into the storm and let the fierce spray blot out all her thoughts.

When she looked back towards the rocks, she saw another figure come down onto the beach. At first she thought it one of the fishermen, but the figure was dressed like a gentleman. Was it some friend of her father's come to ask of his whereabouts? He came closer so that she could make out his features, and at once a shock went through her. How could it be? She looked again. It was. John Addison was walking towards her, was lifting his hat to greet her. Had her thoughts summoned him? She gathered up her skirts and drew her cloak around her.

"Good morning! I am sorry to have surprised you. Juliana told me where I might find you."

"Mr Addison," she said. "It is certainly a surprise. I'm afraid you have missed my father. He and Mother are taking John to London."

"I am sorry to miss them," he said. Then he stood beside her and there was a moment of silence as they stared out at the bay.

"I think a storm may be blowing up," she said. "But you will know better than I, with your sailor's eye."

"Indeed, you are right. The wind has gone round nor-easterly. That'll send ships running for harbour."

There was a silence.

"Perhaps you are looking out for your ghost ship to come to shore."

He had remembered!

"Indeed I am," she said.

"You have still to tell me the tale."

"It is a tale for a winter's night by the fireside. My grandmother would tell it us every Epiphany, and then all us children would fight over the Epiphany cake."

He laughed.

"Shall we stroll a little further along the shore? Although I would have been pleased to talk to your father, it is you I want to speak with, Elizabeth."

A hot blush started in her belly and spread up to her cheeks. She felt her face on fire. They started to walk along the sand, side by side, so that she was not looking at him directly, but listening to his words.

"We have got to know each other a little, and I want to speak with you frankly. I have been a long time coming to marriage. A sailor's life does not sit easily with it. And now that I am come to it, I fear that I have been so long used to my single state that I will be a poor companion to a wife. My business carries me up and down from Whitby to London so that I am often from home."

Has he come all this way to tell me he does not mean to marry, she thought. But he was not finished.

"I want to put all this to you as truthfully as I can. So that if I were to ask you to be my wife you may decide whether or not you would have me. And not accuse me after of being a poor husband to you."

Without waiting for a response, he walked onwards, starting to rush his words as if they were a set piece he had rehearsed before.

"What I can offer you is a genteel house in Whitby or a country estate some thirty miles from the town. And that in either one you will have the means to live as a gentlewoman. You will want for nothing. And since I have so long a connection with your family, I undertake to support both you and them to the best of my ability."

He came to the end of his speech, stopped and turned to look at her, breathless. She felt the blood rushing to her temples. Was it a proposal? "If I were to ask you to be my wife?" What should she say to such an offer?

"I am obliged to you," she said. "It is a very businesslike proposal."

She turned away from him and looked out to sea. For a few moments, there was silence between them, broken only by the sound of the waves whipped up by the freshening wind breaking along the shore. She looked at the long emptiness of the sand and a sense of loneliness overcame her. She wanted to turn and run away, back up the beach, away from John Addison and his loveless proposal.

"Elizabeth. You must not think . . . "

She glanced round and saw that he was surprised. What had he expected her to say? Was she to be bought and sold like all his other business transactions? Did he think all his possessions would make up for the neglect he was promising her? A flare of temper got the better of her.

"I do not care for your house in Whitby, nor your estate either."

He stood in front of her and took hold of her hand. There was a hint of amusement in his eyes that annoyed her further. She tried to take back her hand, but he had it securely in his grasp.

"You are cross with me. I don't wonder at it. You can see I'm no courtier."

He came closer to her, and stood for a moment, composing himself.

"I want you to be my wife, Elizabeth. If you will have me. If you will have me as the man I am."

He held her hand still, looking down at her, waiting. She felt her temper ebbing, but words refused to come. He leaned down, his face close to hers.

"I want you," he said.

Then he kissed her. All her previous thoughts dissolved so that she was aware only of his coat that smelled of sweat and tobacco, his mouth on hers, his beard against her skin. She felt herself losing hold of her resolution. He lifted his head up.

"Will you have me?"

She looked up at him, at his parted lips and his vivid eyes, and desire overcame her.

"Yes," she said. "Yes I will."

And he drew her close so that she felt his body against hers, and he kissed her again.

As the tide turned in the bay, thicker cloud started to roll in off the sea till the far end of the beach was all but blotted out. A sudden volley of rain stung their faces. Unnoticed, a pale form shimmered for a moment on the shoreline before disappearing in the mist.

CHAPTER 22

St Hilda's Terrace, Whitby

April 1767

Six months after his visit to Cresswell, John Addison sat alone at his mahogany dining table with a slice of veal pie on his plate, some pickled beetroot and a hunk of bread, with a bottle of claret at his elbow. There were candles burning in the sconces, but it was still light enough to see a dim outline of the sky through the window. He had had the dining room painted in blue, though he had found it hard to discover any preference in himself. He hoped to rely on Elizabeth for such matters in the future. Usually, he had company of some kind at dinner—a shipmaster newly docked, a couple of merchant friends, a shipwright or builder. And now most often his partner, Richard Moorsom, for their newly established company gave them a constant source of conversation and debate. That Moorsom, a respected and long-established shipmaster in the town, had chosen to go into partnership with John, was a source of particular satisfaction to him.

But tonight he had told his cook he would have a cold dinner and she might go and visit her family or whatever she pleased. When he was alone, he liked to eat simply, as if he were on board ship again and might be called on deck at any moment. He still found it hard to accustom himself to the unchanging stability of life on land. Nothing stirred the solid foundations and stone walls of his mansion house. The fiercest gale Whitby could throw at it might cause a couple of slates to slide down into the garden, where he would hear his neighbour's wife next morning crying out as if disaster had befallen. As he lay secure in bed listening to the wind howling, he would imagine his crews out at sea with every inch of sail reefed down, hauling hard at the wheel to keep the ship steady, waves ten feet high breaking over her. He had seen out some storms in his time.

But quiet though it might be, his new house filled him with the same joy he had felt for his first ship. He loved the way the blocks of ashlar fitted seamlessly together, loved the balance and bold symmetry of the architecture with its tall pedimented windows and pillared front door. Inside, he had seen to it that the fitting-out was as nearly flawless as the carpenters and plasterers could achieve, with elegant cornices and a sweeping staircase. The Whitby of his youth had been dominated by Quaker masters, who shunned ostentation and lived in modest houses on the waterfront. But since the war and the coming of the whaling trade all that had changed. As the town grew more and more prosperous, merchants and ship-owners like himself were moving uphill, away from the noise of industry and the lowlife of the port. Up here on St Hilda's Terrace there were fine views across the town to the old abbey and the houses were as handsome as any belonging to country-house families in York. A new aristocracy had arrived in the town, and he was part of it.

When he had finished his slice of pie, he refilled his glass and stood up with it in his hand. He strolled first to the window and looked out. The house was set back from the road below, but there was scant space for a garden, and the back of the house had the mews where he kept his carriage and horses. So he had purchased a close on the opposite side of the street, a parcel of land that might in time become a pleasure garden for Elizabeth. And the children.

He had made two trips back to Cresswell since his proposal, the first to ask William formally for his daughter's hand, and the second to discuss the wedding and all the arrangements for his life with Elizabeth. He had still had the idea in his mind that a country seat would be fitting for this new stage in his life and had tried to persuade her of it. But she had been very certain.

"Appleton is a day's drive from Whitby, John. I would never see you. Without you residing there it would be difficult for me to find acquaintance in the area. I should hardly know how to go on."

She must have seen him dashed, for she quickly added, "I'm sure it is a very fine house, and all the grounds and garden would serve very well for children later on . . . perhaps when you are less engaged in business than at present, we might use it in the summer months."

He had hardly known whether to be disappointed or relieved. Now he knew. He was relieved. How could he have thought of it? His life was here, was in the town and his business. He was not ready to be a country squire. He did not quite admit to another motive. To have Elizabeth live out at Appleton, to visit for a spell once or twice a month, would have made marriage easier for him.

It was not that he did not like her very well. His visits had given him no reason to regret his proposal. She might not have Bridget's particular charms, but she was still a handsome woman. And, he acknowledged, strong-minded enough to stand up to him. He had no doubts about his choice. She was his necessary companion in his assault upon gentility. She would know how the drawing room should be furnished, how the curtains should be ordered up, what china should be used in place of his rough crockery. She would run his household and entertain his guests. But he found it hard to imagine how it would be to find her in his house, day after day. They were to be married in June; in three months' time he would be a married man. She would be always at the dinner table. Always in his bed.

He was used to living at close quarters with people. Shipboard life trained a man for that; even as master there was never a moment's privacy. There were men around you all the time. But male company was straightforward. Men were bound together by work, by the constant struggle against the sea, by the business they transacted together. All his deep friendships were with men.

Of course he was used to the company of women. In London, he frequented the houses of two or three women who were pleased to entertain him, and sometimes he would stay for days or even weeks. Not in Whitby, of course. The town still maintained high standards of respectability, and he wanted no scandal attaching to his name. But the women he enjoyed in London had no hold on him. He was generous, he was kind, and he was free to walk from the door whenever he chose. Now those visits must cease. He must have Elizabeth's company constantly, whether he would or not, and she would be his equal. There would be no walking from the door if she displeased him.

But he must do it. A genteel wife would open doors to him that still remained politely closed. One door in particular. He pictured it sometimes as a veritable portcullis. Castle Mulgrave. It was a misnomer; the castle was no more than a picturesque ruin, but the great house built in its place still bore the name. Castle Mulgrave sat high above the cliffs outside Whitby and was home to The Right Honourable The Lord Mulgrave. Lord Mulgrave sat in parliament. His eldest son served in the navy with Lord Hervey, and there were a half-dozen younger children. They had influence in the town, and Lord Mulgrave was showing interest in investing in shipping. Married to Elizabeth, John would have a baronet-to-be for a brother-in-law in Harry Parker and a wife whose lineage was as old as the Mulgraves'. Yes! He exulted interiorly. He must do it. Besides, if he were to go to the trouble of making himself a gentleman, he must have an heir to carry on his name. He must have a son.

A son, yes, sometime in the future. In the meantime, he had his nephew to consider. He had promised Frank Easterby he would write a letter on his behalf. He drank off the last of the wine and walked down to his office.

* * *

He was proud of his nephews, John and Frank Easterby. Jane's boys. They were both quick-witted, tough and able, ready to work their way in the world. But it was possible already to see how different their characters would become. In a criss-cross way, John Easterby, who had been named for him, was the more like his father Francis. He was steady and dutiful, ready to follow his father and work his way up through his father's business. He was twenty now and would soon have his first ship as master. He would be heir to Skinningrove, and already he was settled in his manner. John

Addison saw more of himself in Frank Easterby, the younger boy. His father had made it clear that there was room for him in the business too, but Frank had other ideas. He had just completed his apprenticeship and he was restless in Whitby.

"I want to make my own life, Uncle John. I mean to join the navy. I swear I will be a captain before I'm thirty. I'll make you proud of me."

John Addison had looked at his nephew and seen in his face the same boldness, the same will that he knew in himself. He had agreed to write a letter.

He settled himself at his desk and drew out a sheet of paper, inked his quill and began.

> *My dear Harry*
>
> *I truſt that your New State of Matrimony continues to Afford you every Happineſs and I send sincereſt good Wiſhes to Bridget and Yourſelf.*
>
> *I am Writing to you on Behalf of my Nephew Frank Easterby and I Hope you may Indulge me in hearing this Requeſt. He is a very Worthy and Deſerving young man of Excellent character who now Deſires to enter upon a Career in the Navy.*
>
> *He is Well Qualified for the Profeſsion, having newly Completed his Apprenticeship and has served Six years of Seamanship, however in the Present Time of Peace the Navy is greatly Reduced in Number making Entry less Attainable.*
>
> *I therefore Seek to Preſume upon Your very constant Good Will in Asking if a place as a Midſhipman might be found upon the 'Romney' of which your eſteemed Father Admiral Sir Hyde Parker is currently Commander. I can Aſsure you with the Greatest Certainty that Frank would Serve him with the Greateſt Diligence. Both his Father and Myself would be most Deeply Obliged if you could Offer this Recommendation on hiſ Behalf.*
>
> *With Affectionate regards to Yourself and Lady Parker,*
> *John Addison*

CHAPTER 23

Cresswell, Northumberland

October 1767

It had to be owned, William reflected as he sat musing in the tower on a wet autumn morning, that when he thought of his sons-in-law only two names came at once into his mind. Harry Parker, of course. And now, John Addison. To be sure, his other son-in-law, William Johnston of Woodhorn Grange, was a good enough fellow but retiring by nature. If Catherine had not come to live on his doorstep at the Red House, he might have looked forward to a tranquil life as a bachelor. As for Lelia's Robert Sanderson, the less William saw of the prosing parson the better pleased he was.

But contemplating his most recent sons-in-law, Harry Parker and John Addison, gave him nothing but satisfaction. He felt Harry was a son indeed to him. When he and Grace had travelled to London, he had given them every attention, had been constantly solicitous for their comfort. How pleasant it had been to feel, at last, that they might take their ease and be entertained by their daughter and her husband! And Sir Hyde and Lady Parker had been most condescending in their welcome and pressed them to return for a longer stay in London. The truth was, both he and Grace had found the journey so arduous and uncomfortable that he could not imagine making a habit of it, but the invitation was highly gratifying.

And now John Addison. When he had asked for Elizabeth's hand, he had spoken so feelingly of his attachment not only to Elizabeth, but to his god-daughter Juliana and to the family as a whole, that William had felt at last that sense of support one might expect from a son. It was a relief to him. He felt himself growing older, felt the strain of running the estate with all the demands John's education and extravagance put upon it. When his son was finished at the Inns of Court, he would call him back to Northumberland for a stiff talk about the management of the estate and what it could and could not bear. But for now, Grace pleaded, he was young, he was with other wealthy young men, and he must have a sufficient allowance to keep up with them. He found it hard to gainsay her, but it left him with a constant gnaw of anxiety whenever he came up here to his office in the Tower. A gnawing that now could be allayed by reminding himself of his other sons, albeit sons-in-law.

Of course gaining John Addison had meant losing Lizzie. She had only been gone a few months, but already he missed her presence far more than he had expected. He missed her quick way with the accounts and her prudent housekeeping. Grace, too, had grown used to leaving things to Lizzie. They would have to see what Juliana could do, or maybe Alice, since she was a woman now. His daughters Grace and Dorothy went their own way, Dorothy growing a little stranger all the time and Grace taken up with looking after her. He had no idea how they passed the day. Stitching, perhaps. Sheets and shirts and the like. He often only saw them at dinner. It was very quiet in the house these days, just him and Grace and the four girls. Sometimes he and Grace were abed before eight, and his old enthusiasm for the racecourse was ebbing away. The ride to Morpeth left him stiff and aching these days.

Enough of maudlin thoughts, he declared to himself. He would go to the house and take a cup of tea with Grace.

He entered the house and called for her. There was no reply. He climbed the stair and went to see if she was in her bedroom, but it was empty. As he went back down the corridor, Juliana popped her head out of her room, her face pale.

"She is in the parlour, Father."

What is amiss, he wondered. Why did she not call out to me, if she is in the parlour? He went in and saw she was half-lying on the sofa. She did not look up when he came in. He realized she was weeping.

"My dear Grace!" he said. "Whatever is the matter?"

She turned her head and looked at him with so tragic an expression he thought a death must have occurred.

"What is it? Tell me!"

She half-raised her arm to point at the table.

"There—over there. On the table."

Bewildered, he looked over to the table. He saw there was a letter lying there, seal broken. He picked it up and started to read:

> *My Dear Father and Mother*
>
> *I Write to You with News of a Great Change in my Life. Since I Have Come to Live with the Family of Reverend Dyer I have Conceived a Strong Affection for Catherine, his Eldeſt Daughter. You may Remember Her from your Introduction to the Family Laſt Year. She returns my Affections to the Highest Degree and Since I can Conceive No Female likely to make me a Better Wife I have Earneſtly Required her Father's Consent which he has Approved.*
>
> *I could See no Reason to Delay my Wiſh to Enter upon the State of Matrimony and we were Wed laſt week at Paddington Church.*
>
> *Since Catherine's Conſtitution is not Strong and her Family believe she would be Suited by Country Air, I have Rented a Cottage in Dorking where I Plan to Reſide. I Will no Longer attend the Inns of Court, However you Will very Well underſtand that My Expenſes are Greatly Increaſed in our New Houſehold, and I will Require an Addition to my Allowance of at least 30 guineas a month.*
>
> *I Truſt that You enjoy Good Health*
> *Your affectionate son*
> *John*

William flung the letter down on the table, his face suddenly red with rage. He turned on Grace.

"This is your doing!" he shouted at her. "It has been brought about by your everlasting indulgence of the boy! Your pandering to his every whim and fancy! You have made him believe he must have whatever he wants with no thought for the consequences. Dear God!"

Grace buried her head in the sofa without replying.

"Never mind your weeping! It is too late for tears now. The damage is done, and it will be the ruin of us. A penniless curate's daughter without name or dowry! A thousand plagues upon her father for giving his consent! How could he have so betrayed us!"

Grace, seeing the direction of his fury turning towards the Dyers, lifted her head.

"And she is the oldest of them all! She is twenty-seven and he scarcely twenty."

As he took in her words, comprehension struck William like a bolt of lightning.

"A sister! He cannot do without a sister at his beck and call! Why else has he married her?"

Grace and he stared at each other. He felt tears coming to his eyes. All his hopes for John, all his dreams for the marriage he would arrange for him, were dashed to pieces. He had incurred all the expense of John's education with one aim in view; to enable his son to enter polite society. To find a bride of good family who would have, if not a fortune, at least a substantial dowry and income to lend support to the estate. The future turned to ashes in his mouth.

Tears ran down his cheeks. He flung out of the room, out of the house, seizing his stick on the way. He strode up to the woods, slashing at the ground with the stick as he went, and when he reached the trees he swung the stick against the trunk of a tree again and again, shouting aloud, till he tired of the stick and beat his head against the tree instead. If only his first son had lived! His William was only six when he died, but he had been so quick and clever. So willing. John would have been no more than a harmless younger brother to him, a fool who could waste his life as he pleased. He sank down onto the ground and stared out across his land. What had been the point of it all? All the improvements he had made on the farms, all the effort of building the new hall. In the dark mood that was upon him he felt it had all been for nothing, all that he had done, that John would squander it and the family, the estate, would be no more.

CHAPTER 24

St Hilda's Terrace, Whitby

October 1767

It was a fresh October morning in Whitby with a frost in the air. Elizabeth Addison was two months married and had not so far learned that hers was not the only family marriage of the year. Indeed, her brother might have been the furthest person from her mind as her boots went clattering over the cobbles of the narrow lane between crammed-together wooden houses, down into the town in search of the milliner. She had not the slightest idea where it was to be found, but after the morning's encounter she had had no intention of asking Mrs Norris for directions. There were not so many shops in Whitby. She would walk till she found it. In fact, she decided, it might be as well to look in a few shop fronts or order up some fresh tea, in order to compose herself. Her heart was still beating uncomfortably hard, and her thoughts were disordered. She slowed her walk to allow herself to rehearse again the scene she had just left.

The previous night it had rained very heavily from the south-west. A window had blown open in one of the bedrooms and one of the curtains was pulled half off the rail and soaked through. She had gone into the bedroom that morning intending to see to it. She found Mrs Norris, the housekeeper, already taking it down.

"Good morning, Mrs Norris," she said.

"Good morning, ma'am," said Mrs Norris, her manner somehow managing to be both obsequious and overbearing at once. "I will get this curtain taken down for you and order up some fresh material."

"I don't think that will be necessary, Mrs Norris. I had a look at it earlier, and it is only the lining that has torn. The curtain will be quite serviceable once it has dried out."

"Mr Addison prefers to have everything new, ma'am. He doesn't like to be patching up and making do."

Mrs Norris held the curtain possessively. The two women looked at each other for a moment. Mrs Norris had a small ferret-like face framed with stiff red hair like bristles. When she attempted an ingratiating smile, Elizabeth saw the white gleam of her teeth. Elizabeth did not return the smile.

"I will go to the milliner and get some lining cloth. You need not trouble with it further, Mrs Norris. Leave the Household Book on my desk so that I can enter the cloth when I return."

She had turned on her heel and left the room.

*   *   *

The impertinence of it! To presume to prefer Mr Addison's wishes over her own! It was not to be borne with.

She was so busy with her thoughts she hardly noticed that she had reached the bottom of the lane, and suddenly the harbour was before her, the water shining grey between the ships and the masts rising black against the sky. All at once she felt the milliner might wait, that she would take a walk along the shore and let the sea soothe her agitation. It was not a fine morning but not windy either, so she might go along to the seafront without her hair and bonnet getting blown about. Since she had little acquaintance so far in the town, she would not be remarked upon.

She walked briskly along to the end of the road by the pier and then hitched her skirts to walk through the loose sand and onto the beach. How different it felt to Cresswell! Dirty yellow cliffs loomed up behind her, darkening the shore; there was something forbidding and inhospitable about it that made her shiver. But the sea was the same, the surge of the water up the sand, the slow outbreath of its return, the same rhythm she had always known. Her breath came more easily, and she let herself consider Mrs Norris.

Of course when he was single, John Addison had had a housekeeper, and with so large a house to manage she had thought it wise for Mrs Norris to continue. At first, while she had to learn all the necessities of the place, she had depended on Mrs Norris to explain it all. Living in a town where everything had to be bought in, from milk and cheese to meat and bread, was different in every way to living on an estate. And the house was not yet fully furnished and ordered, so there were plenty of matters to occupy her attention. But it had not taken long to discover that Mrs Norris understood herself to be mistress of the house. She found endless trivial ways to undermine Elizabeth's orders and to insinuate herself with John behind her back. She had had her own way for too long. She would talk to John, she resolved.

It was not always easy to find a time for such discussions. As he had warned her, her husband was always busy—in his offices at the back of the house, down in the harbour overseeing the lading of a ship, in the shipyard where a new one was a-building, meeting in the ale house with other merchants and seamen. He was never still, never alone, and seemed never tired. Even at dinner they were seldom without company. His brother-in-law Francis Easterby and nephew John Easterby often ate with them, and his partner, Mr Moorsom, as well as any number of other men he might have dealings with. So she waited till Sunday. They went to church together; she was shown off to yet more of his acquaintance, and then they returned to a cold collation. He was in a good humour, she judged. He liked to be seen with her. She took the moment.

"John, I have a small matter to speak to you about. About the housekeeping. It is Mrs Norris."

"I hope you are pleased with her."

"No. I fear I am not."

"What has she done to displease you? She has worked for me for years. I've never had occasion to complain of her."

"I do not complain of her work, though it is not always as I would have it done myself. But she has grown used to being in charge of the house.

She would like me to go and sit in the drawing room and gaze out the window while she runs the house for you."

"Would you not like to take your ease in the drawing room?"

"I am not used to it, John. All my life I have helped run the house. I don't like to be idle. Besides . . . "

"Besides what?"

"She is spending money very freely on your behalf. I have required the housekeeping book from her and gone through the expenditure. It doesn't always reckon up correctly, and there are items listed which I do not see in the house."

John laughed.

"Well! Where did you learn to reckon up accounts?"

"I did the estate accounts for my father. And the housekeeping book as well."

He stood up and came over to her and laid his hand on her shoulder.

"So, Lizzie. My wife is a bookkeeper."

She stood up and faced him defiantly. He took hold of her and pulled her towards him. Half of her wished to resist him, but she was quickly overcome.

"Let us go upstairs," he said, and then, looking at her face, "I will deal with Mrs Norris."

* * *

Afterwards, amid the flurry of discarded stays and petticoats and the rumpled linen bedsheets, she lay naked on her husband's shoulder with his arm about her and thought, it is Sunday afternoon and I am abed with my husband. My old self is gone. I am Mrs Addison now. And she lifted up her face to him to be kissed again, to feel the prickle of his beard against her cheek, and felt she wanted nothing more than to lie there beside him all day.

Since her marriage she had discovered a wanton in herself whose existence she had never suspected. After thirty years of living as chastely as a nun, with only sisters for company in her bedroom, she had thought of the marriage bed with apprehension as well as desire. But in the great mahogany bed in the room that looked out over the Abbey, her feelings underwent a transformation. Her husband knew how to find out the secret places of her body, knew how to rouse her passion till she had not a shred of modesty left. Soon she could think only of night-times. The days seemed long till he was at last finished drinking after dinner with his friends and was ready to come to her. She started to lace her stays so that her breasts would rise higher to tempt him; she spent more time than she ever had to dress becomingly; she wore flowers in her hair and pearls round her neck. In the mirror she saw that she seemed to have grown younger, her face smoother, her lips fuller. She felt a kind of fulfilment she had not dreamed of. Soon, she thought, her belly must start to swell.

John Addison was pleased with her, she knew. When she rose to leave the gentlemen at the end of dinner, John would stand too and before them all would put his arm around her waist and kiss her, as if to announce, see my wife!

When she had gone, the men would go on drinking port or brandy and smoking. Elizabeth was used to her father taking a glass or two of brandy, but John would drink a half bottle at a sitting. She grew used to a certain recklessness that came over him when he was drunk, a wild teasing self that sometimes half-frightened her, or would have if she had not been half drunk herself. There was wine on the table every night. She grew used to her glass being filled and refilled. She had only ever drunk on high days and holidays; now she drank fine French wine every night and madeira during the day. She felt as if her old thoughts, her old feelings, had been swept away entirely. She was drunk with her new life.

But John Addison would never linger. He always wanted to be up, to be doing, with more energy than before. Already he was restless.

"Up! Up!" he cried at her, pulling the sheet off. "I cannot have my wife lying abed all day!"

She tried to pull back the sheet, but he was too quick, flapping it away over her head. She felt suddenly abashed, lying naked before him, and jumped out of bed.

"You will have to lace my stays, John. I cannot call Susan to do it in the middle of the afternoon."

So he laced her up, as deft as a lady's maid, and she thought, if my sisters could see this! And she laughed aloud at the thought.

He stood over by the window watching her while she pulled on her stockings and gartered them.

"We have a visit to make next week," he said, suddenly serious.

Another visit, she thought. Every week, it seemed, there was someone they needed to call on. All the way out to Skinningrove to meet the new Mrs Easterby and John's nieces and nephews. Up to Airey Place to call upon Mr and Mrs Moorsom in their rambling old farmhouse. Through the town to call upon the wives of his merchant friends and drink tea politely. Only John's own Addison family were so far left off the list.

"Is it far?"

"No distance at all. We can take the carriage to Sandsend and be there in an hour or two. Lady Mulgrave has invited us to pay a morning call on Wednesday."

"Ah!" She digested this. "Will Lord Mulgrave be there?"

"He is in London. He has matters of government to attend to."

"How must I dress?"

"I could not say at all, my dear. As elegant a turnout as you and Susan can devise."

*   *   *

She summoned Susan early on Wednesday morning. Susan was only a housemaid, not a lady's maid, but she had a good eye and nimble fingers. She loved to help Elizabeth try this gown and that, a different fichu, an amber necklace, and in return Elizabeth let her have remainders of material she did not need or a petticoat that no longer answered. Susan knew everyone in Whitby, it seemed. She had servant friends in all the big houses in town and could relate all that went on in their households. When Elizabeth sat drinking tea with a new acquaintance, she was armed already with the information that, for example, Mrs Coulson was awkward with her servants and could turn her sharp tongue upon her husband too.

"Do you know anything of the Mulgraves, Susan?" she asked.

"Oh no, ma'am, hardly at all. The servants there have houses on the estate, in Sandsend, and they are seldom here. The Mulgraves are very highly regarded in the town. Lord Mulgrave is in government and speaks up for Whitby, so they say."

So there was no more to learn there. They had driven up the steep hill out of Sandsend and past the entrance to the castle once or twice, but it was surrounded by thick woodland so that it was impossible to gain a glimpse of it. She had dreamed of it twice since John gave her the news. In both her dreams it appeared as a great Gothic castle set with battlements and turrets with dark looming walls. Yet, forbidding though it seemed, each time she dreamed she had seen a light appear within the castle, faint at first, that grew steadily in brightness till it streamed out of the windows and doors into all the countryside around, and she woke full of joy. There was nothing to fear from Castle Mulgrave, she told herself.

CHAPTER 25

Mulgrave Hall, Sandsend

October 1767

When their carriage rolled up the drive, Elizabeth saw it was not a castle at all, but a Jacobean mansion three storeys high, built of stone, with long mullioned windows and an imposing front entrance. Lawns stretched away from the front of the house to a wonderful vista of the sea beyond, so that the water appeared to flow seamlessly below them.

They were received at the door by a footman and ushered through a wide panelled hall to the drawing room to one side. Elizabeth was at once surprised. There was none of the heavy gloom she had expected; the room was full of light from the tall windows. The walls were painted and hung, not with dour portraits of ancestors, but landscapes and tapestries. The furniture was all of the most modern kind, with chaises and armchairs and coloured rugs, and on the side tables were vases filled with hothouse roses that filled the room with their perfume. Standing before the marble fireplace was a woman in her forties, dressed in a fashionable blue and silver gown with a necklace of sapphires about her neck. Her skin was rouged and cerused, and her powdered hair curled in carefully dressed waves around her face. She came forward at once to greet them.

"My dear Mrs Addison! How good of you to visit us! We are dreadfully dull up here. I am always in want of company."

"We are very much obliged to your ladyship."

"You are from Northumberland, I believe. You are almost Scottish! I shall desire a full account of it from you." She turned to John. "But Mr

Addison, I am neglecting you. You are very welcome. By good fortune I have two nautical visitors to entertain you."

She turned towards the door.

"Constantine! Where are you hiding with Mr Banks? Come and speak with our visitors."

Almost at once, two men in their early twenties appeared at the door, dressed only in breeches and shirts, still laughing at some private joke. The taller of the two stepped forward to greet the visitors, his light blue eyes at once betraying a resemblance to his mother.

"Joseph has been botanizing in the woods and could hardly be persuaded away," he said.

When she would look back at that first meeting with Constantine, on that mild October afternoon at Mulgrave Hall, Elizabeth would find that she had formed no definite impression of him, other than that he was tall and his nose a little protuberant. Nothing suggested to her then that the encounter would be in any particular way memorable to her. Indeed, her attention was more taken by his friend Joseph Banks. He was smaller and slighter than Constantine; to Elizabeth, the dark hair curling around his face and his expressive brown eyes made him instantly appealing. She felt drawn to him at once. Lady Mulgrave made her introductions.

"My son Constantine and Mr Joseph Banks. They are old schoolfriends from their Eton days. Indeed, Joseph is almost a member of the family."

Mr Banks bowed and smiled.

"They are newly returned from a voyage to Newfoundland and Labrador. Mr Addison, I dare say you may be familiar with those waters?"

"I am not, your ladyship, though I was able to provide a couple of transports for Newfoundland during the war."

"Since he came home, Constantine cannot decide whether he wishes to be a naval hero or a scientific explorer."

"Joseph's company gives me the chance to be both!" said Constantine, smiling at his friend. He turned to speak to John directly.

"My recent posting, Mr Addison, was to the colony in Newfoundland under General Palliser's command, to assist with reinforcements. I arranged for Joseph to accompany us as a scientist and I was forever at his elbow.'

"How did you find the voyage, Mr Banks?" asked John.

Banks sighed and shook his head.

"I expect, sir, that like my friend here you started your life at sea at an early age and so became inured to seasickness. But this was the first voyage I ever undertook, and I fear the slightest swell was enough to make me queasy. I spent much time in my cabin."

"It is an arduous voyage," said John. "Even the most hardened sailor suffers on occasion. Did you encounter bad weather?"

"Indeed we did—a most terrible storm off the Azores. I was certain we would never survive it. The water came rushing in and filled my cabin entirely. My boxes of seeds were all washed away and the living plants I had upon the deck as well."

"How dreadful!" exclaimed Elizabeth. "Was all your work wasted?"

"No, I thank God. My specimen books miraculously survived undamaged."

"Perhaps you will allow Mr and Mrs Addison to inspect the drawings?" said Lady Mulgrave.

"I should like to, very much," said Elizabeth.

They were led into another room which clearly had once served as the dining room but now was become a sort of artist's studio, with several tables set round it covered with prints and drawings of every kind of flower and plant, and strange birds she did not recognize.

"How beautiful they are!" she exclaimed. "How wonderfully precise and detailed! Are they your own work, Mr Banks?"

"No. I fear I am no artist. When we returned from the voyage, I commissioned a Mr Ehret to illustrate my specimens so that they might be presented to the scientific community more conveniently. Now his work is done, and Constantine prevailed upon me to bring them for his family to inspect."

Elizabeth stared at the illustrations, at the unfamiliar plants whose names she had to try on her tongue. Each leaf was rendered in minute detail, from unfolding to full growth, and delicately coloured. The flowers were drawn with the same careful observation and yet at the same time had a kind of decorous vitality.

"I feel as if I am looking into a new Garden of Eden, Mr Banks. I am astonished that I can scarcely recognize a single specimen. It is truly a wonder."

He smiled at her enthusiasm. She wandered from table to table, absorbed in the drawings. John Addison turned to the two men.

"Do you mean to undertake another voyage?" John enquired.

"I do!" responded Mr Banks. "The Royal Society means to send an expedition to the South Pacific Ocean to observe the Transit of Venus. The astronomers believe it has a vital role to play in the estimation of longitude. I am no astronomer, of course, but it will give me an opportunity for botanizing in those unknown territories."

He turned to John enquiringly.

"Our captain is to be a Whitby man. Perhaps you know him? James Cook is his name."

John grimaced.

"Yes, I know the man. He was captain of the *Pembroke* on the St Lawrence and collided with one of my transports. He cost me some wrangles with the Admiralty over restitution."

Constantine laughed as he joined the conversation.

"I understand you may be left with low regard for his navigation. Nevertheless, he has great talent as a surveyor. His charts of the Newfoundland waters are wonderfully precise and were of great utility to us on our voyage. It is hoped he will undertake similar surveys in the uncharted territories of the South Pacific."

"Do you mean to go with Mr Banks on this voyage, Lord Constantine?"

"My naval duties prevent me. I am to take up command of the *Boreas* on my return to London. I doubt we will be venturing further than the Channel."

As the men talked, Lady Mulgrave went over and joined Elizabeth at the tables.

"Are they not enchanting?"

"I feel as if I have been transported to Newfoundland just in seeing them."

"Are you a lover of plants? You must return on another occasion, and I will show you round the gardens here. When we come here for the summer, the garden is my chief occupation. But we must take tea now—you have driven all the way from Whitby and had no refreshment."

So tea was served, and Elizabeth sat and talked with Lady Mulgrave—"You must call me Lepell, my dear—I know we shall be great friends"—till she felt indeed she had known her for far longer than a single morning visit. But as soon as tea was done John sprang to his feet and declared they should not presume any longer on Lady Mulgrave's kindness, the carriage was ordered, cordial wishes were expressed for further meetings on both sides and the visit was over.

* * *

As they left, Elizabeth sat by the window of the carriage, peering out at the thick woodland that surrounded the estate, imagining Constantine and Joseph searching for rare specimens. How remarkable it would be to go exploring the South Seas! She tried to imagine Mr Banks, hat on head, boxes slung around him, traversing strange forests and mountains with undreamed of plants and creatures. She turned to John.

"How delightful that was! How fortunate we were to meet with Mr Banks and Lord Constantine! Did you not think the illustrations very skilfully done?"

John Addison returned no answer, but she hardly noticed in her enthusiasm.

"I should love to see the artist at his task, to discover how he renders them with so lifelike a touch. Do you think . . . "

But John suddenly interrupted her, the words breaking out of him vehemently.

"I have no time for such fancies. Seafaring is a sport for Mr Banks which he may indulge as he pleases. His only purpose is to bring back trifles for his noble friends to marvel at and to sit in salons telling tales of his adventures. Alas that his precious box of seeds got washed away! I'll wager a few sailors got washed away as well in such a storm, but he makes no note of that."

His words were like a sudden shock to Elizabeth. She sat quite still, unable to speak. She was aware of a sundering sensation. She felt herself on one continent and John Addison on the other, drifting away from each other. She wanted to clutch at him, to pull him across, but she knew it was no use to try. For all his fine house and country estate, she saw at that moment that John was still a merchant, a ship-owner at heart and that he always would be. He had won all his wealth from the sea, and it meant only one thing to him: trade and profit. For Elizabeth, the taste of exploration and discovery she had just experienced was intoxicating. The two young men brought a whiff of another world, of science and enquiry. She was at once in love with it. But from John it won only contempt.

She turned back to the window, all her animation frozen. They sat apart and exchanged not another word all the long drive back to Whitby.

CHAPTER 26

Whitby

July 1768

Although John Addison was in London for the first anniversary of their marriage almost a year later, he had not forgotten it. When he came home a fortnight later, he brought Elizabeth a Chinese rose bowl, carefully wrapped and boxed; she found it on the breakfast table the morning after his return. When she took it from the box, she felt a shock of delight. How beautiful it was! It had deep rounded sides in fine white porcelain, brightly enamelled with scattered pink and orange blooms. The rim was delicately patterned in dusky pink and inside the bowl was a peony spray encircled by flowers and clouds. She took it carefully in her hands, turning it to see every angle. It was perfectly done.

"It is the loveliest thing I ever saw," she said, looking up at him.

He smiled, pleased.

"It is exotic enough for you, I dare say. It has come all the way from China."

"Oh! To think it has travelled all that way! It is so delicate." She put the bowl down and went to kiss him.

"Dear John. How kind you are!"

He held her tight for a long kiss, till a knock came at the door and the maidservant entered.

"Oh, excuse me, sir."

John released Elizabeth.

"What is it, Mary?"

"You are wanted at the door, sir."

"I will be there in a moment."

He turned back to Elizabeth and held her again, but already he was distracted.

"You must go and see to your caller. I will see you this afternoon."

And he was gone. She stood alone in the breakfast room, turning the bowl in her hands, feeling the fineness of the porcelain, marvelling at the lovely delicacy of the painted flowers. She felt a rush of affection for her husband, that he had troubled to find her something she would like so much. A whole year of marriage. Of John. Sometimes she felt she had lowered herself by becoming a ship-owner's wife, whose fine house and lavish table depended on trade, and whose husband thought of nothing but money. But it was impossible not to see beyond that, into John Addison with all his contradictions. He was so strong, so capable, and yet there were times when he depended on her. He could not rid himself of a kind of subservience when he dealt with the gentry and nobility who invested in his company. It made him at once angry and ill at ease. He needed her presence, her assurance in society. She understood that now, understood why there were sometimes angry outbursts against the very people he most desired to impress. It made her feel unexpectedly protective towards him. She was determined on his behalf that the Addisons would present a genteel face to the world.

And he was a generous man—generous to his people, and generous to her. She turned the bowl in her hands again. Nor did he reproach her, although . . . but she would not give such thoughts space, not now, when she had so much to see to. Lady Mulgrave was to call that afternoon with her boys, so that John Addison could take them down to the yard to see their father's ship. John had convinced Lord Mulgrave that he could increase his profits from the alum works at Sandsend if he could ship the alum himself. John Addison would have the *Mulgrave* built and fitted out for him, find him a crew and a master, and thereafter his shipping costs would be halved. Lord Mulgrave's interest in his ship was only commercial. But his sons, like their older brother Constantine, were in love with the sea, and full of excitement at the prospect of a ship bearing their name.

So Lepell had begged Elizabeth, would Mr Addison take them down to the yard?

When the maid showed the family into the drawing room that afternoon, Elizabeth saw at once that, although she was as elegantly dressed as ever, Lepell was flustered. The two elder boys, Charles and Henry, came and stood beside their mother and bowed politely to Elizabeth. Both were in their early teens and already young gentlemen. But the younger boys, Edmund and Augustus, only six and eight, burst into the room like a whirlwind, with the nursemaid grabbing futilely first at one and then the other.

"Edmund has my soldier!" yelled Augustus. "He took it off me in the carriage! Tell him to give it back to me!"

"He shall not have it, it was mine in the first place, I only lent it to him."

"Give it back!" Augustus broke free of the nursemaid and threw himself upon his brother. The two of them fell upon the floor and started to roll towards the table on which the rose bowl stood. Elizabeth started forward.

"Stop it at once, boys!" said Lepell. They paid her no heed at all. Augustus started screaming, clutching his face.

"He has hit me! He has hit me!"

Then, suddenly, a man's voice cut through the uproar.

"Boys!"

It was so loud, so commanding that Augustus stopped in mid-scream and turned to look. John Addison stood in the doorway, smiling broadly, his arms outstretched.

"Augustus! Edmund! Here you are!"

The boys scrambled to their feet and ran towards him. He swung Augustus up in his arms.

"What a big boy you are become! I swear I can hardly lift you!"

Then it was Edmund's turn and more exclamations. Putting him down, he turned to Charles and Henry and shook their hands very warmly. Then he turned to them all.

"I have some exciting news. You have come on a special day."

He held them in suspense for a moment, looking from one face to another.

"The *Mulgrave*'s mainmast is to be stepped today. It is a special day for the ship and all the men will be there for it. Would you like to see it?"

"Yes!" shouted all four.

"You must mind your manners, now. Remember, it is your ship, the *Mulgrave*. You must show how your family behaves."

Augustus and Edmund stood straight, the soldier forgotten.

"Sir, afterwards, will you take us out in the yawl?" said Charles.

"It will depend on the tide. But if not today, you may come down again very soon, if your mother agrees." John Addison paused. He looked to Lepell.

"Lady Mulgrave, may I take the boys down to the yard?"

"Indeed, I would be delighted if you would. Shall Annie go with you?"

"Better not, in the yard. We will manage very well."

And they were gone, the boys clustering around him, all eager to have his ear.

"Oh!" said Lepell, sinking down into a chair. "Thank God for that." She turned to the nursemaid.

"Annie, you may go down to the kitchen and see what they have for you there."

Elizabeth rang for the maid to bring tea, and the two women settled into their chairs.

"Mr Addison is so good with the boys," said Lepell. "What a wonderful father he will be!"

"If I am able to oblige him," said Elizabeth, before she could stop herself.

"You are not worried, are you, my dear? It is hardly a year since you married."

"My sister Bridget has miscarried and is pregnant again in that time. And my brother's wife Catherine is due to give birth any day, though she was wed three months after us."

"You must not dwell on it. After Constantine was born, I did not conceive again for ten years! I thought he would be my only child. Although it's true that Charles saw more of his mistress than he did of me during that time." A thought struck her. "Is Mr Addison . . . attentive?"

Elizabeth nodded.

"Good. But you must consider, why should the fault be yours? It is always the way of it. If a woman does not conceive, it must be some female condition to blame. But why should it not be laid at the husband's door? Mr Addison is not a young man. He has lived a hard life at sea, and I dare say he is no more of a saint than any other sailor. If a man contracts disease, it may damage his virility altogether."

Elizabeth felt the blood rising hot into her cheeks.

"Have I surprised you? You must forgive me. We Herveys are shockingly loose in our manners. My brother Augustus is a wicked philanderer. I have learned to be surprised at nothing in the naval line."

Lepell took a sip of the tea that had been set before her and warmed to her theme.

"Perhaps you should take a lover, my dear, and put the matter to the test! No no—I am truly joking now. But I beg you not to take all the blame upon yourself. And do not repine—Mr Addison will find a way. He is a great man for finding a way, whatever difficulty is presented to him."

She looked at Elizabeth, who could find nothing to say.

"But it is too early to talk of that. A year is nothing. And maybe there are things that may be tried. When will you go down to London?"

The talk turned to London and the news Lepell had from Constantine of Mr Banks' expedition to the South Seas, and since they were speaking of plants Elizabeth took Lepell to see the latest additions to the pleasure garden across the road. She had sent to a garden nursery in York for every kind of rose—moss roses, sweet scented rosa gallica, centifolias, even the new china roses that were all the rage. But she had borders, too, and Lepell had sent down her gardener with clumps of stachys and germander, tall daisies and slips of lavender. This was only the garden's first year, but already, as June turned into July, it was bright with blossom and scent. The two women stood in the garden, looking out across the valley to the old Abbey on the promontory. Elizabeth thought of St Hilda and her nuns. For a moment she half-wished herself one of them.

When the visit was over and the Mulgraves' carriage had lurched along the narrow mews cobbles, she was relieved to go inside. She went upstairs to their bedroom and sat on the chair in the window. Lepell's frankness was shocking to her. She said aloud things that Elizabeth shrank even from thinking. But now said, they could not be unsaid. Was it true, what Lepell implied? She had not thought very much about John's life before they married. Had not thought how it was he was so familiar with a woman's body. But now she thought it and the thought froze her heart. She had to ask him. She had to know.

That night when they lay together in the great bed he fell asleep almost at once. But she shook him awake.

"John. John."

He didn't stir, but his eyes opened.

"What's the matter?"

"When you go to London . . ."

"Yes?"

"Do you see other women?"

He was immediately awake.

"What has put that into your mind?" He pulled himself up onto his elbow and looked at her. "Have you been talking to Lepell?"

She stared back at him dumbly. She felt tears start to squeeze out of her eyes and run saltily down to her lips.

"No, Lizzie, since you ask. I do not see other women."

He took her in his arms. The relief of feeling his arms around her and the darkness of her face against his chest made the tears flow faster.

"I am surprised you feel the need to ask. Why would you think I am not content with you? The nobility—Lepell and the rest—they do things differently. The Herveys are known for their loose living. I do not mean to imitate them. And you should not listen to her."

Relief spread through her in a warm cloud. She buried her head in his shoulder. It was all right. There was still the question of his earlier life, and whether what Lepell said might be true. But that life was before, and now was after, and that was where they lived. She knew he told her the truth. That was enough for now.

* * *

It was the very next day that Isaac came.

She was called for down to the kitchen, and there he was, sitting at the table, looking just as he always had but older than she remembered. For a moment, she hardly knew where she was, at Whitby or at Cresswell.

"Why, Isaac! Whatever are you doing here?"

She remembered, afterwards, that at the very moment she came into the kitchen Catherine Dyer, her brother's wife, had been in her thoughts, and whether she had been delivered yet. As if it were a premonition.

"The master has sent me down very urgent to see you, Miss Elizabeth."

She felt a sudden dread grip her.

"We'll go to the parlour," she said. Whatever the news he had brought, she didn't want to hear it with Cook and the scullery maid staring round-eyed at her.

Once they were in the parlour and private, she closed the door and stood facing him.

"So, Isaac. What is it?"

"It is Mrs Cresswell." Then, seeing her face, he hurried on, "No, not your mother. Young Mrs Cresswell. Mr John's wife."

"Is she delivered?"

"Yes, ma'am. Twins."

Dear God, she thought, thinking of her mother's sufferings.

"Do they live?"

"Both of them were living when the master had word. But Mrs Cresswell . . . " His voice trailed off.

"What, Isaac?"

"She is dead, ma'am. The birth was very long, and the midwife couldn't save her, so it seems, nor the doctor either."

Elizabeth sat down suddenly in an armchair, unable to take in the news. Catherine dead! And she and John not a year married. How terrible a blow! How would John sustain it?

"This is dreadful news, Isaac. Did John send word to my parents?"

"It was Reverend Dyer sent word, young Mrs Cresswell's father." He pulled out a letter from his jacket. "You had best read this."

He handed her a letter. Elizabeth broke the seal and read:

> *My Dear Lizzie*
>
> *We have learned from Reverend Dyer that John's Wife Catherine has Given Birth to Twin Girls who live so Far but the Birth was very Arduous. Catherine Suffered greatly and Defpite the Strongeft Efforts of the Phyficians she Survived long Enough only to Know her Babes. It is a Very Great Blow to all your brother John's hopes of Happinefs and it Seems He is Diftraught beyond Caring for his New-born Infants.*
>
> *Reverend Dyer Begs us to Haften to Support Him but Since your Mother is not Well I am Sending Isaac to You with the Carriage to Entreat You to Go to Your Brother's side. I would Not have Troubled you with Such a Matter but since Bridget is with Child again and Delicate she Must Not Stir from the House.*
>
> *Your loving Father*
> *William*

She read it twice, thrice, then looked up at Isaac.

"So you have brought the carriage?"

"Yes, ma'am."

"I will send for Mr Addison. Have you eaten, Isaac?"

"Not yet, ma'am."

"Cook will find something for you." She took his hands. "If it were not for your news, I would be so happy to see you, Isaac, and to hear of Cresswell. We'll speak again when you're rested."

CHAPTER 27

Newman Street, Marylebone

July 1768

In the end John Addison had insisted that she take their carriage and Isaac had been sent home.

"I can manage very well without it. You'll be more comfortable," he said.

Her gratitude to him had increased with every day of the journey. She felt half shaken to pieces as it was and how much worse it would have been in her father's ancient coach! By the time they drew up in Newman Street where she was to stay, she was ready for nothing but a good bed and a night's undisturbed sleep. But Bridget was in high spirits at her arrival, ready to sit up half the night chattering.

"Poor Lizzie, you are quite worn out! You must have a glass of port; it will set you to rights. You cannot imagine how pleased I am to see you! The doctor will not let me stir from the house and I am bored to death."

"Is it all going well?"

"I believe so. I felt it move yesterday, which I never did before, with the one I lost. I believe it will be all right this time. You have nothing yet, Lizzie?"

"No."

"I'm sure it will not be long. And then, they will be cousins and they will have each other to play with sometimes!"

"Shall we talk more in the morning, Bridget? I am all done up with the journey."

"Oh, but you must wait till Harry gets home! He is so eager to see you! He will be here very soon."

"Indeed, I will be better company for a night's sleep. And there is much to attend to."

"Do you mean to go and see the Dyers? And the babies? Oh, poor Catherine! What a dreadful thing to happen. It makes me so afraid, Lizzie. She must have suffered horribly."

"I heard her health was never strong."

"Indeed, it is true. When we went to visit them in Dorking, she scarcely moved from the sofa all afternoon. And she was very pale. She gave way to John in everything. She had not the strength to resist him."

"Have you seen the babes?"

"I may not, Lizzie. It will be too affecting, the doctor says. He has forbidden it for now. But you will bring me all the news."

* * *

The next morning Bridget was up before her, full of talk again, and it was afternoon before she stepped out of the door at last.

"You will have a pleasant drive. Reverend Dyer is curate of St James' Church at Paddington; Hyde Park is close by and there are meadows beyond it. How I wish I could come with you! How I should love to walk there!"

An hour later Elizabeth got out of the carriage in Sussex Gardens, in front of the curate's house, a tall thin house squeezed in between two others like it. As soon as the housemaid opened the door to her, she heard the familiar sounds of family life. Two children were chasing each other down the stairs, female voices were raised in disagreement over a piece of stitching, someone was practising on a spinet, and a man's voice, deep and with a Welsh accent, spoke continuously through it all. The maid disappeared, the man's voice paused, and a few moments later the Reverend Dyer appeared. He was a tall, spare man with ascetic cheekbones, whose surplice hung loosely on him. All his energy seemed to be devoted to his hair, black and luxuriant, curling in long waves around his face and shoulders. He moved swiftly towards her and grasped her hands.

"It must be—you are so like Mr Cresswell—it is Mrs Addison, is it not?"

"It is. I am very pleased to make your acquaintance."

"I will call Mrs Dyer at once."

Mrs Dyer appeared from the kitchen, wiping her hands, and with an apron still about her. She was much smaller than her husband, with a tired face and dark circles beneath her eyes. She is exhausted, thought Elizabeth, with a sudden spring of pity.

She took Elizabeth up the narrow stairs to an attic room in the roof, where a small dirty window let in a dim light. The wet-nurse was stooped over a bed, and Elizabeth saw the two small forms below her. An uncomfortable apprehension gripped her, remembering the sickly pallor of her mother's dying infants. She could hardly bear to look.

The two baby girls lay close together, sleeping. The first impression Elizabeth received was of the utmost tranquillity. Their tiny faces were smooth and rosy, their lips pink as tiny rosebuds, with a fuzz of fair hair on their heads. A little dribble of milk ran from a mouth, and on the side where they lay together, their little arms and fists were intertwined.

"How content they look!" she said.

"They are the very image of Catherine. They have her sweet nature too." Mrs Dyer's voice broke, and tears started to run down her face.

"I am very sorry for your loss." Elizabeth took Mrs Dyer's hand in her own. As they stood looking down at the sleeping infants, she felt tears springing to her own eyes. Why was she weeping? She had never known Catherine. Did she weep for the babies, poor motherless girls that they were? Or did she weep for herself, for her empty womb? She pulled a handkerchief from her fichu and dried her eyes. She looked up at the wet-nurse.

"They look very well," she said.

"Oh yes, ma'am, they are fine strong babes, both of them. They were small at first, but you would hardly know that now."

Elizabeth bent down and picked up one of them. How warm and sweet she felt in her arms! She bent down and kissed the smooth soft forehead.

"Which one is this?"

"Frances. The other one is Catherine, after her mother."

Frances stirred in her arms. Her eyelids flickered open, and she looked up at Elizabeth in a sudden glimpse of blue before sighing back to sleep.

"She is beautiful. Beautiful."

At that moment the door swung open and John Cresswell lurched through it. He stood there, swaying slightly.

"You are holding my daughter."

"I am."

"Why did you not come and see me? I only just heard you were here!"

He came closer, so that she could smell the brandy on his breath. She laid Frances back on the bed.

"Come, John. Let us go downstairs."

He went down the stairs before her. He lost his footing on the bottom step, lurched forward and fell suddenly, face down on the floor. One of the younger children ran out from the parlour, saw what had happened and returned inside. Elizabeth kneeled down beside him.

"Are you hurt?"

He gave a groan and turned his head away.

"Come, John, you must get up."

There was no response. She shook his shoulder.

"Up, John!"

"You will not move him," said Mrs Dyer, coming down the stairs. "He has been drinking since morning."

Elizabeth scrambled upright. Mrs Dyer looked down at John Cresswell and a great sigh escaped her. Her face was still streaked with tears. She held tightly to the banister as if she might otherwise collapse altogether.

"I am at my wits' end, Mrs Addison. He cannot stay here. Somewhere else must be found."

"I understand, Mrs Dyer. I will make arrangements as quickly as I am able." She paused. "May I go into the kitchen?"

Mrs Dyer shrugged. Elizabeth followed the smell of boiling mutton along the corridor to the kitchen, went in and took up a pitcher. Returning, she dashed the contents onto John's head, soaking his head and shoulders. He sat up suddenly with a roar.

"Who did that?"

"Get up, John. You must get up."

He staggered to his feet. As soon as he was upright, she tucked her arm into his.

"We will take a walk. You can direct me to the park."

*   *   *

They got only as far as St John's Church, but since it had pleasant gardens all about where they might sit, she gave up her desire to see Hyde Park. John slumped down onto a bench and took his head in his hands.

"You do not realize, Lizzie. You have no notion how frightful it has been. To see my poor Catherine suffer so—to hear her crying out in anguish—and the doctor doing nothing, nothing at all for her! And now she is gone! I cannot bear it, Lizzie!"

"I feel for you with all my heart, John. It is a most dreadful loss, both for you and for the Dyers."

"The Dyers? They do not feel it as I do. They have other daughters and to spare. But I had only Catherine."

"But think, John. You had known her only for a year or two, and they have known her all her life. She was their eldest daughter. I do believe they are as broken-hearted as yourself."

"It may be so." He turned away petulantly. "But she was all to me. I cannot live without her. Oh, it is insupportable, Lizzie!"

He burst into sobs, indifferent to the other people strolling through the gardens. Elizabeth put her arm around him and let him lay his head on her shoulder. What was to be done, she asked herself. What would her husband do? And she thought suddenly of a dinner they had had in their home in Whitby a few nights before she left. John's nephew Frank Easterby had joined them, newly made a midshipman on the *Romney*, full of high spirits and tales of his new life in the navy. Frank Easterby was three years younger than her brother John, but he had already served six years at sea.

He was become a man long ago. And here was John Cresswell, weeping on her shoulder like a child. She took her arm away and sat to face him.

"You must show fortitude. For her sake. For your daughters' sake. She has left something of herself behind for you. They are the bonniest babes I ever saw, John."

"Are they so?" he said, raising his head.

"They are. I see in them how beautiful their mother must have been."

He wept anew, but she felt her words had struck him.

"It must be all for them now, John. You are both mother and father to them. They will repay your love in every way."

"But how am I to care for them? How am I to live?"

"Do you mean to return to your house in Dorking?"

"I cannot bear to be there. Everything in it reminds me of her—the chair she sat on to do her stitching, the bed where I lay beside her. Even her clothes are there! It is as if she were still alive!"

"Did you have a servant there? Did you give notice?"

"No. I gave it no thought."

She would speak to Bridget, Elizabeth decided. Someone would have to go down there. Probably herself.

"Well. We will see what needs to be done. But you cannot stay at the Dyers', John. They have had to make space for the babies and the wet-nurse, and the house is so small. Why not come back north with me, and then home to Cresswell?"

"And listen to my father's reproaches all day? I couldn't abide it. I live in London now, Lizzie."

"Do you mean to find some occupation here? Perhaps Harry Parker might help you to a post."

He stared at her.

"Occupation? I am a gentleman. When Father dies, I shall have three thousand a year. Why should I have an occupation?"

"It would be of great utility to distract you from your grieving."

"Yes. Well, I plan to attend a race meeting on Saturday with some acquaintance of mine. I believe that will serve the purpose. I shall wear mourning bands of course. No one will expect me to be light-hearted."

Elizabeth stood up abruptly.

"Let us walk a little further. Then I must return to the Parkers."

*   *   *

She sat up late that night with Bridget and Harry. A lodging must be found, they agreed. Somewhere in Marylebone, so it would be easy for John to visit the Dyers or for the twins to be brought to see him.

"Better a lodging. He is no use at keeping house for himself, Catherine attended to all that for him. He must have some pleasant woman who will take care of him," said Bridget.

"And a manservant," said Harry. "A man who can keep him right. I will ask around and see what can be managed."

They were right, of course. But the expense of it all, thought Elizabeth. He was to be lodged in his own apartment, and money would have to be found for the Dyers to help with the care of the twins. She imagined her father bent over his ledgers, struggling to find a little extra rent, increasing a mortgage. By the time the estate came to John Cresswell, he might find himself disappointed in his inheritance.

"Will you go to Dorking to see to the cottage, Lizzie? I should so dearly love to come with you! Do you not think the country air would do me good, Harry?"

"My dearest love, it is fully twenty miles! It is a day's journey. I cannot imagine what the doctor would have to say about that." He turned to Elizabeth.

"Indeed, Elizabeth, it will be a long journey for yourself. And you have had so much travelling already."

"I will see if one of Catherine's sisters will come with me. There will be Catherine's clothes—her possessions—whatever she had. They should go to the Dyers."

"I am sorry that the burden of this has fallen upon you. Could not John see to it himself?"

"Oh," said Bridget. "You don't understand, Harry. Our brother John is perfectly helpless."

Elizabeth could not disagree. She thought of the sleeping infants on the bed, of the soft warmth of Frances in her arms and the sudden blue of her open eyes gazing so directly at her. What will become of them, she thought.

PART FOUR

1773–4

The North-West Passage

Extracts from *A Voyage Towards the North Pole: undertaken by His Majesty's Command 1773: Constantine John Phipps Mulgrave*

Journal

> April 19th, 1773 *I received my commiſion for the* Racehorse, *with an order to get her fitted with the greateſt diſpatch for a voyage of diſcovery towards the North Pole and to proceed to the Nore for further orders.*

Three months later:

> June 9th. *About noon Flamborough Head bore NW b N diſtant about ſix miles; we were by obſervation in latitude 54 degrees 4' 54", longitude 0 degrees 27' 15". In the afternoon we were off Scarborough. Almoſt calm in the evening.*
>
> June 10th. *Anchored in the morning for the tide in Robin Hood's Bay, with little wind at NW; worked up to Whitby Road next tide, and anchored there at four in the afternoon, at fifteen fathom, with very little wind.*
>
> June 11th. *Calm in the morning; completed our water, live stock and vegetables. At nine in the morning longitude obſerved by the watch 1 degree 55' 30" W; Whitby Abbey bore S ¼ W. Weighed with the wind at SE and ſteered NE b N to get ſo far into the mid-channel as to make the wind fair Eaſterly or Weſterly, without being too near either ſhore, before we were clear of Shetland and the coaſt of Norway.*

CHAPTER 28

St Hilda's Terrace, Whitby

June 1773

They were like ghosts in the house, John Addison thought of them so often. He would half-imagine a glimpse of fair hair in sunlight, a snatch of a song in the corridor or a curtain pushed aside in an empty bedroom. Their traces vanished when he and Elizabeth had company, and when the Mulgrave boys were around the house the noise of their boisterous games left them no space. But when the house was empty and he was alone, he would let his mind slide away into fantasy. Would there be two of them, or three? After six years of marriage, one might expect two children at least, even allowing for a death or a miscarriage. Bridget and Harry Parker, for instance; they had two now, William and Louise. After his old friend Francis Easterby married again a few years ago, he soon found himself with three more children to fill his empty rooms at Skinningrove.

What would he have called them? John and William? Or were there too many Johns in the family already? But no, he felt certain, the eldest should be John, the next John Addison. Was not one of them going to be a girl? Jane, he thought. For his sister. Unless Elizabeth wanted Grace, for her mother.

Did Elizabeth have the same imaginings? He couldn't ask her. They didn't speak of it. The slow disappointment of childlessness dragged at the edges of their life day in, day out. Of course, he could not reproach her. She had been to see physicians in London, had followed all their advice, taken their medicine. For sure, she felt it as keenly as did he. But although he knew the injustice of it, somewhere in his heart he was angry with her. He had given her everything she could have asked of him, everything. The one thing he asked of her she would not, could not, give him. When they slept together a shadow had fallen between them. The old carefree pleasure had gone. Their lovemaking had become a task, a fruitless task that had nevertheless to be repeated again and again, in the fading hope that one day the miracle would happen, and she would conceive. The ghosts waited behind the bed-hangings, in the dark corners where the candlelight could not reveal them, whispering, rustling, waiting to be born.

Sometimes he asked himself whether he could be to blame. Did people gossip behind his back? He mistrusted Lepell. She was all amiability to his face, of course, especially when he relieved her of her sons.

"You are so good with them! The first question they have for me in the morning is, shall we see Mr Addison today? If only their father was half as interesting to them! But I fear Charles cannot be prised away from his papers."

"As your ladyship knows, I am happy to oblige them. I am always eager to escape my office."

If taking the boys out for a day's sailing helped to bind him close to the Mulgraves, it was worthwhile in every way. Mulgrave's interest in the company was providing the investment that was seeing it outstrip all its competitors. Besides, he liked the boys. They were plucky and bold and as unlike their bookish father as it was possible to be. But he was still wary of Lepell and her loose tongue.

She was coming this very day, he reminded himself, to watch *Racehorse* and *Carcass* come in. Whitby was the expedition's final call for provisioning before Lord Constantine's voyage to the Pole, and John Addison had the contract. If Constantine's quest for the North-West Passage were successful, he would be famous and a hero. The Mulgrave boys could talk of little else. In John's opinion, if such a passage were to be found, the whaling captains would have known of it long ago. But the expedition was undertaken at Royal command, so he kept his views to himself. He would take the boys out to see the ship, if he had time between the tenders. And he would meet them in the harbour, he decided. So that he wouldn't be troubled by any exchanges with Lady Mulgrave.

✷   ✷   ✷

Elizabeth was in the kitchen with Cook, looking over the vegetables that had come up from the market that morning, when Susan came all in a rush to find her.

"Lady Mulgrave is at the door, ma'am. And the two boys with her."

"The ships must be expected. I will come directly."

Elizabeth felt a pulse of excitement as she pulled off her apron and hurried to the hall. Lepell was already there.

"I could not persuade the boys to wait in the carriage! I fear we have broken into your house without ceremony."

"It is no matter, I am delighted to see you! Are the ships come?"

"Constantine sent word from Scarborough that we might expect to see them this afternoon."

"We are going up to the Abbey to watch them come in, Mrs Addison," said Edmund. "And then Augustus and I will take the yawl out to see Constantine and the *Racehorse*."

"If Mr Addison thinks you are able," Lepell corrected him.

"It is quite calm," said Augustus. "I was looking out all the way from Sandsend."

"Let me fetch my bonnet," said Elizabeth. "I will come up to the Abbey with you. Mr Addison has to attend to the provisioning, but you can find him in the harbour later."

When they had climbed up the endless steps to the top of the East Cliff and looked out over the great expanse of the ocean beyond, it was clear that Augustus was correct. There was hardly a ruffle of white on the deep blue of the sea nor a cloud in the sky above. It was a glorious June afternoon. Edmund and Augustus ran ahead, eager for the first glimpse of the ships and, suddenly, there they were on the horizon, a glimpse of white sails catching the sunlight. The boys leaped in the air and shouted huzzahs. Elizabeth and Lepell let them run. It would be another hour or more before the ships were alongside and the women had leisure to find a bench and watch as they drew closer.

"Does Mr Banks sail with him this time?" asked Elizabeth.

"No. The North Pole was too arduous a prospect for him, though he has given Constantine full instruction as to what he must observe. Joseph is become quite famous, you know, after his South Sea voyages. Now he will only embark on voyages of his own choosing."

"Perhaps there is little for him to discover in such a frozen wilderness."

"Indeed, but if Constantine should discover the Passage to the Pacific, who knows what marvels might await him? I say it is poor-spirited in Joseph." Lepell turned to look at Elizabeth and spoke more seriously.

"It is a dangerous voyage, you know. Constantine will not tell me all of it, but I hear tales of the perils that the Greenland whalers encounter. Great icebergs can bear down upon a ship with their mass hidden beneath the surface, so the ship is struck unaware. Or a sudden frost and freezing can cause ice to form around the ship till it is stuck fast. There are many dangers. Truly, I will not sleep easy in my bed till I see his sails returning."

"John says Lord Constantine will take a Greenlander for a pilot. A man familiar with the waters."

"Yes, so he tells me. But Constantine means to push further north than the Greenlanders ever go."

"Look," said Elizabeth, to distract her. "The ships are drawing closer."

They turned and stared out to sea. Elizabeth had lived in Whitby for six years now, but still the sight of a pair of ships in full sail beating down the coast quickened her pulse. It was a perfect scene—the calm weather, the June sunshine, the beautiful symmetry of the sails. It was impossible to imagine the ships running before an Arctic gale or locked in pale sheets of ice.

The boys came running back.

"She will be coming into anchor very soon!" cried out Augustus.

"You can go down to the harbour by yourselves. Mr Addison is waiting for you."

Lepell laughed as they ran helter-skelter down the steps.

"And now your husband is turning all my boys into sailors! I shall never have a moment's rest for fearing storms and shipwrecks!"

*   *   *

Since John had the contract for the provisioning of Lord Constantine's ships, he was occupied with sending tenders out to the *Racehorse* and the boys were soon out of patience with him. He would let them go alone, he decided.

"Can we go now, Mr Addison? They've been at anchor above an hour."

"Don't worry. There's plenty of time. It'll be light till ten tonight."

"Are you coming with us?"

"No. You've got a south-westerly to take you out. It's calm beyond the cliffs. You can show your brother what fine sailors you've become."

Edmund was thirteen now. He could be trusted to keep them right. The two boys looked up at him from the ship, excited and nervous. He would give them no time to think about it. He started to shout instructions at them to ready the boat while he untied the mooring rope. It took the current and moved gently down the Esk towards the sea.

"Remember! Don't drop sail till you are clear of the harbour. Keep her well south of the Rock. And mind to come up squarely alongside the *Racehorse*."

And they were gone. John Addison smiled inwardly. It was a part of his shipboard life that he missed, having youngsters around. Ships always had young boys on board learning the ropes, whether merchant or navy. They brought a freshness and eagerness to please, just as the Mulgrave boys did. But what names! Augustus—Edmund—Constantine. How could you burden a boy with such a name? Of course the nobility loved them, the stranger the better it seemed. Ordinary people made do with ordinary names.

*   *   *

When it was time for the last tender of the day to go out with its cargo of bleating sheep, John Addison looked up at the sky. It was close to seven o'clock; the sun was still strong, but the wind had gone round easterly. With the tide on the turn, the currents would be strong across the harbour entrance and oars might be needed. He should fetch the boys back himself, he decided. He climbed down to join the sheep.

As they came alongside the *Racehorse*, he saw at once that additional strengthening had been carried out to her external timbers—against the ice, he supposed. It gave the ship a portly appearance, as if an ample coat had been tucked around her. He swung himself up the ladder, in a more ungainly manner than he would have liked on account of the old injury, and found his footing on the deck. He looked up at the masts to see how neatly she was reefed and found himself satisfied.

"Do you judge it all in order, Mr Addison?" said a voice beside him. He turned to find Lord Constantine beside him, with Edmund and Augustus close behind.

"It is very neatly done. My compliments to the captain."

Constantine laughed.

"I am fortunate in my crew. And the new members who joined us today!" he said, turning to his brothers. "They did a fine job of bringing out the yawl this afternoon and brought her alongside without a scratch." He lowered his voice slightly. "But I am pleased to see you here. Do you mean to go back with them?"

John Addison nodded.

"Good. The wind has gone about, as you'll have noticed. It might be a more arduous journey home." He paused. "Do you care to take a turn around the ship before you go?"

As they strolled round the deck together discussing every detail of the fitting out, John found himself at ease. The man was not a dilettante like Banks. He knew his ship, and time and again John found himself approving his judgement. Lord Constantine had changed into Captain Phipps and was the better for it.

"Since it is a scientific expedition, we are carrying all manner of instruments," said Constantine. "Would you care to come into my cabin and look them over?" He turned to the boys trailing behind them.

"Edmund—Augustus—we will not be much longer. You can stay up on deck if you prefer."

There was a long desk in the cabin covered with papers and logbooks. Constantine gestured towards them.

"In the interests of science, I must keep several additional logs, meteorological, astronomical and all the rest, as well as the ship's journal. We will be trying out a new timepiece for measuring longitude. Have you heard of Mr Harrison's chronometer?"

John shook his head.

"The Royal Society has offered a prize of £20,000 for a system that will accurately measure longitude and put an end to the navigational hazards that cause such loss of shipping. Mr Harrison is a clockmaker who has produced several different timepieces that are very remarkable in the accuracy of measurement they can produce."

He paused.

"But we also have an astronomer on board, Mr Israel Lyons. There are still many in the Royal Society who doubt Mr Harrison and would prefer to navigate by the celestial bodies."

"It was the only way when I was a mariner."

"Yes indeed, and ship masters like yourself have more practical knowledge than many astronomers. But hush—we must not allow Israel to hear us."

He bent down and unlocked a glass case that sat on the desk.

"Here are the timepieces. We have one made by Mr Kendal after Mr Harrison's principles, because Mr Harrison is unable to produce them himself in any quantity. And this one is by Mr Arnold, suspended between gimbals."

John Addison stared at the two watches. Mr Kendal's looked hardly different to an overgrown pocket watch, perhaps five or six inches in diameter and two inches deep, held between two cushions. The beautiful craftsmanship of it at once interested him.

"As I understand it," Constantine said, lifting it out for John to inspect, "the balance is unconnected with the wheel-work, except at the time it receives the impulse to make it continue its motion, which is only while it vibrates 10 degrees out of 380 degrees, which is the whole vibration; and during this small interval it has little or no friction but what is on the pivots, which work in ruby holes on diamonds. It has but one pallet, which is a plane surface formed out of a ruby and has no oil on it. It cannot rust."

John Addison stared at the watch, trying to understand.

"Watches of this construction keep the same rate of going in every position and are not affected by the different forces of the spring; the compensation for heat and cold is absolutely adjustable. They suffer very little or no change from the vicissitudes of the weather."

A timepiece crafted with rubies and diamonds that might unlock the secret of longitude. John marvelled at it.

"I would never have thought that such a thing might be possible. I wish that Mr Moorsom, my partner, might have seen it too. He has a greater knowledge than I in navigational matters."

"I believe they will soon be more generally known of. But we have yet to discover if it is wholly accurate. I will be taking measurements all through the voyage. I hope Mr Harrison may be found worthy of his prize, for he devoted half his life to it."

He closed the lid and locked the box again.

"And this . . . an ingenious device for distilling fresh water from brine, which may be very useful to us if it is found serviceable . . . and here . . . "

He produced one marvel after another for John's interest, till the boys came running back into the cabin.

"Oh—Edmund! Augustus! It is time you were gone. I have been showing Mr Addison my instruments, and it put everything from my mind."

He came with them to the side of the ship to see them off, embracing each of his brothers in turn.

"There are still some provisions left to come on board tomorrow, are there not, Mr Addison?"

"Yes. We'll fetch them out on the early tide."

"Good. We'll weigh anchor around nine if the wind allows. Keep a watch out for us from the castle, boys. I'll run an ensign up the mast for you."

Once in the yawl John Addison took the helm, sang out instructions to the boys and sent the little craft skimming home for harbour. How pleasant it was to have occasion to be out on the water, and on such a summer night! In spite of himself he felt a new involvement with the *Racehorse* and her polar exploration. And with her captain. The Greenland waters were no easy voyage. The whaling profits were hard won; there were many tales of ships crushed in ice or men frozen to death. Constantine could not be ignorant of the dangers. He was a brave man. God speed to them, he thought.

CHAPTER 29

Cresswell, Northumberland

July 1773

William sat at his desk in the Tower, staring out of the window. It was raining steadily from an iron-grey sky that reflected the utter dereliction of his spirits. The sound of it brought about a kind of lethargy from which he had no wish to rouse himself. He had no fire in the room; the dank cold sank into him and deadened any feeling in his body. Harry Parker coughed politely.

"Well, Father . . . " he said.

He would have to speak, William knew. Would have to make one last effort. Grace had been so long a-dying that it had used up the last dregs of his vitality. At least his son John had come up, those last weeks. Had been with her. Not with himself, of course. John avoided any conversation with him. As soon as the funeral was over, he was gone to his race meeting in York, with nothing discussed, nothing settled. William had not the strength left to care.

But now, his sons-in-law sat before him, and he must open his mind to them. He turned to look at them, Harry Parker and John Addison, so urbane in their frilled linen shirts and silk waistcoats that they seemed quite out of place in the ancient stone room. He found they were both looking at him intently. He hardly knew whether to be encouraged or dismayed.

"It is a sad time," said John Addison. "Perhaps you would sooner wait a while."

"No," he said. "I cannot be asking Harry to spend his time to-ing and fro-ing from London. Let us do it now. Have patience with me."

He leaned over the desk, shuffling among his papers, and finally pulled out a document.

"My will," he said, and then lost concentration as an image of Grace lying on the bed came into his mind, of his hand in hers, and he was overwhelmed. Slow tears rolled down his cheeks.

"My will," he said again, trying to rally himself. John Addison got up and went to the closet for the brandy. He poured three glasses. Putting one into William's hand he stood close beside him, so William could feel the warmth of his son-in-law's presence beside him. It was steadying. He took a gulp of the liquor and felt it burning down his throat. It stirred something in him, and at last he could remember what it was he had to say.

"The estate," he said, 'is entailed. It will go to my son John Cresswell. But the Red House and my house in Morpeth are my own possession. If I leave them to John, he will only sell them to pay his racing debts. So I mean to leave them in trust to you, Harry Parker and John Addison, if you will do me this service."

There was a silence as stony as the walls as John and Harry exchanged glances. John Addison spoke.

"What do you wish for them?"

"Sell them. Sell them both for the best price you can get." He took another gulp of the brandy and a flush spread over his cheeks. "In the first place pay the money for which the estate stands chargeable. I incurred a very sizeable loan for the building of the new Hall and I have not had the means to repay it. But the properties will cover it. Then John will inherit the estate free of debt. Whatever happens after that, I will have done my duty."

"And the second place?" said Harry.

"The second place. Yes. The girls. Grace and Dorothy will never marry, and I cannot rely on my son John to look after them. They must have an annuity out of the sale; I have set it at £250 apiece. And any overplus to be divided between them all, share and share alike."

"Very well." It would not be enough, John Addison thought. William did not realize how prices had risen. But that could be attended to. "And the other girls?"

"The rector at Bothal has spoken for Alice. She will be wed soon. And Juliana, why should she not be wed also? She is a sweet girl. She and Grace and Dorothy may have all my household goods, the plate and furniture and so forth. As you know I mean to close up this house. John has no interest in living here and I have no heart for it without Grace. The expense of it is too great in any case. I will rent it out and move to Morpeth with the girls."

There. It was done. He looked up at John Addison beside him, and Harry Parker on his chair. They were both nodding gravely.

"You will do it?"

Another glance between them. Then John Addison spoke for both.

"Of course. We are happy to be of service to you."

What excellent men they are, William thought, feeling a surge of gratitude.

"You are very good. I am very much obliged to you. Although my own son has not answered to my expectations, I count myself more than fortunate in my sons-in-law. I cannot express how highly I esteem you . . . "

To his dismay he found himself becoming maudlin, his voice breaking and yet more tears springing from his eyes. He shook his head and looked away. But John Addison dropped onto one knee beside him and, taking hold of his hand, clasped it tightly.

"I am proud to be part of your family. You have done so much, all your life, for the estate. I mean to do everything in my power to preserve it."

His vehemence surprised William. He turned towards him, and pressed his other hand on top of John's, as if they were swearing an oath together. Harry got up and stood with his hand on William's shoulder.

"I, too, Mr Cresswell. Between us, John Addison and I will see it all to rights."

* * *

Afterwards John Addison thought of another oath he had sworn, all those years ago, at Skinningrove, when he and Francis Easterby and his young nephews, John and Frank, had drunk a toast together to his dead sister Jane. He had bound himself to look after the boys, his nephews, in her memory. How was it that he found himself tied by oath to these two families, the Easterbys and the Cresswells? What did it mean? The emotion he had felt when William asked him to be his trustee took him by surprise. He had the strongest sense he could not endure to see this family to which he now belonged fall into ruin. He felt protective towards the sisters as if he were somehow responsible for them. This was the family he wanted for himself. Not the family he had come from. Never. He hated the meanness and the hunger he had known, the bitter violence of his feckless father, his mother too sick to protect him. He would not recognize his own family. He would build it new and see his son become a gentleman, like his partner, Richard Moorsom, whose boy was sent off to be educated like a gentleman at a school in York. But if a son was to be denied to him, what then? Must he realize his dreams through the families of others?

* * *

Three months later John Addison and Harry Parker were together again in a room distant in every way from the cold tower office. The panelled apartment in the Inns of Court was warmed with a bright fire in the grate, and the window looked out over the quadrangle where men in robes and wigs scurried to and fro. The lawyer they had come to see was a corpulent man whose robes seemed to take up most of the width of his desk. He had a clean-shaven, rosy-cheeked face beneath a flowing wig and an expression of great solemnity. He had documents spread out before him and was waiting for the latest arrival into the room to settle himself. John Cresswell had kept them waiting for a half an hour but did not trouble himself with apologies on arrival. Instead, he stood in the doorway and stared for several moments at his two brothers-in-law.

"Good day, gentlemen," he said at last. "I am somewhat surprised to find you here. I believe my father's will concerns me alone."

Although he was three and twenty now and dressed like a man about town in a fashionably cut coat and powdered wig, his pink-and-white colouring gave him still a boyish look. The annoyance of finding Harry Parker and John Addison in attendance brought a high spot of colour to his cheeks. He chewed at his bottom lip discontentedly, unwilling to come in.

"Mr Cresswell, let me welcome you to the offices of Driscoll and Ward," said the lawyer. "Please be seated. Mr Addison and Sir Harry Parker are here at my invitation as they are nominated in the will. Perhaps your father did not make you aware of this."

"No," said John Cresswell. "He did not." He sat down abruptly, removed his hat and glowered suspiciously at his brothers-in-law. "Well, let us get on with it then."

The lawyer made a stately movement in his chair and drew himself up, as if to assert that he would not allow his dignity to be compromised by such impatient instruction. With due ceremony he took hold of the document containing William's will.

"Gentlemen," he intoned. "I have before me the last will and testament of William Cresswell of Cresswell in Northumberland, and our task today is to see this will proved as a legal document binding in all its particulars on those mentioned therein."

He paused.

"Since there is an entail upon the Cresswell estate which ensures that the hereditary possessions appertaining to the estate may not be broken up or sold in any particular and must by law be inherited in whole and total by the eldest son of the legatee, there is no requirement for this to be further mentioned herein. This will therefore appertains solely to those properties and possessions owned by William Cresswell on his own account which he was at liberty to dispose of according to his own desires."

John Cresswell pulled himself forward in his chair.

"There is no need to differentiate between the two," he said. "All my father's possessions must come to me."

The lawyer did not answer at once, allowing his face to register his displeasure at the interruption. He allowed the silence to deepen for a couple of minutes before he inclined himself slightly in John's direction.

"Regrettably, Mr Cresswell, such is not the case. I must ask you to keep any further questions until I have completed the reading of the will, according to legal precedent and requirement."

With suitable ceremony he unrolled the parchment and began to read, adopting a slow droning tone that made the formal language of the will even harder to understand:

> *This is the last will and testament of me, William Creſswell of Creſswell in the County of Northumberland.*
>
> *First my will is that money charged upon the Creſswell Estate and the interest thereof shall continue and be charged and chargeable upon the said estate.*
>
> *Secondly I give and devise to my sons-in-law Harry Parker Esquire and John Addison Esquire and to the survivors of them and to the heirs and assigns of such survivors all those my messuages, land, tenements and hereditaments and all and singular other the premisses with their and every of their appurtenances commonly called Woodhorn Demesne or Red House, situate lying and being in the parish of Woodhorn and County of Northumberland. And also that messuage, burgage house or tenement garden which I purchased of Nicholas Cooper deceased situate, standing and being in the town of Morpeth in the said county of Northumberland.*
>
> *To have and to hold the said messuages burgages lands tenements hereditaments and all and singular other the premises abovementioned with their and every of their appurtenances and every part and parcel thereof unto the said Harry Parker and John Addison and to the survivors of them and to the heirs and assigns of such survivors in trust to sell the said estates and premises and every part and parcel thereof with all convenient speed after my decease for the best and highest price that can be got for the same and in the first place to pay the money for which my said estate stands*

> *chargeable and then also to pay out of the money for which my said estate shall be sold the sum of two hundred and fifty pounds of useful money of Great Britain with interest for the same to my daughter Dorothy Cresswell her executors or assigns and the further sum of two hundred and fifty pounds of lawful money with interest for the same to my daughter Grace Cresswell her executors administrators or assignees according to the bonds which I have given them for the payment of the said several sums of money and interest.*
>
> *And my will and mind is and I hereby direct that the receipt or receipts of my said trustees and executors and the survivors of them their heirs executors administrators to be made and given to such person or persons as shall become Purchaser or Purchasers of my said estates at Redhouse and Morpeth of the purchase money shall be a good and sufficient discharge both in law and equity to such Purchaser or Purchasers for the same notwithstanding a misapplication or non application thereof...*

It took at least three paragraphs before the import of the endless sentences became clear to John Cresswell. Then he could contain himself no longer.

"Say it in plain language, man! The Red House and Nicholas Cooper's house are going to be sold over my head! And money paid out to my sisters whether I will or no."

Before the lawyer could reprove him, Harry Parker leaned forward placatorily.

"But it is in your interests, John. Your father did this in order to clear the debts on the estate, so that you might inherit it unencumbered. He has done you a great service."

"I could have done the same thing for myself had I so desired! You have been scheming with him behind my back to thwart my wishes! I take it very ill that you have used me so. We will see what my lawyer has to say to it. I will not endure another word of it." He picked up his hat and stood up.

Despite his injury, John Addison moved remarkably swiftly. He strode to the other side of the room and positioned himself between the door and John Cresswell, arms and legs akimbo, looking suddenly threatening.

"We are not finished, John. The will has not been read in full," he said. "If you had taken the trouble to engage your father's confidence, you might have found yourself less surprised today."

John Cresswell was halted. He stood a little shocked, twisting his hat in his hands. As he hesitated, the lawyer intervened.

"Thank you, Mr Addison. I will continue reading."

The slow drone resumed, through the funeral expenses and the household goods, the furniture, plate and linen, the division of the overplus profits and all possible detail a legal mind could conceive till at last it was done.

"Thank you, gentlemen. That concludes the reading of the will. Now, if . . . "

"Are you satisfied now, Addison?" said John, making to push past him to the door.

John Addison took him by the shoulder and held him very firmly.

"Your signature is required to witness the will."

"I do not wish to witness it."

"I believe you do. I believe, in your heart, you are a dutiful son to a father who has supported you unfailingly throughout your life."

John Cresswell turned bright red, trying to free himself from John Addison's grip. Harry Parker jumped to his feet and came over. He took John's hand.

"John, my dear fellow, we all mean the best for you. You must believe that. It is the simplest thing in the world, just to do your duty here, as we all must. John and I have not the slightest interest in the outcome beyond your wellbeing. I assure you that nothing but good will come of it."

John Addison slackened his grip on John Cresswell's shoulder, and John shrugged him off petulantly, ignoring him and turning instead to Harry in an attempt to retrieve his dignity.

"Yes, well . . . I am happy to oblige YOU, Harry . . . " giving an angry look to John Addison and pulling his coat up ostentatiously. The lawyer had quill and ink ready.

"Just there, Mr Cresswell, if you would be so kind."

John leaned over and scrawled some indecipherable approximation of a signature. When he turned round John Addison was back in his seat, smiling amiably as if nothing had occurred.

CHAPTER 30

St Hilda's Terrace, Whitby

October 1773

It was already evening on the day of John Addison's return to Whitby. Elizabeth was upstairs. She sat in a dressing gown in the chair by the windowsill, reading a novel in the last light of the day. She looked up, startled, when he came into the room.

"Why, John!" she said. "I did not expect you."

He came over and kissed her head.

"Shall I put you up some dinner?"

"I'm not hungry."

"Will you sit? We can go downstairs if you wish."

"I've had my fill of sitting these last few days. I'm content to stand."

He stood close to the window, looking out across the valley. The harbour was hidden from view from this height; there was only the headland and the skeleton of the old Abbey.

"Well," he said. "We read the will."

"Yes?"

"It was exactly as your father told us, in every detail. We had a hard job to get through it for your brother John's indignation. He had no notion of your father's intentions."

"Was he angry?"

"Yes! He could not contain himself. He came close to striking me but thought better of it. Peaceable Harry Parker persuaded him to put his signature to it. It is done."

"So the Red House is to be sold."

"Yes."

John took a turn around the room, stretching his lame leg.

"I have been thinking, Lizzie. I have had plenty of leisure to do so with so much travelling."

He paused, taking a moment to watch the last sunlight fading from the headland.

"I'm going to annoy your brother a little more. I mean to buy the Red House myself."

In her astonishment Elizabeth let the novel slip from her hand, and it fell to the floor. She took no heed, staring up at John Addison.

"Why not?" he said, in response to her stare. "Your brother means to rent out the Hall. He'll never go near the place. There should be somewhere for the family on the estate. Somewhere for your sisters to live."

He looked at her.

"Perhaps you might like to go there too."

"To go there? What—to live there, do you mean?"

"No—what are you thinking? To visit."

"I thought you might mean to be rid of me. Since you are disappointed in me."

He stood quite still, shocked by her words. After a long silence he spoke again.

"No, Lizzie. I did not mean that."

She dropped her gaze to the floor. He felt as if a piece of ordnance had suddenly exploded in front of him. What was he to say?

"I am disappointed. I cannot conceal that from you."

She was silent. He tried again.

"You are a good wife to me in every way, except . . . "

"Except in the only way that matters," she finished for him.

Suddenly a dam within him six years in the making was breached and could no longer be contained. Without warning he threw himself away from her across the room, the air becoming heavy with curses.

"God damn you! God damn my soul! A curse on it, a thousand curses . . ."

He pulled at his heavy travelling coat as if it were suffocating him and ripped open the buttons, tearing it off and dropping it down on the floor, shouting curses all the while. He whirled around the room in his shirt and breeches, smashing his fists against the walls, the bedposts, the cupboards, striking at anything in reach. Elizabeth shrank back against the window, fearing to come within reach of his fists. He stopped for a moment, leaned over unsteadily and pulled the shoes off his feet, hurling them one after another at the door. Then he straightened himself and was suddenly still, standing in his stockinged feet, staring about him unseeingly. He staggered over to the bed and flung himself down, all at once racked with sobs.

After a long interval his passion ebbed and his body grew still. Elizabeth moved away from the window and went over to the bed and sat by him. He didn't stir. Tentatively she reached out and laid her hand on his shoulder. Neither spoke for a long time. She became aware of the room darkening, the sound of a distant bell chiming, a few gulls still calling in the harbour.

"God knows why we must suffer so," she said. "Perhaps we are needed in other ways."

John opened his eyes, too spent to respond. Her words surprised him. These days he attended service on a Sunday morning as a good citizen should. But it didn't mean he had ceded control to God. He, John Addison, controlled his own destiny. But now his wishes were denied. He was being moved in ways he did not understand. Was a different Will at work? Clearly Lizzie thought so. But then, women were accustomed to resignation.

"Perhaps," he said at last. He shifted towards her, twisting himself round till his head was lying in her lap and she was holding him.

"My neck cloth is soaked through."

"Do you want me to untie it for you?"

He nodded.

"It is too much starched," she said, struggling to loosen it.

"I know. It has been chafing me all day." When she got it off, he took it from her and blew his nose on it noisily.

"Would you take a hot toddy, if I can bring the fire up? You have had nothing since you got home."

"Yes."

She got up, went over to the washstand, lit a candle for him and for herself and went out, down the dark stairs to the kitchen to rake the ashes up and boil a kettle.

When she got back with the toddy, she found he had already taken his clothes off and was sitting in bed in his nightshirt. She gave him his drink, turned over the covers and got in beside him. He blew on it, took a long draught and turned towards her.

"You quite put me from my point," he said. "What do you think of my plan to buy the Red House?"

She paused for a moment.

"I think it a fine idea. If you have the means."

"I will need a loan. But my credit is good, and that can easily be arranged."

"We all loved that house. Better than the Hall, though you could not tell my father that. My sisters will be grateful to you. And I am too."

"Will you visit sometimes? Shall we visit sometimes?"

She nodded. They were both silent for a moment, listening to the wind outside. He stretched out his arm towards her.

"And you are wrong, Lizzie. I do not wish you gone, nor ever have."

She moved closer to him till his arm was about her, and he held her tightly to him.

In the morning she woke to find him up already. They did not speak of it again. But afterwards an understanding came about between them, like men at sea facing into foul weather who must depend on each other to see the ship home. What sailor would blame another for the storm? There was nothing for it but to weather it together.

CHAPTER 31

Woodhorn and Cresswell

May 1774

"No," said Elizabeth. "I don't believe it. It can't be true." Her sister's words suddenly distracted her from the worn springing of the sofa that was protruding so uncomfortably into her thigh. She was aware only of astounded outrage.

"See for yourself," said Catherine, throwing the newspaper over to her. And there it was, on the first page, with a box around it for greater prominence: a notice for sale of the lands known as Dene Farm, Longframlington, five hundred and fifty acres of improved pasture and arable land. Elizabeth read every detail twice over before laying down the paper, unable to believe it.

"How can he do so? It is entailed, like every other property on the estate. He cannot sell it."

"Who knows what a crafty lawyer might do?"

"Father said it would take an Act of Parliament to change the entail."

"Lizzie, I believe he will stop at nothing. Our brother John is so incensed at Father's will that he is determined to outwit him. Besides, he has done nothing these past few years but run up debts in the expectation of selling off the Red House. And the Morpeth house. Dear knows where he thought Grace and Dorothy were to live."

"But Longframlington! Father had so improved it that the income outstripped all the others. Without it the estate will yield far less. It will hardly support the family. Does John have no regard for his Cresswell heirs?"

"John means to make his fortune on the Turf. I heard from Bridget that he has three racehorses now and thinks of nothing but the next Meeting. There is even a notice here in the *Courier*."

Catherine picked up the paper again and turned the pages till she came to the reports of the race meetings in York and Newcastle.

"Here—you can see it—Mr Cresswell's *Icelander*. Fourth in the £50 Stake at York. So that will have done nothing to decrease his debts."

Elizabeth sat back on the sofa and stared at Mr Johnstone's bookshelves in a daze. What would her father have thought? For the first time she was grateful that he was dead. Grateful that he did not have to endure John's folly.

"Well," said Catherine, "you have no need to repine. You are become mistress of the Red House."

There was a sharp edge to her voice. Catherine is jealous, Elizabeth saw. Mr Johnstone was a gentleman, but his means were modest. Woodhorn Grange, where she now sat, was at least a hundred years old, and for all her sister's scrubbing and polishing it had a dank and dusty smell. The furniture in the parlour where they sat was worn and the carpet was threadbare. The small windows allowed little light into the room, giving it a gloomy feel. Now Catherine had to watch her younger sister take possession of the Red House.

"Mr Addison's intention is that it should be a home for all the family, where any of us can stay, or live even—Grace and Dorothy, Juliana and Alice till they marry." She paused. Perhaps a mention of John's Addison relations might even the balance.

"His own family mean little to him. His mother is long dead now and he does not see his father. Our family—the Cresswells—are dear to him."

Catherine inclined her head without comment before returning to the attack.

"And what of a family of your own, Lizzie?"

"No, alas. It is not for want of trying."

"I thought maybe our mother's example had put you from the idea altogether." She sighed and stared out the window at the May sunshine. "Do you remember our brother John's birth?"

Elizabeth nodded.

"I do."

"I could not forget it. I feared it so! And now I have Grace I will not have another. You cannot imagine the torments I suffered giving birth to her. I thought I would never live through it."

"Does Mr Johnstone not trouble you for an heir?"

"Mr Johnstone? No. He is happy enough with Grace."

As with everything else Catherine decreed, Elizabeth reflected. William Johnstone was a gentle, kindly man who was accustomed to defer to his wife's wishes. They had been married for twenty years. He was over forty when they married, and now he seemed an old man.

"She is a lovely girl. She must be a joy to you both."

"Yes, she is a good girl."

"I look forward to getting to know her better now we have the Red House."

There they were, back at the Red House. Elizabeth got to her feet.

"I must leave you in peace, Catherine. Please come over to the house whenever you wish."

* * *

Then, at last, the carriage was driving down the lane past the old church, and there was white blossom on the hedgerows and the verges were full of Queen Anne's lace, just as they had been twenty-four years ago when her mother and father had first brought them to see their new house, when John Cresswell was still an infant, and the family had been all together still. They had run round the house and eaten a picnic in the garden, the sun had shone, and her father had sat with his beer bottle in one hand and the other arm around her mother. It seemed like a lost vision of felicity.

When she stepped out of the carriage in front of the house it was all just as she had remembered, the red brick façade and the high view to the sea, although the gardens were unkempt and the windows needed painting. She felt a surge of joy. It was hers. Theirs. She would always, now, have a home on Cresswell land. Would always be part of it, whatever John Cresswell's profligacy led to. It was, she felt at that moment, her real place of belonging. Her marriage—her life in Whitby—seemed to slip away from her as if they had never really existed, as if they were nothing more than a strange eventful dream. She was seized suddenly with a desire to walk along the coast, back to Cresswell and to the long sands at Druridge Bay, to look out over the ocean for a glimpse of a white form moving in the surf.

She would, she would—but later, she reproved herself. She was Mrs Addison now, and there were things to do on John Addison's behalf, to inspect the house and see what needed putting to rights now that the tenants were gone, to choose what rooms they would reserve as theirs and make a list for furnishing. Her father had left all his furniture and effects to her sisters; all of it could be moved from the Morpeth residence, and should be sufficient for the rest of the house. She went up the steps, opened the front door and went inside to start work.

CHAPTER 32

St Hilda's Terrace, Whitby

May 1774

The whole journey from the Red House to Whitby could easily be accomplished in three days, Elizabeth decided as she travelled back to Yorkshire. The road from Morpeth to Newcastle was so much improved that it had caused the carriage little delay, and Peter, the coachman, kept the horses at a very steady pace that occasioned her scarcely any discomfort. Indeed, it had been delightful to travel through the countryside in all its spring greenery and freshness. Her lodgings last night at the inn in Guisborough had been very respectable and clean. The joy she still felt from her return to the Red House buoyed her spirits.

"We'll take the road through Sandsend, Peter," she said. "I will pay a visit to Lady Mulgrave on the way home."

Why not, she thought. Lepell was always eager for news, and she had been interested to know more of the Red House. With her sisters, Catherine and the others, she had to be restrained. But Lepell was so far beyond envy that she would rejoice wholeheartedly in Elizabeth's good fortune.

It was afternoon when they reached Mulgrave Castle.

"I won't stay above an hour or two," she told Peter, and went to the front door to announce herself.

The housemaid who greeted her seemed uncertain—looked around—turned back to her.

"Please wait a moment, ma'am," she said, and scuttled away down a corridor. A few minutes later the housekeeper arrived and greeted her pleasantly.

"Her ladyship is occupied, Mrs Addison, but I am sure she will like to know of your visit. Would you be so good as to wait in the drawing room?"

What is afoot, wondered Elizabeth, suddenly uneasy. Had it been a mistake to call without appointment? She sat and waited—stood up, walked to the window—took a turn around the room. Should she leave?

She was about to call a maid when Lepell came into the room. At once Elizabeth understood that something was amiss. Lepell's hair was undressed, bundled up in a mob cap; her face was unrouged, unpainted; she wore an old gown with a stain down the front. She looked suddenly old and ordinary.

"My dear Elizabeth! If it were anyone else, I should hide myself in my boudoir, but I know you will not judge me."

"I am so sorry—I am imposing on you—I will leave you at once."

"No, do not go, you may do me a very great service, if you will. Do sit down."

Lepell sank down into a chair as if exhausted. Elizabeth sat herself opposite.

"It is Charles. My dear husband. He is very sick, so he says—I cannot tell what is the matter with him. I was up half the night listening to his groans and complaints. He is the very worst of patients! Nothing I can do seems to satisfy him."

"Is it a sudden malady?"

"He has had pains for days. First his stomach grieves him, then it is his chest, or his arms, or dear knows what. He cannot sleep for the pain, and he will not let me from his sight. He thinks he is dying."

"What do the doctors say?"

"That's the thing, Elizabeth. If you would carry a message down to Whitby to the doctor, it would be a very great help to me. Charles insists that he must see a different man; he is not content with Doctor Ramsbottom. It must be another, and I have scarce an idea of who to ask."

"The Moorsoms have been very satisfied with Doctor Hill."

"There—I knew you would have the answer for me. Would you send word to him?"

PART FOUR: THE NORTH-WEST PASSAGE

"Yes indeed, as soon as we get home." She got to her feet. "I'll be gone right away."

"You are so kind!—oh, and I have something for Mr Addison. And for you—I know you like to hear of distant lands."

She picked up a book from a side table.

"It is Constantine's *Journal*. He didn't discover his North-West Passage, so his journey won him little renown, but at least he returned safe. The *Journal* is full of navigation and instruments and the like. I made little of it, but Mr Addison may find something of interest in it."

Elizabeth took the book.

A Voyage Towards The North Pole, she read. *Undertaken By His Majesty's Command 1773 By Constantine John Phipps.* In spite of the distress of the circumstances she felt a shiver of excitement.

"He will be most interested, I am sure. As will I."

She embraced Lepell, feeling her suddenly vulnerable.

"Perhaps you should take some rest now."

Lepell shrugged. "Thank you, my dear. Perhaps I should. If I could."

* * *

Elizabeth did not give Lord Constantine's *Journal* to John right away, as Lepell had bidden her. Indeed, there were so many things to discuss with John on her return that she persuaded herself she had quite forgotten it. But a few days later, when the house was quiet and she had an afternoon to herself, she took it out from her desk and settled to read it.

Lepell was right, of course. It was a plain account of the voyage and mainly taken up with navigational and scientific matters—records of wind direction, depth of anchorage, observations of latitude and longitude. From time to time the captain permitted himself some more personal observations that at once appealed to Elizabeth's imagination.

> *June 29th.*
> *The wind Northerly; stood close in with the land. The Coast appeared to be neither habitable nor accessible; it was formed by*

> *high barren black Rocks without the least marks of vegetation. This prospect would have suggested the idea of perpetual Winter, had not the mildness of the weather, the smooth Water, bright sunshine and constant Daylight given a Cheerfulness and novelty to the whole of this striking and Romantick scene.*

As she read on, Elizabeth discovered a dramatic tale hidden beneath the plain language of the log. In their efforts to discover the fabled Passage, the *Racehorse* and her companion ship, the *Carcass*, essayed any opening in the ice, constantly balancing the risk of the ice closing in behind with the hope of breaking through into undiscovered waters.

At the beginning of August the worst happened. The favourable wind they had enjoyed suddenly dropped and both ships found themselves caught in shifting ice, unable to make headway. For days they were stuck fast with the weather worsening. Knowing it would be impossible to survive the coming winter on the ships, Constantine had taken the decision to abandon ship and attempt to carry the ship's boats across the ice to the nearest clear water.

Mercifully, before they had to resort to such desperate measures, a fresh wind got up and the crew hacked enough ice clear to give the ship traction. Two days later they were free.

Their adventures were not over. The Journal recorded laconically:

> *From the 7th of September when we were off Shetland, till the 24th, when we were off Orford Ness, we had very Hard gales of Wind with little intermission. In one of these Gales, the Hardest I think I was ever in, and with the Greatest sea, we lost three of our Boats and were obliged to heave two of our Guns overboard, and bear away for some time, though near a Lee shore, to clear the Ship of water.*

How fearful it must have been! At such times there could be no danger, no privation that the crew endured that their captain did not also suffer. Of course, she reminded herself, John had suffered just such ordeals when he was a seafaring man. But there was something romantic to her in Lord

Constantine's voyage, that he would risk such perils and hardship for the sake of science and discovery. How admirable a man he was! And how unfeeling was Lepell to dismiss his enterprise so carelessly! Or perhaps she was as proud of him as any mother but did not care to boast of it.

He had not neglected natural history either, for the sake of his friend Mr Banks—a long appendix was filled with his botanical observations, laid out with all the appropriate Latin terminology.

She left the book lying for John to pick up.

"Have you looked at it?" he asked her.

"Yes. It is the log of his voyage, and much more besides."

He opened it, read through the first few pages, skipped on to the appendices and scrutinized them carefully before closing it again.

"I believe I will let Moorsom take a look at it. He is a great man for navigation. He will like to read of the longitude measurements."

"Will you not read it yourself?"

"I have read enough ships' logs to content me forever and I have no time for all his tables and charts. Does it work or not? What else do we need to know?"

He looked at her face and laughed.

"Don't worry, Lizzie. I can read a set of accounts and fit out a ship as well as the next man. And that has advanced me further than understanding longitude."

Elizabeth thought of the Red House and all that John's talents had brought them. She should be grateful.

"Indeed," she said.

John put the book down on the table with a snap.

"I fancy it will be the last of Lord Constantine's adventures," he remarked.

"Why so?"

"The town is full of rumours about his father's health. If half of them are true, Constantine will be the new Lord Mulgrave before the year is out." He dropped his voice confidentially. "We must hope that he will continue his father's interest in our business, or we shall all suffer for it. You must use your influence with Lepell, Lizzie."

Elizabeth felt a shock pass through her. What a simpleton she was! Her fascination with Constantine's voyage of discovery, her friendship with Lepell, John's sailing adventures with the Mulgrave boys, served one purpose only in John's eyes: to bind the wealth and patronage of the Mulgraves closer to his business. She might have remonstrated, but did she not depend on it? Was it not her bread and butter too? She turned her face so that John might not see a tear stain her cheek. For so long she had liked to see Constantine in a romantic light, as a heroic explorer and adventurer. But she must learn to look more coldly. One day Constantine would be the lord of Mulgrave Castle. One day he would hold the keys to their prosperity.

PART FIVE

1781

The Orphans

CHAPTER 33

Marylebone, London

10 January 1781

How he disliked these dreary January evenings, John Cresswell sighed to himself. The air in the street was so heavy with smoke that he could hardly step outside without setting off the dreadful coughing that had afflicted him since Christmas. And, indeed, what was there to do if a fellow was to venture forth? He could not return to Brooke's till he had the means to pay what he owed for the misfortune he had suffered at the tables before Christmas. He had been so certain—it could not fail—he was still at a loss to understand it. He could not charge himself with recklessness. And yet, it had gone against him.

It was the bad luck that had dogged him all his life. He had struggled against it, God knows. But even his own father had turned against him. Had taken from him the only part of his inheritance he might have realized without difficulty and put it into the hands of John Addison. What a calculating schemer the man was! He had planned it all along, John Cresswell was certain; had persuaded his father to change his will so that he, Addison, might have the Red House. And now, not satisfied with stealing the Red House from him, he and Elizabeth had taken up residence in Bedford Square. A brand-new house in one of the most exclusive squares in London! There was no denying it, Addison was brazen in his ambitions. The man had come from nowhere—he had no family, he was nothing but a jumped-up deckhand, and he presumed to buy his way into society. There should be a law, John felt, a law that prevented such low types acquiring property. It should be available only to the gentry. Otherwise, any elegant neighbourhood in the town risked being dragged down.

All Addison's fortune was due to the Mulgrave family, according to Harry Parker. Since Harry worked at the Admiralty, he knew what went on: knew how, since Constantine, now Lord Mulgrave, was Parliamentary spokesman for the Admiralty and had influence, contracts fell into Addison's pockets like ripe plums. And since the start of the American War, those contracts had made him a fortune. Of course Harry was such an innocent, gullible fellow he could see no harm in it. And Addison and Elizabeth had so ingratiated themselves with Lord Mulgrave and his brothers that they countenanced them as acquaintance far beyond the limits of their business connection. They might mix in society without anyone making the least objection.

He leaned forward to poke the fire and at once it set off a bout of coughing so violent that he felt it might tear his lungs out of his chest altogether.

"Mrs Stock!" he called out, as soon as he recovered himself. There was no response. He pulled himself out of his chair, went to open the door and called again. A few moments later he heard a footstep on the stair.

"There now, Mr Cresswell, you have caught me napping! I declare the day is so dreary there is nothing for it but to doze till it is done."

"Indeed, Mrs Stock, I envy you your repose. My chest is so tight—so dreadfully painful—that I can take no rest."

"Oh dear, that is very unpleasant for you. Should you be more comfortable in your bed, do you think?"

"No, no—I can find no rest. My spirits are very low, Mrs Stock."

"Let me turn your chair around, Mr Cresswell, so that you can take satisfaction from your lovely portrait. It will make you think of your girls. There's nothing surer to restore you to spirits."

She didn't understand, thought John. She had no idea of the difficulties he laboured under. Charming though his daughters were, they could hardly free him of those. But he would oblige her. He would allow her to turn the chair.

"How well you look in it, sir! Anyone can see you are a gentleman."

It was true, he thought, and it did afford him some satisfaction. The new filly had won him £50 at the September meeting in York and rather than let it drain away on his debts he had commissioned a portrait of himself with his girls, which now hung on the wall of the parlour. He was pictured at the centre, with the girls on either side of him. It was a fair likeness of the girls, Fanny demure and dark-haired, Catherine with her bolder smile and reddish curls. They were not at all alike, twins though they were. As for himself, it would be immodest to pass comment, though he felt his lips were shown a little thin, and there was a certain puffiness to his cheeks. But on the whole, as Mrs Stock rightly said, it portrayed him in a very gentlemanly manner.

The truth was, he was starting to feel proud of his daughters. When he took them out for a stroll in Hyde Park or sat taking tea with them, he was often complimented on their looks. Several of the ladies of his acquaintance took an interest in them and he felt that his role as a father increased their respect for him. He had sometimes worried that the Dyers would not bring them up with sufficient accomplishments, but he need not have feared. Although they had no money the Dyers were a very artistic household. The girls could sing and draw and write an elegant hand. After all, had not his beloved Catherine possessed every charm and delicacy of manner? The girls did him credit.

"Thank you, Mrs Stock. I believe I should have a posset of some sort—you will know what would be best. To soothe the pain in my chest."

"I will put it up for you right away. Why don't you take this shawl and wrap it round your throat to keep it warm? I will bring the fire up so that you are cosy."

He liked to have her tucking the shawl around him and fussing at the fire. His mood lifted a little. Really, she suited him very well. He had grown used to having her around. Harry and Bridget were for ever urging him to find a wife—to make a home for his daughters—but he found it hard to imagine. And yet he must. There was nothing else for it. When he had met with the steward, the man had nothing but ill news. The tenant of the Hall had given notice, complaining that it was inconvenient. Indeed, his father had made a very poor job of it, but there was nothing to be done about that now. It was to be divided up and let out as rooms to labouring men who would make no complaints about their lodging. The income from the estate was hardly enough to service all the charges on it from the mortgages he had taken out and now there was nothing left to mortgage. Where was he to turn? It was a desperate case. He had already borrowed from the Parkers to pay Mrs Stock and the Dyers, but Bridget had been very ill-tempered about it and made a great fuss about Harry having to earn a living. She need hardly have troubled herself since they would have a fortune when the Admiral died. He had been forced to listen to it all with a patient face. He didn't wish to repeat the experience.

So there was nothing for it but marriage. A pleasant widow, he thought. With an inheritance. A woman who was already accustomed to looking after a man. Who would have established her own interests and occupations and would not be looking to him for her entertainment. No children. Or grown up at least. He could not be expected to look after another man's brood. He had his own girls to think of.

There was no one in his acquaintance who seemed to fit with his requirements. It would be back to Bridget and Harry, he supposed. They seemed to be acquainted with half of London.

Mrs Stock came back into the room with a pitcher and cup.

"Here we are, this will put you to rights, and maybe you will have a sleep afterwards. I'll come up later and see what you might have for your dinner."

She put down the posset before him.

"The newspaper is come, I have brought it up for you," she added, and she put it down on the table with the posset.

The hot liquor in the posset made his eyes water, but he gulped it down gratefully. A little glow of warmth spread down his throat. He picked up the paper and scanned the newspaper. A name caught his eye. No, surely it was not, he had only now been thinking of the man, he must have imagined it. But a closer look confirmed that yes, indeed it was. Constantine. Lord Mulgrave.

January 7th 1781

Capture of French frigate off Brest.

We have learned of a successful naval action this week in the English Channel. The French frigate Minerve, *formerly the English ship* Minerva *taken by the* Concorde *on 22nd August 1778, was recaptured in a bold and daring action by the* Courageux, *commanded by Lord Mulgrave with support from the* Valiant *and Captain Francis Easterby. The action took place on January 4th in rough seas whose ferocity prevented the* Courageux *from opening her lower gunports, and which met with fierce resistance from the Chevalier de Grimouard. The* Minerve *suffered the loss of all her masts and 50 men dead, 23 wounded, while the* Courageux *lost 10 men and 7 wounded.*

The successful recapture of an English ship must inspire patriotic sentiments in every loyal heart, and the courage and resolve of Lord Mulgrave and Captain Easterby are deserving of the warmest commendation.

John threw the newspaper back on the table. The news brought no glow of patriotic pride to his breast, he thought. After six years of war with one country or another, one grew weary of heroes and commendations. Why could they not put an end to it? He was sick of there being no news but that of the war, as if nothing else were deemed of any importance in the country. And since there was no racing news to be had in January what use was the paper to him? He felt a headache coming on. Soon the pain was so severe he could not read a word.

* * *

By the time Mrs Stock returned to ask what he would have for dinner, he was very much worse.

"No, I will have nothing—nothing at all. My throat is on fire and my head aches terribly. Water—a pitcher of water, Mrs Stock. Pray take it upstairs. I am become so hot I believe I have a fever. I will go to bed directly."

Mrs Stock looked at him a little closer and then backed out of the room quite swiftly.

She brought him the water and a nightshirt to his chamber and left him. Since Timothy had gone home, he was forced to undress himself, which was very inconvenient, and he found his fingers stumbling over the buttons. It took a great deal of time. He dropped his clothes on the floor as he discarded them. Timothy would have to deal with them in the morning since he was inconsiderate enough to have absented himself when his master was unwell. At last he got the nightshirt over his head and got into bed. He was asleep in five minutes.

After a few hours of dream-filled sleep, during which he flung every one of the covers from him, he seemed to wake. He could not tell where he was. Then he saw before him his wife Catherine, as distinctly as if she had left him only yesterday. Her face was quite pale, her eyes dark, and she wore a long robe. He knew she had something of great importance to tell him, but no matter how he called out to her, she did not speak. She seemed to mean for him to follow her and he got up at once from the bed and went after her. She went down the stairs, through the hallway to the door and vanished through it. He wrenched it open and hastened outside. He burned with such heat that the bitter cold of the night did not trouble him in the least though he wore only his nightshirt. He looked down the street and yes! There she was again, very close, and smiling to him. He ran towards her, ran and ran until he lost sight of her. Suddenly he could go no further. He sank down to the ground, to the sweet coolness of the paving stones. He would lie there for a little while, he told himself. He would lie and rest. Then he would find her, and they would be together at last.

CHAPTER 34

Bedford Square

March 1781

On a frosty morning in March a postboy brought a package of documents to the pedimented front door of the Addisons' house in Bedford Square. When John Addison untied it, the heading stood out in florid letters:

High Court of Chancery, Lincoln Inn Fields
Guardianship of Orphans

He took the papers into his office and settled to his desk. A couple of hours later he sent the parlourmaid for his wife.

"And some coffee," he added.

Elizabeth came into the room in a rustle of grey silk. Now that she spent every winter in London she availed herself of the services of a London dressmaker. They often entertained Lord Mulgrave and his brothers, as well as other distinguished guests, and it would not do for her to be dressed like a provincial matron. John Addison was not a connoisseur of ladies' fashions, but it pleased him to see her handsomely dressed. As she grew older, she had started to have a regal air in her fine laces and silks, with the dull sheen of pearls around her neck.

"The documents have come."

"Well?"

"I believe it must be you, Lizzie. I can see no other way."

She sat down heavily beside him.

"If it had but come ten years ago. Dear God—I am old enough to be their grandmother."

"For my part I have quite a fancy to be a grandfather."

"Don't tease, John. Tell me what it says."

"It is confirmed that your brother John Cresswell left no will. And that he made no provision for the twins. Although there was an agreement that the Dyers should care for them, and he did, sometimes, pay them an allowance for their pains, nothing was put in writing."

He paused.

"There is no problem with the estate. The entail takes care of the inheritance. Since they are of the same age, and are both females, the estate goes in equal shares to them both."

She nodded.

"The guardianship is another matter. The law decrees that if the father has not made a legal deed naming a guardian, then it must be a paternal relative, with no inheritable interest in the estate. Since you have no brothers, paternal relative means one of you girls. One of the sisters."

"The eldest?" Perhaps Catherine could have them, she thought.

"No, there is no requirement for the eldest. Only that the guardian be able to undertake their care, and the care of their estate."

Elizabeth remembered again the scene at her brother's graveside. The Reverend Dyer had read the Offices for the Dead as her brother's coffin was lowered into the grave, and the twins stood one either side of Mrs Dyer, clinging to her as Reverend Dyer's sonorous Welsh voice battled with the icy January wind. The two girls shed no tears, but their faces were pale and frightened. Afterwards Bridget had gone to embrace them, for the twins had sometimes visited the Parkers' home in Newman Street. But Elizabeth hardly knew them. Since the falling-out over the Red House, her brother had forbidden the Addisons from seeing his daughters. And now, there they were, young misses of thirteen who she scarcely recognized. Like Bridget, she had gone up to offer her condolences, but they had looked back at her blankly and clung closer to Mrs Dyer.

"Could they not go to Bridget? They are acquainted already."

"She has her own family to manage. And the Parkers never go north. The girls must get to know their estate. You can take them to the Red House. Your sisters will help look after them. And from time to time, they can come back here to London and spend time with the Dyers."

In her heart she knew he was right. Knew it must be her. But after all these years of wishing for children, now it was upon her she felt only apprehension. They were part of the Dyers' family—they looked like Dyers; they were nothing like her Cresswell younger sisters. And she had established her own life, her own acquaintance, her visits to concerts and readings and to the endlessly fascinating halls of the British Museum. Was she to give it all up to take on her brother's girls?

"There are other things to consider," said John Addison. "The guardian must look after her wards' estate in their best interests till they reach their majority. Who better than you, Lizzie? You helped your father run the place."

"I would look after the estate?"

"Yes. On their behalf."

An image came to her mind from the last time she had been in Northumberland. She had paid a visit to Cresswell Home Farm, to the Kyles, who had farmed it for generations as Cresswell tenants, had always supplied the Hall with milk and meat and grain. But she had found Thomas Kyle full of complaint about her brother's steward, who did nothing for them, let everything go but kept putting up the rents. On and on he went. It had pained her to the core, that John Cresswell had become the worst kind of absentee landlord who took no care of his land or his people. This would give her a chance to set things right. To teach the girls how things should be done. A sudden impulse of interest raised her spirits.

"I would need your help, John."

"Yes. I swore to your father that we would set the place to rights. I will do whatever is needed. It will take some doing. John mortgaged every field and stone he could lay his hands on."

He sat back in his chair.

"One more thing. The guardian must give their assent to any marriage that may be arranged. Who knows? There may be possibilities there as well."

Elizabeth was thinking about Northumberland and did not take heed of his words. They would return to her later.

* * *

Their next task was to visit the Dyers. Their house in Sussex Gardens was just as Elizabeth remembered it, tall and thin between others like it, with peeling paint on the windowsills and bits of street rubbish blowing around the front door. The Reverend Dyer was, it seemed, truly a Perpetual Curate who would never have a living of his own.

One of the daughters opened the door to them and took them into the parlour where the Reverend Dyer was at work upon a sermon. Mrs Dyer came in from the kitchen without troubling to remove her apron or offer tea. From somewhere in the house came the sound of singing. Girls' voices. Was it the twins, Elizabeth wondered.

"You have done John a great service with Fanny and Kitty," she began.

"Are you come to take them away, Mrs Addison?" said Mrs Dyer. "They are part of our family. They are my granddaughters. Do we have no rights of kinship?"

Elizabeth wanted to reply, no, I have not the slightest wish to take them from you, but she choked the words in her throat. John Addison took over. He explained all the requirements of the law, how there was no choice in the matter regardless of the bonds and ties that existed between them and which would nevertheless always be respected, how it was in the interest of the girls now they were become heiresses to spend some time at least on their estate, how they would also spend time in London and be at liberty to visit their grandparents and aunts and uncles as often as they wished . . . on and on he went, till Mrs Dyer's resistance slackened somewhat.

"You know," said Elizabeth, "it was always our wish to be close to the girls, but after my father's death we had a falling out with my brother. He would not allow us to visit them."

Mrs Dyer nodded. "Yes. I knew that."

"Well," said the Reverend Dyer, "Perhaps you had better meet them now." He got up and went out into the hall. "Kitty! Fanny! Come down please."

A few moments later the girls came into the room, a little breathless, and went to stand beside their grandmother's chair.

"This is your Uncle John Addison and your Aunt Elizabeth. Aunt Elizabeth is one of your father's sisters."

The girls curtsied to them. You would hardly have known they were twins, thought Elizabeth. Fanny was a little taller and very slender, with curling brown hair and a gentle expression. Kitty was smaller, stockier; more like her brother John, she thought, with fair hair that had a definite reddish tinge and a way of thrusting her chin forward that gave her a defiant look. They were on the cusp of womanhood, still childish in their smooth open faces, but both starting to develop.

"What young ladies you are become!" said Elizabeth. "When I saw you last you were both tiny babies, as sweet as could be."

The girls smiled politely.

"We are very happy to make your acquaintance," said John. "We live not very far away in Bedford Square, though Mrs Addison spends some of her time in Northumberland. I am a ship man and my ships keep me busy in London."

He leaned forward towards them.

"Have you ever been upon a ship?"

"No, sir!" they said together.

"We have a new ship come into dock. It is called after your aunt. The *Elizabeth*. It has been in dock just two days and is waiting to unload. Would you like to take a carriage ride to Deptford and have a look?"

Kitty and Fanny looked at each other, suddenly animated, and turned eager faces to their grandparents.

"Could we go?"

Taken by surprise, Mrs Dyer nodded.

"We should like it very much," said Kitty. "Shouldn't we, Fanny?"

"Is it—ah—quite respectable?" asked Reverend Dyer.

"Mr Addison is very well known on the docks, and we will travel in the carriage. It will give us an opportunity to get to know one another."

"Very well."

"We will call for you tomorrow in the carriage and drive down to the docks. You'll need a warm cloak—there's always a sharp wind down there."

* * *

Elizabeth did her best to converse with the girls in the carriage. She learned that their Dyer aunts and uncles acted as their tutors and that they were all very fond of reading and music. Their grandfather taught them scripture. They had never been to the seaside, but they had once been to visit their relatives in Wales and they had liked it very much. They had easy, unaffected manners, she decided. They answered her questions politely but could hardly restrain their eagerness to pull down the carriage window and stare outside. Once they reached the dock and were alongside the ship, John helped them out and showed them the ship, bare-masted, tied up against the dock. He pointed to the bow.

"There's the name!"

Elizabeth, they read, staring at her. The name had been Lord Mulgrave's doing. The first ship he and John owned jointly had been the *Constantine*. The second, Constantine himself insisted, must be the *Elizabeth*. What joy it had given her!

"Yes," she said. "And look, there is her figurehead. She is like the spirit of the ship."

They stared at the woman's head and shoulders reaching forward to the sea, her buxom chest half-covered in a blue dress and her long yellow hair streaming out behind her.

"Is it you, Aunt Elizabeth?" said Fanny uncertainly.

"No, not really. She is a ship spirit."

Once the girls were aboard, they lost their shyness and ran around the decks exclaiming over everything. The crew were all ashore and, since the ship was waiting to be unloaded, they could roam unchecked. They looked in the hold at the cargo: the logs stacked over and over and the longer tree trunks that would become bowsprits and masts, the tightly strapped bales of furs and the sacks of grain; they ran through the sailors' quarters and tried to balance themselves in hammocks; they stood in the galley and pretended to be cooks; they peeped in the captain's cabin and pointed at all his instruments and charts; and then they were out on the deck again, staring out across the Pool of London at all the other ships moored hard up against the *Elizabeth*.

"Uncle John, we can sing a sailors' shanty! Would you like to hear it?"

"I would! I'm sure your aunt would too!"

The two girls positioned themselves in front of the mast, back-to-back, and crossed their arms to imitate sailors. Their voices were clear and sweet, and the shanty was accompanied by many actions of hauling up sail and weighing anchor and waving flags. At the end, letting their cloaks slip off, they performed a little hornpipe to round off the show.

"Bravo!" cried out John Addison, clapping. "You are fine sailors! You may join the crew whenever you please. Here is sixpence for your song."

He fished in his purse and brought out two silver sixpences. The girls swooped on them like hungry seagulls.

Elizabeth watched, surprised at their easy confidence. The Dyers were Welsh, of course, and the Welsh loved to sing. She observed the girls' clothes, the worn cloaks and threadbare gowns that had clearly served others before them. It would be a household of hand-me-downs. She felt a pang of protectiveness towards them. How young they were! How innocent! If their father had not died, they might have grown up in the obscurity of the curate's family, loved and unremarked. Now they were to be sprung out into a new world, into a new family, two young heiresses whose estate would draw predatory eyes towards them.

They understood nothing of it yet. It was clear that their father had never been at the centre of their lives and there was no reason they knew of that anything would change. Next time, she thought, she must talk to them directly. The outing with their new Uncle John had helped to break the ice and it was clear he was enjoying his new young nieces. But they must know sooner or later. And once they had had time to apprise themselves of their new destiny, she would take them to the Red House.

CHAPTER 35

Sussex Gardens, London

June 1781

The Reverend Dyer went to answer his front door early one morning in June, a few weeks after the twins had gone away to Northumberland. He found the post-boy waiting, gave the boy a penny and took the letter inside to the kitchen, where his wife was taking breakfast with two of his daughters.

"A letter," he said to her noncommittally.

"Oh, let me have it," she said, plucking it from his hand. The upright childish hand on the front was unmistakeable. She took a knife and slit open the letter.

"Pray read it aloud," said her husband. "We are all eager for the news."

Mrs Dyer unfolded the thin paper and started to read, with some hesitation due to smudges and some misspelled words.

> *Dear Grandmother*
>
> *I hope you and Grandfather are very well. I think of you and all our family very often.*
>
> *We are living at the Red House, it is very large, there are more rooms than our house at Suſsex Gardens and there is a garden all round it. We can see the sea from the window of our bedroom. We have four aunts here, Aunt Dorothy, Aunt Grace, Aunt Juliana, and Aunt Alice, as well as Aunt Elizabeth. In the morning we do leſsons*

and in the afternoon we do stitching and other things. I can make cheese from milk.

We have a Cousin too, she is called Grace and she is four years older than us. She lives nearby at Woodhorn, her mother is Aunt Catherine. We are friends. Kitty and I like her very well. Grace takes us for walks to the seashore and we can go to Morpeth sometimes with her in the carriage. It is a town but not so big as London.

The Red House is four miles away from Creſswell, there is a Hall there but the Creſswells don't live in it anymore. Part of it is an old Tower and Aunt Elizabeth is going to show us inside it. The people at Creſswell are fishermen and when they bring the boats in you can see all the fish in baskets.

Kitty sends Affectionate greetings, she will write very soon.
Your loving grand-daughter
Fanny Creſswell

When she had read it aloud Mrs Dyer took the letter and read it again to herself, several times.

"You see?" said the Reverend Dyer. "You are not forgotten."

Mrs Dyer tucked the letter into her fichu and wiped the tears from her cheeks.

"No," she said. "She is a good girl."

"They have aunts enough to care for them very well, I should say."

"That may be, but we are their grandparents. How unjust it is! The law cares for nothing but property and estate."

"The girls will have a better life than ever we could have given them."

"Better? How better? Have you no regard for your own household?"

"Come now, my dear. How can we know what God has decreed in our lives, or their lives? How can we know why John Cresswell was taken so suddenly? We must bear our lot with fortitude."

Mrs Dyer took a piece of bread without responding further to her husband. She buttered the bread with considerable attack and bit sharply into it, filling her mouth and making further conversation impossible.

PART SIX

1785–7

The Shadow of the Tower

CHAPTER 36

Lloyds Coffee House, Tower Street, London

March 1785

The Brethren of Trinity House

At Deptford is a Mariners Society known as the Brethren of Trinity House founded in honour of the Blessed Trinity and St Clement for the increase and perpetual augmentation of their cunning.

Their principal task is to take cognizance of all sea marks and to erect lighthouses upon the several coasts of the kingdom, for the security of navigation; to direct replacing or repairing of such as may be removed and to prosecute everyone who wilfully and maliciously destroys them.

This corporation is governed by a master, four wardens, and eighteen elder brethren. The rest are called younger brethren, the number of them is unlimited. Out of these the elder brethren are chosen, except that there are always among them a few honorary members, generally nobleman or other persons of rank; these currently comprise the Duke of Marlborough, the Marquis of Downshire and the Rt. Hon. Lord Mulgrave.

*A place falling vacant, we are pleased to announce that **Captain Francis Easterby** was elected on the 13th day of March 1785 to serve as an Elder Brother of Trinity House.*

John Addison put the newspaper down on the coffee-house table in front of him for a moment, the better to relish the notice he had just read.

Frank was become an Elder Brother of Trinity House! There could be no more influential body in shipping than the Corporation. It governed the Thames and the Port of London, as well as navigation further afield. What connections it would open to Frank! Of course he had Lord Mulgrave's patronage to thank for it, but all the patronage in the world would be to no purpose if he not been deserving.

John felt his heart full; truly, he was as proud as if Frank had been his own son. His sister Jane's boy, and somehow of all her children, it was with Frank he felt the most particular kinship. Frank was more of an Addison than an Easterby, more like himself, John Addison, than his father. He had repaid Admiral Parker's patronage in the navy with diligence and application. But a captain needed more; he needed a cool head and a quick wit. It was Frank's own daring and seamanship during the American War that had earned him his captaincy. Now he was an officer and a gentleman, who could be at home in any company.

He had profited from his naval career in other ways too: he had ended the war with his pockets full of prize money as well as his captain's pay and bought himself a fine house in Blackheath. Park House had pleasant views over Greenwich Park and was convenient for the docks. And now, thanks to Lord Mulgrave, he was an Elder Brother of Trinity House. He could hardly be better connected.

It was already agreed between them that Frank would take over the London side of the business now the war was over. Over the last year John Addison had started to feel himself growing old. This war had been even more lucrative for the business than the last, with the helter-skelter into the Baltic trade as the North American timber imports suddenly dried up, leaving His Majesty with an endless stream of ships to commission and refit and not enough timber and pitch to do it. But the constant long hours in the office and the endless paperwork from the Admiralty had worn him out. And invaluable though Lord Mulgrave's investment was, he was demanding.

John Addison wanted to live more in Whitby. He could take care of that end of the business while Frank managed the London offices. He also wanted to spend time in Northumberland at the Red House with his wife and Fanny and Kitty when they were there for the summer. He loved to have the girls around him; loved to tease them about suitors and watch them blush, loved to buy little trifles for them and see their smiles. Elizabeth was severe with the twins, so he felt himself at liberty to be indulgent.

He meant to bind them to himself as close as he could. Was it not obvious? His nephew Frank would marry one of Elizabeth's nieces. The son or daughter of the marriage would carry the blood of both Cresswell and Addison. It was as near as he and Elizabeth could come to having a grandchild of their own. It would be a kind of fulfilment of his dreams. He meant to make Frank his heir. And the marriage to one of the twins would bring Frank half the Cresswell estate.

The girls were sixteen, close to marriageable age, and John Addison had decided there was nothing to be gained by waiting. Now Frank was become a gentleman with a large house he would be looking about him for a wife and the opportunity might be lost. When John had put the idea to him one night over a few glasses of brandy, Frank had declared himself very pleased with the notion. Now he had only to convince Elizabeth since she was their guardian and must consent to any marriage. She could see the advantages, of course, but insisted that the girls must not be forced into a marriage of convenience. They must not be persuaded against their wishes. But what young girl would refuse Captain Easterby? In anyone's view, he was a fine-looking man, good-humoured and kind-hearted. What girl could hope for better?

Which one? He loved both the girls, but Kitty had something more of her father in her. She was more prone to fits of temper if she was crossed and could sulk for half a day. Whereas Fanny was the most sweet-tempered young woman imaginable—always willing and obliging, with a pair of blue eyes that lit up his heart. Fanny was the one—and did they not share the same name, Frances and Francis? But it would be for Frank to decide. He was coming to dine that very night.

CHAPTER 37

Bedford Square

March 1785

While John Addison sat with his newspaper at the coffee house, Elizabeth was at her desk in the house in Bedford Square. But she could not pretend to be engaged in the documents before her. Since she had returned to London for the winter with the girls, Elizabeth frequently found herself as distracted as a foolish girl. Sometimes when she might have been supposed to be reckoning up the household accounts she sat staring blankly at the columns, pencil motionless, recollecting, for example, how Constantine had questioned her at the table about the Red House, with such a lively manner that she could not help but feel he was truly interested. Or she pondered again his description of the new opera he had attended at the King's Theatre, how well he had liked the soprano, how elegant the ensemble was. He urged her to persuade Mr Addison to take her and the girls. Of course, he never would—John had no taste for such things—but she loved to hear of it.

Was Constantine a handsome man? she had sometimes asked herself recently, as if trying to account for the sudden rapidity of her heartbeat she experienced when he came into the drawing room. One could hardly say so. His face was weathered by his years at sea and his nose was often mocked as over-large. But to her, it gave his face character and distinction, echoed in the firmness of his jaw and lips. His presence was highly distinguished, if not conventionally handsome.

She thought very often of Lepell's words to her before she died. Lepell had taken ill quite suddenly, only months after John Cresswell's death. It was a dropsy of some kind that caused strange growths to appear on her body and took all the life from her. The doctors wanted to bleed her, but she had no time for that.

"I have sent them away, Elizabeth. It is not the slightest use. I am not going to spend my last days with leeches sucking out my blood."

"Have they no other treatment for you?"

"One of them wanted to cut out these things. Can you imagine? What a disgusting idea! No—I shall rely upon laudanum for my consolation."

By the time of Elizabeth's last visit, she found Lepell drifting in and out of dreams. She sat with her for half an hour before Lepell was momentarily awake. Her face was very pale and thin, her eyes unnaturally bright from the drug.

"Constantine," she said. "I worry about Constantine. It is always duty, duty, duty. Why will he not take a wife and have a family?"

Her gaze drifted past Elizabeth towards the window, and she was silent for a time. Then she looked back at her, quite directly.

"You must look after him for me when I am gone. Will you do so, Elizabeth? Will you?"

For a moment she was agitated, but before Elizabeth could answer, her head dropped back on the pillow and her eyes closed. She was already dreaming again.

Lepell's words had seemed very strange to her then. The war was at its height; Constantine was commanding the *Courageux* in the Channel and could not even get leave to be at his mother's side. It seemed very unlikely that he would require her services. But she had whispered to Lepell, "I will. Don't worry. It will all be well."

Now, four years later, Lepell's words had stayed with her. In the strangest way, it sometimes seemed to her that they were coming true. Lord Mulgrave was often at Bedford Square to dine and talk business with John Addison and he had taken to asking her advice on all manner of topics. Where could his housekeeper buy fish like the fine turbot she served him? Would she advise him on a wedding gift for his sister? What was to be done about Mr Pitt's constant interference in his procurement? He was an MP now, a member of the Privy Council and elevated in every way, and yet he would ask her views on the decisions of the Council as if he valued her opinion as much as any lord or bishop. He deferred constantly to her seniority—she almost wished he would not—she was after all only eight years older than him. But it was all part of the consideration with which he treated everyone, whatever their rank or sex. How modest he was in spite of all his gifts and accomplishments! How amiable in his manners!

One afternoon when she was lost in such thoughts, Kitty came looking for her. She was sitting at her desk with pen poised over a letter to her sister, and immediately composed her face into an expression of forbidding severity as she looked up.

"What is it? I am busy."

Kitty sighed respectfully.

"Fanny and I want to know what we should wear tonight."

Suddenly she was galvanized. How could she sit here dreaming? It was tonight! Frank was to come and dine, together with Constantine and his protégé from the navy, young Richard Moorsom. The girls had met Frank already, at a concert and on a visit to Greenwich Park. But it was the first time they would dine with him. John believed Captain Frank Easterby might be ready to make up his mind. She must see to their dresses and to all the other business.

*   *   *

Lord Mulgrave, Richard Moorsom and Frank Easterby were old comrades from their navy days, though Richard was the only one still serving, and for the first course the talk was all of the American war and stories of their engagement with the heroic *Minerva*, dramatically retold for the benefit of the ladies. But when the soup plates had been cleared away Constantine, who was sitting to Elizabeth's right, let them continue the conversation without him. He leaned towards her and spoke in a more confidential tone.

"My mother so often lamented that her example must have turned me from matrimony altogether—it is not true of course, the responsibility is all my own—and now that she is gone I deeply regret she cannot assist me in the matter. So you must advise me, Mrs Addison, if you will."

Matrimony! He planned to marry! She was at once thrown into confusion. Rallying herself, she responded, "I am sure that any young lady would count herself fortunate in your attentions, Lord Mulgrave."

She allowed herself to imagine for the smallest instant the feelings of such a lady before returning resolutely to the discussion. How strange that he should have raised such a matter this evening of all evenings!

"I am not so sure!" he said. "I must seem an old man to your nieces here, and the young lady in question—Anne Elizabeth—is a year or two younger than them."

Elizabeth was shocked for a moment—she could not help it—but concealed it at once.

"It is a considerable difference, it is true. But if there is sincere affection on both sides and a compatibility of spirit it may answer very well."

"You are very consoling, Mrs Addison. May I explain the case to you? Anne Elizabeth is a Cholmley. The family, you know, once owned much of Scarborough and Whitby, but their estates suffered greatly in the Civil War. The family used to live in Abbey House in Whitby—you may be acquainted with it?"

"Yes—it is become quite ruinous."

"The family removed to their estates elsewhere, to Howsham Hall in Yorkshire."

"Howsham Hall?" cried out John Addison from the other end of the table, catching at their conversation. "I know Howsham Hall—it is near my place at Appleton." He looked at the girls dramatically.

"It has a curse upon it."

Elizabeth wished he would not interrupt so thoughtlessly. But the girls looked back at him, eager for a story.

"When King Henry sold off the monasteries, a great Earl bought the land of Kirkham Priory. He tore down the Priory and used the stone to build himself a mansion. The Prior of Kirkham placed a curse upon the house, saying that no family that lived there would have issue. And so it proved for the Earl and for every family that has lived there after."

The girls stared, wide-eyed.

"But it will not, I trust, be so for the Cholmleys," said Constantine dryly. Elizabeth feared he was offended.

"Every old house has some such legend to go with it," she said. "My old home at Cresswell Hall has a White Lady in the Tower who walks the shore on stormy nights."

"She threw herself from the top of the tower to try to save her lover," said Kitty.

"Yes, and at the very moment she was to be reunited with him and thought herself happiest, everything was lost to her!" added Fanny, and Elizabeth saw her blue eyes fixed earnestly upon Frank Easterby.

"I hope she is not a vengeful ghost," said Frank, smiling back at Fanny.

"Not the slightest," said Elizabeth. "I always fancied her as my protectress—our protectress."

Frank leaned across the table to say something more to Fanny. Elizabeth turned back to her conversation with Constantine. In a low voice she said, "I am sorry. Mr Addison loves to tell a tale and had no notion what we were speaking of."

"I have heard the tale before and in any case, it does not concern Miss Cholmley. I will speak plainly to you, Mrs Addison. My purpose in the marriage is to unite the two families who have so long a connection with Whitby. Miss Cholmley is their only daughter, so I am hopeful that the difference in our ages may not be too great an obstacle. But you must tell me frankly if you think I may be odious to her."

She laughed. "I guarantee that you will not."

So. It was to be a dynastic union. Where he felt his duty lay. For some reason she was relieved that it was not a passionate affair of the heart. But still, in the days that followed, the news lay on her heart like a stone. Once he was married, there would be no more intimate conversations and discussions. He would be always with his wife. A wife who was younger than the twins, from a noble family as great as his own.

PART SIX: THE SHADOW OF THE TOWER 233

*   *   *

After the meal, when she had withdrawn and the girls had been sent up to bed, the four men continued in the dining room with the port into the early hours. When John finally came upstairs to bed, he was in tearing spirits.

"Ah—what good fellows they are! What good fellows!" He seized her by the waist and twirled her unsteadily about the room. He was quite drunk, she perceived. He stopped, held her close and kissed her. Then he took a pace back and looked at her.

"Frank will have Fanny!" he said. "I was never so glad of anything in all my life."

CHAPTER 38

Bedford Square

April 1785

As spring drew on, Captain Easterby became a regular visitor to Bedford Square and often accompanied Mrs Addison and her two nieces to Assemblies and concerts or on carriage outings to Regent's Park. Elizabeth found she could not help but like him. He reminded her of John Addison in his younger days—he had the same indefatigable energy and liveliness, though he had an assurance and ease that had always eluded her husband. He was taller than John, clean-shaven with a wide mouth that curved unevenly when he smiled, giving him a lopsided, humorous look. He was so easy and unaffected in his manner, so entertaining with his stories of his life at sea and so full of funny observations that they were always entertained in his company. It was clear to Elizabeth where his preference lay, but he took care to pay equal attention to both the girls.

A fortnight before Elizabeth planned to take the girls up to Northumberland for the summer, Captain Easterby called at Bedford Square and requested a private audience with Fanny in the drawing room. Elizabeth already knew to expect him and left the room, taking Kitty with her. As soon as they were out of the room, Kitty flung away from her and ran upstairs in a very unladylike manner, sobbing loudly. She could hardly be blamed, Elizabeth thought. She remembered standing in Woodhorn Church, watching one sister after another wed before her. The pain of the memory was as sharp as ever. She followed Kitty up the stairs and went into her bedroom, where Kitty was sobbing on the bed. She looked up at her aunt with a tragic expression.

"He has chosen Fanny! Why should it be her? He doesn't like me!"

"That's not true. He likes you very well, Kitty. He told your uncle that he loved you both. But he must choose one of you."

"But why Fanny? Why not me?"

"I know it seems hard to you now. But I believe you will come to be grateful for it in time. Captain Easterby is not the only gentleman in the world, and you will have the opportunity to make a much wider acquaintance, to attend Assemblies and Balls and the like and to choose someone you truly love."

"But I love Captain Easterby!"

"He is the first man who has paid you attentions. You will receive many more."

She sat down beside her niece and stroked her hair.

"The truth is, Kitty, I believe Fanny is better suited to marrying a man so much older than herself. He is thirty-three and you girls are only sixteen. Captain Easterby is quite settled in his ways, in his views and preferences; Fanny will have to adapt to those. It would be a trial to your lively disposition. I do believe you will be better suited to a husband closer to yourself in age."

Kitty stopped her tears to stare at her aunt, taken aback by her words. Of course she had given no thought at all to how it might be to actually live with Captain Easterby. Elizabeth pressed home the consolation.

"You are a very pretty girl, Kitty, and you have an inheritance. You will make a very great match. I am certain of it."

*   *   *

They would have to make changes, Elizabeth thought afterwards. It was time for the girls to be apart, to start the separation that Fanny's marriage would bring, though it would not take place straight away. She would insist, as her guardian, that the marriage wait till Fanny was eighteen, at least. She was too young, too unformed still. She needed to be more in society and become acquainted with the circles Frank Easterby moved in. She needed to know how to run a household such as Frank's where there would be frequent entertaining, to be confident and assured in her command, to become familiar with the services of a lady's maid. She was only a girl still.

Fanny could spend some time with John Addison and herself in Whitby over the next two summers, she decided, after they had all spent time together at the Red House. Kitty could stay on at the Red House. She would have Grace Johnson, Catherine's daughter, for company and learn to be independent of her sister.

Constantine, it seemed, was also planning to spend time in Whitby that summer—or at least, at Mulgrave Hall. His early discussions with Miss Cholmley's parents had, she learned, been very cordially received. He might pay his addresses to Miss Cholmley—Elizabeth Anne—though it was jointly agreed between the families that the marriage should be delayed till she was sixteen. In the meantime, in anticipation of his family life, he meant to carry out some alterations and enlargements to Mulgrave Hall. Howsham Hall was one of the first houses in the county and he did not wish his bride to feel her new home was in any way inferior. He had engaged Mr John Soane as his architect; perhaps Mrs Addison would care to visit Mulgrave Hall and give him her opinions on the plans?

Mrs Addison would, she confirmed, be delighted.

CHAPTER 39

The Red House, Woodhorn Demesne, Northumberland

June 1786

John Addison sat at the head of the table in the dining room at the Red House, with a glass of claret at his elbow and a plate of stewed hare in front of him. His first hunger satisfied, he paused for a moment to look down the table. On one side of him sat Elizabeth's nieces Kitty, Fanny and Grace, on the other his sisters-in-law Alice and Juliana, and facing him at the other end was his wife Elizabeth. Was ever a man so surrounded by women? he asked himself. Until lately there might have been Grace and Dorothy as well, but they were independent women now, thanks to the jointure settled on them by their father. They had removed to Morpeth and set up their own household. Alice was still at the Red House, in spite of all the talk of her marrying the curate at Bothal. The man kept putting it off—he must find a living of his own, he couldn't support a wife yet—and Alice showed no great signs of impatience. She and Juliana seemed quite content to live indefinitely at the Red House, supported by whatever income he and Elizabeth could scrape together from the estate. John Addison did not begrudge it them for a moment. He felt protective of them all. They were a family of women. By default, he had become the head of the family, and it pleased him very well. He had the greatest affection for them all, but in particular for the twins. They seemed to him like two lovely flowers coming into bloom—their skin so smooth and creamy, their lips rosy, their hair bright, both of them so slender and graceful. They were unspoilt and innocent, always laughing, always teasing, till Elizabeth called them to order. Then they would be so sober and respectful that he could not resist a wink at them, if only to watch the smiles trying to break back.

What would old William Cresswell say if he could see me now, he sometimes wondered. He remembered the visits of his youth to Cresswell Hall, when the girls were children lined up on benches in their pinafores and pigtails, when Juliana would jump for joy to see him and cry out for sugar plums. He was no more than an apprentice then, a smuggler's hand, dreaming of making his fortune. Well, so he had. And now, he was sitting here in William Cresswell's seat, head of the family.

He bent his head back to his plate and finished off his meal. When all the eating was done, he sat back in his chair.

"Well then," he said. "I received a letter this morning. You can guess who it might be from."

At once Fanny was upright in her seat. "Is it from Frank?"

"You have guessed first time! It is. And here's the news. Captain Frank Easterby is taking pity on me, lost as I am in the company of women. He means to pay us a visit."

At once there were cries and exclamations. John Addison held up his hand.

"He will be here in a week, so you have time to make all the plans you want for his entertainment."

* * *

When Cresswell Hall became empty, the steward had been unable to find a gentleman willing to tenant it and had resorted to making it a kind of rooming house for labourers' families. It would be the ruin of the house—it would have to be put to rights when Fanny and Frank were married—but with so much else to see to, Elizabeth had decided to let it be for the time.

But she had given notice to the tenants living in the old Tower. She could not bear the thought of strangers using it. She had the door between the Tower and the house sealed up, so that she and the family could use the Tower whenever they wished. It had been cleaned out and fresh hangings put on the walls, a table, some chairs. It was too cold to go there in the winter, but in the summer, when she came up to the Red House with the girls, she would walk over to Cresswell on her own. She liked to climb up the stone spirals of the staircase, linger in the room where her grandparents had lived, go back into the office and sit again at the table where she had spent so many hours with her father, staring out of the narrow window, wondering if she would ever marry. Last of all she would climb out onto the roof and stand looking down at the bay, at the slow-moving lines of surf, and search for an extra gleam of whiteness along the shore.

As soon as the news of Frank's visit was announced, Fanny, Kitty and Grace had started planning a special visit to the Tower with an impromptu rendering of the old story of the White Lady. Elizabeth was still taken by surprise by their liveliness. They were forever writing songs and poems, making up plays and charades, dressing up in costumes made from old cast-offs. Their cousin Grace could play the fiddle and was their always-willing accomplice. Had she and her sisters ever done such things, Elizabeth wondered. She could remember nothing like this. It was the Dyer heritage, she thought. Poor Mrs Dyer could hardly be called artistic, but the Reverend certainly had a poetical look.

Fanny and Kitty were writing a ballad, or a play, it seemed to change very often. It was to be performed at the Tower and would tell the story of the White Lady and her lost lover.

"It is very Gothic," Kitty declared, when asked about their writing. "The Tower will make a perfect setting."

It seemed to require a great deal of practice. Cousin Grace came over from the Grange every day, and all week long the girls asked to be excused from their usual tasks. Elizabeth might not have relented but as usual John Addison took their part. He was rewarded with a part in the play.

"You shall be her wicked brother, Uncle John. You will come in at the end of the story and stab the prince to death."

"Must I do it with a sword?" he inquired. "Or will a dagger suffice?"

"Oh, we must not have a real sword! A stick will do very well."

* * *

On the third day of Frank's visit the sun was up at breakfast time and the sky was cloudless. It was declared the day for the outing. Frank would ride over to Cresswell with the young ladies, and Uncle John and all the aunts would come in the carriage to be an audience and to bring the picnic. Although Aunt Alice wished to come, she was inclined to disapprove on behalf of her absent curate.

"Do you think it quite proper to countenance such entertainments? Gerald believes that play-acting encourages loose morals in the young."

"I am afraid they are so far gone, Alice, that it is quite beyond me to restrain them," said John.

Elizabeth repressed a smile. Even Catherine had been persuaded to come, to see Grace perform her part. Only Bridget and Harry were missing.

* * *

Frank and the girls were already at the Tower when the carriage arrived. Kitty ran over to greet them.

"We have shown Frank the Tower, and he knows what his part is to be. We are all ready; you have just to make yourselves comfortable."

The coachman brought rugs and cushions for the audience and laid them out on the grass in front of the Tower. When they were settled Kitty stepped forward and announced:

"This is the tale of the Tragedy of the Tower, told in a ballad in the style of former times."

She took up her sheet and started to declaim:

> Oh rocky shore,
> oh fearsome cliffs,
> what peril you foretell,
> no ship however strong or fair
> can 'scape your dreadful swell.

"Louder!" called out John. "I can scarcely hear you."

Kitty favoured him with a dark look and beckoned cousin Grace to help her. They repeated the verse and the audience clapped encouragingly. The ballad continued—the storm blew fierce, the ship was wrecked, and the prince half drowned. Frank obligingly staggered from the woods and fell in front of the Tower. Fanny ran from the Tower to his aid and Kitty joined her to sing a song in praise of love, accompanied by Grace on the fiddle.

The familiar story unfolded poetically—the prince was restored to health; he swore his undying love and promised his return:

> "My dearest love, I must be gone,
> home to my native land,
> but I swear I will return again,
> with gold to claim your hand."

Fanny ran up and stood on top of the Tower, scanning the bay, waiting impatiently for his return. Kitty continued:

> At last his sail came into view,
> with joy her heart o'erflowed,
> the kindly waves bore him to shore,
> with treasure safely stowed.

Elizabeth hardly heard the words. A sensation arose in her—out here, in the sunshine, with all the merriment of the day and with her family around her—that the ghostly spirit itself was somehow present with them. With her. She could see nothing—no pale glimmer against the dark stone of the Tower, no movement in the air—but it was palpable to her. All at once she found herself abstracted from what was going on, as if she were seeing the charade from far away. There was none of her usual sense of joy or consolation in the spirit's presence. Instead Elizabeth was affected with such a lowering of her spirits that tears stood in her eyes. What was happening to her? What did the spirit mean to tell her, if indeed it were her?

The play rolled onwards. Frank came marching on again, returned from his country to claim his bride. Fanny was hauled away by her wicked brother and locked in the Tower. She ran to the top to call out a warning to her lover, but too late. John Addison set upon Frank with his stick and felled him to the ground with many blows. Fanny gave a dreadful shriek from the top of the Tower and made to throw herself off it.

"I cannot guarantee to catch you!" shouted John, only half in jest.

But she disappeared inside; Kitty and cousin Grace held up a blanket before the front door to screen her from view, and then she was discovered lying dead beside her lover. Frank however, finding her beside him, sat up, took her in his arms and kissed her.

"Oh no!" cried Kitty. "You must not revive! You are to be dead, for we have still to sing the lament!"

Frank was rather slow to obey her commands, but he eventually relinquished his beloved and expired once more. Kitty and cousin Grace stepped forward beside them and sang an affecting lament for their tragic deaths. Then the blanket was brought out once more—there was a short interlude—and very soon Fanny reappeared at the top of the Tower, entirely clad in a white sheet to represent the ghost. She waved her arms, pointed to the seashore, and made many eloquent gestures towards the corpse of her lost lover.

Elizabeth saw nothing of it. She was no longer conscious of the spirit but of the dark shadow of the Tower. It seemed to loom closer and closer to her till she felt it would engulf her entirely. John, she thought, clutching at shadows. Where is he gone? She looked around her—tried to rise to her feet to go and look for him—but she could not move. A kind of desperation afflicted her. At last she managed to pull herself half upright—staggered sideways—and then suddenly she was falling, down and down, as if from a great height. She felt herself a child again, toppling down the staircase of the Tower, but this time no kind hands stayed her. She fell headlong into darkness.

In front of her the players came forward to take their bow and the audience clapped and laughed, until suddenly Kitty cried out and pointed, "Uncle John! Oh look! Aunt Elizabeth has fainted quite away!"

CHAPTER 40

New Mulgrave Hall

September 1786

By the time the Addisons returned to Whitby with Fanny two months later Elizabeth was quite recovered from the fainting fit that had afflicted her during the picnic. It was a kind of sunstroke, the doctor said, and certainly when she had rested for a day or two at the Red House she seemed quite recovered. Only Fanny wondered at it. Aunt Elizabeth had grown up in the Tower—she was the one who had told them the story of the White Lady—she had even said, once, that she looked on the spirit as her protector. Had their play-acting stirred up some ghostly echoes in the Tower that only Aunt Elizabeth had been aware of? Was there more truth in the old legend than she had allowed? After Frank left, she went once or twice to the Tower on her own, to see if she might discern some otherworldly intimations. But it remained stubbornly stony, the sky an ordinary blue, and only the chill dampness of the interior provided any atmosphere.

For her part Elizabeth believed the doctor was right. She had sat too long in the sun, that was all. She would think no more about it. She did not mention to anyone that she woke still in the night with the same sense of dread she had known that afternoon, that it gripped so tight about her throat that she would have to get up suddenly from bed to walk along the corridor. When she came back, she would lie close to John, listening to the hoarse rhythmic snuffle of his breath, feeling the slight sweat on his body close against her own till she was calmed by his substantial presence. What was it that she feared?

On their return to Whitby they discovered an invitation card awaiting them that put all such thoughts from her mind. It was elegantly penned in black ink.

> *The Right Honourable The Lord Mulgrave begs leave to inform Mrs Addison that he is presently in residence at New Mulgrave Hall in the company of Miss Cholmley and Lady Cholmley and begs Mrs Addison and Miss Cresswell to do them the honour of a visit on a day of their convenience.*

Mrs Addison lost no time in despatching a response, hoping that it might not be too late to take advantage of Lord Mulgrave's kind invitation and announcing they would be delighted to call on the following Wednesday.

Both she and Fanny were up early, fretting over their dressing, with Susan running to and fro between them.

"It will not do, Fanny," Elizabeth said, looking at the light muslin gown her niece had chosen. "It is September! You will be chilled to the bone if we walk outdoors."

But Fanny just smiled at her. "I have a shawl, Aunt. And you know I do not feel the cold."

Elizabeth sighed. What had happened to the biddable girl who had come to them from the Dyers? What could she say? Fanny was seventeen now. In a year's time she would be a married woman with a household of her own. Elizabeth shrugged and went out to the carriage, turning her thoughts to the visit.

She had seen the plans for the new building last year. There would be two new wings added to the south and north, and the interior of the house was to be remodelled entirely—"to make it more suitable for family life", Constantine had declared. It had puzzled Elizabeth to understand how a new perspective ceiling in the entrance hall with two ornate antechambers might contribute to family life, but she had held her tongue.

But the plans had not prepared her for what awaited them. When they got out of the carriage, she hardly recognized what she saw. The new south wing was complete already, and the north wing half-built. The great extent of the new buildings, the pale stone and the pedimented frontage produced an effect more striking than she could have imagined. The north wing was still covered with scaffolds thronged with workmen, hauling lurching baskets of stone upwards on pulleys, boys carrying buckets of mortar to and fro, masons sliding the stones seamlessly against one another. She stood and stared, Fanny beside her, trying to take it all in.

Then Constantine was coming towards them from the front door, smiling, hands outstretched to them.

"Mrs Addison! Miss Cresswell! How good of you to visit us! Anne Elizabeth will be so delighted to make your acquaintance!"

Then, glancing at Elizabeth's face, he added, "We have made great advances since your last visit! How do you like it?"

"I am still in amazement! I would scarcely have known that I was at Mulgrave Hall. What a transformation you have brought about!"

"There is still much to do, but I own myself pleased with what has been accomplished. We are very fortunate in the masons and the craftsmen—such able men—I am astonished at their skill."

Elizabeth thought for a moment of her father, remembering his endless struggle with the wayward builders of Cresswell Hall. He had dismissed his architect, she remembered. She asked, "Does Mr Soane oversee the works on your behalf?"

"He does. He cannot always be with us, but his supervisor is very well apprised of our wishes."

He turned to Fanny.

"Miss Cresswell, I am neglecting you. Let me take you inside. Anne Elizabeth is waiting for us."

Elizabeth was half-relieved to find the drawing room unchanged. Standing by the window waiting for them was a young woman. Elizabeth knew her to be sixteen, but it would have been impossible to judge her age, powdered and painted as she was, with her brown hair elaborately dressed. Her stays were tightly drawn to force a slender and statuesque pose on her body, which was adorned with a silk gown elaborately interstitched with lace. Elizabeth felt a moment of anxiety for Fanny—Miss Cholmley was so haughty in her demeanour—but Fanny stepped forward directly to make her greetings. Then it was Elizabeth's turn.

"Mrs Addison was a great friend to my mother," Constantine said, "and she has been kind enough to take an interest in our plans for the house."

"Oh! It is very inconvenient, Mrs Addison. The workmen are forever round the house and one can scarcely get any rest. And I never saw so much dust in all my life!"

"I'm sure the inconvenience will be soon forgotten when you are able to enjoy your new home. Is it your first visit to the Hall?"

"It is. I fear the sea air is too damp for my mother. She is quite indisposed."

Constantine interposed.

"My dear, perhaps you might care to show Miss Cresswell the gardens? Or such parts of the house that are suitable for visitors."

"Oh! Well if you should like it, Miss Cresswell?"

"I would like it very well, thank you."

"I must have another wrapper, Constantine. I do not mean to take my mother's cold."

Constantine went from the room and returned with a shawl, placing it around her shoulders. She looked up at him and smiled, suddenly coquettish. Then with a rustle of her skirts she was out of the door, with Fanny at her heels.

Elizabeth glanced at Constantine. His expression was composed.

"How charming your niece is become!" he said. "I am happy for Anne Elizabeth to have some company of her own age. She is missing her friends in London."

But she has you for company, thought Elizabeth.

"I confess that I have sent them off together so that I may show you my new library. Anne Elizabeth is quite tired of it already, but I believe it will be of interest to you."

The library was in the completed south wing. It was a high room, the ceiling decorated with plaster motifs of flowers and leaves and two walls lined with bookcases filled with volumes. The other walls were hung with pictures of his ships and scenes from his voyages to the Arctic and Newfoundland, with prints of plants and birds, with framed charts and, in front of them, display cabinets holding navigation and scientific instruments. She felt again the excitement that had filled her all those years ago, when she had first met with Joseph Banks and Constantine.

"It is a treasure house! How wonderful a collection you have made! I hardly know where to begin!"

"I have lately received a collection of prints from my friend Mr Banks—do you remember him?"

"Indeed I do."

"He has become a scientific advisor to the colony in Australia and receives many extraordinary records of the flora and fauna of that country. Quite unlike anything we might see in Europe. This shrub, for example—it bears his name now, Banksia. It is quite unique to that country."

They stood together before the display table, going through print after print. He turned to one of the display cases.

"This may interest you too. It is a timepiece from the *Racehorse*—a chronometer as they call them now. At that time their use was doubted, but now the worthy Mr Harrison has received his prize and every shipmaster is eager to possess one."

Elizabeth bent over the watch, admiring the elegant crafting of it.

"It is wonderful that so small a device may prevent great loss of life."

"Indeed. I remark upon it because Harry Parker, your brother-in-law, is newly appointed Admiralty secretary to the Board of Longitude. Had you heard of it?"

"I did. And I heard that it was on your recommendation."

"Truly, Harry needs no recommendation. He is so diligent and obliging. If anyone can keep the peace between Mr Maskelyne and his lunar distances and the clockmakers, it will be him."

An hour later they were still absorbed, when a maid came to tell Lord Mulgrave that the two young ladies were in the drawing room and desired his company.

"We must go and drink chocolate," he said. "I have detained you far too long."

* * *

When the visit was over and Elizabeth and Fanny were back in the carriage, Elizabeth looked at her niece.

"I'm sorry we kept you. You must have been half-frozen out in the garden."

Fanny laughed.

"We didn't stay out there very long. Miss Cholmley took me to her dressing room to show off all her gowns to me. So I have seen very little of the garden, or the house either."

"Did she speak of Lord Mulgrave?"

"Yes, a great deal. She believes he is too serious, that he should go less to Parliament and all the rest. She is quite discontented with all his London engagements and means to have him attend on her more frequently when they are married."

The carriage rolled out of the great gates of the hall and started on the descent into Sandsend. Fanny looked at her aunt.

"Do you know, Aunt? She makes a great show of her discontent, but I believe she is afraid. Lord Mulgrave is so very much older than her. Much older than Frank. And he is so very distinguished."

Elizabeth was too surprised to answer for a moment. At last she said, "Well, Fanny. Maybe you are right."

How unexpected Fanny was, she thought.

* * *

When they returned to St Hilda's Terrace, Elizabeth looked through the window of the carriage towards the mews. She caught sight of John, standing alone, leaning against the wall at the back door. He looked strangely stiff and haggard. What was he doing? Why was he standing there? A swift pang of dread went through her, as if she were caught in one of her night terrors. She shook it away before Fanny could see it.

"Why, there is Uncle John!" said Fanny. "He must be waiting to hear the news."

But when they got down from the carriage John went and spoke directly to the coachman without greeting them, telling the man to change the horses. Only when he was done did he turn towards them, his face unsmiling.

"What's the matter?" she asked.

"It is Francis Easterby. He is sick. Very sick. A man came from Skinningrove with the news. I must have the carriage directly."

"Oh, Uncle!" said Fanny. "I will come with you."

"No, my dear. I'll go alone. Keep your aunt company for me."

He turned away and as soon as the horses were changed, he was gone. As she and Fanny turned into the house, Elizabeth found herself suddenly cold and pulled her shawl around her.

"Oh, Fanny!" she said. "This is sad news indeed. I suppose it is too soon for Frank to know that his father is unwell."

"Shall I write to him, do you think?"

"Better wait till Uncle John returns and we know better how Mr Easterby is."

It was only later that she thought, why did he wait for us? Why did he not take a horse and ride to Skinningrove? Why did he want the carriage? She reminded herself: he is getting old, that's all.

Certainly, when he returned home two days later, he seemed exhausted. He hauled himself up the stairs on the banister and sat heavily down on the chair in his office.

"Yes, I'm tired, though I have done nothing but sit in a carriage. It has quite worn me out. I will take some brandy."

For the first time she wondered, is it quite good for him? But she said nothing and fetched him the drink. When he was settled, he told her the news.

"It is his heart, the doctors say. He collapsed in the garden—he said the pain in his chest near enough crushed the life out of him. But he came round. The doctors say he is improving, though he looks like a cadaver. He can hardly shift himself from his chair and they are at him dawn to dusk. 'You must rest, Mr Easterby. Take it slowly, Mr Easterby. Eat up your gruel, Mr Easterby.' And there he sits, pale as a sheet, doing their bidding." He shook his head.

"What a business. It gave me quite a shock to see him, Lizzie. Francis and I grew up as close as brothers. And now he is sixty years old and death has been knocking at his door. Please God he rallies. He must see Frank and Fanny wed."

He took her hand and held it for a moment close to his heart, staring at her. Then he gulped down the brandy and held out his glass for more.

CHAPTER 41

Bedford Square, London

October 1786

Was it the shock of Francis Easterby's illness that started it? It seemed fanciful, yet there was so strong a bond between them that she half believed it.

The first signs of it were there in Whitby, but it was not till they returned to London for the winter that it was clear. At first it was fatigue. He was constantly complaining of how tired he was, that he must go to bed sooner. He would come home at noon and lie down. She couldn't comprehend it. John was never tired. He was always active, always doing. Of course he was getting older, he would soon be sixty, but the fatigue seemed to come upon him suddenly. It was not the gradual decline of old age.

At table he sent his food away half-eaten.

"It is no use," he would say. "I cannot stomach it. I feel I have lost my sea-legs and am ready to puke."

She had Cook prepare plain broths and junket for him. If he would eat them, he was better for them, she thought, but he was stubborn. Meat was what a man ate, in his view. Even if could not swallow it.

When one of the Mulgraves came to visit, Augustus or Edmund or Charles, he would have a fine dinner set for them and drink more heavily than usual to try and make himself a jovial host. The next day he would be far worse, complaining of pains in his belly.

He started to wake in the night with strange fevers that would make him burning hot one moment, then suddenly racked with shivering and cold. She put covers on him—took them off again—fetched him cold water one minute, a hot drink the next. One morning she sat up in bed.

"You must have the doctor, John."

He didn't argue.

The man spent two hours with him, taking urine and blood and writing down several pages of notes. Elizabeth waited for him in the hall and took him into the drawing room before he left. He looked at her for a few moments.

"I fear it is his liver, Mrs Addison. It may be damaged. If you look at his eyes and skin, you may see that he has some jaundice."

"His liver? He is tired because of his liver?"

"It is one of the symptoms, Mrs Addison. Loss of appetite, nausea, tiredness, fever—all these things may occur, and others too."

"What do you mean to do?"

"The cure must be in his hands. He must stop drinking altogether. The damage is caused by alcohol. If he stops now, he may recover somewhat. He must have plain but nourishing food to build his constitution and plenty of rest. Nothing that will strain his nerves unduly."

Elizabeth's mind refused to take in the words she was hearing. This could not be. John could not be sick. She tried to grasp what the man was telling her.

"He may recover somewhat?"

"Yes. I cannot tell how far it is advanced at present; I will need to visit regularly for a few weeks."

He nodded gravely to conclude the interview and turned to go.

"Remember," he said. "It is in his own hands. No brandy, no spirits. Nor wine."

After he had gone, she stood quite still in the hall, trying to collect herself. The so-familiar dread gripped her so that she could not move or breathe. Darkness seemed to gather at the edges of the room, closing in towards her. Was it this the spirit had warned her of? What should she do? What was she to say to John?

He was still sitting on the side of the bed, staring out of the window. She went over to him and dropped down onto her knees beside him.

"I'm a sick man, Lizzie."

"It may not be so bad. He said he couldn't tell just yet."

"I've kept out of the hands of doctors all my life. I don't mean to have him hanging round me measuring every drop of urine that I pee."

"You must take heed of what he tells you, John."

He didn't answer her. Could he do it, she wondered. She could not imagine her husband abstinent.

* * *

So it began.

His first preoccupation was his will. He started making regular visits to the Inns of Court. He summoned Harry Parker and the Mulgraves to help him—not one only, but Charles, Henry, Edmund and Augustus, whenever they were in town and he could avail himself of their services. Constantine, he seemed to acknowledge, was too occupied. He meant to set up a Trust, he told her, that would contain all his properties and effects. It appeared to be extraordinarily complicated and he would explain nothing to her.

"You have nothing to worry about," he liked to tell her. "You will be taken care of."

"I don't want to be taken care of. I want you to get better. I wish you would think more about what your doctor tells you and less about what your lawyer puts into your head."

It seemed to her that he had become set upon dying, that if he would but take heed of the physician's advice, all might be well. But she did not want to create discord between them.

Soon abstinence was forced upon him. A single glass of brandy made him instantly unwell, so that he was compelled to withdraw from the table. After a few hours he would start to shake. He accepted, at last, that he must stop. Must stop altogether.

Elizabeth was hopeful then. She watched his eyes, his skin, to see if they would lose their yellow tinge. She tried to cheer his spirits with news and stories, to find delicacies to tempt his appetite again. But he was listless and irritable.

One day Frank came to visit and the two men were closeted together for a long time in John Addison's office. Afterwards she found him in better spirits.

"I shall go to Whitby. Frank wants me to see to a few things before the winter sets in. And he wants me to keep company with his father. He's worried about him."

She felt immediate gratitude to Frank. He had found reasons for John to leave London. Had given him a purpose.

"Very well," she said. "Should you like Fanny and I to come with you? We can stay with you a few weeks in Whitby. Perhaps we could all go to the Red House for Christmas."

"Yes. Yes, come with me. Why not?"

*   *   *

Halfway through the journey north she regretted the decision, regretted that they had ever set out, and wished with all her heart they had stayed in London. The movement of the carriage upset him terribly. He suffered stabbing pains in his back that made every rut in the road a torment. He was nauseous and frequently needed to have the carriage stopped in order to relieve himself. She dosed him with laudanum, but the effect was so strong she feared she had killed him; he lay slumped across the seat with glassy eyes, unable to move or speak. Fanny understood for the first time that her uncle was very sick. All her customary liveliness deserted her. She sat with him—tried to give him sips of water—wiped his head, but he was hardly able to recognize her. After one overnight stop at a coaching inn, when he woke more coherent than before, Elizabeth said to him, "Should you rather return to London? We have more than half the journey still."

But he shook his head.

"Whitby," he said. "I long for sea air." She took his hand then and held it close to her.

At last they got there. He lay in bed for days, recovering, and for all the bitter weather of November would have the window open and the sea air blowing in.

"I am a seaman, after all," he said to her. "All I need is salt air and a smell of the sea, and I will be better."

And indeed, he managed to rally, to have his man dress him in the morning and go down with him to the harbour, though he could scarcely drag himself back up the hill. The doctor came to see him very often with medications for him and encouraged her.

"He is a strong man, Mrs Addison. We cannot get him back to quite his old self, but I believe we are seeing an improvement."

But when December came and she asked the doctor, might he travel to Northumberland for Christmas, there was a decided refusal.

"No, no. There must be no more travelling at all. Rest is the thing. He must live quietly till he regains his strength."

So it was decided that she and Fanny would go to the Red House for Christmas without him. Fanny had spent long enough in an invalid household, Elizabeth thought, and John Addison was content to spend Christmas at Skinningrove with Francis Easterby.

After Christmas a spell of bitter weather and heavy snowfall made the roads impassable, so that January was almost over when she set out again for Whitby. She found John eager to see her.

"How long you have been! I can hardly manage without you."

"I have come back as soon as I could. The roads were dreadful. Has Betty not taken care of you?"

"She does well enough, but she doesn't have your touch." He stared at her reproachfully. "I need my wife about me."

He looked grey and old. He is out of spirits, she thought. Or had he worsened in her absence? She rallied herself to make extra efforts to keep him warm and comfortable, to entertain him with tales of the young people and the Christmas charades, to read him the letters she had brought from Fanny and Kitty. But she had not been back in Whitby above a week when news came from Skinningrove.

The man said only that he had a message for Mr Addison, so she took him straight into the drawing room where John was drowsing. He woke with a start when the man entered.

"Mr Addison, sir. I am sent from Skinningrove with a message for you."

"What is it?"

"It is Mr Easterby, sir. He has died, just last night. He fell all of a sudden when he got up from his chair after dinner. There was nothing the doctor could do to help him. He was dead at once."

Horrified, Elizabeth wanted to seize the man, to hush him at once, to have him tell only herself so that she might consider how to break it to John. But it was out before she could stop him.

John listened without expression. When the message was done, there was a long silence in the room. The manservant looked at Elizabeth and she nodded for him to leave. When he was gone John hauled himself upright and left the room without a word. He went to his office and shut the door. Hour after hour went by. At dinner time she told the maid to take some soup to him, but he turned her away. He refused lights. At last she took up a lamp and went in to him. The room was so dark she could hardly make him out. Then he saw he was in a chair, slumped forward over his desk. There was a foul smell in the room. She took the lamp over and held it above him. She saw that there was a pool of black bile by his face. She became conscious of a slow dripping sound as it spilled over onto the floor. Frozen with fear, she stood quite still for a moment. Then she put her hand to his forehead. It was still warm. She found his hand, felt the wrist; the pulse was beating still.

"John," she said. He didn't move. She turned away, out of the room, down to the kitchen and called out for the maid, for John's man, to bring lights, to bring water, to come, come quickly, now!

They got him moved at last, up to the bedroom and into bed. She sat with him all night, coaxing him to drink a little whenever he stirred. When the late January dawn brought some light into the room he woke and tried to sit up.

"It is gone first watch," he said. "Where is Mr Ainsley?"

"You are dreaming, John," she said, but he looked past her unseeing.

* * *

Fanny's birthday, which was to have been her wedding day, came and went. With Frank's father dead and John mortally ill, there could be no talk of weddings. For two more months John lay on his sickbed, his legs and belly horribly swollen, unable to eat or drink. He was constantly confused, as if his mind had refused to accept the news of Francis' death. Every day was a torment to Elizabeth, helpless to relieve his suffering. Towards the end of April a new fever took him, worse than before; his breathing grew laboured and the restlessness left him.

"It is pneumonia," the doctor told her. "It will not be long now."

He slipped away in the night without her knowing and without a farewell. She was so exhausted that she felt nothing at first. And then, a kind of relief that it was done. The priest came and gave last rites, although he was already gone. She prayed with the priest and begged God that since he had suffered so very greatly in his dying that he might be spared the pains of purgatory, that his sins be already forgiven. How else could you make sense of such suffering? Why had he had to endure such torments? She felt as if half her heart had been burned away, that she had no feelings left, no pity or sorrow or regret, but only emptiness. What did people mean when they counselled fortitude? She had no faith or courage left, only numbness.

Of course people mistook it for resignation, and praised her for it, how dignified Mrs Addison was at the funeral, how calm she was. It was meaningless to her. She felt the illusion of happiness and joy had been pulled away from under her, and beneath it was only darkness. She knew it for the same darkness of the Tower, the darkness that lay under all the innocence of life, that destroyed all hope and joy before they could be realized.

After the funeral she stayed in Whitby for some weeks, to be alone. Every day the postboy brought letters of condolence for her from London. All the Musgraves wrote, Augustus, Charles, Edmund . . . and Constantine wrote, two long pages, so kindly and delicately expressed, full of his regard and admiration for John, and his sadness and sympathy for herself. He made no mention of his wedding.

But a few weeks later the papers in the town were full of it—the marriage of the two great families of North Yorkshire, the Mulgraves and the Cholmleys, of the distinction of the bridegroom and the beauty of the bride, lately painted by Mr Gainsborough, on and on. When she read it, Elizabeth felt the last light go out of her spirit. He had married her. It was irrevocable. Why had she ever supposed it might be otherwise? Constantine and Anne Elizabeth were man and wife.

She went to her bureau and took out the letter of condolence he had sent her. She took it to the open window, read it through one more time, then tore it into pieces, letting them flutter away through the window. Why hold on to false consolation? She knew herself to be utterly alone.

PART SEVEN

1788–92

Time's Changes

CHAPTER 42

Bedford Square, London

5 May 1788

On the first anniversary of John Addison's death Elizabeth was in London, at Bedford Square. Perhaps she should have been at his graveside, but the house in Whitby with all its memories was still too raw for her.

John's will had given her unexpected freedoms. He had promised her that she would want for nothing, but she had thought that might mean a generous annuity. She knew he meant to make Frank his heir so, when the will was read, she had not understood it. There was page upon page concerning a Trust involving Edmund, Augustus, Henry and Charles Mulgrave, as well as Harry Parker. Had he left his property to them? She was bewildered. The lawyer had to explain to her that she was the beneficiary of the Trust, that John Addison had left his property in trust to her, for her use in her lifetime. Only the estate at Appleton went directly to Frank. He would have to wait till she was gone for the rest.

If Frank was disappointed, he concealed it; indeed, it seemed to come as no surprise to him. So she found herself with three houses at her disposal, several ships, and other investments to provide her an income. She could choose where she was to live, whether at Whitby, the Red House or Bedford Square. She was immensely grateful now for the ease it gave her. She preferred to be here in London, where she could be alone, but could distract herself with talks and exhibitions, with visits to her sister Bridget and her family. And, now, with visits to Fanny.

Fanny and Frank had married at the start of December, when mourning for Francis Easterby and John Addison could be said to be over. It was meant to be a quiet affair, but there was no subduing Frank's high spirits. He was overjoyed to have Fanny at last and she was radiant. Their happiness would have melted a heart of stone, Elizabeth thought and, in spite of her grief that John was not there to witness it, she could not help but be glad for them.

It had brought other, unlooked for consequences. Kitty and cousin Grace had been there, of course, as bridesmaids, and Frank's elder brother John Easterby as the groom's man. John Easterby was a quieter, more sober man than his brother. When Frank gave his speech at the wedding feast he teased his older brother, that he, Frank, had outstripped him on the way to the altar, and when was John going to delight them with a bride? It seemed that John Easterby had heeded his brother's words, or else he had fallen suddenly in love with the quiet charms of the second bridesmaid. Within weeks of his return north, he had presented himself at Woodhorn Grange to ask permission to pay his respects to cousin Grace.

Today Elizabeth had ordered up the carriage for a visit to Blackheath, to Park House. Fanny was so kind to her—so considerate of her feelings—and where else would John Addison have wanted her to be on this anniversary? Elizabeth hardly knew what she believed concerning the survival of the soul—for herself, she experienced only absence—but she prayed with all her heart that if John did continue in some way, that he might haunt Blackheath and slip disembodied through the walls and windows of Park House. He would be eager to hear more of John Easterby and Grace's courtship, but even more of another piece of news. Last time Elizabeth had visited, Fanny had whispered to her that she had suspicions—that she could not be sure—but she would see the doctor before she made any mention of it.

So although Elizabeth set out from Westminster soberly enough, the spring weather could not help but lift her spirits. After all the darkness and sorrow of the past year she felt a quickening within herself, as if, after all, life might be a possible thing, even if it were the continuance of the family rather than her own life. And when she arrived at Park House, it was impossible not to be pleased by the lovely prospect of Greenwich

Park, the great trees all newly come into leaf and the long grassy sward of the hill. Fanny came out to greet her—brought her inside to the new drawing room with its freshly painted walls and hangings and fine Turkey carpet—and they sat down together over tea.

They talked first of John Addison and Fanny asked her very kindly for her memories and stories of him, though she had heard them a score of times before. Elizabeth found it did ease her to speak of him, as if it did indeed bring him into the room to be with them, and when she felt tears coming to her eyes, Fanny saw it straight away and took her hand. When she was composed, she said, "And now, my dear Fanny. You must tell me what your news is."

"The doctor has been." Fanny paused for a moment. "I am with child, Aunt! Is it not exciting? He thinks it may be three or four months so far and I am to be quiet and not go out for a few weeks in case there is a risk of miscarriage. I cannot feel it yet—but I feel a sort of difference in my body."

Elizabeth looked at her, and indeed, her skin was very smooth and fresh and her figure a little fuller than before.

"It is wonderful news. Nothing would have delighted your Uncle John more."

"I know. I am very happy, Aunt. But I am . . . I cannot help it . . . I have not said so to Frank . . . " She broke off.

"You are what?"

"Frank told me such sad news last night. It made me so afraid. Perhaps you have heard it already? About Lord Mulgrave?"

A sudden chill gripped Elizabeth's heart.

"I have heard nothing."

"Do you remember, when we visited Mulgrave Hall two summers ago? And we met Miss Cholmley, and how very young she was?"

"I do."

"She is dead, Aunt. She died in childbirth."

"Oh God! Oh no!"

"Yes. The baby daughter lives."

Elizabeth could find no words. Fanny leaned forward to her, suddenly intense.

"It is just as it was for my mother. Like Miss Cholmley, it was her first confinement. She and my father had not been wed a year."

They were both silent.

"I cannot say this to anyone but you, Aunt, but I am so fearful. What if it should happen to me, as it did to my mother? What if I should die at my first confinement? Like Miss Cholmley. What would Frank do?"

Elizabeth rallied herself.

"You must not listen to such fears. You are very well. And you are strong—your poor mother was delicate, and then to have twins—she could not endure it. But it will be different for you. Frank will make sure that you have the best attention." She paused.

"As for Miss Cholmley . . . " she searched for words, her heart loud in her chest, trying to conceal her own agitation. "She was very young, Fanny. A full two years younger than you, scarcely seventeen. I believe it is too young; a girl may not be fully formed at that age. You must not compare yourself. Think of your Aunt Bridget, or Aunt Catherine. Their confinements passed easily enough."

Fanny clutched at her hand.

"Yes. You are right. It is silly of me."

But Elizabeth could see the fear in her eyes. She thought of her own mother's sufferings and of poor Catherine Dyer. How cruel a business it was to enter the world, as well as to leave it.

Between Fanny's fear and the shock of the news, her feelings were in turmoil. Constantine, a widower, and not a year wed! It was inconceivable. What must he be suffering? After all the months and years of preparation, of the rebuilding of the Hall, of joyful anticipation of matrimony, for it to end like this! How savage a blow Fate had dealt him.

* * *

That evening she sat at her bureau, pen in hand. To be writing a letter of condolence to Constantine, on the very anniversary of John Addison's death! Do you see it, John? she asked him. Do you see what darkness the world is made of? Pray for us, wherever you are. Pray that we find light!

CHAPTER 43

St Hilda's Terrace, Whitby

5 May 1789

The following spring it was a shock to remember that it would soon be the second anniversary of John Addison's death. This time she must go north, she decided. It had been too long since she had visited the house in Whitby. Since John's death she had had a dread of the place, of the memories it might stir up in her. But she was stronger now and it was not right for her to have neglected his grave. She would stay at St Hilda's Terrace for a few weeks on her way to the Red House. She would take Hetty, her maid, with her, and the coachman could bring his lad to share the driving and run errands in the town. There was no need to have the whole house opened up. They would use only the rooms they needed and fetch a woman up from the town to do the cooking.

Once they left the London Road, the long drive across the moors to Whitby took all morning and into the afternoon. Even on a bright May morning there was a desolation about the high moors, with a few peat-stacked cottages the only habitations. How bleak it was! The drive seemed to separate her from all the ordinary consolations of her life. She kept her gaze from the window—tried to pay attention to the novel she had with her—but the grim starkness of the moors gave the lie to its frivolity. At last, she laid down the book. It was no use to resist. She stared out of the window and endured the journey.

It was not a great deal more cheerful when they reached the house. It was so silent. So empty. She regretted she had not given orders to have it opened up for them. The coachman went up to the front door, carried the trunk inside and laid it down in the hall. She went into the parlour and stared about her. It was so familiar, and yet strange. There was a smell of musty furniture and stale air. A lone butterfly fluttered to and fro before the window. She walked over and opened it up, letting a sudden breeze into the room. She could hear the distant sounds of the town, the familiar banging and clattering from the dockyards, the cries of people in the street. At once she wanted all the windows open, to bring life back into the place, to let the wind blow through it and carry away all its memories. All of the past. She went from one room to another, drawing back curtains, opening windows. The house had slept for long enough.

Hetty fetched in provisions from the coach and set them out on the kitchen table. They sat all together, Peter the coachman and his lad, Hetty and herself, eating bread and ham and drinking beer, with Peter teasing the lad for the size of his mouthfuls and Hetty bewailing the lack of a fire set ready, and where were they to buy milk at this hour? And the dreariness of the drive began to dispel, till their arrival felt like a more hopeful adventure, and it was no longer the house she had left but another.

* * *

She would pay some visits, she decided. To John Addison's grave first of all, of course. To the Moorsoms, who she had not seen since the funeral. And to Skinningrove, to visit her dear niece, Grace, now married to John Easterby and mistress of the house.

But first, to John Addison. She went over the road to her garden to see what flowers there might be to carry to his grave. How overgrown it was! The roses had quite taken over the ground, though they were not in flower yet. But there were some narcissi still, that John had always liked. She would take those to the churchyard with her.

His grave lay in a corner shaded by trees, and she was shocked to see that already, moss had started to form at the edges of his gravestone. She would have to come back with a trowel and scrape it off. And there were dead leaves settled on the ground in front, though that could not be helped. She pushed them away with her hands and laid the narcissi in their place. Then she stood beside the grave and waited; waited to see if she would have a sense of John's presence, if she would, somehow, hear his voice or know him to be there. But she heard nothing apart from the cawing of the rooks, swaying on the branches of the overhanging tree. She felt the fresh mildness of the May morning, of the spring life moving in the ground. A life he was no longer part of.

I must begin, she thought.

"John," she said. "John, I am here. It is two years since you were gone. I pray you have found ease. You are with us, in all our hearts. I love you still." She paused. "There is very great news I have come to tell you. Fanny is delivered of a fine boy, and he is thriving. And so is she. They have named him for you. He is Addison John Easterby. How happy it would have made you! Addison John! I wish you might have seen him. But perhaps you do."

She paused, distracted by the thought of Addison John. He was, she thought, incomparably the most handsome child she had ever seen. It was a marvel to her that a slip of a girl like Fanny could have borne such a fine boy. He was six months old now, with a head of golden curls and the same sweet temper as his mother. Already she could sit him on her lap and let him play with his rattle while she sang to him or bounced him on her knee, while Fanny looked on smiling. She could never have imagined she would feel such intense love for a child.

"I feel him truly to be ours, John. He is like a grandson for us. I cannot express how much joy he has brought me."

Frank and Fanny were so kind to her. She might visit whenever she pleased, might hold him, and play with him as much as she chose. And she had been so stern a guardian to Fanny! John had always been more indulgent an uncle than she an aunt, had so much more deserved Fanny's love.

"I like to spend time in London, John. So that I may be near them. Or at the Red House, if they come to Cresswell for the summer. I do not know that I will spend time again in Whitby. I hope it will not grieve you if I sell the house. Frank has no objection."

She waited to see if he would express any displeasure, for he had always loved his Whitby house. But he said nothing.

"You will want to hear news of the girls," she said. "Kitty has taken up with a soldier. He is in the 21st Regiment of Foot. She is suddenly become an expert on military matters. He is said to be a natural son of the Duke of Hamilton, but whether he will have an estate settled on him I don't know. Of course he is very dashing and may suit Kitty very well. She will be of age before long and may make her own mind up, but she has asked my opinion. And Cousin Grace has married John Easterby! Is it not wonderful? There is a double union now between the Cresswells and the Easterbys. I shall go and see them and give you all the news when I return."

She looked around her. She felt quite at ease, here in the churchyard, talking to John, but it might seem strange to others. She stood a little straighter, bowed her head and said a prayer or two before she left.

* * *

A few days later Elizabeth took the carriage to pay a visit to Skinningrove. The carriage passed out along the coast road, down through Sandsend and past the woods surrounding New Mulgrave Hall. The Moorsoms had told her that the house had been shut up since Miss Cholmley's death, but as they drove past the entrance to the long drive, she saw the gates standing open. She let herself dwell for a moment on a fancy that Constantine might be there, that she might visit the house that held so many memories for her. But she pushed it quickly from her mind. He held important positions in government now: he was an MP and a privy counsellor and Frank had told her that he was paymaster-general of the army and navy. He was a Fellow of the Royal Society. He sat on the Board of Longitude with Harry Parker. He had no time for Mulgrave Hall. She had seen him once or twice in London when he dined at the Parkers'. He was as solicitous and kind as ever, but she could see the fatigue in his eyes. He did not speak of Anne Elizabeth. What had happened to his infant daughter, she wondered. Had the Cholmleys taken charge of her? Constantine was making himself so busy he would scarcely have time for a child.

Her niece Grace and John Easterby received her very kindly and insisted that she spend the night with them. In the evening they strolled down to the little bay beyond the house. While they watched the tide come in, John Easterby told her of his memories of his Uncle John Addison, how much they had loved their uncle's visits. And how, one night after his mother's death, the four of them, two Johns and two Francises, had vowed an oath together to preserve her memory. Elizabeth had not heard the tale before, and it moved her to tears. What a faithful uncle John Addison had been to the boys!

She returned the next morning and had hardly been home two hours before the front doorbell rang. Peter was over in the stables and she had sent Hetty down into town to buy some fish. Who could it be? A neighbour, perhaps, noticing that she was at home. She would answer it herself. She drew back the bolt and pulled open the heavy door.

Constantine was standing on the doorstep. It took her a moment to take it in.

"Lord Mulgrave!"

"Mrs Addison—you must forgive me, to call on you so unexpectedly."

"Pray come in. You must excuse me—we are here only for a short time—the house is all shut up."

"It is of no consequence, if it is inconvenient . . . "

"Oh no! I am very happy to see you. As you see, I am become both doorkeeper and housemaid, but if you are content with simple entertainment, I should like nothing more than to receive you."

She took him into the parlour, ran down to the kitchen to have the woman make some tea for them, and then forced herself to go slowly up the stairs to calm herself.

He was standing by the window.

"What a fine view of the abbey you have!"

"We have. I am often reminded of how chilly a life St Hilda must have led."

He smiled and turned back into the room. She gestured to a seat and took one herself at a proper distance for a widow entertaining a lord.

"The Moorsoms told me you were in town," he said. "I felt I must do myself the honour of visiting you. I have neglected our friendship since John died. I wish I could have supported you more in your loss."

"You have suffered as great a loss of your own," she said.

He nodded.

"This past year I fear I have been poor company for anyone, it has so oppressed my spirits. I had thought myself inured to death—shipboard life brings many dreadful sights—but this! To think of the poor creature—her suffering—and that I was powerless to help her even though I was the cause of it."

"You have no cause to blame yourself."

"And yet I do. I was impatient to be wed, but she was still so young! If I had waited . . . "

He was silent for a moment, then looked again at her.

"I remember that your brother had a like misfortune."

"He did. It was a terrible blow to him. His was the opposite case—he was scarcely nineteen, and Catherine eight years his elder.

"You have been a very true and constant guardian to his daughters," he said.

At that moment the tea was brought and the conversation paused while teacups were found and a bowl for the sugar before it could be served. It was almost as if they were picnicking, she thought; it made for a kind of ease that could not have been there in a formal visit. He took his cup and sucked at the sugar.

"I see Frank Easterby sometimes at Trinity House, and he is the proudest man in the world of his young son. He is to be Addison John, I hear."

"Yes, we are all delighted. And Frank's brother John has married my niece Grace, so there is a second union of our families. I have but lately been to Skinningrove to see them."

A sudden impulse took hold of her, to tell him something more of what was in her heart.

"While I was in London I had occasion to visit the theatre to see *A Winter's Tale*, in the adaptation by Mr Garrick. Do you know the play?"

"I don't believe I do."

"The first half of it is all darkness and tragedy. In a jealous rage the king believes his wife unfaithful with his friend. He orders her imprisonment and the casting away of their new-born babe. It is all death and heartbreak, and it seems that nothing can be redeemed at all. But the second half skips onwards several years. The castaway babe has been rescued and grows into a lovely maiden. The son of the king's friend discovers her; they fall in love. Their union reconciles the past, and all is joy and hope once more."

She took a breath. He must be wondering at her long story, but there was no turning back now.

"I have told it very poorly, but when I saw it, it struck me deeply. What wisdom Shakespeare has! And how true it seemed to me, that time finds ways to repair our suffering. Younger spirits take our place and life springs up again. My orphaned niece has married, and now little Addison John renews John's memory. Do you not think that one day you may find some such consolation in the babe Anne Elizabeth has left behind for you?"

He said nothing for a moment, gazing at her. Then he spoke.

"I believe I understand you, though it is hard to conceive now that the darkness of this time might one day be redeemed. But you are right. One should have faith in that."

He sighed deeply.

"I hardly see my daughter. She is with her grandmother."

"You are very much occupied in London, I suppose."

"I am. Too much occupied, Anne Elizabeth often told me. But I am not used to leisure."

They talked then of other matters, of the Board of Longitude and Harry Parker, and the great house in Suffolk the Parkers had bought with the Admiral's prize money, which Elizabeth had not yet seen, till the tea was drunk and Constantine rose to his feet.

"I have kept you too long, Elizabeth, when you have so much to attend to. But I mean to think more on what you said. I believe I may desire your counsel once more if you are willing."

"Of course," she said, wondering.

"I will not be at Mulgrave Hall for more than a few days now. I am come only to deal with some matters on the estate the steward needs me for and I will be away again. But I hope we may meet when you are returned to London."

CHAPTER 44

Bedford Square, London

October 1789

Elizabeth did not want for occupation that summer at the Red House. Fanny and Kitty had their twenty-first birthdays in June, marking the end of her eight-year guardianship. Fanny and Frank came up from London with the baby to stay at the Red House and celebrate the occasion. Frank had bought out Kitty's share in the estate and now she had reached her majority, he would take over the Cresswell estate from Elizabeth. He would take all the cares from her shoulders, he told her. But not yet, she soon discovered. There was so much she needed to explain to him. They spent afternoons closeted in the parlour with the estate records or riding off to visit one of the farms. He meant to put the Hall to rights; the tenants had been given notice and builders brought in to start repairs, and she must advise him on how the Hall had originally been laid out.

Meanwhile the Red House was in a constant turmoil, with all the preparations for Kitty's wedding to her Lieutenant Brown. They were to live in Morpeth, so there were constant trips to and from the house to advise Kitty on her curtains or her dining table or how the kitchen was to be set up. And there was Addison John, to be cooed over by all his great-aunts, Juliana, Alice, Catherine, Grace and Dorothy, till Elizabeth was ready to drive them all away and claim him as her sole possession. There were picnics and expeditions, evening soirees and visits to Assemblies—in short, such constant distraction and business that Elizabeth might have supposed herself to have no space in her thoughts for anything else. And yet, when she retired at last to her own room for the night, or when she found herself for a brief time alone, Constantine's visit was always in her mind. What might he want to say to her when she returned to London? Or were his words no more than a passing thought that he would have long since forgotten?

*   *   *

When at last she returned to London, the house in Bedford Square seemed empty after the constant company of the Red House. She could not forever be calling at Park House and the Parkers were still in Suffolk. She would call on other friends, she told herself. She would see what talks and concerts were proposed for the season. But for a fortnight she lived very quietly, going out only to take a stroll through Russell Square or further, to Regent's Park.

When she returned from one of these walks, the housemaid told her that Lord Mulgrave had called and had regretted that she was from home. She read the note he had left. Would Mrs Addison do him the honour of paying a visit to Harley Street the following morning?

She took the carriage, though the Mulgraves' house in Harley Street was hardly distant enough to warrant it and, when Lepell was alive, she had often walked across town to visit her. But today there was a cold breeze blowing and she had taken extra care over her dressing, to make up for her shabbiness when Constantine had called on her in Whitby. She reminded herself that she was a widow, an old woman of fifty-three, and that the agitation of her spirits was foolish. But when she arrived at the familiar house, knocked on the door and was shown inside to find Constantine waiting for her in the hall, she could not subdue them.

"Mrs Addison! Elizabeth, if I may? How good of you to come."

Here in Harley Street he was his London self, she saw, with powdered wig and an expensively tailored brocade coat. For a moment she felt intimidated at her own boldness, in presuming to come and call upon a Baron. But she looked up at his face and forgot the Baron. It was

Constantine, with his kind smile and light blue-and-hazel eyes looking at her in the quizzical way he had.

"I am happy to be here."

He took her to the drawing room with its pleasant outlook onto the gardens behind; a maid came with cake and madeira, and they settled to the visit.

"I have thought very often of your words when we last met, concerning my daughter Anne," he said. "I feel my obligation to her very keenly—to her, and to her mother. She is all that is left to me of my wife and I know that Anne Elizabeth would expect me to be a loving father—for the sake of her memory, if for no other reason." He paused.

"But I am ill-equipped for fatherhood. I have spent my life aboard ship or in society, and I have had little opportunity to learn the tender arts. I have no conception what might entertain an infant—a girl—"

"Where is she now?"

"She is at Howsham. My mother-in-law has taken charge of her. Of course, I have made every provision for her care, but I hardly see her. And when I do, she is put into my arms for a few moments till the nursemaid judges she has seen enough of me, and she is carried off again to the nursery."

He made a kind of grimace. How he suffers, Elizabeth thought. He leaned forward.

"Elizabeth, I have the greatest favour in the world to beg of you. You must not hesitate for a moment to deny me, for it is far beyond the bounds of friendship or good counsel. And if you do, I beg you will put it from your mind as soon as you leave the house."

She nodded, waiting.

"Here it is, then. I want my daughter to be part of my household. I want her to be here, with me, in this house, as Anne Elizabeth and I had planned it. But I need help."

"Yes."

"My mother-in-law knows very well that I have not the least idea of how to run a nursery. I can employ a nursemaid, but she will not be satisfied with that. It must be properly overseen if she is to relinquish her granddaughter to me." He hesitated.

"Nor is that the end of it. It is very well to have her with me, to be a father to her. But when a nursemaid brings her to me, I have no notion what to do. Should I hold her? Should I speak to her? What am I to do when she starts to cry? I am at a loss. I cannot ask a nursemaid to teach me how to be a father. And so I hand her back very quickly and get to know her no better than before."

Elizabeth understood. How different he was from John Addison! For all his wealth and consequence, there had been a part of John that was still a child. He loved to play, to tell stories, to take an infant on his knee and chant a rhyme. He always had a treat in his pocket or a silver sixpence for a forfeit. But Constantine had forgotten his childhood altogether. She remembered Lepell's words: "It is all duty, duty, duty with Constantine." He would have to learn how to play with his daughter.

"I am sure we can arrange something," she said. "Do you have a room or two set up as a nursery in the house already?"

He took a quick glance at her.

"I will show you."

They climbed the stairs to the top of the house, and there it was, the empty nursery, with its cradle that Anne might already have outgrown, the nurse's rocking chair, the nursery table and highchair, the dolls waiting on the dresser, the fire set in the grate. Elizabeth felt tears rising to her eyes. The room spoke so eloquently of abandoned hope and expectation. But she made herself look carefully to take in what was there and what might be needed.

"Where will the nursemaid sleep?" she asked.

He showed her an adjoining chamber, with a neatly made bed and chest. It was all well done, all suitable. Had Anne Elizabeth seen to it, she wondered. Or her mother? She did not ask.

When they were downstairs again, she was businesslike.

"I cannot be here every day," she said. "I must be to Blackheath every week, and I have other obligations to see to. But if I can be here three or four times a week, I believe it will answer, and perhaps I may stay sometimes if the need arises—if Anne is ill or suchlike. It will all depend upon securing an excellent nursemaid. Can the nursemaid from Howsham come with her or must we look about us? It would be better still if there is a second—one of the housemaids, perhaps, who can help out."

"I will make enquiries."

"If you appoint yourself certain evenings where you will take no invitations to dine abroad, that you may spend with Anne, I will arrange to be in attendance so the nursemaid will not be required. And many families keep some part of Sunday for domestic use."

He looked at her and she saw there was both relief and amusement in his eyes. He smiled at her and gave a little bow.

"I am at your command, Mrs Addison."

CHAPTER 45

Harley Street, London

November 1789

The nursemaid brought the baby down to the drawing room, fresh and clean in a white dress. With a glance at Constantine she gave her to Elizabeth.

"There you are, ma'am. I will be upstairs should you need me."

Elizabeth put the baby on her shoulder and took a turn or two about the room, letting little Anne get used to her new surroundings. She showed her the window and pointed to the oak tree outside. She walked past the pictures and let her peep in the mirror. Constantine stood by the mantelpiece and watched them. Elizabeth felt the soft weight of the baby on her chest and breathed in the soapy, milky smell of her. When they were grown familiar with each other, she sat down on the sofa and put Anne on her knee so they could look at each other. She was a bright little thing, Elizabeth decided. There was no whingeing for her nursemaid or sudden bashfulness. She beckoned to Constantine to come and sit beside them.

With the baby on her knee, face to face, holding both tiny hands in hers, Elizabeth sang her a dandling song, bouncing her gently up and down to the rhythm of the song:

> Gee up Neddy to the fair
> What shall we have when we get there
> A halfpenny bun and a glass of wine,
> Gee up Neddy, home it's time.

The infant smiled and laughed. When it was done, she held out her arms for more. Elizabeth picked her up and put her on Constantine's knee.

"Now you."

Uncertain, he positioned Anne on his knee and jiggled her about awkwardly. She gave a little pout and looked back at Elizabeth.

"You must do it with the song. I will sing it with you."

Together they sang

> Gee up Neddy . . .

The rhythm of the song overcame his awkwardness and soon Anne was trotting along happily enough on her father's knee.

"Once more!" Elizabeth said.

And now Constantine grew confident and the trot broke into a canter, bouncing higher and higher. The little girl looked straight at her daddy and crowed with delight. At the end of the song he took her in his arms, stood up and swung her up above his head, father and daughter laughing to each other. At last she came down. Constantine, breathless, looked at Elizabeth.

"What now?"

"We had better not make her too excited. Let us take her downstairs and put on her coat. We can take a little stroll around the park and feed the pigeons."

Down the stairs they went. She gave him Anne's coat and let him struggle with the baby's flailing arms till a little wail started and she judged it time to rescue him. But once Anne was ready, Elizabeth declared he must carry her, she was far too heavy for Aunt Elizabeth, and out they went into the London dusk.

* * *

As the weeks went by, the easy playfulness of the nursery brought about a new intimacy between Elizabeth and Constantine. They watched Anne's first steps—taught her to say da-da and endured her tantrums. The winter afternoons and evenings they spent together became comfortable and familiar. When Constantine walked into the nursery, his daughter gave a cry of delight and held her arms out to him. He learned to keep little treats in his pocket, to plan little surprises for her, to bring a little toy or a book for her. Sometimes they would do nothing more than sit together before a great fire in the drawing room, making toast and roasting chestnuts.

Sometimes, as Elizabeth sat with the baby on her lap, rocking and singing to her, she felt Constantine's eyes upon her. She knew he wanted her. Why not, she thought, singing to the baby. Both of them were lost and heartsore. Why should they not console each other?

One evening, when Constantine was standing at the mantelpiece and she was sitting and singing to Anne, she felt his gaze upon her once again. This time she got up and set Anne down on the carpet with her doll. She went and stood in front of him without speaking and looked at him directly, till she was aware of nothing but his gaze and the beating of her heart.

"Elizabeth," he said. "You are . . . "

He stopped—took her hand—held it for a moment to his lips. She felt as if she might stop breathing altogether. Then he took her in his arms and kissed her.

*   *   *

She knew she could expect nothing of him. If he were to marry again, it would be for duty, for the sake of an heir. It would be another dynastic match, and she was neither titled nor of childbearing age. If he did marry, she would have to suffer again a thousand times worse than the first time. But for now, she would not think of that. It was enough, to snatch from Fate a moment of perfect happiness. She had neither looked for it nor expected it. She knew the darkness was still there, the shadows lapping at the edge of this moment of radiance. But for now, it was at bay.

She started, sometimes, to stay overnight in Harley Street. The coachman knew to call for her early in the morning, without presuming to comment on Mrs Addison's arrangements. The little girl sometimes had night fears, Elizabeth mentioned, and she wished to be near the nursery to soothe her.

In Lord Mulgrave's intimate circle, which included his four brothers, it was understood that Mrs Addison had become a kind of family companion to enable Constantine to have his daughter's company. Perhaps out of respect for the eminence the Baron enjoyed in public life, no one troubled to enquire too closely as to the exact nature of his relationship with Mrs Addison. Constantine and Elizabeth were, in turn, discreet and seldom ventured forth into society without Anne's company to confer respectability. Besides, Constantine had so many demands upon his time that his domestic life was often curtailed. Elizabeth understood very well why his wife might have grown impatient with his many obligations.

Fanny, however, was a more astute observer.

"How well you are looking, Aunt Elizabeth!" she said. "I declare you are growing younger by the day! You are becoming a second mother to baby Anne. Addison John and I are growing jealous."

"You have no need. I am fond of Anne, but she cannot hold a candle to Addison John, I assure you. Why, she is six months older than him, but already he is as advanced as she. You know he will always be first in my affections."

Fanny laughed.

"I didn't truly doubt it, Aunt. It is for the sake of her father, I suppose, that you are helping out. I met him only once on our visit to Mulgrave Hall, but Frank tells me he is a very amiable gentleman."

To her chagrin Elizabeth felt a blush coming to her cheeks.

"I was very fond of his mother," she said. "She was very kind to me. I do it for her sake."

CHAPTER 46

Harley Street, London

April 1790

The first shadow over her happiness fell in the spring. Plans were laid for the summer; Elizabeth would go to the Red House to spend time with her family and baby Anne would go to Howsham, to her grandmother. Constantine would stay in London till July. Then he would travel north, pick up his daughter and meet with Elizabeth at New Mulgrave Hall. The three of them would stay at the Hall for the whole of July and August. It would be the first time since Anne Elizabeth's death that Constantine would stay properly in the house. The first time his little daughter would be there. How Anne would love it! The freedom of the great house, the gardens and all the countryside around, the sea that she had never seen and the shore. Elizabeth looked forward to it on her own behalf as well. The prospect of staying at New Mulgrave Hall with Constantine, to have him constantly beside her in the lovely freedom of the summer months, was completely delightful to her.

But before she could start making preparations to close up her house in Bedford Square, the newspapers brought unwelcome news. There was talk of unconscionable treachery on the part of Spain, of her desire to usurp Britain's colonies, of a strange faraway port named Nootka Sound. Constantine was more than ever from home—she hardly saw him from one week to the next. At last she was forced to go and dine at the Parkers' to see what Harry might be able to tell her.

"Nootka Sound, Harry," she said. "Why are we all talking about it? What a strange barbaric name it is! Is it a Spanish possession?"

"No, it is not, though the Spaniards wish it were. It is a trading post—a very profitable one, serving the fur trade, in North America, near Vancouver Island. A fleet of Spanish ships came into the Sound when three English trading ships were there and used them very ill. They fired upon the ships and took one captive, clapping all the officers in irons. They mean to usurp control of Nootka Sound and all the trade it brings."

"Oh," said Elizabeth. It all seemed very distant. "That is very wrong of them, I suppose."

"It is a challenge. A throwing down of the gauntlet, you might say, to express their intentions. The Spanish ambassador refuses to apologize for the incident or to make any reparation."

"What will happen?"

"It is for the King and Privy Council to decide."

She knew she would get no more from him. Harry was incurably discreet. She would have to wait for Constantine.

A week later he came to call on her at Bedford Square. When she saw him standing in the hall, she felt not her usual delight but a sharp stab of fear. Why had he called? What did he have to tell her?

He did not keep her waiting. As soon as they were seated in the drawing room he began.

"My dear, I came directly here to let you know the news. I fear our plans for the summer must be set aside."

He paused.

"You will have read the news. A crisis has arisen over the incident at Nootka Sound. The Privy Council believe that it is an act of provocation that may lead to war. The fleet is to be mobilized immediately and Lord Admiral Howe wants it to be out into the Channel by June."

Elizabeth tried to understand what he was telling her.

"It is so sudden."

"It is. More than half the fleet is laid up—no one was expecting them to be called upon. It will be a huge task. We will have to press for sailors. The Admiralty will be at full stretch."

"And you?"

"I have been offered a command. The ship is the *Leviathan*. I am undecided where my duty lies, whether with the *Leviathan* or at the Admiralty and with the government. I believe Lord Howe may decide for me."

He hesitated.

"But whichever it is, Elizabeth, I am going to be absent from home very often. All the time if I take command of the *Leviathan*. This is only the beginning—we have not declared war yet—it may be months away. I fear I will not see New Mulgrave Hall this summer."

Elizabeth wanted to weep, to cry her protest against the folly of it all. But she held herself tightly in. He owed her nothing, she reminded herself.

"It is the greatest kindness in you, to come and give me this news so directly. I am sorely disappointed . . . "

"And indeed, my dear, so am I—more than you can imagine."

"If God wills, other occasions will be found. I know that you have no choice, that you must do your duty."

A little rush of fear suddenly possessed her.

"But oh, Constantine, I cannot help but pray you are not called upon to command the *Leviathan*. Surely there are scores of young captains eager for a command? Are you not more wanted in the government? How dreadful it would be if Anne were to lose her father too!"

She could not stop tears starting from her eyes.

"My dear," he said. "Come here." He took her in his arms and let her shed her tears into his fresh linen shirt.

"Don't be afraid. Have I not done a fine job of staying alive all these years?"

CHAPTER 47

London

May 1790–May 1791

Suddenly North America was at the forefront of all Elizabeth's thoughts. She became an avid reader of newspapers. The Spanish were planning to ally with France, she learned, to make war on British colonies in Canada and the East and West Indies. King Louis had given orders to prepare his fleet of forty ships of the line. War, it seemed, was inevitable.

But then other news came from France. There was said to be great unrest in the country and spies reported mutiny spreading through the French ships. On 14 July a great mob in Paris stormed the Bastille prison and executed its governor. The old parliament, the Estates Generales, was abolished and a new Assembly was set up. All at once revolution was taking hold, with riots in Paris and the countryside in wholesale disorder. King Louis had more to think about than Spain's colonies.

Elizabeth knew little of France and its troubles, but she blessed the revolutionaries with all her heart. Yet still the mobilization of the English fleet continued. On 27 July the newspapers brought a new blow to her hopes. The launch of the *Leviathan* from Chatham was announced, commissioned by Lord Mulgrave; it would make its way to Torbay to join the fleet. A fortnight later there was more unwelcome news. The *London Gazette* reported it:

> *Before thousands of spectators lining the shore, and under a fresh breeze in the west-north-west, Lord Admiral Howe set sail from*

> *Torbay on 17th August with His Majesty's fleet, being thirty-one sail of the line, nine frigates and some twenty additional vessels to patrol the Channel.*

The *Leviathan* was a ship of the line. She must be part of the fleet, with Constantine commanding her.

Yet war was still not declared. Although the Spanish fleet had been sighted off Cadiz, they made no attempt to enter the Channel. Both fleets were in readiness but still neither made a move. Were the Spaniards waiting for the French fleet?

By September it was clear that the French would never put to sea. Half the English fleet was stood down and returned to Portsmouth. British strength and resolve had seen off the Spaniards! the papers trumpeted. Before the end of October, negotiations between Britain and Spain produced the *Nootka Sound Convention*, giving Britain full access to the anchorage. Spain dropped all claims and recompensed the British traders she had mistreated. Britain had won a great victory, church bells were rung and the nation rejoiced, none more heartily than Elizabeth. It was over. Constantine would come home.

But their reunion was not as she had imagined. Early in November she received a visit in Bedford Square from Constantine's manservant, Louis Catt. She knew Louis well from her stays at Harley Street and they were on easy terms. He had been a sailor, had served Constantine for years and had a devoted if caustic regard for his master.

"Why, Louis. Do you have news of Lord Mulgrave?"

"Yes, ma'am. He is safe returned and wishes me to convey his greetings."

"May I call upon him?"

"You are to be told that he is unwell."

"Unwell? What is it?"

"It is some trouble with his lungs that pains him very bad. The doctor has told him he will have to rest if it is to clear."

"Oh, Louis! Is he very sick?"

"Since he takes heed of the doctor, I should say he is. I never knew him heed the man before."

"May I call on him?"

"He doesn't wish to trouble you but I daresay he will not turn you away. The little girl is not sent for, till he grows stronger."

"I will write a note to him, Louis. Will you take something in the kitchen till I am ready?"

She sat at her desk and took paper and pen. She was greatly distressed to hear of his illness—she wished she might offer any assistance she was able—if he were not too indisposed, she hoped he might receive her on the morrow. She sealed it up and gave it to Louis.

* * *

When she arrived at Harley Street the next day she was taken up to his private rooms. He was lying in bed, propped up on pillows with a shawl over his chest, his eyes closed. Louis Catt was making up the fire. He turned when he saw her enter.

"Good day, Mrs Addison. There you are, a good fire for you. I'll bring up a chair for you beside his Lordship. He'll be awake directly."

She thanked him and stood for a moment watching Constantine. She saw the rise and fall of his chest beneath the shawl and listened to the shallow sighing of his breath. How could it be that Constantine was unwell? He was never sick, or if he was, would pay not the slightest attention to it. How was he content now to lie abed?

Louis returned with a chair and withdrew quietly; at the sound of the door closing, Constantine's eyes opened. For a moment he stared at her unseeing before he woke fully. Then with a little jolt of his attention he saw her.

"Elizabeth! You've come!" He held out a hand to her. She drew the chair close to him so that she could take it. She took his hand, held it to her cheek for several moments. He was ill, but he was here; she was with him after the long months of absence and her joy was very great. She kissed his hand and for a few moments her feelings were too full for words. Then anxiety rose up.

"You are sick!" she accused him.

"I am. It is very wrong of me. I had meant to come and call on you at Bedford Square, but I am forbidden movement."

"Have you suffered some injury?"

"No, no. *Leviathan* never saw action. I have spent months sailing the Channel with not a cannon fired. I was happy to be under sail, but it has set off this trouble again."

"You've had it before?"

"Many years ago. I thought myself entirely cured."

Elizabeth looked more closely at him. His face was weathered from the last few months at sea, but she could discern the pallor beneath. He might be feverish, she thought. His eyes were glassy and sweat rimmed his forehead.

"Do you have a fever?"

"Very likely." He pulled himself up a little higher on the pillows. "It is a disorder in the lungs. I cough a great deal and I am often feverish, as you have noticed. I had the first symptoms of it while I was at sea, but I paid no heed to it. Now it has forced itself upon me."

As if to verify his words, a coughing fit took hold of him. He fumbled beside him for a napkin and held it to his mouth. When he took it away, she saw it was stained red. She felt a sudden horror. He saw her face.

"Yes," he said. "That is why I must lie here, to avoid aggravating it further. I suffered a worse haemorrhage on the journey back to London. The doctor was very severe."

Might he have died? she thought. Will it—could it—cause his death? She could find nothing to say, no comforting and thoughtful words.

"Don't be afraid. I have over-spent myself, that is all. It is my own folly in choosing to ignore it. I will have to spend some time very quietly, but I will soon be rid of it, just as before."

"Are you sure, Constantine? What does the doctor say?"

"I will let you speak with him yourself. But don't let his words dismay you."

She visited very regularly in the following weeks. There was no question of bringing Anne down to London while he was sick, but he had other tasks for her. There was an office in an adjoining room where documents were stacked up on the desk, and every day brought new ones to add to the pile. On days when he was well enough, he would have her bring in the latest papers and read them through to him. Then she would sit at a table and write letters for him. There were so many people who required his attention, from admirals and ministers to his many friends and his tenants at Mulgrave. For Elizabeth it was like a window into his life. Other days he was too exhausted to do anything more than lie in bed and have her read a newspaper to him. If he had a fever, she would take a basin and cloth to wipe the sweat from his face, and sit with him for the morning. The old easy intimacy between them returned, but it was undershot now with a new tension.

Louis Catt was her informant and co-conspirator. Did he cough last night, she would interrogate him. Was there blood? What had the doctor said? Had he eaten well at dinner? The doctor had impressed on her that he must have nourishing food, very frequently, in order to regain his strength. He had grown shockingly thin, but no matter how well he ate, he seemed to grow no fatter. She consulted with Louis.

"What do you think, Louis? Is he improving?"

"His Lordship would like to say so, ma'am, but I can't see it. It is a cruel time of year for his lungs with the air so dank and dirty. I reckon we'll not see him right till the spring."

Surely Louis was right, she thought. How could his lungs heal in the stuffy sickroom air? The doctor would not let her set the windows open for fear of the sooty air setting off his coughing. Once spring came and the weather grew warmer, he might sit outside, might take a little walk to strengthen his legs again.

But April came, and May, and though he sometimes had Louis dress him so that he could take a turn in the garden, he was soon exhausted. He no longer insisted that he would soon be better. His mood was sober. When she brought government papers to him, he would look at them for a short while, then hand them back to her, saying he could not deal with them. One morning she arrived to find him in a new mood of resolution.

"I have a new plan, Elizabeth. I have spoken to the doctor and he does not disapprove of it."

Does not disapprove, she thought. Or has not found a way to gainsay Lord Mulgrave. She waited.

"When I suffered from this trouble in my youth, my mother sent me to take the waters at Spa. It is a place of resort much frequented by noble families of Europe, near Liège in Belgium. It is blessed with hot springs and chalybeate waters that are beneficial for many illnesses. I confess I found it tedious then—I was impatient of both the illness and the cure—but after a few months I was rid of it entirely."

He looked at her directly.

"As you know, I had believed that with rest I would shake it off again in the same manner. But we can all see it is not so. I believe I must take more drastic measures."

He started to cough.

"Should you rest a little?"

He took up a napkin, shaking his head, and spat out the matter from his lungs, sputum tinged with blood. It was too familiar now for Elizabeth to remark on it.

"No, it's nothing. So. Here it is. I mean to resign my government positions. I regret it very much, but I cannot continue in this state. Once I am free of obligations, I mean to return to Liège to try if the waters will cure me."

He looked at her.

"Will you come with me?"

* * *

When Elizabeth returned to Bedford Square, her thoughts were in turmoil. She had given Constantine no answer. She would need to consider it, was all she had said. She had been thrilled, instantly, at the idea; at the thought of the journey, of visiting Europe, of travelling with Constantine. But she had managed to put that aside till she had thought more carefully about it. Of course, Constantine was the first consideration—whether he was well enough to manage such a journey, whether the difficulty of it might outweigh any benefit. But she had to consider herself as well. Was it the long months of isolation in his sickroom that had made Constantine think so little about society, she wondered. Was his illness so much at the forefront of his thoughts that he had not considered her position? While she lived scarcely a mile from his house and continued, in the eyes of the world, to live as a respectable widow in her own household, no questions were asked about her frequent visits to Harley Street. But how would it seem if Mrs Addison were to accompany Lord Mulgrave on his journey to Liège? She could not—would not—be seen as his housekeeper. She was a gentlewoman of independent means. Was she his nurse? His companion? His mistress? What would the family think?

She did not return to Harley Street the next day, or the next. But in the evening she received a visitor. The Honourable Henry Phipps was announced. Elizabeth was not entirely surprised. Henry was Constantine's younger brother—younger by twelve years, so he seemed a young man to Elizabeth. John Addison had been close to him and often had him to dine at Bedford Square. Privately she thought him less able—less accomplished—than his elder brother, but he had the same kindness of manner.

"I have lately come from Harley Street," he said.

"Has Constantine told you his plan?"

"He has, and I gave it every encouragement. Spa is frequented by some of the best families in Europe and it has effected some remarkable cures. Constantine went there, you know, as a young man when he first had this trouble with his lungs."

"Yes. Is it a very arduous journey, do you think?"

"There is the Channel crossing, to be sure, but he is a hardened sailor. Once you are to Ostend, it is hardly one hundred and fifty miles to Liège. It can be done in steady stages."

"He has quite won you over."

Henry laughed.

"You're right. He is persuasive. But the thing is this, Mrs Addison. Is he to spend the rest of his days cooped up in his rooms at Harley Street, constantly thinking of all the things he can no longer do? It would have a lowering effect on any man's spirits. Since he hit on this plan his old enthusiasm has returned. I believe that in itself will help to bring about a cure."

"Perhaps you're right."

Henry paused, looking at her.

"Mrs Addison, Constantine has told me of his wish that you might accompany him. It is a very great thing to ask of you. But if you were prepared to consider it, it would be the greatest consolation to all of us, not just to Constantine. To know that he had with him a companion with whom he was able to converse, to share his interests—and for whom he has so great an affection—why, Mrs Addison, it would be the best thing in the world for him. It would be a lonely business otherwise."

"Do you not think that it may attract censure for me to accompany him?"

"I do not believe so. My brothers, sister and I are fully in favour of the idea, and we will resist any imputation of impropriety. It is well known that Constantine is an invalid since he resigned his ministerial posts. It can simply be put about that you are accompanying him as a companion."

Why does he not marry me? thought Elizabeth, and put an end to such discussions?

As if he read her thoughts Henry said, "It is a great deal to ask of you, Mrs Addison, and perhaps one might wish for him to arrange it otherwise. But I believe he thinks that as an invalid he must make no claim on anyone."

Elizabeth sighed. She must not think about herself at this time, she rebuked herself. Her sole concern must be Constantine. If he were to be cured by their visit to Liège, why then . . . She stopped herself.

"Thank you, Lord Henry. You are very kind. You have reassured me." She hesitated.

"I believe I will undertake this independently. I have the means to do so. I do not wish to be seen as part of his household."

"As you wish. Constantine would be more than content to pay for all expenses, but it is for you and he to decide, I believe. So you will go?"

"I will."

* * *

When Henry was gone Elizabeth sat for some time on her own in the drawing room, watching the twilight slowly fading outside in the square. She was, she realized, a free woman. Her guardianship of the twins was over; they were both married with homes of their own. Frank had taken over the Cresswell estate and, although he still turned to her for advice, her responsibility for it was at an end. The Red House was shut up; Alice had finally married her curate, and as Juliana did not care to live there alone, Elizabeth and Frank had helped her buy a house in Newcastle where she might have more company. The house in Whitby would soon be sold and Frank would take care of that. Indeed, it was all Frank now. He was the head of the family. She could slip into the background; she was an independent woman of means and might do as she pleased. If she chose to travel to the Continent and take the waters, why, she was at liberty to do so. Even, in whose company she pleased.

* * *

But when she told Fanny, she still felt some hesitation. She had been so insistent on propriety when she was Fanny's guardian.

"I hope you will not think the arrangement improper," she said.

"Improper? My dear Aunt, the nobility may do as they please. Did you not know that?"

Elizabeth blinked. Fanny's way of speaking was a little modern sometimes.

"Maybe so, but I do not regard myself in that light."

"No? But later perhaps, when you return from Liège—if the Baron is restored to health—who knows?"

Goodness, thought Elizabeth. Is this what the family think? Are they expecting me to marry Constantine? And all at once, in front of the niece who had been her ward and who was thirty years her junior, she felt as bashful as a girl. She could think of nothing to say. Fanny took pity on her.

"It will be wonderful, Aunt. I am so envious of you! Just think—you will have your first taste of life aboard ship! I believe I will stow away in your luggage."

Then she looked down at her belly.

"But not yet. By the time you come home, we may have a new member of the family for you to meet."

"Are you . . . you are? Oh Fanny! I am so delighted for you! When is it expected?"

And for the rest of the visit they talked about babies and confinements and whether it might be a brother or a sister and no more was said about Elizabeth's expedition.

CHAPTER 48

Spa, Belgium

1791–2

The voyage was not at all as she had imagined. For sure, it had been thrilling to feel the heave and lift of the ship as they sailed out of Chatham, down the Medway and past the fort at Sheerness. But as soon as the ship moved out into the open sea, she felt quite unwell. The swell was far greater than she had expected. No one appeared to think anything of it, but the rise and fall of the waves was alarming to her. The ship heeled over to the side in the wind till she thought it might tip over altogether. How did such vessels contrive to stay afloat in all weathers? she asked herself. She regretted having eaten breakfast before coming aboard; she was feeling altogether nauseous. Louis Catt appeared at her side.

"How are your sea legs, Mrs Addison?"

"Oh Louis—I feel quite unwell. How is Constantine?"

"Better than you, I should say"

"I think I will go down to my cabin, Louis."

"You would be better to stay up here in the air."

"I cannot endure it, Louis. The way the ship heaves so, as if it might go over at any moment. I believe I will go below."

She turned away from the rail and Louis went with her down to her cabin, a little cramped cell with room for no more than a bed and a small table. She had imagined her cabin would be like the captain's quarters John had shown her. But she cared nothing for it now—all she wanted was to lie down—to close her eyes—and try to ignore the heaving of the ship.

"Not to worry," said Louis. "We've got a good fresh breeze behind us that will see us to Ostend in no time. You'll not have to endure it long."

He left her but was back very shortly with a basin and cloth that he placed beside her. She was soon to discover why.

*   *   *

When they came into harbour at Ostend, her relief was short-lived. After she left the ship, she found herself unable to walk properly. The solid ground beneath her had become unreliable and seemed to rise and fall like the ocean. She forgot that Constantine was the invalid and clung tightly to his arm.

"Poor Elizabeth," he said, unfeelingly cheerful. "I'm afraid it is often the way on a first voyage. You will feel better directly."

She looked at him and at Louis. How were they so unaffected?

"Was it not quite rough?" she asked.

"Very rough," Constantine assured her. "But now you are become a sailor."

Oh no, she thought, I will never set foot on board ship again. But after a quiet night in Ostend, she woke in the morning and found that the sickness had gone. Even, that she was ready to eat breakfast. She had survived. The crossing was a necessary ordeal and now, she was there, in Europe—in Belgium—and the adventure was begun.

*   *   *

Everything was unfamiliar in her new life. The streets, the buildings, the houses looked different. The meals that were set before her tasted unlike English dishes. All around her were the strange sounds of a language she had never heard before.

She would have no need to bring a lady's maid, Constantine had told her; the hotels they would stay in en route for Spa would provide one for her and once there she might hire a woman locally. But she had not allowed for the language. She could not tell what the maids in the hotels were saying. She had no idea whether the strange words were Flemish or French, but it would have made no difference.

"Could they not speak English?" she asked Constantine as they sat drinking tea together in his hotel rooms in Aalter. "You have Louis to attend to you, but I cannot make myself understood. I can hardly get them to set a cap straight on my head."

"You are too unkind," said Constantine. "I think you are very properly turned out. Charmingly, indeed!"

She smiled in spite of herself.

"It is all Flemish here," he added, "but in the area around Liège, French is spoken. I believe you will soon pick it up."

"Do you speak it?"

He nodded. "I do. And Louis Catt is a master of languages from his seafaring days. He can make himself understood in Flemish, French, German . . . even some Spanish, I believe."

How little she had seen of the world, she thought. Everything was new and strange to her. But more than any of that to her was the change it had wrought in Constantine. Their fears that the journey would be too arduous for him had proven unfounded. Rather, it seemed to rally him, to bring about a new energy and eagerness. They travelled slowly, taking a day or two to rest between each stage of the way, but he suffered no worsening of his condition.

When they reached Ghent, they decided to spend a week there, so that Elizabeth might visit the lace-makers' workshops and buy lace to send home to Fanny and Kitty. She found the town very curious and charming, with its old houses and guildhalls along the riverside, the white-walled castle that seemed to rise out of the water, the busy shops and lace markets. Some days Constantine was well enough to take a stroll with her to the town square and drink a cup of chocolate, or to escort her to one of the ancient churches and explain its architecture to her. A new hopefulness filled them both. It seemed that the journey might be the very restorative that Constantine required.

By the time they reached their destination, the town of Spa where Constantine would take the waters, she was ready for an end to travel, impatient to settle into their new life and to have the cure begin. The town was not large, but it was full of very handsome buildings serving as hotels for visitors to the famous springs. Constantine was familiar with the town—knew already where he wished to stay, on the outskirts, where he might have a view to the wooded hills that lay above the town. Louis Catt made all the arrangements—a set of rooms in a grand hotel for Constantine, and a more modest apartment in an adjoining establishment for Elizabeth. Then there was all the business of trunks and unpacking and finding a lady's maid to serve her; then doctors must be found to supervise Constantine and oversee his treatment, and for a few weeks everything was still new, still unfamiliar.

But as the summer wore on, the days started to take on a predictable sameness that was not so different from the London ones, except for the regular taking of the waters. At first she had expected—hoped—that Constantine might be quickly cured, or at least make steady progress back to health. But, after the euphoria of the journey had worn off, he seemed to lapse back into the old fatigue. He started to suffer bouts of fever and coughing again.

"You must be patient," the doctors told her. "His case is quite advanced. It may take many months for him to recover."

As he relapsed, her own spirits declined. This will not do, she told herself. She would set herself tasks—she would learn French—she would take walks every day in the pine forests. She would find a way to be patient.

CHAPTER 49

Spa, Belgium

1792

Afterwards all she would remember of the long weeks and months in Spa was a room with two tall windows and outside shutters, one facing west with a view of the hills, the other south, looking out onto a terrace where other guests would take the air in the afternoon. Against the wall opposite the west window was a four-poster bed with silk damask hangings, always drawn back during the day so that Constantine could see the hills, on the other wall a grate with a log fire burning on all but the warmest days. There was a table set back from the south window with writing paper, pen and ink and a little pile of letters, and a chair beside it. Between the two windows was a chaise longue upholstered in yellow brocade where Elizabeth was accustomed to sit, reading or stitching. There was a chair next to the bed too, so she could sit close if necessary. Sometimes she felt as if she had spent half a lifetime in that room.

Unless it was very cold, Constantine liked the windows to be open so that he could smell the pine from the forests. One of the doctors had given her an embrocation made with pine oil and, when Constantine's chest pained him, he liked her to rub his chest with it. For the rest of her life the smell of pine oil would take her back to that room, to the feel of his rough-haired skin beneath her fingers, his shallow breath close to her face. Sometimes she would have him roll onto his stomach so she could rub it on his back, and she would see again how slack and shrunken his muscles had become. It was hard to believe he would ever be strong again.

For the first few months of their stay, Louis Catt would often dress Constantine and go with him to the bath house and to the salons where visitors gathered to drink the waters. Constantine sometimes seemed to enjoy conversing with his companions there, and the attendants would advise on how often he should visit, and how much he should drink. Elizabeth visited the hot springs too, but found it hard to make acquaintances, although there were English women among the visitors. In the main they were of noble family, with a large entourage waiting upon them, and liked to socialize with others like themselves. They were unsure how to place plain Mrs Addison. A companion of some sort; a secretary, perhaps. But not an equal.

As winter approached, they both withdrew more and more into Constantine's apartments. He grew weary of attending the salons and preferred to have the waters brought to him, to have the doctor attend him privately. Elizabeth wanted to avoid the casual disdain of the English visitors. They read books and newspapers together and the letters that came from their families, from Fanny and Kitty and her sisters, from his brothers. Sometimes Constantine wrote letters to little Anne, with drawings to amuse her. As time went on, even the letters seemed to come from a distant, half-forgotten world. It felt to Elizabeth as if they had spent their whole lives there, in that room, in the little town. They seldom talked about his illness. It was obvious that he was not cured, though neither of them would admit that he was worse. Instead, all their conversation assumed that he would be better very soon. When the summer came. When a different physician was found. They would talk sometimes about returning to London, what they would do, the people they would visit, the theatres they would go to, but the discussions had an unreality about them. London had become a kind of mirage.

She started to have strange vivid dreams of long-forgotten places and people. One night she dreamed that she was in the Tower at Cresswell. The furnishings were not as she remembered them, though a great fire burned in the hearth of the main room. She found herself in a side chamber and saw a girl leaning over a pallet in the corner where a man was lying. She was holding a drink to his lips, and when he had drunk it, he took her hand and smiled at her. In her dream Elizabeth knew at once who it was and felt a great urge to warn them both of the danger that awaited them. "Have a care!" she cried. "Have a care!" But they could not see her, could not heed her, and she woke hot with sweat as if it were herself and Constantine she had seen. She shook the image from her, but a sense of foreboding stayed with her. In the days following, she dreamed again and again of the Tower, menacing and brooding, its looming darkness coming ever closer towards her.

She would take a walk, she thought, one morning when she awoke from another night of dreams. She would go up into the hills and shake these dark thoughts from her. It was a pleasant day, and she would take a basket to gather up some fir cones to burn on the fire for Constantine. She was gone all morning and returned with a rosy flush on her cheeks, eager to tell him of her adventures.

She found him slumped sideways on the bed, groaning. She turned him over, towards her, but his eyes were tightly closed and his face contorted with pain. She hurried to the closet for the laudanum and made up a dose for him.

"Drink this," she said, holding it to his mouth, and even as she did, the image of her dream returned to her and she heard herself cry out, "Have a care!"

He took it, and in a little while it eased him.

"The pain is very bad, Elizabeth. I think I must see a doctor."

When the man came, he bent over Constantine, listening to his lungs, peering into his eyes. Constantine coughed suddenly, and a spurt of bright red blood stained the sheet. The doctor turned away.

"Mrs Addison."

He took her into another room.

"He does not have long to live. There is nothing we can do now. If there are any arrangements you would like me to make . . . "

She shook her head. It was upon her, the day she had tried so hard to deny. She was calm with shock. All that she could think of now was to be with him, to make it easy for him. But when she went back into the room, the laudanum had taken effect and he was sitting up.

"I believe I am dying. I must arrange . . . my affairs . . . " He paused, gasped horribly for breath. "I must have a lawyer."

Suddenly it was all commotion. Louis Catt was sent off to find an English lawyer, or anyone who could string a legal sentence together, and witnesses. She and Louis could be two; they would need two more.

"If . . . they are too late . . . " he said, "tell them . . . I make Henry my heir, to the estate and the title. Anne must go into the care of her grandparents . . . oh, God . . . " He bent his head over and wept.

"Do not distress yourself. The lawyer will be here very soon. Rest and save your strength."

He nodded and lay back. He looked so still and white she had to take his wrist and feel for the little pulse still fluttering.

He lingered for two days, and she saw it was only his will that kept him living, forced the breath to keep passing in and out of his failing lungs, so that the will might be done. And when it was done, he called the man back again, as he desired one codicil after another, so that all his obligations might be fulfilled, and no one should think themselves forgotten. When it was done, at last he was at peace. She sat beside him through a long evening and into the night, expecting every moment that the fragile lift and fall of the covers would cease and yet praying for another moment more. Sometime after midnight he pulled himself upright. She saw his whole body was wracked with spasms that made him agonizingly rigid. He turned towards her and called out. She jumped up from her seat, took him in her arms and held him while he suffered them. Blood ran from his mouth. Then suddenly he was still. His body went limp and heavy in her arms. He was gone.

As she clung to him, she felt the darkness drawing in around her. Was it not unbearable? She had been brought to the very brink of happiness, only for it to be torn from her grasp! Her heart was breaking, here, in this room far from all she knew. She let the dead weight of Constantine's body fall back onto the pillows, and then, burying her head in his chest, wept out long paroxysms of grief and bitterness.

Much later, when her first grief was spent, she lifted her head. It seemed that the room was growing lighter, though the curtains were still drawn.

There was a glimmer of whiteness, a light, pale as the stars, that she had always known, and a salt smell, as if a breath from the sea had somehow blown into the room. In spite of all she felt herself stayed. The tears dried on her face. She sat up and looked down at Constantine. After all the anguish of his last days his face was serene, his forehead unlined. There was even the trace of the old smile about his lips. He was at peace. A thought came from somewhere: love is never lost. She would love him always. Always. She leaned over and arranged his arms by his sides, gave him a last kiss and closed his eyes. Taking up a cloth she dampened it and washed the blood from his face. He had had no priest, she thought. She should say the prayers for the dead, but only the old hymn came to her lips:

> *Ave, maris stella,*
> *Dei mater alma,*
> *atque semper virgo,*
> *Felix cæli porta.*

When she had sung the verses for him, she got up and went to the windows. She pulled back the curtains and let the light come in.

* * *

> *Will of Constantine John Lord Mulgrave of Mulgrave, Yorkshire*
> *Deceased 10 October 1792 at Liège*
> *This my Will signed Sealed Published and Witnessed in Presence of the Testator and each other at Liege this Eighth day of October One thousand Seven hundred and Ninety two*
> *Witnesses: Robert Clifford Elizabeth Addison William Clay Louis Catt*

Will dated:	*08-October-1792*
6 Codicils all dated	*08-October-1792*
Will proved:	*10-November-1792*

EXTRACTS
Codicil No 1
2. I Do Appoint Mrs Anne Jesse Cholmley and in case of her
3. death Mrs Dorothy Coulton and in case of her Death Mrs Maria
4. Phipps Wife of my Brother Augustus to be Guardian of my
5. Daughter to receive Quarterly the amount of her fortune and
6. not to be Accountable for the Expenditure of her fortune or
7. the Conduct of her Education to any Person whatsoever
28. Codicil No 4
29. I leave to Mrs Elizabeth Addison five hundred pounds as
30. a Grateful Testimony of her unexampled Goodness to be
31. paid immediately
32. to Captain Robert Moorson the Care of all my Sea Papers Charts Journals and   Memorandums for
33. his use and inspection till the Honorable Charles Paget
34. Stell shall be a Post Captain and then to him as well as
35. Nautical Instruments I leave to my dear Friend Captain
36. Nathan Brunton My Spy Glasses
43. Codicil No 5
44. I leave to my Servant Louis Cat Fifty pounds to John Sproson
45. thirty pounds to my House keeper One hundred pounds to
46. All my other Servants one Years Wages to be paid out of the
47. Current Produce of the Estate

EPILOGUE

The Red House, Woodhorn Demesne, Northumberland

1 December 1807

A weak heart, the doctor said. She did not contradict him, but she thought it nonsense. She knew for certain that her heart was very strong. How else could she have endured the sorrows life had brought her?

She did have dropsy. That was obvious. Her feet and legs were swollen up very unpleasantly and had to be treated with leeches. And she was weary. When she tried to do anything or walk anywhere, she became breathless and fatigued as she never had before. It was old age, that was all. She was sixty-eight. It was twenty years since John died. Fifteen since Constantine. Perhaps her time was drawing close.

So, she had summoned the lawyers to take care of her will. Of course, the provisions of John's will would take care of everything that was to go to Frank. But over the years she had managed her affairs astutely; John had always said she would make a good businessman. She had bought an estate at East Lilburn, which she meant to leave to Addison John. Fanny had five boys now, but Addison John had first claim on her heart. The rest of the money would go to supporting the boys' education. It gave her an extra little leverage. If any of them refused to use the surname Cresswell, they would get nothing.

Truly, her greatest wish now was for the family name to endure. She understood that it was humiliating for a man to take his wife's surname but, if Frank could but swallow his pride, what advantages would accrue for his son and heir! He would be Addison John Cresswell of Cresswell

Hall. He would be a gentleman of distinction in the county. Who had ever heard of the Easterbys in Northumberland? Whereas the name Cresswell would immediately command recognition and respect.

She had worn Frank down till he agreed. It was for his son's sake, she told him. It couldn't be denied that she had made use of the mortgage, too: the still-unpaid loan left by her brother John. If Frank were to agree, she could make sure the estate would pass to him without debt. It had helped to clinch the argument. He had, at last, taken the name and arms of Cresswell by act of parliament.

Fanny was not as encouraging as she might have hoped.

"Why, Aunt—you are becoming quite a tyrant!" she had said.

It wasn't true. None of this was done on her own behalf. Why should she trouble herself? No. She did it for Addison John. The astounding love she had felt for him when he was a baby had never faltered; rather it had grown as he did. It was quite different to the love she had had for John, or even Constantine. It was completely altruistic. She wanted nothing from her eldest great-nephew, only to see him flourish and prosper. That he was constantly affectionate and considerate towards her was only an added joy. It was, she thought, how her mother must have felt towards her son John, but that had only led to his spoiling. The business of Addison John's upbringing was in the hands of his mother and father. She had no responsibility other than to love him, and she knew certainly that the change of name would be right for him.

Would her husband John Addison not have approved? Had he not always wanted to be a gentleman? And now, here was his great-nephew, bearing his own name, on the way to achieving it. His name, and now hers. Addison John Cresswell.

Yes, she thought, she had done her duty by the family. And she felt justified in directing in her will that she was to be buried in the family vault at Woodhorn church, with her parents and their parents. Frank thought it disloyal of her, said that she should be buried with John. But she didn't care to spend eternity in Whitby. It had never been her real home. John would understand.

PART SEVEN: TIME'S CHANGES 307

The Red House, in the end, was home. After all the years in Whitby, in London—in Belgium, even—this was the only place she truly belonged. Sometimes she allowed herself to dream, what if Constantine had been cured? What might have happened? Where might she have ended up? But they were idle, idle thoughts she had given up long ago. She had locked them away in a secret part of her heart that no one else, none of the family, had any idea about. Except for Fanny. Fanny knew. But she kept her own counsel.

It was the last thing she needed to resolve. She took the miniature from the drawer and looked at it again, at Constantine's loved familiar face, as he had been then. Henry, his brother, had given it to her after she returned from Liège. It was beautifully made, with a border of diamonds. They would find it when they went through her possessions. They would not know who it was. It might be sold, and it would mean nothing to anyone. They would strip off the diamonds and throw the portrait away. She had decided what she would do. She would have a codicil to her will. She wouldn't let the lawyer do it, in their tortured rambling phrases. She would write it herself as elegantly as Constantine would have liked. It was time to close the door forever.

She sat down at her desk and began:

> *I request that my Executors in my said Will named will return to the Right Honorable Henry Lord Mulgrave the original Miniature Picture set with Diamonds of his Brother the late Lord Mulgrave which he gave to me soon after his said Brothers decease. I make this request because I do not know anyone to whom I can give it with so much Propriety as his Lordship who I request will accept along with it the Assurance which I now give him of the sincere respect and regard which to the latest period of my life I entertained for himself and his Family.*
>
> *I Give to General Edmund Phipps the Picture of his late Mother Lady Mulgrave and I Give and bequeath to the Honorable Anna Elizabeth Murray Daughter of the said late Lord Mulgrave and now the Wife of General Murray to and for her own Sole and separate use*

the Sum of Five Hundred Pounds being the amount of a Legacy left me by the said late Lord Mulgrave and which I request she will lay out in any Token of her remembrance of me as one who had always the highest esteem for her.

✷   ✷   ✷

There. It was done. Her will was complete. All her obligations were fulfilled. She felt a lightness of spirit. Was she ready to die, she wondered. Her body was, for sure. But herself?

She would like to go and sit for a little in Woodhorn church, she decided. Could she walk that far? She called for one of the housemaids to help her.

"Are you sure, Mrs Addison? With your bad legs? And the breathlessness?"

"We will go slowly."

It was true, she was very tired when she got there. But she sent the girl away and settled herself into a pew close to the front. There it was, the old wooden statue of the Virgin, so dark and worn you could no longer make out her expression, only the wide brow and watchful eyes. Stella Maris, Star of the Sea, the sailors' protectress and friend.

She no longer needed to go down to the shore as she used to in her younger days, looking for a glimpse of white, a hint of the spirit's presence. She was here too. Would anyone else see her, Elizabeth wondered, when she was dead? Would Fanny? Or the little girls she had started producing after her five sons, would they play in the Tower or on the shore and catch a glimpse of the White Lady and run home to tell their mother? She would still be there, whether they saw her or not.

She stared at the statue, and beyond, into the white spaces of the little church. She felt herself, finally, at peace. She muttered a Hail Mary to the statue. She would have liked to light a candle, but her legs were unwilling to move. She would have to rest here for a while. She might as well get accustomed to it. She would soon be resting here for eternity, and indeed she was so tired she felt ready to enter it. Her thoughts slipped away and her head sagged forward on her chest. She slept on and on, as the shadows lengthened through the windows. The statue stood quite still above her, looking down with dark eyes.

IN WOODHORN CHURCH

Memorial to Elizabeth Cresswell

*In a vault to the north side of this wall are deposited
the remains of Elizabeth Addison daughter of William
Cresswell of Cresswell in this county, Esq and wife of John
Addison of Whitby in the county of York, esquire
Who departed this life on the 1st day of
December 1807 aged 68 years.
This monument was erected by her nephew Addison John
Cresswell in remembrance of her unbounded kindness to him.*

ACKNOWLEDGEMENTS

My thanks are due to:

- Terry and Anne Sancroft Baker, for giving me access to their extensive research into the Baker Cresswell family tree and for their untiring help with my enquiries
- Constantine, Lord Normanby for allowing me access to the family archives held at Mulgrave Castle
- My first readers, Joyce Miller and Harry Baker Cresswell, for their invaluable feedback and suggestions
- Richard Rutherford Hilton and Natalie Watson at Sacristy Press for their continuing interest and support
- my ever-patient husband and editor-in-chief Michael Tiernan, for sharing his life with my eighteenth-century family and their impossibly complicated family relationships.

Documents quoted in the text

Letter of Marque: John Addison
Letter dated   *July 31 1756*
Archive   *The National Archives of the UK (TNA), Kew*

Will of John Addison of Whitby, Yorkshire
Will dated: *10-June-1786*
Codicil dated: *24-March-1787*
Will proved: *24-May-1787*

Archive: *The National Archives of the UK (TNA), Kew Records of the Prerogative Court of Canterbury (PCC)*

Will of Constantine John Lord Mulgrave of Mulgrave, Yorkshire
Will dated: 08-October-1792
6 Codicils all dated 08-October-1792
Will proved: 10-November-1792
Archive: *The National Archives of the UK (TNA), Kew Records of the Prerogative Court of Canterbury (PCC)*

Will of Elizabeth Addison, Widow of Woodhorn Demesne, Northumberland
Will dated: 03-October-1807
First Codicil dated: 14-November-1807
Second Codicil dated: 14-November-1807
Will proved: 07-January-1808
Archive: *The National Archives of the UK (TNA), Kew Records of the Prerogative Court of Canterbury (PCC)*

CRESSWELL TOWER

The Tower has recently been restored and is open to visitors. Refer to their website for opening times and visitor information.

www.cresswellpeletower.org.uk

Novels by Katharine Tiernan

STAR OF THE SEA
ISBN: 9781789592887

CUTHBERT OF FARNE
ISBN: 9781789590098

PLACE OF REPOSE
ISBN: 9781789590784

A NEW HEAVEN AND A NEW EARTH
ISBN: 9781789591255

www.sacristy.co.uk

Ingram Content Group UK Ltd.
Milton Keynes UK
UKHW020611250523
422330UK00010B/268